Praise for the novels of
#1 *New York Times* bestselling author
Debbie Macomber

"Virtually guaranteed to please."
—*Publishers Weekly*

"It's impossible not to cheer for Macomber's characters…. When it comes to creating a special place and memorable, honorable characters, nobody does it better than Macomber."
—*BookPage*

"Macomber's writing and storytelling deliver what she's famous for—a smooth, satisfying tale with characters her fans will cheer for and an arc that is cozy, heartwarming and ends with the expected happily-ever-after."
—*Kirkus Reviews* on *Starting Now*

"No one writes stories of love and forgiveness like Macomber."
—*RT Book Reviews*

"It's clear that Debbie Macomber cares deeply about her fully realized characters and their families, friends and loves, along with their hopes and dreams. She also makes her readers care about them."
—*Bookreporter.com*

"Romantic, warm, and a breeze to read—one of Macomber's best."
—*Kirkus Reviews* on *Cottage by the Sea*

"Macomber is a skilled storyteller."
—*Publishers Weekly*

DEBBIE MACOMBER

Winning Hearts

mira

ISBN-13: 978-0-7783-3154-4

Recycling programs for this product may not exist in your area.

Winning Hearts

Copyright © 2020 by Harlequin Books S.A.

Laughter in the Rain
First published in 1986. This edition published in 2020.
Copyright © 1986 by Debbie Macomber

Love by Degree
First published in 1987. This edition published in 2020.
Copyright © 1987 by Debbie Macomber

This edition published by arrangement with Harlequin Books S.A.

For questions and comments about the quality of this book, please contact us at CustomerService@Harlequin.com.

Mira
22 Adelaide St. West, 40th Floor
Toronto, Ontario M5H 4E3, Canada
www.Harlequin.com

Printed in Lithuania

Also available from Debbie Macomber and MIRA

Blossom Street

The Shop on Blossom Street
A Good Yarn
Susannah's Garden
Back on Blossom Street
Twenty Wishes
Summer on Blossom Street
Hannah's List
"The Twenty-First Wish"
  (in *The Knitting Diaries*)
A Turn in the Road

Cedar Cove

16 Lighthouse Road
204 Rosewood Lane
311 Pelican Court
44 Cranberry Point
50 Harbor Street
6 Rainier Drive
74 Seaside Avenue
8 Sandpiper Way
92 Pacific Boulevard
1022 Evergreen Place
Christmas in Cedar Cove
  (*5-B Poppy Lane* and
  A Cedar Cove Christmas)
1105 Yakima Street
1225 Christmas Tree Lane

The Dakota Series

Dakota Born
Dakota Home
Always Dakota
Buffalo Valley

The Manning Family

The Manning Sisters
  (*The Cowboy's Lady* and
  The Sheriff Takes a Wife)

The Manning Brides
  (*Marriage of Inconvenience* and
  Stand-In Wife)
The Manning Grooms
  (*Bride on the Loose* and
  Same Time, Next Year)

Christmas Books

A Gift to Last
On a Snowy Night
Home for the Holidays
Glad Tidings
Christmas Wishes
Small Town Christmas
When Christmas Comes
  (now retitled *Trading
  Christmas*)
There's Something About Christmas
Christmas Letters
The Perfect Christmas
Choir of Angels
  (*Shirley, Goodness and Mercy*,
  Those Christmas Angels and
  Where Angels Go)
Call Me Mrs. Miracle

Heart of Texas

Texas Skies
  (*Lonesome Cowboy* and
  Texas Two-Step)
Texas Nights
  (*Caroline's Child* and
  Dr. Texas)
Texas Home
  (*Nell's Cowboy* and
  Lone Star Baby)
Promise, Texas
Return to Promise

CONTENTS

LAUGHTER IN THE RAIN

One

"I'm so late. I'm so late."

The words were like a chant in Abby Carpenter's mind with every frantic push of the bike pedals. She was late. A worried glance at her watch when she paused at the traffic light confirmed that Mai-Ling would already be in Diamond Lake Park, wondering where Abby was. Abby should have known better than to try on that lovely silk blouse, but she'd seen it in the store's display window and couldn't resist. Now she was paying for the impulse.

The light turned green and Abby pedaled furiously, rounding the corner to the park entrance at breakneck speed.

Panting, she stopped in front of the bike stand and secured her lock around a concrete post. Then she ran across the lush green lawn to the picnic tables, where she normally met Mai-Ling. Abby felt a rush of relief when she spotted her.

Mai-Ling had recently immigrated to Minneapolis from Hong Kong. As a volunteer for the World Literacy Movement, Abby was helping the young woman learn to read English. Mai-Ling caught sight of her and waved eagerly.

Abby, who'd been meeting her every Saturday afternoon for the past two months, was impressed by her determination to master English.

"I'm sorry I'm late," Abby apologized breathlessly.

Mai-Ling shrugged one shoulder. "No problem," she said with a smile.

That expression demonstrated how quickly her friend was adapting to the American way of speaking—and life.

Mai-Ling started to giggle.

"What's so funny?" Abby asked as she slid off her backpack and set it on the picnic table.

Mai-Ling pointed at Abby's legs.

Abby looked down and saw one red sock and one that was blue. "Oh, dear." She sighed disgustedly and sat on the bench. "I was in such a rush I didn't even notice." No wonder the salesclerk had given her a funny look. Khaki shorts, mismatched socks and a faded T-shirt from the University of Minnesota.

"I am laughing with you," Mai-Ling said in painstaking English.

Abby understood what she meant. Mai-Ling wanted to be sure Abby realized she wasn't laughing *at* her. "I know," she said as she zipped open the backpack and took out several workbooks.

Mai-Ling sat opposite Abby. "The man's here again," she murmured.

"Man?" Abby twisted around. "What man?"

Abby couldn't believe she'd been so unobservant. She felt a slight twinge of apprehension as she looked at the stranger. There was something vaguely familiar about him, and that bothered her. Then she remembered—he was the same man she'd seen yesterday afternoon at the grocery store. Had he been following her?

The man turned and leaned against a tree not more than twenty feet away, giving her a full view of his face. His tawny hair gleamed in the sunshine that filtered through the leaves of the huge elm. Beneath dark brows were deep-set brown eyes. Even from this distance Abby could see their intense expression. His rugged face seemed to be all angles and planes. He was attractive in an earthy way that would appeal to a lot of women and Abby was no exception.

"He was here last week," Mai-Ling said. "And the week before. He was watching you."

"Funny, I don't remember seeing him," she murmured, unable to disguise her discomfort.

"He is a nice man, I think. The animals like him. I am not worried about him."

"Then I won't worry, either," Abby said with a shrug as she handed Mai-Ling the first workbook.

In addition to being observant, Mai-Ling was a beautiful, sensitive and highly intelligent woman. Sometimes she became frustrated with her inability to communicate, but Abby was astonished at her rapid progress. Mai-Ling had mastered the English alphabet in only a few hours and was reading Level Two books.

A couple of times while Mai-Ling was reading a story about a woman applying for her first job, Abby's attention drifted to the stranger. She watched in astonishment as he coaxed a squirrel down the trunk of the tree. He pulled what appeared to be a few peanuts from his pocket and within seconds the squirrel was eating out of his hand. As if aware of Abby's scrutiny, he stood up and sauntered lazily to the nearby lakeshore. The instant he appeared, the ducks squawked as though recognizing an old friend. The tall man took bread crumbs from a sack he carried and fed them. Lowering himself to a crouch, he threw back his head and laughed.

Abby found herself smiling. Mai-Ling was right; this man had a way with animals—and women, too, if her pounding heart was anything to judge by.

A few times Mai-Ling faltered over a word, and Abby paused to help her.

The hour sped by, and soon it was time for the young woman to meet her bus. Abby walked Mai-Ling to the busy street and waited until she'd boarded, cheerfully waving to Abby from the back of the bus.

Pedaling her bicycle toward her apartment, Abby's thoughts again drifted to the tall, good-looking stranger. She had to admit she was enthralled. She wondered if he was attracted to her, too, since apparently he came to the park every week while she was there. But maybe she wasn't the one who attracted him; perhaps it was Mai-Ling. No, she decided. Mai-Ling had noticed the way the handsome stranger studied Abby. He was interested *in her.* Great, she mused contentedly; Logan Fletcher could do with some competition.

Abby pulled into the parking lot of her low-rise apartment building and climbed off her bike. Automatically she reached for her backpack, which she'd placed on the rack behind her, to get the apartment keys. Nothing. Surprised, Abby turned around to look for it. But it wasn't there. Obviously she'd left it at the park. Oh, no! She exhaled in frustration and turned, prepared to go and retrieve her pack.

"Looking for this?" A deep male voice startled Abby and her heart almost dropped to her knees. The bike slipped out from under her and she staggered a few steps before regaining her balance.

"Don't you know better than to sneak up on someone

like that? I could have..." The words died on her lips as she whirled around to face the stranger. With her mouth hanging half open she stared into the deepest brown eyes she'd ever seen—the man from the park.

Her tongue-tied antics seemed to amuse him, but then it could have been her mismatched socks. "You forgot this." He handed her the backpack. Speechless, Abby took it and hugged it to her stomach. She felt grateful...and awkward. She started to thank him when another thought came to mind.

"How'd...how'd you know where I live?" The words sounded slightly scratchy, and she cleared her throat.

He frowned. "I've frightened you, haven't I?"

"How'd you know?" She repeated the question less aggressively. He hadn't scared her. If anything, she felt a startling attraction to him, to the sheer force of his masculinity. Logan would be shocked. For that matter, so was she. But up close, this man was even more appealing than he'd been at a distance.

"I followed you," he said simply.

"Oh." A thousand confused emotions dashed through her mind. He was so good-looking that Abby couldn't manage another word.

"I didn't mean to scare you," he said, regret in his voice.

"You didn't," she hurried to assure him. "I have an overactive imagination."

Shaking his head, he thrust his hands into his pants pockets. "I'll leave before I do any more damage."

"Please don't apologize. I should be thanking you. There's a Coke machine around the corner. Would you like to—"

"I've done enough for one day." Abruptly he turned to go.

"At least tell me your name." Abby didn't know where

the request came from; it tumbled from her lips before she'd even formed the thought.

"Tate." He tossed it over his shoulder as he stalked away.

"Bye, Tate," she called as he opened his car door. When he glanced her way, she lifted her hand. "And thanks."

A smile curved his mouth. "I like your socks," he returned.

Pointedly she looked down at the mismatched pair. "I'm starting a new trend," she said with a laugh.

Standing beside her bike, Abby waited until Tate had driven away.

Later that night, Logan picked her up and they had hamburgers, then went to a movie. Logan's obligatory goodnight kiss was…pleasant. That was the only way Abby could describe it. She had the impression that Logan kissed her because he always kissed her good-night. To her dismay, she had to admit that there'd never been any driving urgency behind his kisses. They'd been dating almost a year and the mysterious Tate was capable of stirring more emotion with a three-minute conversation than Logan had all evening. Abby wasn't even sure why they continued to date. He was an accountant whose office was in a building near hers. They had many of the same friends, and did plenty of things together, but their relationship was in a rut. The time had come to add a little spice to her life and Abby knew exactly where that spice would be coming from….

After Logan had left, Abby settled into the overstuffed chair that had once belonged to her grandfather, and picked up a new thriller she'd bought that week.

Dano, her silver-eyed cat, crawled into her lap as Abby opened the book. Absently she stroked the length of his spine. Her hand froze in midstroke as she discovered the hero's name: Logan. Slightly unnerved, she dropped the book and jumped up from her chair to look for the remote. Turning on the TV, she told herself she shouldn't feel guilty because she felt attracted to another man. The first thing she saw on the screen was a commercial for Logan Furniture's once-a-year sofa sale. Abby stared at the flashing name and hit the off button. This was crazy! Logan wouldn't care if she was interested in someone else. He might even be grateful. Their relationship was based on friendship and had progressed to romance, a romance that was more about routine than passion. If Abby was attracted to another man, Logan would be the first to step aside. He was like that—warm, unselfish, accommodating.

Her troubled thoughts on Saturday evening were only the beginning. Tate dominated every waking minute, which just went to prove how limited her social life really was. She liked Logan, but Abby longed for some excitement. He was so staid—yes, that was the word. *Staid.* Solid as a rock, and about as imaginative.

Logan came over to her apartment on Sunday afternoon, which was no surprise. He always came over on Sunday afternoons. They usually did something together, but never anything very exciting. More often than not Abby went over to his house and made dinner. Sometimes they watched a DVD. Or they played a game of backgammon, which he generally won. During the summer they'd ride their bikes, some of their most pleasant dates had been spent in Diamond Lake Park. Logan would lie on the grass and rest his head in her lap while she read whatever thriller or mystery she was currently devouring.

They'd been seeing each other so often that the last time they had dinner at her parents', Abby's father had suggested it was time they thought about getting married. Abby had been mortified. Logan had laughed and changed the subject. Later, her mother had tactfully reminded Abby that he might not be the world's most exciting man, but he was her best prospect. However, Abby couldn't see any reason to rush into marriage. At twenty-six, she had plenty of time.

"I thought we'd bike around the park," Logan said.

The day was gloriously sunny and although Abby wished Logan had proposed something more inventive, the idea *was* appealing. She enjoyed the feel of the breeze in her hair and the sense of exhilaration that came with rapid movement.

"Hi!" Abby and Logan were greeted by Patty Martin just inside the park's boundaries. "How's it going?"

"Fine," Logan answered for them as they braked to a stop. "How about you?"

Patty had recently started to work in the same office building as Logan, which was how Abby had met her. Although Abby didn't know her well, she'd learned that Patty was living with her sister. They'd talked briefly at lunch one day, and Abby had invited her to join an office-league softball team she and Logan had played in last summer.

"I'm fine, too," Patty answered shyly and looked away.

In some ways she reminded Abby of Mai-Ling, who hadn't said more than a few words to her the first couple of weeks they'd worked together. Only as they came to know each other did Mai-Ling blossom. Abby herself had never been shy. The world was her friend, and she felt certain Patty would soon be comfortable with her, too.

"I can't talk now. I saw you and just wanted to say hello. Have fun, you two," Patty murmured and hurried away.

Confused, Abby watched her leave. The girl looked like a frightened mouse as she scurried across the grass. The description was more than apt. Patty's drab brown hair was pulled back from her face and styled unattractively. She didn't wear makeup and was so shy it was difficult to strike up a conversation.

After biking around the lake a couple of times, they stopped to get cold drinks. As they rested on a park bench, Logan slipped an affectionate arm around Abby's shoulders. "Have I told you that you look lovely today?"

The compliment astonished Abby; there were times she was convinced Logan didn't notice anything about her. "Thank you. I might add that you're looking very good yourself," she said with twinkling eyes, then added, "but I won't. No need for us both to get conceited."

Logan smiled absently as they walked their bikes out of the park. His expression was oddly distant; in some ways he hadn't been himself lately, but she couldn't put her finger on anything specific.

"Do you mind if we cut our afternoon short?" he asked unexpectedly.

He didn't offer an explanation, which surprised Abby. They'd spent most Sunday afternoons together for the past year. More surprising—or maybe not, considering her recent boredom with Logan—was the fact that Abby realized she didn't care. "No, that shouldn't be any problem. I've got a ton of laundry to do anyway."

Back at her apartment, Abby spent the rest of the afternoon doing her nails, feeling lazy and ignoring her laundry. She talked to her mother on the phone and promised to stop by sometime that week. Abby had been on her own ever since college. Her job as receptionist at an orthopedic clinic had developed with time and specialized training into a position as an X-ray technician. The advancement had included a healthy pay increase—enough to start saving for a place of her own. In the meanwhile, she relished her independence, enjoying her spacious ground-floor apartment, plus the satisfactions of her job and her volunteer work.

Several times over the next few days, Abby discovered herself thinking about Tate. Their encounter had been brief, but had left an impression on her. He was the most exciting thing that had happened to her in months.

"What's the matter with you?" Abby admonished herself. "A handsome man gives you a little attention and you don't know how to act."

Dano mewed loudly and weaved between her bare legs, his long tail tickling her calves. It was the middle of June and the hot summer weather had arrived.

"I wasn't talking to you." She leaned over to pet the cat. "And don't tell me you're hungry. I know better."

"Meow."

"You've already had your dinner."

"Meow. Meow."

"Don't you talk to me in that tone of voice. You hear?"

"Meow."

Abby tossed him the catnip mouse he loved to hurl in the air and chase madly after. Logan had gotten it for Dano. With his nose in the air, the cat ignored his toy and sauntered into Abby's room, jumping up to sit on the windowsill, his back to her. He ignored Abby, obviously pining after whatever he could see outside. In some obscure way, Abby felt that she was doing the same thing to Logan and experienced a pang of guilt.

Since it was an older building, the apartments didn't have air-conditioning, so Abby turned on her large fan. Then, settling in the large overstuffed chair, she draped one leg over the arm and munched on an apple as she read. She was so engrossed in her thriller that when she glanced at her

watch, she gasped in surprise. Her Tuesday evening painting class was in half an hour and Logan would arrive in
less than fifteen minutes. He was always punctual, and although he seldom said anything, she could tell by the set of
his mouth that he disliked it when she was behind schedule.

The "I'm late, I'm late" theme ran through her mind as
she vaulted out of the chair, changed pants and rammed
her right foot into her tennis shoe without untying the
lace. Whipping a brush through her long brown hair, she
searched frantically for the other shoe.

"It's got to be here," she told the empty room frantically.
"Dano," she cried out in frustration. "Did you take my shoe?"

She heard a faint indignant "meow" from the bedroom.

On her knees she crawled across the carpet, desperately
tossing aside anything in her path—a week-old newspaper,
a scarf, a CD case, the mismatched pair of socks she'd worn
last Saturday and a variety of other unimportant things.

She bolted to her feet when her apartment buzzer went
off. Logan must be early.

She automatically let him into the building, threw open
her door—and saw *Tate* standing in the hallway.

Abby felt the hot color seep up from her neck. He *would*
come now, when she wasn't prepared and looking her worst.

He approached her apartment. "Hello," he said, staring
down at her one bare foot. "Missing something?"

"Hello again." Her voice sounded unnaturally high. She
bit her lip and tried to smile. "My shoe's gone."

"Walked away, did it?"

"You might say that. It was here a few minutes ago. I was
reading and…" She dropped to her knees and lifted the skirt-
ing around the chair. There, in all its glory, was the shoe.

"Find it?" He was still in the doorway.

"Yes." She sat on the edge of the cushion and jerked her foot into the shoe.

"It might help if you untied the laces," he said, watching her with those marvelous eyes.

"I know, but I'm in a hurry." With her heel crushing the back of the shoe, Abby hobbled over to the door. "Come on in." She closed it behind him. "I'm—"

"Abby."

"Yes. How did you know?"

"I heard your friend say it at the park. And when I got to the lobby, I asked one of your neighbors." He frowned. "You should identify your guests before you let them in, you know."

"I know. I will. But I—was expecting someone else and…" Her words drifted off.

Smiling, he offered her his hand. "Tate Harding," he said.

A tingling sensation slipped up her arm at his touch.

Tate's hand was callused and rough from work. She successfully restrained her desire to turn it over and examine the palm. His handsome face was tanned from exposure to the elements. Tate was handsome, compellingly so.

"It looks as if I came at an inconvenient time."

"Oh, no," she hurried to assure him. She noticed that he'd released his grip, although she continued to hold her hand in midair. Self-consciously she lowered it to her side. "Sit down," she said, motioning toward her favorite chair. The hot color in her face threatened to suffocate her with its intensity.

Tate sat and lazily crossed his legs, apparently unaware of the effect he had on her.

Abby was shocked by her own reaction. She'd dated a number of men. She was neither naive nor stupid. "Would

you like something to drink?" she asked as she hastily re-
treated to the kitchen, not waiting for his answer. Pausing,
she frantically prayed that for once, just once, Logan would
be late. No sooner had the thought formed than she heard the
apartment buzzer again. This time she listened to her speaker.

"Abby?"

Logan. Abby hesitated, but let him in.

Tate had stood and opened the door by the time she
turned around. Logan had arrived. When he stepped inside,
the two men eyed each other skeptically. A slight scowl
drew Logan's brows together.

"Logan, this is Tate Harding. Tate, Logan Fletcher."
Abby flushed uncomfortably and darted an apologetic
look at them both.

"I thought we had a class tonight." Logan spoke somewhat defensively.

"This is my fault," Tate said, his gaze resting on Abby's
face and for one heart-stopping moment on her softly parted
lips. "I dropped by unexpectedly."

Logan's mouth thinned with displeasure and Abby
pulled her eyes from Tate's. Logan had never been the jealous type, but then he'd never had reason or opportunity to
reveal that side of his nature. Still, it surprised her. Abby
hadn't considered this a serious relationship. It was more of
a companionable one. Logan had understood and accepted
that, or so she'd thought.

"I'll come back another time," Tate suggested. "You've
obviously got plans with Logan."

"We're taking classes together," Abby rushed to explain.
"I'm taking painting and Logan's studying chess. We drive
there together, that's all."

Tate's smile was understanding. "I won't keep you, then."

"Nice to have met you," Logan stated, sounding as if he meant exactly the opposite.

Tate turned back and nodded. "Perhaps we'll meet again."

Logan nodded briskly. "Perhaps."

The minute Tate left Abby whirled around to face Logan. "That was so rude," she whispered fiercely. "For heaven's sake—you were acting like you owned me...like I was your property."

"Think about it, Abby," Logan said just as forcefully, also in a heated whisper. His dark eyes narrowed as he stalked to the other side of the room. "We've been dating exclusively for almost a year. I assumed that you would've developed some loyalty. I guess I was mistaken."

"Loyalty? Is that all our relationship means to you?" she demanded.

Logan didn't answer her. He walked to the door and held it open, indicating that if she was coming she needed to do it now. Silently Abby followed him through the lobby and into the parking lot.

The entire way to the community center they sat without speaking. The hard set of Logan's mouth indicated the tight rein he had on his temper. Abby forced her expression to remain haughtily cold.

They parted in the hallway, Logan taking the first left while Abby continued down the hall. A couple of the women she'd become friends with greeted her, but Abby had difficulty responding. She took twice as long as normal setting up her supplies.

The class, which was on perspective, didn't go well, since Abby's attention kept returning to the scene with Logan and Tate. Logan was obviously jealous. He'd revealed more emotion in those few minutes with Tate than in the past twelve months. Logan tended to be serious and reserved, while she was more emotional and adventurous. They were simply mismatched. Like her socks—one red, one blue. Logan had become too comfortable in their relationship these last months, taking too much for granted. The time had come for a change, and after tonight he had to recognize that.

After class they usually met in the coffee shop beside the center. Logan was already in a booth when she arrived there.

Wordlessly, Abby slipped into the seat across from him. Folding her hands on the table, she pretended to study her nails, wondering if Logan was ever going to speak.

"Why are you so angry?" Abby finally asked. "I hardly know Tate. We only met a few days ago."

"How many times have you gone out with him?"

"None," Abby said righteously.

"But not because you turned him down." Logan shook his head grimly. "I saw the way you looked at him, Abby. It was all you could do to keep from drooling."

"That's not true," she denied vehemently—and realized he was probably right. She'd never been good at hiding her feelings. "I admit I find him attractive, but—"

"But what?" Logan taunted softly. "But you had this old boyfriend you had to get rid of first?" The hint of a smile touched his mouth. "And I'm not referring to my age." He was six years older than Abby. "I was pointing out that we've been seeing each other two or three times a week and suddenly you're not so sure how you feel about me."

Abby opened, then closed her mouth. She couldn't argue with what he'd said.

"That's it, isn't it?"

"Logan." She said his name on a sigh. "I like you. You know that. Over the past year I've grown very...fond of you."

"Fond?" He spat the word at her. "One is *fond* of cats or dogs—not men. And particularly not me."

"That was a bad choice of words," Abby agreed.

"You're not exactly sure what you feel," Logan said, almost under his breath.

Abby's fingers knotted until she could feel the pain in her hands. Logan was right; she *didn't* know. She was attracted to Tate, but she knew nothing about him. The problem was that she liked what she saw. If her feelings for Logan were what they should be after a year, she wouldn't want Tate to ask her out so badly.

"You aren't sure, are you?" Logan said again.

She hung her head so that her face was framed by her dark hair. "I don't want to hurt you," she murmured.

"You haven't." Logan's hand reached across the table and squeezed her fingers reassuringly. "Beyond anything else, we're friends and I don't want to do anything to upset that friendship because it's important to me."

"That's important to me, too," she said and offered him a feeble smile. Their eyes met as the waitress came and turned over the beige cups and filled them with coffee.

"Do you want a menu?"

Abby couldn't have eaten anything and shook her head.

"Not tonight. Thanks, anyway," Logan answered for both of them.

"I don't deserve you," Abby said after the waitress had moved to the next booth.

For the first time all night Logan's lips curved into a genuine smile. "That's something I don't want you to forget."

For a few minutes they sipped their coffee in thoughtful silence. Holding the cup with both hands, she studied him. Logan's eyes were as brown as Tate's. Funny she hadn't remembered how brown they were. Tonight the color was intense, deeper than ever. They made quite a couple; she was so emotional—and he wasn't. Abby noticed that Logan's jaw was well-defined. Tate's jaw, although different, revealed that same quality—determination. With Logan, Abby recognized there was nothing he couldn't do if he wanted. Instinctively she knew the same was true of Tate.

She sensed that there were definite similarities between Logan and Tate, and yet she was reacting to them in different ways.

It seemed unfair that a man she'd seen only a couple of times could affect her like this. If she fell madly in love with someone, it should be Logan.

"What are you thinking about?" His words broke into her troubled thoughts.

Abby shrugged. "Oh, this and that," she said vaguely.

"You didn't even add sugar to your coffee."

Abby grimaced. "No wonder it tastes so awful."

Chuckling, he handed her the sugar canister.

Pouring some onto her spoon, Abby stirred it into her coffee. Logan had a nice mouth, she reflected. She couldn't remember thinking that in a long time. She had when they'd first met, but that was nearly two years ago. She watched him for a moment, trying to figure him out. Logan was so—Abby searched for the right word—sensible. Nothing ever seemed to rattle him. There wasn't an obstacle he couldn't overcome with cool reason. For once, Abby wanted him to do something crazy and nonsensical and fun.

"Logan." She spoke softly, coaxingly. "Let's drive to Des Moines tonight."

He looked at her as if she'd lost her mind. "Des Moines, Iowa?"

"Yes. Wouldn't it be fun just to take off and drive for hours—and then turn around and come home?"

"That's not fun, that's torture. Anyway, what's the point?"

Abby pressed her lips together and nodded. She shouldn't have asked. She'd known his answer even before he spoke.

The ride home was as silent as the drive to class. The tension wasn't nearly as great, but it was still evident.

"I have the feeling you're angry," Logan said as he parked in front of her building. "I'm sorry that spending the whole night on the road doesn't appeal to me. I've got this silly need for sleep. From what I understand, it affects older people."

"I'm not angry," Abby said firmly. She felt disappointed, but not angry.

Logan's hand caressed her cheek, curving around her neck and directing her mouth to his. Abby closed her eyes, expecting the usual feather-light kiss. Instead, Logan pulled her into his arms and kissed her soundly. Deeply. Passionately. Surprised but delighted, Abby groaned softly, liking it. Her hands slipped over his shoulders and joined at the base of his neck.

Logan had never kissed her with such intensity, such unrestrained need. His mouth moved over hers, and Abby sucked in a startled breath as pure sensation shot through her. When he released her, she sighed longingly and rested her head against his chest. Involuntarily, a picture of Tate entered her mind. This was what she'd imagined kissing *him* would be like....

"You were pretending I was Tate, weren't you?" Logan whispered against her hair.

Two

"Oh, Logan, of course I wasn't," Abby answered somewhat guiltily. She *had* thought of Tate, but she hadn't pretended Logan's kiss was Tate's.

He brushed his face along the side of her hair. Abby was certain he wanted to say something more, but he didn't, remaining silent as he climbed out of the car and walked around to her side. She smiled weakly as he offered her his hand. Logan could be such a gentleman. She was perfectly capable of getting out of a car by herself, but he always wanted to help. Abby supposed she should be grateful—but she wasn't. Those old-fashioned virtues weren't the ones that really mattered to her.

Lightly, he kissed her again outside her lobby door. Letting herself in, Abby was aware that Logan waited on the other side until he heard her turn the lock.

After changing into her long nightgown, Abby went into the kitchen and poured a glass of milk. She sat at the small round table and placed her feet on the edge of a chair, pulling her gown over her knees. Did she love Logan? The answer came almost immediately. Although he'd taken offense, "fond" had aptly described her feelings. She liked

Logan, but Tate had aroused far more emotion during their short acquaintance. Downing the milk, Abby turned off the light and miserably decided to go to bed. Dano joined her, purring loudly as he arranged himself at her feet.

Friday evening, she begged off when Logan invited her to a movie, saying she was tired and didn't feel well. He seemed to accept that quite readily. And, in fact, she watched a DVD at home, by herself, and was in bed by ten, reading a new mystery novel, with Dano stretched out at her side.

Saturday afternoon, Abby arrived at the park a half-hour early, hoping Tate would be there and they'd have a chance to talk. She hadn't heard from him and wondered if he'd decided Logan had a prior claim to her affection. However, Tate didn't seem the type who'd be easily discouraged. She found him in the same spot as last week and waved happily.

"I was hoping you'd be here," she said eagerly and sat on the grass beside him, leaning her back against the massive tree trunk.

"My thoughts exactly," Tate replied, with a warm smile that elevated Abby's heart rate.

"I'm sorry about Logan," she told him, weaving her fingers through the grass.

"No need to apologize."

"But he was so rude," Abby returned, feeling guilty for being unkind. But she'd said no less to Logan himself.

Tate sent her a look of surprise. "He didn't behave any differently than I would have, had the circumstances been reversed."

"Logan doesn't own me," she said defiantly.

A smile bracketed the edges of his mouth. "That's one piece of news I'm glad to hear."

Their eyes met and he smiled. Abby could feel her bones melt. It was all she could do to smile back.

"Do you like in-line skating?"

"I love it." She hadn't skated since she was a teen at the local roller rink, but if Tate suggested they stand on their heads in the middle of the road, Abby probably would have agreed.

"Would you like to meet me here tomorrow afternoon?"

"Sure," she said without hesitating. "Here?" she repeated, sitting up.

"You *have* skated?" He gave her a worried glance.

"Oh, sure." Her voice squeaked, embarrassing her. "Tomorrow? What time?"

"Three," Tate suggested. "After that we'll go out for something to eat."

"This is sounding better all the time," Abby teased. "But be warned, I do have a healthy appetite. Logan says—" She nearly choked on the name, immediately wishing she could take it back.

"You were saying something about Logan," Tate prompted.

"Not really." She gave a light shrug, flushing involuntarily.

Mai-Ling stepped off the bus just then and walked toward them. Abby stood up. Brushing the grass from her legs, she smiled warmly at her friend.

"Why do you meet her every week?" Tate asked. The teasing light vanished from his eyes.

"I do volunteer work with the World Literacy Movement. Mai-Ling can read perfectly in Chinese, but she's an American now so I'm helping her learn to read and write English."

"Have you been a volunteer long?"

"A couple of years. Why? Would you like to help? We're always looking for volunteers."

"Me?" He looked stunned and a little shocked. "Not now. I've got more than I can handle helping at the zoo."

"The zoo?" Abby shot back excitedly. "Are you a volunteer?"

"Yes," Tate said as he stood and glanced at his watch. "I'll tell you more about it tomorrow. Right now I've got to get back to work before the boss discovers why I've taken extended lunch breaks the past four Saturdays."

"I'll look forward to tomorrow," Abby murmured, thinking she'd never known anyone as compelling as Tate.

"You met the man?" Mai-Ling asked as she came over to Abby's side and followed her gaze to the retreating male figure.

"Yes, I met him," Abby answered wistfully. "Oh, Mai-Ling, I think I'm in love!"

"Love?" Mai-Ling frowned. "The American word for love is bad."

"Bad?" Abby repeated, not comprehending.

"Yes. In English one word means many kinds of love."

Abby turned her attention from Tate to her friend and asked, "What do you mean?"

"In America, love for a husband is the same as…as love for chocolate. I heard a lady on the bus say she *loves* chocolate, then say she is in love with a new man." Mai-Ling shook her head in astonishment and disbelief. "In Chinese it is much different. Better."

"No doubt you're right," Abby said with a bemused grin. "I guess it's all about context."

Mai-Ling ignored that. "You will see the man again?"

"Tomorrow," Abby said dreamily. Suddenly her eyes widened. Tomorrow was Sunday, and Logan would expect her to do something with him. Oh, dear, this was becoming a problem. Not only hadn't she skated in years, but she was bound to have another uncomfortable confrontation with Logan. Her eager anticipation for tomorrow was quickly replaced by a sinking feeling in the pit of her stomach.

Abby spent another miserable night. She'd attempted to phone Logan and make up another excuse about not being able to get together, but he hadn't been home. She didn't feel it was right to leave a message, which struck her as cowardly. Consequently her sleep was fitful and intermittent. It wasn't as if Logan called and arranged a time each week; they had a simple understanding that Sundays were *their* day. Arrangements for most other days were more flexible. But Abby couldn't remember a week when they hadn't gotten together on a Sunday. Her sudden decision would be as readable as the morning headlines. Logan would know she was meeting Tate.

Abby's first inclination was not to be there when he arrived, but that was even more cowardly. In addition, Abby knew Logan well enough to realize that her attempts to dodge him wouldn't work. Either he'd go to the park and look for her or he'd drive to her parents' house and worry them sick.

By the time he did arrive, Abby's stomach felt as if a lead balloon had settled inside.

"Beautiful afternoon, isn't it?" Logan came over to her and slipped an arm around her waist, drawing her close to his side. "Are you feeling better?" he asked in a concerned voice. So often in the past year, Abby had longed for him to hold her like this. Now when he did, she wanted to scream with frustration.

"Yes, I'm...okay."

"What would you like to do?" he asked, nuzzling her neck and holding her close.

"Logan." Abby hesitated, and cleared her throat, feeling guilty. "I've got other plans this afternoon." Her voice didn't even sound like her own as she squeezed her eyes shut, afraid to meet his hard gaze.

A grimness stole into his eyes as his hand tightened. "You're seeing Tate, aren't you?"

Abby caught her breath at the ferocity of his tone. "Of course not!" She couldn't look at him. For the first time in their relationship, Abby was blatantly lying to Logan. No wonder she was experiencing this terrible guilt. For one crazy minute, Abby felt like bursting into tears and running out of the apartment.

"Tell me what you're doing, then," he demanded.

Abby swallowed at the painful lump in throat. "Last week you cut our time together short," she said. "I didn't ask where you were going. I don't feel it's too much to expect the same courtesy."

Logan's grip on her waist slackened, but he didn't release her. "What about later? Couldn't we meet for dinner? There's something I wanted to discuss."

"I can't," she said quickly. Too quickly. Telltale color warmed her face.

Logan studied her for a long moment, then dropped his arm. She should've been glad. Instead she felt chilled and suddenly bereft.

"Let me know when you're free." His words were cold as he moved toward the door.

"Logan," Abby called out to him desperately. "Don't be angry. Please."

When he paused and turned around, his eyes flickered over her. She couldn't quite read his expression but she knew it wasn't flattering. Wordlessly, he turned again and left.

Abby wanted to crawl into a hole, curl up and die. Logan deserved so much better than this. Any number of women would call her a fool—and they'd be right.

* * *

Dressed in white linen shorts and a red cotton shirt, Abby studied her reflection in the full-length mirror on the back of the bedroom door. Her hair hung in a long ponytail, practical for skating, she figured. Makeup did little to disguise the doubt and unhappiness in her eyes. With a jagged breath, Abby tied the sleeves of a sweater around her neck and headed out the door.

Tate was standing by the elm tree waiting for her. He was casually dressed in jeans and a V-neck sweater that hinted at curly chest hair. Even across the park, Abby recognized the quiet authority of the man. His virile look attracted the attention of other women in the vicinity, but Tate didn't seem to notice.

He started walking toward her, his smile approving as he surveyed her long legs.

"You look like you've lost your best friend," Tate said as he slid a casual arm around her shoulder.

Abby winced; his comment might be truer than he knew.

"Problem?" he asked.

"Not really." Her voice quavered, but she managed to give him a broad smile. "I'm hoping we can rent skates. I don't have a pair."

"We can."

It didn't take long for Tate's infectious good mood to brighten Abby's spirits. Soon she was laughing at her bungling attempts to skate. A concrete pathway was very different from the smooth, polished surface of the rink. Either that, or it'd been longer than she realized since her last time on skates.

Tate tucked a hand around her hip as his movements guided hers.

"You're doing great." His eyes were smiling as he relaxed his grasp.

Laughing, Abby looked away from the pathway to answer him when her skate hit a rut and she tumbled forward, wildly thrashing her arms in an effort to remain upright. She would have fallen if Tate hadn't still been holding her. His hand tightened, bringing her closer. She faltered a bit from the effect of his nearness.

"I'm a natural," she said with a grin.

"A natural klutz," he finished for her.

They skated for two hours. When Tate suggested they stop, Abby glanced at her watch and was astonished by the time.

"Hungry?" Tate asked next.

"Famished."

The place Tate took her to was one of those relatively upscale restaurants that charged a great deal for its retro diner atmosphere, but where the reputation for excellent food was well-earned. Abby couldn't imagine Logan bringing her someplace like this. Knowing that made the outing all the more enticing.

When the waitress came, Abby ordered an avocado burger with a large stuffed baked potato and strawberry shortcake for dessert.

Tate smiled. "I'll have the same," he told the waitress, who wrote down their order and stepped away from the table.

"So you do volunteer work at the zoo?" Abby was interested in learning the details he'd promised to share with her.

"I've always loved animals," he began.

"I could tell from the way you talked to the ducks and the squirrels," Abby inserted, recalling the first time she'd seen Tate.

He acknowledged her statement with a nod. "Even as a

child I'd bring home injured animals—rabbits, raccoons, squirrels—and do what I could to make them well."

"Why didn't you become a veterinarian?"

Tate ignored the question. "The hardest part was setting them free once they were well. I might have been a veterinarian if things in my life had gone differently, but I'm good with cars, too."

"You're a mechanic?" Abby asked, already knowing the answer. The callused hands told her that her guess couldn't be far off.

"I work at Bessler's Auto Repair."

"Sure. I know it. That's across the street from the Albertsons' store."

"That's it."

So it *had* just been a coincidence that she'd seen Tate in the store; he worked in the immediate vicinity.

"I've been working there since I was seventeen," Tate added. "Jack Bessler is thinking about retirement these days."

"What'll happen to the shop?"

"I'm hoping to buy it," Tate said as he held his fork, nervously rotating it between two fingers.

Tate was uneasy about something. He ran his fingers up and down the fork, not lifting his gaze from his silverware.

Their meal was as delicious as Abby knew it would be. Whatever had bothered Tate was soon gone and the remainder of the evening was spent talking, getting to know each other with an eagerness that was as strong as their mutual attraction. They talked nonstop for hours, sauntering lazily along the water's edge and laughing, neither of them eager to bring their time together to a close.

When Abby finally got home it was nearly midnight. She floated into the apartment on a cloud of happiness. Even as she readied for bed, she couldn't forget how wonderful the night had been. Tate was a man she could talk to, really talk to. He listened to her and seemed to understand her feelings. Logan listened, too, but Abby had the impression that he sometimes felt impatient with her. But perhaps that wasn't it at all. Maybe she was looking for ways to soothe her conscience. His reaction today still shocked her; as far as she was concerned, they hadn't made any commitment to each other beyond that of friendship. Sometimes Abby wondered if she really knew Logan.

The phone rang fifteen minutes after she was in the door.

Assuming it was Tate, Abby all but flew across the room to answer it, not bothering to check call display. "Hello," she said in a low, sultry voice.

"Abby, is that you? You don't sound right. Are you sick?" It was Logan.

Instantly, Abby stiffened and sank into the comfort of her chair. "Logan," she said in her normal voice. "Hi. Is something wrong?" He wouldn't be phoning this late otherwise.

"Not really."

"I just got in… I mean…" She faltered as her thoughts tripped over each other. "I thought you might be in bed, so I didn't call," she finished lamely. He was obviously phoning to find out what time she got home.

Deftly Logan changed the subject to a matter of no importance, confirming Abby's suspicions. "No," he said, "I was just calling to see what time you wanted me to pick you up for class on Tuesday."

Of all the feeble excuses! "Next time I go somewhere without you, do you want me to phone in so you'll know the precise minute I get home?" she asked crisply, fighting her temper as her hand tightened around the receiver.

His soft chuckle surprised her. "I guess I wasn't very original, was I?"

"No. This isn't like you, Logan. I've never thought of you as the jealous type."

"There's a lot you don't know about me," he answered on a wry note.

"I'm beginning to realize that."

"Do you want me to pick you up for class this week, or have you...made other arrangements?"

"Of course I want you to pick me up! I wouldn't want it any other way." Abby meant that. She liked Logan. The problem was she liked Tate, too.

Logan hesitated and the silence stretched between them. Abby was sure he could hear her racing heart over the phone. But she hoped he couldn't read the confusion in her mind.

After work on Monday afternoon, instead of heading back to her apartment and Dano, Abby stopped off at her parents' house.

"Hi, Mom." She sauntered into the kitchen and kissed her mother on the cheek. "What's there to eat?" Opening the refrigerator door, Abby surveyed the contents with interest.

"Abby," her mother admonished, "what's wrong?"

"Wrong?" Abby feigned ignorance.

"Abby, I'm your mother. I know you. The only time you show up in the middle of the week is if something's bothering you."

"Honestly, aren't I allowed an unexpected visit without parental analysis?"

"Did you and Logan have a fight?" her mother persisted.

Glenna Carpenter's chestnut hair was as dark as Abby's but streaked with gray, creating an unusual color a hairdresser couldn't reproduce. Glenna was a young sixty, vivacious, outgoing and—like Abby—a doer.

"What makes you say that? Logan and I never fight." Abby chewed on a stalk of celery and closed the refrigerator. Taking the salt from the cupboard beside the stove she sprinkled some on it.

"Salt's bad for your blood pressure." Glenna took the shaker out of Abby's hand and replaced it in the cupboard. "Are you going to tell me what's wrong?" She spoke in a warning tone that Abby knew better than to disregard.

"Honest, Mom, there's nothing."

"Abby." Sapphire-blue eyes snapped with displeasure.

Abby couldn't hold back a soft laugh. Her mother had a way of saying more with one glare than some women did with a tantrum.

Holding the celery between her teeth, Abby placed both hands on the counter and pulled herself up, sitting beside the sink.

"Abby," her mother said a second time.

"It's Logan." She gave a frustrated sigh. "He's become so possessive lately."

"Well, thank goodness. I'd have thought you'd be happy." Glenna's smiling eyes revealed her approval. "I was wondering how long it would take him."

"Mother!" Abby wanted to cry. Deep in her heart, she'd known her mother would react like this. "It's too late—I've met someone else."

Glenna froze and a shocked look came over her. "Who?"

"His name is Tate Harding."

"When?"

"A couple of weeks ago."

"How old is he?"

Abby wanted to laugh at her mother's questions. She

sounded as if Abby was fifteen again and asking for permission to date. "He's twenty-seven and a hardworking, respectable citizen. I don't know how to explain it, Mom, but I was instantly attracted to him. I think I'm falling in love."

"Falling in love," Glenna echoed, reheating the day's stale coffee and pouring herself a cup. Her hand shook as she lifted the mug to her mouth a couple of minutes later.

Abby knew her mother was taking her seriously when she drank coffee, which she usually reserved for mornings. A smile tugged at Abby's mouth, but she successfully restrained it.

"I know what you must be thinking," Abby said. "You don't even have to say it because I've already chided myself a thousand times. Logan's the greatest man in the world, but Tate is—"

"The ultimate one?"

The suppressed smile came to life. "You could say that."

"Does Logan know?"

"Of all the luck, they ran into each other at my apartment last week. It would've helped if they hadn't met like that."

"I think having Logan and Tate stumble into each other was more providential than you realize," Glenna murmured with infuriating calm. "I've always liked Logan. I think he's perfect for you."

"How can you *say* that?" Abby demanded indignantly. "We aren't anything alike. We don't even enjoy the same things. Logan can be such a stuffed shirt. And you haven't even met Tate."

"No." Her mother ran the tip of one finger along the rim of her mug. "To be honest, I could never understand why Logan puts up with you. I love you, Abby, but I know your faults as well as your strengths. Apparently Logan sees the same potential in you that I do."

"I can't believe my own mother would talk to me like this." Abby spoke to the ceiling, venting her irritation. "I come to her to pour out my heart and seek her advice and end up being judged."

Glenna laughed. "I'm not judging you," she declared. "Just giving you some sound, motherly advice." An ardent light glowed from her eyes. "Logan loves you. He—"

"Mother," Abby interrupted. "How can you be so sure? If he does, which I sincerely doubt, then he's never told me."

"No, I don't imagine he has. Logan is waiting."

"Waiting?" Abby asked sarcastically. "For what? A blue moon?"

"No," Glenna said sharply and took a long, deliberate sip of her coffee, which must have tasted foul. "He's been waiting for you to grow up. You're impulsive and quick-tempered, especially when it comes to relationships. You expect him to take the lead and yet you resent him for it."

Abby gasped; she couldn't help it. Rarely had her mother spoken this candidly to her. Abby opened her mouth to deny the accusations, then closed it again. The words hurt, especially coming from her own mother, and she lowered her gaze to hide the onrush of emotional pain. Tears gathered in her eyes.

"I'm not saying these things to hurt you," Glenna continued softly.

"I know that." Abby grimaced. "You're right. I should be more honest, but I don't want to hurt Logan."

"Then tell him what you're feeling. Stringing him along would be unkind."

"But it's hard," Abby protested, wiping her eyes. "If I told him yesterday that I was going out with Tate he would've been angry. And miserable."

"And do you suppose he wasn't? I know Logan. If you

said anything to him, he'd immediately step aside until you've settled things in your own mind."

"I know," Abby breathed in frustration. "But I'm not sure I want that, either."

"You mean you want to have your cake and eat it, too," Glenna said. "As the old cliché has it..."

"I never have understood that saying."

"Then maybe you'd better think about it, Abby."

"In other words you're telling me I should let Logan know how I feel about Tate."

"Yes. You can't have it both ways. You can't keep Logan hanging if you want to pursue a romance with this other man."

The seriousness of her mother's look, her words, transferred itself to Abby.

"Today," Glenna insisted. "Now, before you change your mind."

Slowly Abby nodded. She hopped down from the counter, prepared to talk to Logan. "Thanks, Mom."

Glenna Carpenter gave Abby a motherly squeeze. "I'll be thinking about you."

"You'll like Tate."

"I'm sure I will. You always did have excellent taste."

Abby's smile was tentative.

She knew Logan was working late tonight, so she drove straight to his accounting firm, which was situated half a block from her own office. Karen, his assistant, had gone home, and Abby knocked at the outer office. Almost instantly the door opened and Logan gestured her inside.

"Abby." He beamed her a warm smile. "What a nice surprise. Come in, won't you."

Abby took the leather chair opposite his desk.

"Logan." Her fingers had knotted into a tight fist in her lap. "Can we talk?"

He looked down at his watch.

"It won't take long, I promise," she added hurriedly.

Leaning against the side of his desk, he crossed his arms. "What is it, Abby? You never look this serious about anything."

"I think you have a right to know that I was with Tate Harding yesterday." Her heart was hammering wildly as she said this.

"Abby, you're as readable as a child. I was aware from the beginning who you were with," he told her. "I only wish that you'd been honest with me."

"Oh, Logan, I do apologize for that."

"Fine. It's forgotten."

How could he be so generous? So forgiving? Just when she was about to explain that she wanted to continue seeing Tate, Logan reached for her, drawing her into his embrace. As his mouth settled over hers, he drew from her a response so complete that Abby was left speechless and all the more confused. He kissed her as if he couldn't get enough of her mouth, of *her*.

"I've got a client meeting in five minutes," Logan whispered as he massaged her shoulders. "But believe me, holding you is far more appealing. Promise me you'll drop by the office again."

Then he let her go, and she sank back into the chair.

Three

Abby punched the pillow and determinedly shut her eyes. She shouldn't be having so much trouble falling asleep, she thought, fighting back a loud yawn. Ten minutes later, she wearily raised one eyelid and glared at the clock radio. Two-thirty! She groaned audibly. Logan was responsible for this. He should've taken the time to listen to her. Now she didn't know when she'd work up the courage to talk to him about Tate.

And speaking of Tate... He'd phoned after dinner and suggested going to the zoo that weekend. Abby couldn't refuse him. Now she was paying the price—remorse and self-recrimination. Worse, it was all Logan's fault that she hadn't been able to explain the situation to him. She didn't mean to do anything behind his back. She liked both men, but the attraction she felt toward Tate was far more intense than the easy camaraderie she shared with Logan.

Bunching the pillow, Abby forced her eyes to close. She'd gone to Logan to tell him she wanted to date other men. She'd tried, really tried. What else could she do?

When the radio went off at six, Abby wanted to scream. Sleep had eluded her the entire night. The few hours she'd managed to catch wouldn't be enough to see her through the day. Her eyes burned as she tossed aside the covers and sat on the edge of the bed.

More from habit than anything, Abby brushed her teeth and dressed. Coffee didn't help. And the tall glass of orange juice tasted like tomato, but she didn't open her eyes to investigate.

Half an hour later, she let herself into the clinic. The phone was already ringing.

"Morning." Cheryl Hansen, the receptionist, smiled at Abby before answering the call.

Abby returned the friendly gesture with a weak smile of her own.

"You look like the morning after a wild and crazy night," Cheryl said as Abby hung her jacket in the room off the reception area.

"It was wild and crazy, all right," Abby said after an exaggerated yawn. "But not the way you think."

"Another late night with Logan?"

Abby's eyes widened. "No!"

"Tate, then?"

"No. Unfortunately."

"I'm telling you, Ab, keeping track of your love life is getting more difficult all the time."

"I haven't got a love life," she murmured, unable to stop yawning. Covering her mouth, Abby moved to the end of the long hallway.

The day didn't get any better. By noon, she recognized that she couldn't possibly attend tonight's class with Logan. For one thing, she was too tired to concentrate on painting theory and technique. For another, as soon as he saw her troubled expression, he'd know immediately that she was deceiving him and seeing Tate again. And something she didn't need today was another confrontation with Logan. She didn't want to hurt him. But more than that—she didn't want to lie to him.

On her way back from lunch, Abby decided to call his office. Her guilt grew heavier at the pleasure in his voice.

"Abby! What's up?"

"Hi, Logan." She groaned inwardly. "I hope you don't mind me phoning you like this."

"Not at all."

"I'm not feeling well." She paused, her hand tightening around the receiver. "I was thinking that maybe it'd be best if I skipped class tonight."

"What's wrong?" His genuine concern was nearly her undoing. "You weren't well on Friday, either."

Did he really believe her excuse of Friday evening, which had been nothing but a way of avoiding him?

"You must be coming down with something," he said.

"I think so." *Like a terminal case of cowardice*, her mind shot back.

"Have you seen a doctor?"

"It isn't necessary. Not yet. But I thought I'd stay home again tonight and go to bed early," Abby mumbled, feeling more wretched every second.

"Do you need me to do anything for you?" His voice was laced with gentleness.

"No," she assured him quickly. "I'm fine. Really. I just thought I'd nip this thing in the bud and take it easy."

"Okay. But promise me that if you need anything, you'll call."

"Oh, sure."

Abby felt even worse after making that phone call. By the time she returned to her apartment late that afternoon her excuse for not attending her class had become real. Her head was throbbing unmercifully; her throat felt dry and scratchy and her stomach was queasy.

With her fingertips pressing her temple, Abby located the aspirin in the bathroom cabinet and downed two tablets. Afterward she lay on the sofa, the phone beside her, head propped up with a soft pillow, and closed her eyes. She didn't open them when the phone rang and she scrabbled around for it blindly.

"Hello." Her reluctant voice was barely above a whisper.

"Abby, is that you?"

She breathed easier. It was her mother.

"Hi, Mom."

"What's wrong?"

"I've got a miserable headache."

"What's bothering you?"

"What makes you think anything's bothering me?" Her mother displayed none of the sympathy Logan had.

"Abby, I know you. When you get a headache it's because something's troubling you."

Breathing deeply, Abby glanced at the ceiling with wide-open eyes, unable to respond.

"Did you talk to Logan yesterday?" Her mother resumed the interrogation.

"Only for a little while. He was on his way to a meeting."

"Did you tell him you want to continue seeing Tate?"

"I didn't get the chance," Abby said more aggressively than she'd intended. "Mom, I tried, but he didn't have time to listen. Then Tate phoned me and asked me out this weekend and… I said yes."

"Does Logan know?"

"Not yet," she mumbled.

"And you've got a whopper of a headache?"

"Yes." The word trembled on her lips.

"Abby." Her mother's voice took on the tone Abby knew all too well. "You've *got* to talk to Logan."

"I will."

"Your headache won't go away until you do."

"I know."

Dano strolled into the room and leaped onto the sofa, settling in Abby's lap. Grateful to have one friend left in the world, Abby stroked her cat.

It took her at least twenty minutes to work up enough fortitude to call Logan's home number. His phone rang six times, and Abby sighed, not leaving a message. She assumed he'd gone to class on his own, that he was on his way, so she didn't bother trying his cell. She'd talk to him tomorrow.

She closed her eyes again, wondering how—if—she could balance her intense attraction to Tate with her feelings of friendship for Logan. Friendship that sometimes hinted at more. His ardent kiss yesterday had taken her by surprise. But she *had* to tell him about Tate....

The apartment buzzer woke Abby an hour later. She sat up and rubbed the stiff muscles of her neck. Dano remained on her lap and meowed angrily when she stood, forcing the cat to leap to the floor.

"Yes?" she said into the speaker.

"It's Logan."

Abby buzzed him in. Her hand was shaking visibly as she unlocked the door. "Hi," she said in a high-pitched voice.

Logan stepped inside. "How are you feeling?"

"I don't know." She yawned, stretching her arms. "Better, I guess." Her attention was drawn to a white sack Logan was holding. "What's that?"

A crooked smile slanted his mouth. "Chicken soup. I

picked some up at the deli." He handed her the bag. "I want to make sure you're well enough for the game tomorrow night."

Abby's head shot up. "Game? What game?"

"I wondered if you'd forgotten. We signed up a couple of weeks ago for the softball team. Remember?"

This was the second summer they were playing in the office league. With her recent worries, softball had completely slipped Abby's mind. "Oh, *that* game." Abby wanted to groan. She'd *never* be able to avoid Logan. Too many activities linked them together—work, classes and now softball.

She took the soup into the kitchen, removing the large plastic cup from the sack. The aroma of chicken and noodles wafted through the small room. Logan followed her in and slipped his arms around her waist from behind. His chin rested on her head as he spoke. "I woke you up, didn't I?"

She nodded, resisting the urge to turn and slip her arms around his waist and bury her face in his chest. "But it's probably a good thing you did. I've gotten a crick in my neck sleeping on the couch with Dano on my lap."

Logan's breath stirred the hair at the top of her head. The secure feeling of his arms holding her close was enough to bring tears to her eyes.

"Logan." She breathed his name in a husky murmur. "Why are you so good to me?"

He turned her to face him. "I would've thought you'd have figured it out by now," he said as he slowly lowered his mouth to hers.

A sweetness flooded Abby at the tender possession of his mouth. She wanted to cry and beg him *not* to love her. Not yet. Not until she was sure of her feelings. But the gentle caress of his lips prevented the words from ever forming. Her hands moved up his shirt and over his shoulders, reveling in his strength.

His hands, at the small of her back, arched her closer as he inhaled deeply. "I've got to go or I'll be late for class. Will you be all right?"

Speaking was impossible and it was almost more than Abby could do to simply nod her head.

He straightened, relaxing his grip. "Take care of yourself," he said as his eyes smiled lovingly into hers.

Again it was all Abby could do to nod.

"I'll pick you up tomorrow at six-thirty, if you're up to it. We can grab a bite to eat after the game."

"Okay," she managed shakily and walked him to the door. "Thanks for the soup."

Logan smiled. "I've got to take care of the team's first-base player, don't I?" His mouth brushed hers and he was gone.

Leaning against the door, Abby looked around her grimly. If she felt guilty before, she felt wretched now.

Shoving the baseball cap down on her long brown hair, which she'd tied back in a loose ponytail, Abby couldn't stifle a sense of excitement. She did enjoy softball. And Logan was right—she was the best first-base player the team was likely to find. Not to mention her hitting ability.

Logan wasn't as good a player but enjoyed himself as much as she did. He just didn't have the same competitive edge. More than once he'd been responsible for an error. But no one seemed to mind and Abby didn't let it bother her.

As usual he was punctual when he came to pick her up. "Hi. I can see you're feeling better."

"Much better."

The game was scheduled to be played in Diamond Lake Park, and Abby was half-afraid Tate would stumble across them. She wasn't sure how often he went into the park and— She reined in her worries. There was no reason to assume he'd show up or that he'd even recognize her.

Most of the team had arrived by the time Abby and Logan sauntered onto the field. The Jack and Jill Softball League was recreational. Of all their team members, Abby was the one who took the game most seriously. The team positions alternated between men and women. Since Abby played first base, a man was at second. Logan was in the outfield.

The team they were playing was from a local church that Abby remembered having beaten last summer.

Dick Snyder was their office team's coach and strategist. "Hope that arm's as good as last year," Dick said to Abby, who beamed at him. It was gratifying to be appreciated.

After a few warm-up exercises and practice pitches, their team left the field. Logan was up at bat first. Abby cringed at the stiff way he held himself. He wasn't a natural athlete, despite his biking prowess.

"Logan," she shouted encouragingly, "flex your knees."

He did as she suggested and swung at the next pitch. The ground ball skidded past the shortstop and Logan was safe on first.

Abby breathed easier and sent him a triumphant smile.

Patty Martin was up at bat next. Abby took one look at the shy, awkward young woman and knew she'd be an immediate out. Patty was new to the team this year, and Abby hoped she'd stick with it.

"Come on, Patty," she called out, hoping to instill some confidence, "you can do it!"

Patty held the bat clumsily and bit her lip as she glared

straight ahead at the pitcher. She swung at the first three balls and missed each one.

Dick pulled Patty aside and gave her a pep talk before she took her place on the bench.

Abby hurried over to Patty and patted her knee. "I'm glad you decided to play with us." She meant that honestly. She suspected Patty could do with some friends.

"But I'm terrible." Patty stared at her clenched hands and Abby noticed how white her knuckles were.

"You'll improve," Abby said with more certainty than she felt. "Everyone has to learn, and believe me, every one of us strikes out. Don't worry about it."

By the time Abby was up to bat, there were two outs and Logan was still at first. Her standup double and a home run by the hitter following her made the score 3–0.

It remained the same until the bottom of the eighth. Logan was playing the outfield when a high fly ball went over his head. He scrambled to retrieve it.

Frantically jumping up and down at first base, Abby screamed, "Throw the ball to second! Second." She watched in horror as Logan turned and faced third base. "Second!" she yelled angrily.

The woman on third base missed the catch, and the batter went on to make it home, giving his team their first run.

Abby threw her glove down and, with her hands placed defiantly on her hips, stormed into the outfield and up to Logan. "I told you to throw the ball to second."

He gave her a mildly sheepish look. "Sorry, Abby. All your hysterics confused me."

Groaning, Abby returned to her position.

They won the game 3–1 and afterward gathered at the local restaurant for pizza and pitchers of beer.

"You're really good," Patty said, sitting beside Abby.

"Thanks," she said, smiling into her beer. "I was on the high-school team for three years, so I had lots of practice."

"I don't know if I'll ever learn."

"Sure you will," Logan insisted. "Besides, we need you. Didn't you notice we'd be one woman short if it wasn't for you?"

Abby hadn't noticed that, but was pleased Logan had brought it up. This quality of making people feel important had drawn Abby to him on their first date.

"I'm awful, but I really like playing. And it gives me a chance to know all of you better," Patty added shyly.

"We like having you," Abby confirmed. "And you *will* improve." Patty seemed to want the reassurance that she was needed and appreciated, and Abby didn't mind echoing Logan's words.

They ate their pizzas and joked while making plans for the game the following Wednesday evening.

Dick Snyder and his wife gave Patty a ride home. Patty hesitated in the parking lot. "Bye, Abby. Bye, Logan," she said timidly. "I'll see you soon."

Abby smiled secretly to herself. Patty was attracted to Logan. She'd praised his skill several times that evening. Abby didn't blame her. Logan was wonderful. True, he wasn't going to be joining the Minnesota Twins any year soon—or ever. But he'd made it to base every time he was up at bat.

Logan dropped Abby off at her apartment, but didn't accept her invitation to come in for a glass of iced tea. To be honest, Abby was grateful. She didn't know how much longer she could hide from Logan that she was continuing to see Tate. And she refused to lie if he asked her. She planned to tell him soon…as soon as an appropriate opportunity presented itself.

The remainder of the week went smoothly. She didn't

talk to Logan, which made things easier. Abby realized that Sunday afternoon with him would be difficult after spending Saturday with Tate, but she decided to worry about it then.

She woke Saturday morning with a sense of expectation. Tate was taking the afternoon off and meeting her in the park after she'd finished tutoring Mai-Ling. From there they were driving out to Apple Valley and the Minnesota Zoo, where he did volunteer work.

She wore a pale pink linen summer dress and had woven her long brown hair into a French braid. A glance in the mirror revealed that she looked her best.

Mai-Ling met her and smiled knowingly. "You and Tate are seeing each other today?"

"We're going to the zoo."

"The animal place, right?"

"Right."

Abby's attention drifted while Mai-Ling did her lesson. The woman's ability was increasing with every meeting. Judging by the homework Mai-Ling brought for Abby to examine, the young woman wouldn't be needing her much longer.

They'd finished their lesson and were laughing when Abby looked up and saw Tate strolling across the lawn toward her.

Again she was struck by the sight of this ruggedly appealing male. He was dressed in jeans, a tight-fitting T-shirt and cowboy boots.

His rich brown eyes seemed to burn into hers. "Hello, Abby." He greeted Mai-Ling, but his eyes left Abby's only for a second.

"I'll catch my bus," said Mai-Ling, excusing herself, but Abby barely noticed.

"You're looking gorgeous today," Tate commented, taking her hand in his.

A tingling sensation shot up her arm at his touch. Her nerves felt taut just from standing beside him. Abby couldn't help wondering what kissing Tate would be like. Probably the closest thing to heaven this side of earth.

"You seem deep in thought."

Abby smiled up at him. "Sorry. I guess I was."

They chatted easily as Tate drove toward Apple Valley. Abby learned that he'd been a volunteer for three years, working at the zoo as many as two days a week.

"What animals do you care for?"

Tate answered her without taking his eyes off the road. "Most recently I've been working with a llama for the Family Farm, but I also do a lot of work with birds. In fact, I've been asked to assist in the bird show."

"Will you?" Abby remembered seeing Tate that first day with the ducks....

"Yes."

"What other kinds of things do you do?"

Tate's returning smile was quick. "Nothing that glamorous. I help at feeding time and I clean the cages. Sometimes I groom and exercise the animals."

"What are you doing with the llama?"

"Mostly I've been working to familiarize him with people. We'd like Larry to join his brother in giving children rides."

Tate parked the car and came around to her side to open the passenger door. He kept her hand tucked in his as he led the way to the entrance.

"You love it here, don't you?" Abby asked as they cleared the gates.

"I do. The zoo gives us a rare opportunity to discover nature and our relationship to other living things. We have a responsibility to protect animals, as well as their habitats. Zoos, good zoos like this, are part of that." A glint of laughter flashed in his eyes as he turned toward her. "I didn't know I could be so profound."

Someone called out to Tate, and Abby watched him respond with a brief wave.

"Where would you like to start?"

The zoo was divided into five regions and Abby chose Tropics Trail, an indoor oasis of plants and animals from Asia.

As they walked, Tate explained what they were seeing, regaling her with fascinating bits of information. She'd been to the zoo before, but she'd never had such a knowledgeable guide.

Three hours later, it was closing time.

"Promise you'll bring me again," Abby begged, her eyes held by Tate's with mesmerizing ease.

"I promise," he whispered as he led her toward his car.

The way he said it made her feel weak in the knees, made her forget everything and everyone else. She lapsed into a dreamy silence on the drive home.

Tate drove back to Minneapolis and they stopped at a Mexican restaurant near Diamond Lake Park. Abby had passed it on several occasions but never eaten there.

A young Hispanic waitress smiled at them and led them to a table.

Tate spoke to the woman in Spanish. She nodded her head and turned around.

"What did you ask?" Abby whispered.

"I wanted to know if we could eat outside. You don't mind, do you? The evening is lovely."

"No, that sounds great." But she did mind. Because it immediately occurred to her that Logan might drive past and see her eating there with Tate. Abby managed to squelch her worries as she sat down at a table on the patio and opened her menu. She studied its contents, but her appetite had unexpectedly disappeared.

"You've got that thoughtful look again," Tate remarked. "Is everything okay, Abby?"

"Oh, sure," she said.

Abby decided what she'd order and took the opportunity to watch Tate as he reviewed the menu. His brow was creased, his eyes narrowed in concentration. When he happened to glance up and found her looking at him he set the menu aside.

An awkwardness followed. It continued until the waitress finally stopped at their table. Abby ordered cheese enchiladas and a margarita; Tate echoed her choice but asked for a Corona beer. "I had a good time today," Abby said in an attempt to breach the silence after the waitress left.

"I did, too." Tate sounded stiff, as if he suddenly felt uneasy.

"Is something wrong?" Abby asked after another silence.

It could have been Abby's imagination, but she sensed that Tate was struggling within himself.

"Tate?" she prompted.

He leaned forward and pinched the bridge of his nose before exhaling loudly. "No...nothing."

Long after he'd dropped her off at the apartment, Abby couldn't shake the sensation that something was troubling him. Twice he'd seemed about to speak, but both times he'd stopped himself.

Abby's thoughts were heavy as she drifted into sleep. Tomorrow she'd be spending the afternoon with Logan. She had to tell him she'd decided to see Tate; delaying it any longer was a grave disservice to them both—to Logan *and* to Tate.

* * *

Sunday afternoon, Logan sat on the sofa beside Abby and reached for her hand. She had to force herself not to snatch it away. So often in the past Abby had wanted Logan to be more demonstrative. And now that he was, it caused such turmoil inside her that she wanted to cry.

"You're looking pale, Abby. Are you sure you're feeling all right?" he asked her, his voice concerned.

"Logan, I've got to talk to you," she blurted out miserably. "I need to—"

"What you need is to get out of this stuffy apartment." He stood up, bringing her with him. Slipping an arm around her waist, Logan directed her out of the apartment and to his car.

Abby didn't have time to protest as he opened the door. She climbed inside and he leaned across to fasten her seat belt.

"Where are we going?" she asked, confused and unhappy as he backed out of the parking area.

"For a drive."

"I don't want to go for a drive."

Logan glanced away from the road long enough to narrow his eyes slightly at her. "Abby, what is it? You look like you're about to cry."

"I am." She swallowed convulsively and bit her bottom lip. "I want to go back to the apartment."

Logan pulled over and cut the engine. "Abby, what's wrong?" he asked solicitously.

Abby got out and leaned against the side of the car. The blood was pounding wildly in her ears. She hugged her waist with both arms.

"Abby?" he prompted softly as he joined her.

"I tried to tell you on Monday evening," she said. "I even went to your office, but you had some stupid meeting."

He didn't argue with her. "Is this about Tate?"

"Yes!" she shouted. "I went to the zoo with him yesterday. All week I've felt guilty because I know you don't want me to see anyone except you."

Abby chanced a look at him. He displayed no emotion, his eyes dark and unreadable. "Do you want to continue seeing him?" he asked carefully.

"I like Tate. I've liked him from the time we met," Abby admitted in a low whisper. "I don't know him all that well, but—"

"You want to get to know him better?" His eyes seemed to draw her toward him like a magnet.

"Yes," she whispered, gazing up at him.

"Then you should," he said evenly.

"Oh, Logan," she breathed. "I was hoping you'd understand."

"I do, Abby." He placed his hands deep inside his pants pockets and walked around the car, opening the passenger door.

"Where are we going?"

He looked mildly surprised. "I'm taking you home."

The smile that touched the corners of his mouth didn't reach his eyes. "Abby, if you're seeing Tate, you won't be seeing me."

Four

Shocked, Abby stared at him, and her voice trembled slightly. "What do you mean?"

"Isn't it obvious?" Logan turned toward her. His eyes had darkened and grown more intense. There was an almost imperceptible movement along his jaw. "Remind me. How long have we been dating?" he asked, but his voice revealed nothing.

"You know how long we've been dating. About a year now. What's that got to do with anything?"

Logan frowned. "If you don't know how you feel about me in that length of time, then I can't see continuing a relationship."

Abby clenched her fist, feeling impotent anger well up within her. "You're trying to blackmail me, aren't you?"

"Blackmail you?" Logan snapped. He paused and breathed in deeply. "No, Abby, that isn't my intention."

"But you're saying that if I go out with Tate, then I can't see you," she returned with a short, bitter laugh. "You're not being fair. I like you both. You're wonderful, Logan, but...but so is Tate."

"Then decide. Which one of us do you want?"

Logan made it sound so simple. "I can't." She inhaled a shaky breath and raked a weary hand through her hair. "It's not that easy."

"Do you want Tate and me to slug it out? Is that it? Winner takes the spoils?"

"No!" she cried, shocked and angry.

"You've got the wrong man if you think I'll do that."

Tears spilled from Abby's eyes. "That's not what I want, and you know it."

"Then what *do* you want?" The low question was harsh.

"Time. I… I need to sort through my feelings. When did it become a crime to feel uncertain? I barely know Tate—"

"Time," Logan interrupted, but the anger in his tone didn't seem directed at her. "That's exactly what I'm giving you. Take as long as you need. When you've decided what you feel, let me know."

"But you won't see me?"

"Seeing you will be unavoidable. Our offices are half a block apart—and we have the softball team."

"Classes?"

"No. There's no need for us to go together or to meet each other there."

Tilting her chin downward, Abby swiped at her tears, trying to quell the rush of hurt. Logan could remove her from his life so effortlessly. His apparent indifference pierced her heart.

Without a word, he drove her back to the apartment building and parked, but didn't shut off the engine.

"Before you go," Abby said, her voice quavering, "would you hold me? Just once?"

Logan's hand tightened on the steering wheel until his knuckles were strained and white. "Do you want a comparison? Is that it?" he asked in a cold, stiff voice.

"No, that wasn't what I wanted." She reached for the door handle. "I'm sorry I asked."

Logan didn't move. They drew each breath in unison. Unflinching, their eyes held each other until Logan, his clenched jaw, hard and proud, became a watery blur and Abby lowered her gaze.

"Call me, Abby. But only when you're sure." The words were meant as a dismissal and the minute she was out of his car, he drove away.

Abby's knees felt so weak, she sat down as soon as she got inside her apartment. She was stunned. She'd expected Logan to be angry, but she'd never expected this—that he'd refuse to see her again. She'd only tried to be fair. Hurting Logan, or Tate for that matter, was the last thing she wanted. But how could she possibly know what she felt toward Tate? Everything was still so new. As she'd told Logan, they barely knew each other. They hadn't so much as kissed. But she and Logan were supposed to be friends....

She moped around the house for a couple of hours, then thought she'd pay her parents a visit. Her mother would be as shocked at Logan's reaction as she'd been. Abby needed reassurance that she'd done the right thing, especially since nothing had worked out as she'd hoped.

The short drive to her parents' house was accomplished in a matter of minutes. But there was no response to her knock; her parents appeared to be out. Belatedly, Abby recalled her mother saying that they were going camping that weekend.

Abby slumped on the front steps, feeling enervated and depressed. Eventually she returned to her car, without any clear idea of where she should go or what she should do.

Never had a Sunday been so dull. Abby drove around

for a time, picked up a hamburger at a drive-in and washed her car. Without Logan, the day seemed empty.

Lying in bed that night, Dano at her feet, Abby closed her eyes. If she'd missed Logan, he must have felt that same sense of loss. This could work both ways. Logan would soon discover how much of a gap she'd left in *his* life.

The phone rang Monday evening and Abby glanced at it anxiously. It had to be Logan, she thought hopefully. Who else would be calling? She didn't recognize the number, so maybe he had a new cell, she told herself.

"Hello," she said cheerfully. If it *was* Logan, she didn't want him to get the impression that she was pining away for him.

"Abby, it's Tate."

Tate. An unreasonable sense of disappointment filled her. What was the matter with her? This whole mess had come about because she wanted to be with Tate.

"How about a movie Friday evening?"

"I'd like that." She exhaled softly.

"You don't sound like yourself. Is something wrong?"

"No," she denied quickly. "What movie would you like to see?"

They spoke for a few more minutes and Abby managed to steer the conversation away from herself. For those few minutes, Tate helped her forget how miserable she was, but the feelings of loss and frustration returned the moment she hung up.

Tuesday evening, Abby waited outside the community center hoping to see Logan before class. She planned to give him a regal stare that would show how content she was without him. Naturally, if he gave any hint of his own unhappiness, she might succumb and speak to him. But either he'd arrived before her or after she'd gone into the building, because Abby didn't catch a glimpse of him anywhere. Maybe he'd even skipped class, but she doubted that. Logan loved chess.

The painting class remained a blur in her mind as she hurried out the door to the café across the street. She'd met Logan there after every class so far. He'd come; Abby was convinced of it. She pictured how their eyes would meet and intuitively they'd know that being apart like this was wrong for them. Logan would walk to her table, slip in beside her and take her hand. Everything would be there in his eyes for her to read.

The waitress gave Abby a surprised glance and asked if she was sitting alone tonight as she handed her the menu. Dejectedly Abby acknowledged that she was alone...at least for now.

When Logan entered the café, Abby straightened, her heart racing. He looked as good as he always did. What she didn't see was any outward sign of unhappiness...or relief at her presence. But, she reminded herself, Logan wasn't one to display his emotions openly. Their eyes met and he gave her an abrupt nod before sliding into a booth on the opposite side of the room.

So much for daydreams, Abby mused. Well, fine, he could sit there all night, but she refused to budge. Logan would have to come to her. Determinedly she studied the menu, pretending indifference. When she couldn't stand it any longer, she glanced at him from the corner of her eye. He now shared his booth with two other guys and was chatting easily with his friends. Abby's heart sank.

"I'm telling you, Mother," Abby said the next afternoon in her mother's kitchen. "He's blown this whole thing out of proportion."

"What makes you say that?" Glenna Carpenter closed the oven door and set the meat loaf on top of the stove.

"Logan isn't even talking to me."

"It doesn't seem like there's been much opportunity. But I wouldn't worry. He will tonight at the game."

"What makes you so sure of that?" Abby hopped down from her position on the countertop.

Glenna straightened and wiped her hands on her ever-present terry cloth apron. "Things have a way of working out for the best, Abby," she continued nonchalantly.

"Mom, you've been telling me that all my life and I've yet to see it happen."

Glenna chuckled, slowly shaking her head. "It happens every day of our lives. Just look around." Deftly she turned the meat loaf onto a platter. "By the way, didn't you say your game's at six o'clock?"

Abby nodded and glanced at her watch, surprised that the time had passed so quickly. "Gotta rush. Bye, Mom." She gave her mother a peck on the cheek. "Wish me well."

"With Logan or the game?" Teasing blue eyes so like her own twinkled merrily.

"Both!" Abby laughed and was out the door.

Glenna followed her to the porch, and Abby felt her mother's sober gaze as she hurried down the front steps and to her car.

Almost everyone was on the field warming up when Abby got there. Immediately her gaze sought out Logan. He was in the outfield pitching to another of the male players. Abby tried to suppress the emotion that charged through her. Who would've believed she'd feel so lost and unhappy without Logan? If he saw that Abby had arrived, he gave no indication.

"Hi, Abby," Patty called, waving from the bench.

Abby smiled absently. "Hi."

"Wait until you see me bat." Patty beamed happily, pretending to swing at an imaginary pitch. Then, placing her hand over her eyes as the fantasy ball flew into left field, she added, "I think I'll be up for an award by the end of the season."

"Good." Abby was preoccupied as she stared out at Logan. He looked so attractive. So vital. Couldn't he have the decency to develop some lines at his eyes or a few gray hairs? He *had* to be suffering. She was, although it wasn't what she'd wanted or expected.

"Logan took me to see the Twins play on Monday night and he gave me a few pointers afterward," Patty continued.

Abby couldn't believe what she was hearing. *A few pointers? I'll just bet he did!* Logan and Patty?

The shock must have shown in her eyes because Patty added hurriedly, "You don't mind, do you? When Logan phoned, I asked him about the two of you and he said you'd both decided to start seeing other people."

"No, I don't mind," Abby returned flippantly, remembering her impression last week—that Patty had a crush on him. "Why should I?"

"I... I just wanted to be sure."

If Patty thought she'd get an award for baseball, Abby was sure someone should nominate *her* for an Oscar. By the end of the game her face hurt from her permanent smile. She laughed, cheered, joked and tried to suggest that she hadn't a care in the world. At bat she was dynamite. Her pain was readily transferred to her swing and she didn't hit anything less than a double and got two home runs.

Once, Logan had patted her affectionately on the back

to congratulate her, Abby had shot him an angry glare. It'd taken him only one day. *One day* to ask Patty out. That hurt.

"Abby?" Logan's dark brows rose questioningly. "What's wrong?"

"Wrong?" Although she gave him a blank look, she realized her face must have divulged her feelings. "What could possibly be wrong? By the way, Tate said hello. He wanted to be here tonight, but something came up." Abby knew her lie was childish, but she couldn't help her reaction.

She didn't speak to him again.

Gathering the equipment after the game, Abby tried not to remember the way Patty had positioned herself next to Logan on the bench during the game and how she made excuses to be near him at every opportunity.

"You're coming for pizza, aren't you?" Dick asked Abby for the second time.

Abby wanted to go. The get-togethers after the game were often more fun than the game itself. But she couldn't bear the curious stares that were sure to follow when Logan sat next to Patty and started flirting with her.

"Not tonight," Abby responded, opening her eyes wide to give Dick a look of false candor. "I've got other plans." Abby noticed the way Logan's mouth curved in a mirthless smile. He'd heard that and come to his own conclusions. Good!

Abby regretted her hasty refusal later. The apartment was hot and muggy. Even Dano, her temperamental cat, didn't want to spend time with her.

After a cool shower, Abby fixed a meal of scrambled eggs, toast and a chocolate bar. She wasn't the least bit hungry, but eating was at least a distraction.

She couldn't concentrate on her newest suspense novel, so she sat on the sofa and turned on the TV. A rerun of an old situation comedy helped block out the image of Patty in Logan's arms. Abby didn't doubt that Logan had kissed Patty. The bright, happy look in her eyes had said as much.

Uncrossing her legs, Abby released a bitter sigh. She shouldn't care if Logan kissed a hundred women. But she did. It bothered her immensely—regardless of her own hopes and fantasies about Tate. She recognized how irrational she was being, and her confusion only increased.

With the television blaring to drown out the echo of Patty's telling her about the fun she'd had with Logan, Abby reached for the chocolate bar and peeled off the wrapper. The sweet flavor wouldn't ease the discomfort in her stomach, because Abby knew it wasn't chocolate she wanted, it was Logan. Feeling wretched again, she set the candy bar aside and leaned her head back, closing her eyes.

By Friday evening, Abby was convinced all the contradictory feelings she had about Logan could be summed up in one sentence: The grass is always greener on the other side of the fence. It was another of those clichés her mother seemed so fond of and spouted on a regular basis. She was surprised Glenna hadn't dragged this one into their conversations about Logan and Tate. The idea of getting involved with Tate had been appealing when she was seeing Logan steadily. It stood to reason that the reverse was also true—that Logan would miss her and lose interest in Patty. At least that was what Abby told herself repeatedly as she dressed for her date.

With her long brown hair a frame around her oval face, she put on more makeup than usual. With a secret little smile she applied an extra dab of perfume. Tate wouldn't know what hit him! The summer dress was one of her best—a pale blue sheath that could be dressed up or down, so she was as comfortable wearing it to a movie as she would be to a formal dinner.

When Tate arrived, he had on a pair of cords and a cotton shirt, open at the neck, sleeves rolled up. It was undeniably a sexy look.

"You're stunning," he said appreciatively, kissing her lightly on the cheek.

"Thank you." Abby couldn't restrain her disappointment. He'd looked at her the way one would a sister and his kiss wasn't that of a lover—or someone who intended to be a lover.

Still, they joked easily as they waited in line for the latest blockbuster action movie and Abby was struck by their camaraderie. It didn't take her long to realize that their relationship wasn't hot and fiery, sparked by mutual attraction. Instead, it was…friendly. Warm. Almost lacking in imagination. Ironically, that had been exactly her complaint about Logan….

Tate bought a huge bucket of popcorn, which they shared in the darkened theater. But Abby noted that he appeared restless, often shifting his position, crossing and uncrossing his legs. Once, when he assumed she wasn't watching, he laid his head against the back of the seat and closed his eyes. Was Tate in pain? she wondered.

Abby's attention drifted from the movie. "Tate," she whispered. "Are you okay?"

He immediately opened his eyes. "Of course. Why?"

Rather than refer to his restlessness, she simply shook her head and pretended an interest in the screen.

When they'd finished the popcorn, Tate reached for her hand. But Abby noted that it felt tense. If she didn't know better, she'd swear he was nervous. But Abby couldn't imagine what possible reason Tate would have to be nervous around her.

The evening was hot and close when they emerged from the theater.

"Are you hungry?" Tate asked, taking her hand, and again, Abby was struck by how unnaturally tense he seemed.

"For something cold and sinful," she answered with a teasing smile.

"Beer?"

"No," Abby said with a laugh. "Ice cream."

Tate laughed, too, and hand in hand they strolled toward the downtown area where Tate assured her he knew of an old fashioned ice-cream place. The Swanson Parlor was decorated in pink—pink walls, pink chairs, pink linen tablecloths and pink-dressed waitresses.

Abby decided quickly on a banana split and mentioned it to Tate.

"That does sound good. I'll have one, too."

Abby shut her menu and set it aside. This was the third time they'd gone for something to eat, and each time Tate had ordered the same thing she did. He didn't seem insecure. But maybe she was being oversensitive. Besides, it didn't make any difference.

Their rapport made conversation comfortable and light-hearted. They talked about the movie and other films they'd both seen. Abby discussed some of her favorite mystery novels and Tate described animal behavior he'd witnessed. But several times Abby noted that his laughter was forced. His gaze would become intent and his sudden seriousness would throw the conversation off stride.

"I love Minneapolis," Abby said as they left the ice-cream parlor. "It's such a livable city."

"I agree," Tate commented. "Do you want to go for a walk?"

"Yes, let's." Abby tucked her hand in the crook of his elbow.

Tate looked at her and smiled, but again Abby noted the sober look in his eyes. "I was born in California," he began.

"What's it like there?" Abby had been to New York but she'd never visited the West Coast.

"I don't remember much. My family moved to New Mexico when I was six."

"Hot, I'll bet," Abby said.

"It's funny, the kinds of things you remember. I don't recall what the weather was like. But I have a very clear memory of my first-grade teacher in Alburquerque, Ms. Grimes. She was pretty and really tall." Tate chuckled. "But I suppose all teachers are tall to a six-year-old. We moved again in the middle of that year."

"You seem to have moved around quite a bit," Abby said, wondering why Tate had started talking about himself so freely. Although they had talked about a number of different subjects, she knew little about his personal life.

"We moved five times in as many years," Tate continued. "We had no choice, really. My dad couldn't hold down a job, and every time he lost one we'd pack up and move, seeking another start, another escape." Tate's face hardened. "We came to Minneapolis when I was in the eighth grade."

"Did your father finally find his niche in life?" Abby sensed that Tate was revealing something he rarely shared with anyone. She felt honored, but surprised. Their relationship was promising in some ways and disappointing in others, but the fact that he trusted her with his pain, his difficult past, meant a lot. She wondered why he'd chosen her as a confidante.

"No, Dad died before he ever found what he was look-ing for." There was no disguising the anguish in his voice. "My feelings for my father are as confused now as they were then." He turned toward Abby, his expression solemn. "I hated him and I loved him."

"Did your life change after he was gone?" Abby's ques-tion was practically a whisper, respecting the deep emo-tion in Tate's eyes.

"Yes and no. A couple of years later, I dropped out of school and got a job as a mechanic. My dad taught me a lot, enough to persuade Jack Bessler to hire me."

"And you've been there ever since?"

His mouth quirked at one corner. "Ever since."

"You didn't graduate from high school then, did you?"

"No."

That sadness was back in his voice. "And you resent that?" Abby asked softly.

"I may have for a time, but I never fit in a regular class-room. I guess in some ways I'm a lot like my dad. Restless and insecure. But I'm much more content working at the garage than I ever was in a classroom."

"You've worked there for years now," Abby said, con-tradicting his assessment of himself. "How can you say you're restless?"

He didn't acknowledge her question. "There's a chance I could buy the business. Jack's ready to retire and wants out from under the worry."

"That's what you really want, isn't it, Tate?"

"The business is more than I ever thought I'd have."

"But something's stopping you?" Abby could sense this more from his tension than from what he said.

"Yes." The stark emotion in his voice startled her.

"Are you worried about not having graduated from high

school? Because, Tate, you can now. There's a program at the community center where I take painting classes. You can get what they call a G.E.D.—General Education Diploma, I think is what it means. Anyway, all you need to do is talk to a counselor and—"

"That's not it." Tate interrupted her harshly and ran a hand across his brow.

"Then what is it?" Abby asked, her smile determined.

Tate hesitated until the air between them was electric, like a storm ready to explode in the muggy heat.

"Where are you going with this discussion? What can I do to help? I don't understand." One minute Tate was exposing a painful part of his past, and the next he was growling at her. What was it with men? Something had been bothering him all evening. First he'd been restless and uneasy, then brooding and thoughtful, now angry. Nothing made sense.

And it wasn't going to. Abruptly he asked her if she was ready to leave.

He hardly said a word to her when he dropped her off at her apartment.

For a moment, Abby was convinced he'd never ask her out again.

"What about Sunday?" he finally said. "We can bring a picnic."

"Okay." But after this evening, Abby wasn't sure. He didn't sound as if he really wanted her company. "How about three o'clock?"

"Fine." His response was clipped.

Again he gave her a modest kiss, more a light brushing of their mouths than anything passionate or intense. Not a real kiss, in her opinion.

She leaned against the closed door of her apartment, not

understanding why Tate was bothering to take her out. It seemed apparent that his interest in her wasn't romantic—although she didn't know what it actually was, didn't know what he wanted or needed from her. And for that matter, the bone-melting effect she'd experienced at their first meeting had long since gone. Tate was a handsome man, but he wasn't what she'd expected.

Maybe the grass wasn't so green after all.

After a restless Sunday morning, Abby decided that she'd go for a walk in the park. Logan often did before he came over to her place, and she hoped to run into him. She'd make a point of letting him know that their meeting was pure coincidence. They'd talk. Somehow she'd inform him, casually of course, that things weren't working out as she'd planned. In fact, yesterday, during her lesson with Mai-Ling, Tate hadn't come to the park, and she'd secretly been relieved. Despite today's picnic, she suspected that their romance was over before it could really start. And now she had doubts about its potential, anyway. Hmm. Maybe she'd hint to Logan that she missed his company. That should be enough to break the ice without either of them losing their pride. And that was what this came down to—pride.

The park was crowded by the time Abby arrived. Entering the grounds, she scanned the lawns for him and released a grateful sigh to find that he was sitting on a park bench reading. By himself. To her relief, Patty wasn't with him.

Deciding on her strategy, Abby stuck her hands in her pockets and strolled down the paved lane, hoping to look as if she'd merely come for a walk in the park. Their meeting would be by accident.

Abby stood about ten feet away, off to one side, watching Logan. She was surprised at the emotion she felt just studying him. He looked peaceful, but then he always did. He was composed, confident, in control. Equal to any situation. They'd been dating for almost a year and Abby hadn't realized that so much of her life was interwoven with Logan's. She'd taken him for granted until he was gone, and the emptiness he'd left behind had shocked her. She'd been stupid and insensitive. And heaven knew how difficult it was for her to admit she'd been wrong.

For several minutes Abby did nothing but watch him. A calm settled over her as she focused on Logan's shoulders. They weren't as broad or muscular as Tate's, but somehow it didn't matter. Not now, not when she was hurting, missing Logan and his friendship. Without giving it much thought, she'd been looking forward to Sunday all week and now she knew precisely why: Sundays had always been special because they were spent with Logan. It was Logan she wanted, Logan she needed, and Abby desperately hoped she wasn't too late.

Abby continued to gaze at him. After a while her determination to talk to him grew stronger. Never mind her pride—Logan had a right to know her feelings. He'd been patient with her far longer than she deserved. Her stomach felt queasy, her mouth dry. Just when she gathered enough courage to approach him, Logan closed his book and stood up. Turning around he looked in her direction, but didn't hesitate for a second. He glanced at his watch and walked idly down the concrete pathway toward her until he was within calling distance. Abby's breath froze as he looked her way, blinked and looked in the opposite direction. She couldn't believe he'd purposely avoid her and she doubted he would've been able to see her standing off to the side.

The moment she was ready to step forward, Logan stopped to chat with two older men playing checkers. From her position, Abby saw them motion for him to sit down, which he did. He was soon deep in conversation with them. The three were obviously good friends, although she'd never met the other men before.

Abby loitered as long as she could. Half an hour passed and still Logan stayed.

Defeated, Abby realized she'd have to hurry or be late for her picnic with Tate. Silently she slipped from her viewing position and started across the grounds. When she glanced over her shoulder, she saw that Logan was alone on a bench again and watching a pair of young lovers kissing on the grass. Even from this distance, she saw a look of such intense pain cross his face, she had to force herself not to run to his side. He dropped his head in his hands and hunched forward as if a heavy burden was weighing on him.

Abby's throat clogged with tears until it was painful to breathe. They filled her eyes. Logan loved her and had loved her from the beginning, but she'd carelessly thrown his love aside. It had taken only a few days' separation to know with certainty that she loved him, too.

Tears rolled down her face, but Abby quickly brushed them aside. Logan wouldn't want to know she'd seen him. She'd stripped him of so much, it wouldn't be right to take his pride, as well. Today she'd tell Tate she wouldn't be seeing him again. If that was all Logan wanted, it would be a small price to pay. She'd run back to his arms and never leave him again.

By the time she got to her building, Tate was at the front door. They greeted each other and Tate told her about a special place he wanted to show her near Apple Valley.

She ran into her apartment to get a few things, then joined him in the car.

Both seemed preoccupied during the drive. Abby helped

him unload the picnic basket, her thoughts racing at breakneck speed. She folded the tablecloth she'd brought over a picnic table while Tate spread out a blanket under a shady tree. They hardly spoke.

"Abby—"

"Tate—"

They both began together.

"You first," Abby murmured and sat down, drawing up her legs and circling them with both arms, then resting her chin on her bent knees.

Tate remained standing, hands in his pockets as he paced. Again, something was obviously troubling him.

"Tate, what is it?"

"I didn't know it would be so hard to tell you," he said wryly and shook his head. "I meant to explain weeks ago."

What was he talking about?

His gaze settled on her, then flickered to the ground. "I tried to tell you Friday night after the movie, but I couldn't get the words out." He ran a weary hand over his face and fell to his knees at her side.

Abby reached for his hand and held it.

"Abby." He released a ragged breath. "*I can't read.* I'll pay you any amount if you'll teach me."

Five

In one brilliant flash everything about Tate fell into place. He hadn't been captivated by her charm and natural beauty. He'd overheard her teaching Mai-Ling how to read and knew she could help him. That was the reason he'd sought her out and cultivated a friendship. She could help him.

Small things became clear in her mind. No wonder Tate ordered the same thing she did in a restaurant. Naturally their date on Friday night had been awkward. He'd been trying to tell her then. How could she have been so blind?

Even now he studied her intently, awaiting her response. His eyes glittered with pride, insecurity and fear. She recognized all those emotions and understood them now.

"Of course I'll teach you," she said reassuringly.

"I'll pay you anything you ask."

"Tate." Her grip on his hand tightened. "I wouldn't take anything. We're friends."

"But I can afford to pay you." He took a wad of bills from his pocket and breathed in slowly, glancing at the money in his hand.

Again Abby realized how difficult admitting his inability to read had been. "Put that away," Abby said calmly. "You won't be needing it."

Tate stuffed the bills back in his pocket. "You don't know how relieved I am to have finally told you," he muttered hoarsely.

"I don't think I could have been more obtuse," she said, still shocked at her own stupidity. "I'm amazed you've gotten along as well as you have. I was completely fooled."

"I've become adept at this. I've done it from the time I was in grade school."

"What happened?" Abby asked softly, although she could guess.

A sadness stole into his eyes. "I suppose it's because of all those times I was pulled out of school so we could move," he said unemotionally. "We left New Mexico in the middle of first grade and I never finished the year. Because I was tall for my age my mother put me in second grade the following September. The teacher wanted to hold me back but we moved again. And again and again." A bitterness infected his voice. "By the time I was in junior high and we'd moved to Minneapolis, I had devised all kinds of ways to disguise the fact that I couldn't read. I was the class clown, the troublemaker, the boy who'd do anything to get out of going to school."

"Oh, Tate." Her heart swelled with compassion.

Sitting beside her, Tate rubbed his hand across his face and smiled grimly. "But the hardest part was getting up the courage to tell you."

"You've never told anyone else, have you?"

"No. It was like admitting I have some horrible disease."

"You don't. We can fix this," she said. She was trying to reassure him and felt pathetically inadequate.

"Will you promise me that you'll keep this to yourself? For now?"

She nodded. "I promise." She understood how humiliated he felt, why he wanted his inability to read to remain a secret, and felt she had to agree.

"When can we start? There's so much I want to learn. So much I want to read. Books and magazines and computer programs..." He sounded eager, his gaze level and questioning.

"Is tomorrow too soon?" Abby asked.

"I'd say it's about twenty years too late."

Tate brought Abby back to her apartment two hours later. Tomorrow she'd call the World Literacy Movement and have them email the forms for her to complete regarding Tate. He looked jubilant, excited. Telling her about his inability to read had probably been one of the most difficult things he'd ever done in his life. She understood how formidable his confession had felt to him because now she had to humble herself and call Logan. And that, although major to her, was a small thing in comparison.

Abby wasn't unhappy at Tate's confession. True, her pride was stung for a moment. But overall she was relieved. Tate was the kind of man who'd always attract women's attention. For a brief time she'd been caught up in his masculine appeal. And if it hadn't been for Tate, it would have taken her a lot longer to recognize how fortunate she was to have Logan.

The thought of phoning him and admitting that she was wrong had been unthinkable a week ago. Had it only been a week? In some ways it felt like a year.

Abby glanced at the ceiling and prayed that Logan would answer her call. There was so much stored in her heart that she wanted to tell him. Her hand trembled as she lifted the receiver and tried to form positive thoughts. *Everything's going to work out. I know it will.* She repeated that mantra over and over as she dialed.

She was so nervous her fingers shook and her stomach churned until she was convinced she was going to be sick. Inhaling, Abby held her breath as his phone rang the first time. Her lungs refused to function. Abby closed her eyes tightly during the second ring.

"Hello."

Abby took a deep breath.

"Logan, this is Abby."

"Abby?" He sounded shocked.

"Can we talk? I mean, I can call back if this is inconvenient."

"I'm on my way out the door. Would you like me to come over?"

"Yes." She was surprised at how composed she sounded. "That would be great." She replaced the phone and tilted her head toward the ceiling. "Thank you," she murmured gratefully.

Looking down, Abby realized how casually she was dressed. When Logan saw her again, she wanted to bowl him over.

Racing into her room, she ripped the dress she'd worn Friday night off the hanger, then decided it wouldn't do. She tossed it across her bed. She tried on one outfit and then another. Never had she been more unsure about what she wanted to wear. Finally she chose a pair of tailored black pants and a white blouse with an eyelet collar. Simple, elegant, classic.

Abby was frantically brushing her hair when the buzzer went. *Logan.* She gripped the edge of the sink and took in a deep breath. Then she set down the brush, practiced her smile and walked into the living room.

"Hello, Abby," Logan said a moment later as he stepped into the apartment.

Her first impulse was to throw her arms around him and weep. A tightness gripped her throat. Whatever poise she'd managed to gather was shaken and gone with one look from him.

"Hello, Logan. Would you like to sit down?" She gestured toward the chair. Her gaze was fixed on his shoulders as he walked across the room and took a seat.

"And before you ask," he interjected sternly, "no, I don't want anything to drink. Sit down, Abby."

She complied, grateful because she didn't know how much longer her knees would support her.

"You wanted to talk?" The lines at the side of his mouth deepened, but he wasn't smiling.

"Yes." She laced her hands together tightly. "I was wrong," she murmured. Now that the words were out, Abby experienced none of the calm she'd expected. "I'm—I'm sorry."

"It wasn't a question of my being right or your being wrong," Logan said. "I'm not looking for an apology."

Abby's lips trembled and she bit into the bottom corner. "I know that. But I felt I owed you one."

"No." He stood and with one hand in his pocket paced the width of the carpet. "That's not what I wanted to hear. I told you to call me when you were sure it was me you wanted and not Tate." His eyes rested on her, his expression hooded.

Abby stood, unable to meet his gaze. "I *am* sure," she breathed. "I know it's you I want."

His mouth quirked in what could have been a smile, but he didn't acknowledge her confession.

"You have every right to be angry with me." She couldn't look at him, afraid of what she'd see. If he were to reject her now, Abby didn't think she could stand it. "I've missed you so much," she mumbled. Her cheeks flamed with color, and she couldn't believe how difficult this was. She felt tears in her eyes as she bowed her head.

"Abby." Logan's arms came around her shoulders, bringing her within the comforting circle of his arms. He lifted her chin and lovingly studied her face. "You're sure?"

The growing lump in her throat made speech impossible. She nodded, letting all the love in her eyes say the words.

"Oh, Abby…" He claimed her lips with a hungry kiss that revealed the depth of his feelings.

Slipping her arms around his neck, Abby felt him shudder with a longing he'd suppressed all these months. He buried his face in the dark waves of her hair and held her so tightly it was difficult to breathe.

"I've been so wrong about so many things," she confessed, rubbing her hands up and down his spine, reveling in the muscular feel of him.

Lowering himself to the sofa, Logan pulled Abby onto his lap. His warm breath was like a gentle caress as she wound her arms around his neck and kissed him, wanting to make up to him for all the pain she'd caused them both. The wild tempo of her pulse made clear thought impossible.

Finally, Logan dragged his mouth from hers. "You're sure?" he asked as if he couldn't quite believe it.

Abby pressed her forehead against his shoulder and nodded. "Very sure. I was such a fool."

His arm held her securely in place. "Tell me more. I'm enjoying this."

Unable to resist, Abby kissed the side of his mouth. "I thought you would."

"So you missed me?"

"I was miserable."

"Good!"

"Logan," she cried softly. "It wouldn't do you any harm to tell me how lonely *you* were."

"I wasn't," he said jokingly.

Involuntarily Abby stiffened and swallowed back the hurt. "I know. Patty mentioned that you'd taken her to the Twins game."

Logan smiled wryly. "We went with several other people."

"It bothers me that you could see someone else so soon."

"Honey." His hold tightened around her waist, bringing her closer. "It wasn't like you're thinking."

"But...you said you weren't lonely."

"How could I have been? I saw you Tuesday and then at the game on Wednesday."

"I know, but—"

"Are we going to argue?"

"A thousand kisses might convince me," she teased and rested her head on his shoulder.

"I haven't got the willpower to continue kissing you without thinking of other things," he murmured in her ear as his hand stroked her hair. "I love you, Abby. I've loved you from the first time I asked you out." His breathing seemed less controlled than it had been a moment before.

"Oh, Logan." Fresh tears sprang to her eyes. She started to tell him how much she cared for him, but he went on, cutting off her words.

"As soon as I saw Tate I knew there was no way I could compete with him. He's everything I'll never be. Tall.

Movie-star looks." He shook his head. "I don't blame you for being attracted to him."

Abby straightened so she could look at this man she loved. Her hands framed his face. "You're a million things Tate could never be."

"I know this has been hard on you."

"But I was so stupid," Abby inserted.

He kissed her lightly, his lips lingering over hers. "I can't help feeling grateful that you won't be seeing him again."

Abby lowered her eyes. She *would* be seeing Tate, but not in the way Logan meant.

A stillness filled the room. "Abby?"

She gave him a feeble smile.

"You aren't seeing Tate, are you?"

She couldn't reveal Tate's problem to anyone. She'd promised. And not for the world would she embarrass him, especially when admitting he couldn't read had been so difficult. No matter how much she wanted to tell Logan, she couldn't.

"I'd like to explain," Abby replied, her voice trembling.

Logan stiffened and lightly pushed her from his lap. "I don't want explanations. All I want is the truth. Will you or will you not be seeing Tate?"

"Not romantically," she answered, as tactfully and truthfully as possible.

Logan's eyes hardened. "What other explanation could there be?"

"I can't tell you that," she said forcefully and stood up.

"Of course you can." A muscle worked in his jaw. "We're right back where we started, aren't we, Abby?"

"No." She felt like screaming at him for being so unreasonable. Surely he recognized how hard it had been for her to call him and admit she was wrong?

"Will you stop seeing Tate, then?" he challenged.

"I can't." Her voice cracked in a desperate appeal for him to understand. "We live in the same neighborhood..." she said, stalling for time as her mind raced for an excuse. "I'll probably run into him.... I mean, it'd be only natural, since he's so close and all."

"Abby," Logan groaned impatiently. "That's not what I mean and you know it. Will you or will you not be *seeing* Tate?"

She hesitated. Knowing what her promise was doing to her relationship with Logan, Tate would want him to know. But she couldn't say anything without clearing it with him first.

"Abby?"

"I'll be seeing him, but please understand that it's not the way you assume."

For an instant, Abby saw pain in Logan's eyes. The pain she witnessed was the same torment she was experiencing herself.

They stood with only a few feet separating them and yet Abby felt they'd never been further apart. Whole worlds seemed to loom between them. Logan's ego was at stake, his pride, and he didn't want her to continue seeing Tate, no matter what the reason.

"You won't stop seeing him," Logan challenged furiously.

"I can't," Abby cried, just as angry.

"Then there's nothing left to say."

"Yes," Abby said, "there is, but you're in no mood to hear it. Just remember that things aren't always as they appear."

"Goodbye, Abby," he responded. "And next time don't bother calling me unless—"

Abby stalked across the room and threw open the door. "Next time I won't," she said with a cutting edge.

Reaction set in the minute the door slammed behind him. Abby was so angry that pacing the floor did little to relieve it. How could Logan say he loved her in one breath and turn around and storm out the next? Yet, he'd done exactly that.

Once the anger dissipated, Abby began to tremble and felt the tears burning for release. Pride demanded that she forestall them. She wouldn't allow Logan to reduce her to that level. She shook her head and kept her chin raised. She wouldn't cry, she wouldn't cry, she repeated over and over as one tear after another slid down her cheeks.

"Who did you say was responsible for the literacy movement?" Tate asked, leafing respectfully through the first book.

"Dr. Frank Laubach. He was a missionary in the Philippines in the 1920s. At that time some of the island people didn't have a written language. He invented one and later developed a method of teaching adults to read."

"Sounds like he accomplished a lot."

Abby nodded. "By the time he died in 1970, his work had spread to 105 countries and 313 languages."

Tate continued leafing through the pages of the primary workbook. Abby wanted to start him at the most fundamental skill level, knowing his progress would be rapid. At this point, Tate would need all the encouragement he could get and the speed with which he completed the lower-level books was sure to help.

Abby hadn't underestimated Tate's enthusiasm. By the end of the first lesson he had relearned the alphabet and was reading simple phrases. Proudly he took the book home with him.

"Can we meet again tomorrow?" he asked, standing near her apartment door.

"I've got my class tomorrow evening," Abby explained, "but if you like, we could meet for a half hour before—or after if you prefer."

"Before, I think."

The following afternoon, Tate showed up an hour early, just after she got home from work, and seemed disappointed that Abby would be occupied with softball on Wednesday evening.

"We could get together afterward if you want," she told him.

Affectionately, Tate kissed her on the cheek. "I want."

Again she noted that his fondness for her was more like that of a brother—or a pupil for his teacher. She was grateful for that, at least. And he was wonderful to her. He brought over takeout meals and gave her small gifts as a way of showing his appreciation. The gifts weren't necessary, but they salvaged Tate's pride and that was something she was learning more about every day—male pride.

Abby was dressing for the game Wednesday evening when the phone rang. No longer did she expect or even hope it would be Logan. He'd made his position completely clear. Fortunately, call display told her it was her parents' number.

"Hello, Mom."

"Abby, I've been worried about you."

"I'm fine!" She forced some enthusiasm into her voice.

"Oh, dear, it's worse than I thought."

"What's worse?"

"Logan and you."

"There is no more Logan and me," she returned.

A strained silence followed. "But I thought—"

"Listen, Mom," Abby cut in, unwilling to listen to her

mother's postmortem. "I've got a game tonight. Can I call you later?"

"Why don't you come over for dinner?"

"Not tonight." Abby hated to turn down her mother's invitation, but she'd already agreed to see Tate for his next lesson.

"It's your birthday Friday," Glenna reminded her.

"I'll come for dinner then," Abby said with a feeble smile. Her birthday was only two days away and she wasn't in any mood to celebrate. "But only if you promise to make my favorite dish."

"Barbecued chicken!" her mother announced. "You bet."

"And, Mom," Abby continued, "you were right about Logan."

"What was I right about?" Her mother's voice rose slightly.

"He does love me, and I love him."

Abby thought she heard a small, happy sound.

"What made you realize that?" her mother asked.

"A lot of things," Abby said noncommittally. "But I also realized that loving someone doesn't make everything perfect. I wish it did."

"I have the feeling there's something important you're not telling me, Abby," Glenna said on a note of puzzled sadness. "But I know you will in your own good time."

Abby couldn't disagree with her mother's observation. "I'll be at your place around six on Friday," she murmured. "And thanks, Mom."

"What are mothers for?" Glenna teased.

The disconnected phone line droned in Abby's ear before she hung up, suddenly surprised to see that it was time to head over to the park. For the first time that she could remember, she didn't feel psyched up for the game. She wasn't ready to see Logan, which would be more painful than reassuring. And if he paid Patty special attention, Abby didn't know how she'd handle that. But Logan wouldn't do anything to hurt her. At least she knew him well enough to be sure of that.

The first thing Abby noticed as she walked onto the diamond was that Patty Martin had cut and styled her hair. The transformation from straight mousy-brown hair to short, bouncy curls was astonishing. The young woman positively glowed.

"What do you think?" Patty asked in a hurried voice. "Your hair is always so pretty and…" She let the rest of what she was going to say fade.

Abby held herself motionless. Patty had made herself attractive for Logan. She desperately wanted Logan's interest, and for all Abby knew, she was getting it. "I think you look great," Abby commented, unable to deny the truth or to be unkind.

"I was scared out of my wits," Patty admitted shyly. "It's been a long time since I was at the hairdresser's."

"Hey, Patty, they're waiting for you on the field," the team's coach hollered. "Abby, you, too."

"Okay, Dick," Patty called back happily, her eyes shining. "I've gotta go. We'll talk later, okay?"

"Fine." Softening her stiff mitt against her hand with unnecessary force, Abby ran to her position at first base.

Logan was practicing in the outfield.

"Abby," he called, and when she turned, she found his gaze level and unwavering. "Catch."

Nothing appeared to affect him. They'd suffered through the worst four days of their relationship and he looked at her as coolly and unemotionally as he would a…a dish of potato salad. She didn't respond other than to catch the softball and pitch it to second base.

The warm-up period lasted for about ten minutes. Abby couldn't recall a time she'd felt less like playing, and it showed.

"What's the matter, Ab?" Dick asked her at the bottom of the fifth after she'd struck out for the third time. "You're not yourself tonight."

"I'm sorry," she said with a frustrated sigh. Her eyes didn't meet his. "This isn't one of my better nights."

"She's got other things on her mind." Logan spoke from behind her, signaling that he was sitting in the bleachers one row above. "Her boyfriend just showed up, so she'll do better."

Abby whirled around to face Logan. "What do you mean by that?"

Logan nodded in the direction of the parking lot. Abby's gaze followed his movement and she wanted to groan aloud. Tate was walking toward the stands.

"Tate isn't my boyfriend." Abby's voice was taut with impatience.

"Oh, is that terminology passé?" Logan returned.

Stunned at the bitterness in him, Abby found no words to respond. They were both hurting, and in their pain they were lashing out at each other.

Logan slid from the bleachers for his turn at bat. Abby focused her attention on him, deciding she didn't want to make a fuss over Tate's unexpected arrival.

Logan swung wildly at the first pitch, hitting the ball with the tip of his bat. Abby could hear the wood crack as the ball went flying over the fence for a home run. Logan looked as shocked as Abby. He tossed the bat aside and ran around the bases to the shouts and cheers of his teammates. Abby couldn't remember Logan ever getting more than a single.

"Hi." Tate slid into the row of seats behind her. "You don't mind if I come and watch, do you?" he asked as he leaned forward with lazy grace.

"Not at all," Abby said blandly. It didn't make any difference now. She stared at her laced fingers, attempting to fight off the depression that seemed to have settled over her. She was so caught up in her own sorrows that she didn't see the accident. Only the startled cries of those around her alerted her to the fact that something had happened.

"What's wrong?" Abby asked frantically as the bench cleared. Everyone was running toward Patty, who was clutching her arm and doubled over in pain.

Logan's voice could be heard above the confusion. "Stand back. Give her room." Gently he aided Patty into a sitting position.

Even to Abby's untrained eye it was obvious that Patty's arm was broken. Logan tore off his shirt and tied it around her upper body to create a sling and support the injured arm.

The words *hospital* and *doctor* were flying around, but everyone seemed stunned and no one moved. Again it was Logan who helped Patty to her feet and led her to his car. His calm, decisive actions imparted confidence to both teams. Only minutes before, Abby had been angry because he displayed so little emotion.

"What happened?" Abby asked Dick as they walked off the field.

"I'm not sure." Dick looked shaken himself. "Patty was trying to steal a base and collided with the second baseman. When she fell, she put out her arm to catch herself and it twisted under her."

"Will she be all right?"

"Logan seemed to think so. He's taking her to the emergency room. He said he'd let us know her condition as soon as possible."

The captain of the opposing team crossed the diamond to talk to Dick and it was decided that they'd play out the remainder of the game.

But without Logan the team was short one male player.

"Do you think your friend would mind filling in?" Dick asked somewhat sheepishly, glancing at Tate.

"I can ask."

"No problem," Tate said, smiling as he picked up Logan's discarded mitt and ran onto the field.

Although they'd decided to finish the game, almost everyone was preoccupied with the accident. Abby's team ended up winning, thanks to Tate, but only by a slight margin.

The group as a whole proceeded to the pizza parlor to wait for word about Patty.

Tate sat across the long wooden table from Abby, chatting easily with her fellow teammates. Only a few slices of the two large pizzas had been eaten. Their conversation was a low hum as they recounted their versions of the accident and what could have been done to prevent it.

Abby was grateful for Logan's clear thinking and quick actions. He wasn't the kind of skilled softball player who'd stand out, but he gave of himself in a way that was essential to every member of the team. Only a few days earlier she'd found Logan lacking. Compared to the muscular Tate, he'd seemed a poor second. Now she noted that his strengths were inner ones. Again she was reminded that if given the chance, she would love this man for the rest of her life.

Abby didn't see Logan enter the restaurant, but the immediate clamor caused her to turn. She stood with the others.

"Patty's fine," he assured everyone. "Her arm's broken, but I don't think that's news to anyone."

"When will she be back?"

"We want to send flowers or something."

"When do you think she'll feel up to company?"

Everyone spoke at once. Calmly Logan answered each question and when he'd finished, the mood around the table was considerably lighter.

A tingling awareness at the back of her neck told Abby that Logan was near. With a sweeping action he swung his foot over the long bench and joined her.

He focused on Tate, sitting across from Abby. "I wish I could say it's good to see you again," he said with stark unfriendliness.

"Logan, please!" Abby hissed.

The two men eyed each other like bears who'd violated each other's territory. Tate had no romantic interest in her, Abby was convinced of that, but Logan was openly challenging him and Tate wouldn't walk away from such blatant provocation.

Unaware of the dangerous undercurrents swirling around the table, Dick Snyder sauntered over and slapped Logan on the back.

"We owe a debt of thanks to Tate here," he informed Logan cheerfully. "He stepped in for you when you were gone. He batted in the winning run."

Logan and Tate didn't so much as blink. "Tate's been doing a lot of that for me lately, isn't that right, Abby?"

Wrenching her gaze from him, Abby stood and, with as much dignity and pride as she could muster, walked out of the restaurant and went home alone.

The phone was ringing when she walked into the apartment. Abby let it ring. She didn't want to talk to anyone. She didn't even want to know who'd called.

"Abby, would you take the bread out of the oven?" her mother asked, walking out to the patio.

"Okay." Abby turned off the broiler and pulled out the cookie sheet, on which slices of French bread oozed with melted butter and chopped garlic. Her enthusiasm for this birthday celebration was nil.

The doorbell caught her by surprise. "Are you expecting anyone?" she asked her mother, who'd returned to the kitchen.

"Not that I know of. I'll get it."

Abby was placing the bread slices in a warming basket when she heard her mother's surprised voice.

Turning, Abby looked straight at Logan.

Six

A shocked expression crossed Logan's face. "Abby." He took a step inside the room and paused.

"Hello, Logan." A tense silence ensued as Abby primly folded her hands.

"I'll check the chicken," Glenna Carpenter murmured discreetly as she hurried past them.

"What brings you to this neck of the woods?" Abby forced a lightness into her voice. He looked tired, as if he hadn't been sleeping well. For that matter, neither had Abby, but she doubted either would admit as much.

Logan handed her a wrapped package. "I wanted your mother to give you this. But since you're here—happy birthday."

A small smile parted her trembling lips as Abby accepted the brightly wrapped gift. He had come to her parents' home to deliver this, but he hadn't expected her to be there.

"Thank you." She continued to hold it.

"I, uh, didn't expect to see you." He stated the obvious, as though he couldn't think of anything else to say.

"Where else would I be on my birthday?"

Logan shrugged. "With Tate."

Abby released a sigh of indignation. "I thought I'd ex-plained that I'm not involved with Tate. We're friends, noth-ing more."

She shook her head. They'd gone over this before. An-other argument wouldn't help. Abby figured she'd endured enough emotional turmoil in the past few weeks. She still hadn't spoken to Tate about telling Logan the truth. But she couldn't, not with Tate feeling as sensitive as he did about the whole thing.

"Abby." Logan's voice was deadly quiet. "Don't you see what's happening? You may not think of Tate in a roman-tic light, but I saw the way he was looking at you in the pizza place."

"You openly challenged him." Abby threw out a few challenges of her own. "How did you expect him to react? You wouldn't have behaved any differently," she said. "And if you've come to ruin my birthday…then you can just leave. I've had about all I can take from you, Logan Fletcher." She whirled around, not wanting to face him.

"I didn't come for that." The defeat was back in his voice again.

Abby's pulse thundered in her ears as she waited for the sounds of him leaving—at the same time hoping he wouldn't.

"Aren't you going to open your present?" he said at last.

Abby turned and wiped away a tear that had escaped from the corner of her eye. "I already know what it is," she said, glancing down at the package. "Honestly, Logan, you're so predictable."

"How could you possibly know?"

"Because you got me the same perfume for my birthday

last year." Deftly she removed the wrapping paper and held up the small bottle of expensive French fragrance.

"I like the way it smells on you," Logan murmured, walking across the room. He rested his hands on her shoulders. "And if I'm so predictable, you'll also recall that there's a certain thank-you I expect."

Any resistance drained from her as Logan pulled her into his embrace. Abby slid her arms around his neck and tasted the sweetness of his kiss. A wonderful languor stole through her limbs as his mouth brushed the sweeping curve of her lashes and burned a trail down her cheek to her ear.

"I love you, Logan," Abby whispered with all the intensity in her.

Logan went utterly still. Gradually he raised his head so he could study her. Unflinching, Abby met his gaze determined that he see for himself what her eyes and heart were saying.

"If you love me, then you'll stop seeing Tate," he said flatly.

"And if you love *me*, you'll trust me."

"Abby." Logan dropped his hands and stepped away. "I—"

"Oh, Logan." Glenna Carpenter moved out of the kitchen. "I'm glad to see you're still here. We insist you stay for dinner. Isn't that right, Abby?"

Logan held her gaze with mesmerizing simplicity.

"Of course we do. If you don't have another appointment," Abby said meaningfully.

"You know I don't."

Abby knew nothing of the kind, but didn't want to argue. "Did you see the gift Logan brought me?" Abby asked her mother and held out the perfume.

"Logan is always so thoughtful."

"Yes, he is," Abby agreed and slipped an arm around his waist, enjoying the feel of him at her side. "Thoughtful, but not very original." Her eyes smiled into his, pleading with him that, for tonight, they could forget their differences.

Logan's arms slid just as easily around her. "But with that kind of thank-you, what incentive do I have for shopping around?"

Abby laughed and led the way to the back patio.

Frank Carpenter, Abby's father, was busy standing in front of the barbecue, basting chicken.

"Logan," he exclaimed and held out a welcoming hand. "This is a pleasant surprise. Good to see you."

Logan and her father had always gotten along and had several interests in common. For a time that had irked Abby. Defiantly she'd wanted to make it clear that she wouldn't marry a man solely because her parents thought highly of him. Her childish attitude had changed dramatically these past weeks.

Abby's mother brought another place setting from the kitchen to add to the three already on the picnic table. Abby made several more trips into the kitchen to carry out the salad, toasted bread and a glass of wine for Logan.

Absently, Logan accepted the glass from her and smiled, deep in conversation with her father. Happiness washed over Abby as she munched on a potato chip. Looking at the two of them now—Abby busy helping her mother and Logan chatting easily with her father—she figured there was little to distinguish them as unmarried.

Dinner and the time that followed were cheerful. Frank suggested a game of cards while they were eating birthday cake and ice cream. But Abby's mother immediately rejected the idea.

"I think Glenna's trying to tell me to keep my mouth

shut because it's obvious you two want some time alone," Abby's father complained.

"I'm saying no such thing," Glenna denied instantly as an embarrassed flush brightened her cheeks. "We were young once, Frank."

"Once!" Frank scolded. "I don't know about you, but I'm not exactly ready for the grave."

"We'll play cards another time," Logan promised, ending a friendly argument between her parents.

"Double-deck pinochle," Frank prompted. "Best card game there is."

Glenna pretended to agree but rolled her eyes dramatically when Frank wasn't looking.

"Shall we?" Logan successfully contained a smile and held out his open palm to Abby. She placed her hand in his, more contented than she could ever remember being. After their farewells to her parents, Logan followed her back to her apartment, parking his car beside hers. He took a seat while Abby hurried into the next room.

"Give me a minute to freshen up," Abby called out as she ran a brush through her hair and studied her reflection in the bathroom mirror. She looked happy. The sparkle was back in her eyes.

She dabbed some of the perfume Logan had given her to the pulse points at her throat and wrists. Maybe this would garner even more of a reaction. He wasn't one to display a lot of emotion, but he seemed to be coming along nicely in that area. His kisses had produced an overwhelming physical response in Abby, and she was aware that his feeling for her ran deep and strong. It had been only a matter of weeks ago that she'd wondered why he bothered to kiss her at all.

"I suppose you're going to suggest we drive to Des

Moines and back," Logan teased when she joined him a few minutes later.

"Logan!" she cried, feigning excitement. "That's a wonderful idea."

He rolled his eyes and and laid the paper on the sofa. "How about a movie instead?"

Abby gave a fake groan. "So predictable."

"I've been wanting to see this one." He pointed at an ad for the movie she'd seen with Tate.

"I've already been," Abby tossed back, not thinking.

"When?"

Abby could feel the hostility exuding from Logan. He knew. Without a word he'd guessed that Abby had been to the movie with Tate.

"Not long ago." She tried desperately to put the evening back on an even keel. "But I'd see it again. The film's great."

The air between them became heavy and oppressive.

"Forget the movies," Logan said and neatly folded the paper. He straightened and stalked to the far side of the room. "In fact, why don't we forget everything."

Hands clenched angrily at her sides, Abby squared her shoulders. "If you ruin my birthday, Logan Fletcher, I don't think I'll ever forgive you."

His expression was cold and unreadable. "Yes, but there's always Tate."

A hysterical sob rose in her throat, but Abby managed to choke it off. "I... I told you tonight that I loved you." Her voice wobbled treacherously as her eyes pleaded with his. "Doesn't that mean anything to you? Anything at all?"

Logan's gaze raked her from head to foot. "Only that you don't know the meaning of the word. You want both Tate *and* me, Abby. But you can't decide between us so you'd prefer to keep us both dangling until you make up your mind." His voice gained volume with each word. "But I won't play that game."

Abby breathed in sharply as a fiery anger burned in her cheeks. Once she would have ranted, cried and hurled her own accusations. Now she stood stunned and disbelieving. "If you honestly believe that, then there's nothing left to say." Her voice was calmer than she dared hope. Life seemed filled with ironies all of a sudden. Outwardly she presented a clearheaded composure while on the inside she felt a fiery pain. Perhaps for the first time in her life she was acting completely selflessly, and this was her reward—losing Logan.

Without another word, Logan walked across the room and out the front door.

Abby watched him leave with a sense of unreality. This couldn't be happening to her. Not on her birthday. Last year Logan had taken her to dinner at L'Hôtel Sofitel and given her—what else—perfume. A hysterical bubble of laughter slipped from her. He was predictable, but so loving and caring. She remembered how they'd danced until midnight and gone for a stroll in the moonlight. Only a year ago, Logan had made her birthday the most perfect day of her life. But this year he was ruining it.

Angry, hurt and agitated, Abby paced the living-room carpet until she thought she'd go mad. Dano had wandered into the living room when she and Logan came in, but had disappeared into her bedroom once he sensed tension. Figured. Not even her cat was interested in comforting her. Usually when she was upset she'd ride her bike or do something physical. But bike riding at night could be dangerous, so she'd go running instead. She changed into old jeans and a faded sweatshirt that had a picture of a Disneyland castle on the front. She had trouble locating her second tennis shoe, then threw it aside in disgust when the rainbow-colored lace snapped in two.

She sighed. Nothing had gone right today. Tate had been disappointed that she wasn't able to meet him. Because of that, she'd been fighting off a case of guilt when she went to her parents'. Then Logan had shown up, and everything had steadily and rapidly gone downhill.

Ripping a lace from one of her baseball shoes, Abby had to wrap it around the sole of the shoe several times. On her way out the door, she paused and returned to the bathroom. If she was going to go running, then she'd do it smelling better than any other runner in Minneapolis history. She'd dabbed perfume on every exposed part of her body when she stepped out the door.

A light drizzle had begun to fall. Terrific. A fitting end to a rotten day.

The first block was a killer. She couldn't be that badly out of shape, could she? She rode her bike a lot. And wasn't her running speed the best on the team?

The second block, Abby forced her mind off how out of breath she was becoming. Logan's buying her perfume made her chuckle. *Predictable. Reliable. Confident.* They were all words that adequately described Logan. But so were *unreasonable* and *stubborn*—traits she'd only seen recently.

The drizzle was followed by a cloudburst and Abby's hair and clothes were plastered against her in the swirling wind and rain. She shouldn't be laughing. But she did anyway as she raced back to her apartment. It was either laugh or cry, and laughing seemed to come naturally. Laughing made her feel better than succumbing to tears.

By the time Abby returned to her building, she was

drenched and shivering. With her chin tucked under and her arms folded around her middle, she fought off the chill and hurried across the parking lot. She was almost at her building door when she realized she didn't have the keys. She'd locked herself out!

What more could go wrong? she wondered. Maybe the superintendent was home. She stepped out in the rain to see if the lights were on in his apartment, which was situated above hers. His place was dark. Of course. That was how everything else was going.

Cupping one hand over her mouth while the other held her stomach, Abby's laughter was mixed with sobs of anger and frustration.

"Abby?" Logan's urgent voice came from the street. Hurriedly he crossed it, took one look at her and hauled her into his arms.

"Logan, I'll get you wet," she cried, trying to push herself free.

"What happened? Are you all right?"

"No. Yes. I don't know," she murmured, sniffling miserably. "What are you doing here?"

Logan brought her out of the rain and stood with his back blocking the wind, trying to protect her from the storm. "Let's get you inside and dry and I'll explain."

"Why?" she asked and wrung the water from the hem of her sweatshirt. "So you can hurl insults at me?"

"No," he said vehemently. "I've been half-crazy wondering where you were."

"I'll just bet," Abby taunted unmercifully. "I'm surprised you didn't assume I was with Tate."

A grimace tightened his jaw, and Abby knew she'd hit her mark. "Are you going to be difficult or are we going inside to talk this out reasonably?"

"We can't go inside," she said.

"Why not?"

"Because I forgot my keys."

"Oh, Abby," Logan groaned.

"And the manager's gone. Do you have any more bright ideas?"

"Did you leave the bedroom window open?" he asked with marked patience.

"Yes, just a little, but—" A glimmer of an idea sparked and she smiled boldly at Logan. "Follow me."

"Why do I have the feeling I'm not going to like this?" he asked under his breath as Abby pulled him by the hand around to the back of the building.

"Here," she said, bending her knee and lacing her fingers together to give him a boost upward to the slightly open window.

"You don't expect to launch me through there, do you?" Logan glared at her. "I won't fit."

Rivulets of rain trickled down the back of Abby's neck. "Well, I can't do it. You know I'm afraid of heights."

"Abby, the window's barely five feet off the ground."

"I'm standing here, drenched and miserable," she said, waving her hands wildly. "On my birthday, no less," she added sarcastically, "and you don't want to rescue me."

"I'm not in the hero business," Logan muttered as he hunched his shoulders to ward off the rain. "Try Tate."

"Fine, I'll do that." She stalked off to the side of the building.

"Abby?" He sounded unsure as she dragged over an aluminum garbage can.

"Go away!" she shouted. "I don't need you."

"What's the difference between going through the window using a garbage can or having me lift you through?"

"Plenty." She wasn't sure what, but she didn't want to take the time to figure it out. All she wanted was a hot bath and ten gallons of hot chocolate.

"You're being totally irrational."

"I've always been irrational. It's never bothered you before." Her voice trembled as she balanced her weight on the lid of the garbage can. She reached the window and pushed it open enough to crawl through when she felt the garbage can lid give way. "Logan!" she screamed, terror gripping her as she started to fall.

Instantly he was there. His arms gripped her waist as she tumbled off the aluminum container. Together they went crashing to the ground, Logan twisting so he took the worst of the fall.

"Are you okay?" he asked frantically, straightening and brushing the hair from her face.

Abby was too stunned and breathless to speak, so she just nodded.

"Now listen," he whispered angrily. "I'm going to lift you up to the windowsill and that's final. Do you understand?"

She nodded again.

"I've had enough of this arguing. I'm cold and wet and I want to get inside and talk some reason into you." He stood and wiped the mud from his hands, then helped her up. Taking the position she had earlier, he crouched and let her use his knee as a step as his laced fingers boosted her to the level of the window.

Abby fell into the bedroom with a loud thud, knocking the lamp off her nightstand. Dano howled in terror and dashed under the bed.

"Are you okay?" Logan yelled from outside.

Abby stuck her head out the window. "Fine. Come around to the front and I'll let you in."

"I'll meet you at your door."

"Logan." She leaned forward and smiled at him provocatively. "You *are* my hero."

He didn't look convinced. "Sure. Whatever you say."

Abby had buzzed open the front door and unlocked her own by the time he came around the building. His wet hair was dripping water down his face, and his shirt was plastered to his chest, revealing a lean, muscular strength. He looked as drenched and miserable as she felt.

"You take a shower while I drive home and change out of these." He looked down ruefully at his mud-spattered beige pants and rain-soaked shirt.

Abby agreed. Logan had turned and was halfway out the door when Abby called him back. "Why are you here?" she asked, wanting to delay his leaving.

He shrugged and gave her that warm, lazy smile she loved. "I don't know. I thought there might be another movie you wanted to see."

Abby laughed and blew him a kiss. "I'm sure there is."

When Logan returned forty minutes later, Abby's hair was washed and blown dry and hung in a long French braid down the middle of her back. She'd changed into a multicolored bulky sweater and jeans.

Abby smiled. "We're not going to fight, are we?"

"I certainly hope not!" he exclaimed. "I don't think I can take much more of this. When I left here the first time I was thinking…" He paused and scratched his head. "I was actually entertaining the thought of driving to Des Moines and back."

"That's crazy." Abby tried unsuccessfully to hide her giggles.

"You're telling me?" He sat on the sofa and held out his arm to her, silently inviting her to join him.

Abby settled on the sofa, her head resting on his chest while his hand caressed her shoulder.

"Do you recall how uncomplicated our lives were just a few weeks ago?" Logan asked her.

"Dull. Ordinary."

"What changed all that?"

Abby was hesitant to bring Tate's name into the conversation. "Life, I guess," she answered vaguely. "I know you may misunderstand this," she added in a husky murmur, "but I don't want to go back to the way our relationship was then." He hadn't told her he loved her and she hadn't recognized the depth of her own feelings.

He didn't move. "No, I don't suppose you would."

Abby repositioned her head and placed the palm of her hand on his jaw, turning his face so she could study him. Their eyes met. The hard, uncompromising look in his dark eyes disturbed her. She desperately wanted to assure him of her love. But she'd realized after the first time that words were inadequate. She shifted and slid her hands over his chest to pause at his shoulders.

The brilliance of his eyes searched her face. "Abby." He groaned her name as he fiercely claimed her lips. His hand found its way to the nape of her neck, his fingers gently pulling dark strands free from the braid so he could twine them through his fingers.

His breathing deep, he buried his face in the slope of her neck. "Just let me hold you for a while. Let's not talk."

She agreed and settled into the warm comfort of his embrace. The staccato beat of his heart gradually returned to a normal pace and Abby felt content and loved. The key to a peaceful relationship was to bask in their love for each other, she thought, smiling. That, and not saying a word.

"What's so amusing?" Logan asked, his breath stirring the hair at the side of her face.

"How do you know I'm smiling?"

"I can feel it."

Abby tilted her head so she could look into his eyes. "This turned into a happy birthday, after all," she said.

Now he smiled, too. "Can I see you tomorrow?"

"If you weren't going to ask me, then I would've been forced to make some wild excuse to see *you*." Lovingly Abby rubbed her hand along the side of his jaw, enjoying the slightly prickly feel of his beard.

"What would you like to do?"

"I don't care as long as I'm with you."

"My, my," he whispered, taking her hand. Tenderly he kissed her palm. "You're much easier to please than I remember."

"You don't know the half of it," she teased.

Logan stiffened and sat upright. "What's tomorrow?"

"The tenth. Why?"

"I can't, Abby. I've got something scheduled."

She felt a rush of disappointment but knew that if she was frustrated, so was Logan. "Don't worry, I'll survive," she assured him, then smiled. "At least I think I will."

"But don't plan anything for the day after tomorrow."

"Of course I'm planning something."

"Abby." He sounded tired and impatient.

"Well, it's Sunday, right? Our usual day. So I'm planning to spend it with you. I thought that was what you wanted."

"I do."

The grimness about his mouth relaxed.

Almost immediately afterward, Logan appeared restless

and uneasy. Later, as she dressed for bed, she convinced herself that it was her imagination.

The lesson with Mai-Ling the following afternoon went well. It was the last reading session they'd have, since Mai-Ling was now ready to move on. She'd scheduled one with Tate right afterward, deciding that what Logan didn't know wouldn't hurt him. Tate was still painfully self-conscious and uncomfortable about telling anyone else, although his progress was remarkable and he advanced more quickly than any student she'd ever tutored, including the talented Mai-Ling. From experience, she could tell he was spending many hours each evening studying.

On her way back to her apartment late Saturday afternoon, Abby decided on the spur of the moment to stop at Patty's and see how she was recuperating. She'd sent her an email wishing her a rapid recovery and had promised to stop over some afternoon. Patty needed friends and Abby was feeling generous. Her topsy-turvy world had been righted.

She went to a drugstore first and bought half a dozen glossy magazines as a get-well gift, then drove to Patty's home.

Her sister answered the doorbell.

"Hi, you must be from the baseball team. Patty's gotten a lot of company. Everyone's been wonderful."

Abby wasn't surprised. Everyone on the team was warm and friendly.

"This must be her day for company. Come on in. Logan's with her now."

Seven

Abby was dismayed as the sound of Patty's laughter drifted into the entryway, but she followed Patty's sister into the living room.

Patty's broken arm was supported by a white linen sling and she sat opposite Logan on a long sofa. Her eyes were sparkling with undisguised happiness. Logan had his back to Abby, and it was all she could do not to turn around and leave. Instead she forced a bright smile and made an entrance any actress would envy. "Hello, everyone!"

"Hi, Abby!" Patty had never looked happier or, for that matter, prettier. Not only was her hair nicely styled, but she was wearing light makeup, which added color to her pale cheeks and accented her large brown eyes. She wore a lovely summer dress, a little fancy for hanging around the house, and shoes that were obviously new.

"How are you feeling?" Abby prayed the phoniness in her voice had gone undetected.

Logan stood up and came around the couch, but his eyes didn't meet Abby's probing gaze.

"Hello, Logan, good to see you again."

"Hello, Abby."

"Sit down, please." Patty pointed to an empty chair. "We've got a few minutes before dinner." Patty seemed oblivious to the tension between her guests.

"No, thanks," Abby murmured, faking another smile. "I can only stay a minute. I just wanted to drop by and see how you were doing. Oh, these are for you," she said, handing over the magazines. "Some reading material…"

"Thank you! And I'm doing really well," Patty said enthusiastically. "This is the first night I've been able to go out. Logan's taking me to dinner at the Sofitel."

Abby breathed in sharply and clenched her fist until her nails cut into her hand. Logan had taken her there only once, but Abby considered it their special restaurant. He could've taken Patty anyplace else in the world and it would've hurt, but not as much as this.

"Everyone's been great," Patty continued. "Dick and his wife were over yesterday, and a few others from the team dropped by. Those flowers—" she indicated several plants and bouquets "—are from them."

"We all feel terrible about the accident." Abby made her first honest statement of the visit.

"But it was my own fault," Patty said as Logan hovered stiffly on the other side of the room.

Abby lowered her eyes, unable to meet the happy glow in Patty's. A crumpled piece of wrapping paper rested on the small table at Patty's side. It was the same paper Logan had used to wrap Abby's birthday gift the day before. He *couldn't* have gotten Patty perfume. He wouldn't dare.

"You look so nice," Abby said. Her pulse quickened. What *had* Logan brought Patty? She thought she recognized that scent…. "Is that a new perfume you're wearing?"

"Yes, as a matter of fact, Logan—"

"Hadn't we better be going?" Logan said as he made a show of glancing at his watch.

Patty looked flustered. "Is it time already?"

Following her cue, Abby glared at Logan and took a step in retreat. "I should go, too." A contrived smile curved her mouth. "Have a good time."

"I'll walk you to your car," Logan volunteered.

Walking backward Abby gestured with her hands, swinging them at her sides to give a carefree impression. "No, that isn't necessary. Really. I'm capable of finding my own way out."

"Abby," Logan said under his breath.

"Have a wonderful time, you two," Abby continued, her voice slightly high-pitched. "I've only been to the Sofitel once. The food was fantastic, but I can't say much for my date. But I no longer see him. A really ordinary guy, if you know what I mean. And so predictable."

"I'll be right back." Logan directed his comment to Patty and gripped Abby by the elbow.

"Let me go," she seethed.

Logan's grip relaxed once they were outside the house. "Would you let me explain?"

"Explain?" She threw the word in his face. "What could you possibly say? No." She waved her hand in front of his chest. "Don't say a word. I don't want to hear it. Do you understand? Not a word."

"You're being irrational again," Logan accused, apparently having difficulty keeping his rising temper in check.

"You're right," she agreed. "I've completely lost my sense. Please forgive me for being so closed-minded." Her voice was surprisingly even but it didn't disguise the hurt or the feeling of betrayal she was experiencing.

"Abby."

"Don't," she whispered achingly. "Not now. I can't talk now."

"I'll call you later."

She consented with an abrupt nod, but at that point, Abby realized, she would have agreed to anything for the opportunity to escape.

Her hand was shaking so badly that she had trouble sliding the key into the ignition. This was crazy. She felt secure in his love one night and betrayed the next.

Abby didn't go home. The last thing she wanted to do was sit alone on a Saturday night. To kill time, she visited the Mall of America and did some shopping, buying herself a designer outfit that she knew Logan would hate.

The night was dark and overcast as she let herself into the apartment. Hanging the new dress in her closet, Abby acknowledged that spending this much money on one outfit was ridiculous. Her reasons were just as childish. But it didn't matter; she felt a hundred times better.

The phone rang the first time at ten. Abby ignored it. Logan. Of course. When it started ringing at five-minute intervals, she simply unplugged it. There was nothing she had to say to him. When they spoke again, she wanted to feel composed. Tonight was too soon. She wasn't ready yet.

Calm now, she changed into her pajamas and sat on the sofa, brushing her long hair in smooth, even strokes. Reaction would probably set in tomorrow, but for now she was too angry to think.

Half an hour later, someone pressed her buzzer repeatedly. Annoying though it was, she ignored that, too.

When there was a banging at her door, Abby hesitated, then continued with her brushing.

"Come on, Abby, I know you're in there," Logan shouted.

"Go away. I'm not dressed," she called out sweetly.

"Then get dressed."

"No!" she yelled back.

Logan's laugh was breathless and bitter. "Either open up or I'll tear the stupid door off its hinges."

Just the way he said it convinced Abby this wasn't an idle threat. And to think that only a few weeks ago she'd seen Logan as unemotional. Laying her brush aside, she walked to the door and unlatched the safety chain.

"What do you want? How did you get into the building? And for heaven's sake, keep the noise down. You're disturbing the neighbors."

"Some guy from the second floor recognized me and opened the lobby door. And if you don't let me in to talk to you, I'll do a lot more than wake the neighbors."

Abby had never seen Logan display so much passion. Perhaps she should've been thrilled, but she wasn't.

"Did you and Patty have a nice evening?" she asked with heavy sarcasm.

Logan glanced briefly at his hands. "Reasonably nice."

"I apologize if I put a damper on your *date*," she returned with smooth derision. "Believe me, had I known about it, I would never have visited Patty at such an inopportune time. My timing couldn't have been better—or worse, depending on how you look at it."

"Abby," he sighed. "Let me in. Please."

"Not tonight, Logan."

Frustration furrowed his brow. "Tomorrow, then?"

"Tomorrow," she agreed and started to close the door. "Logan," she called and he immediately turned back. "Without meaning to sound like I care a whole lot, let me ask you something. Why did you give Patty the same perfume as me?" Some perverse part of herself had to know.

His look was filled with defeat. "It seemed the thing to

do. I knew she'd enjoy it, and to be honest, I felt sorry for her. Patty needs someone."

Abby's chin quivered as the hurt coursed through her. Pride dictated that she maintain a level gaze. "Thank you for not lying," she said and closed the door.

Tate was waiting for her when Abby entered the park at eleven-thirty Sunday morning. Since her Saturday sessions with Mai-Ling had come to an end, Abby was now devoting extra time on weekends to Tate.

"You look like you just stepped out of the dentist's chair," Tate said, studying her closely. "What's the matter? Didn't you sleep well last night?"

She hadn't.

"You work too hard," he told her. "You're always helping others. Me and Mai-Ling..."

Abby sat on the blanket Tate had spread out on the grass and lowered her gaze so that her hair fell forward, hiding her face. "I don't do nearly enough," she disagreed. "Tate," she said, raising her eyes to his. "I've never told anyone the reason we meet. Would you mind if I did? Just one person?"

Unable to sleep, Abby had considered the various reasons Logan might have asked Patty out for dinner. She was sure he hadn't purposely meant to hurt her. The only logical explanation was that he wanted her to experience the same feelings he had, since she was continuing to see Tate. And yet he'd gone to pains to keep her from knowing about their date. Nothing made sense anymore. But if she could tell Logan the reason she was meeting Tate, things would be easier....

Tate rubbed a weary hand over his eyes. "This is causing problems with you and—what's-his-name—isn't it?"

Abby didn't want to put any unnecessary pressure on

Tate so she shrugged her shoulders, hoping to give the impression of indifference. "A little. But I don't think Logan really understands."

"Is it absolutely necessary that he know?"

"No, I guess not." Abby had realized it would be extremely difficult for Tate to let anyone else learn about his inability to read—especially Logan.

"Then would it be too selfish of me to ask that you don't say anything?" Tate asked. "At least not yet?" A look of pain flashed over his face, and Abby understood anew how hard it was for him to talk about his problem. "I suppose it's a matter of pride."

Abby's smile relaxed her tense mouth. The relationship among the three of them was a mixed-up matter of pride, and she didn't know whose was the most unyielding.

"No, I don't mind," she replied, and opened her backpack to take out some books. "By the way, I want to give you something." She handed him three of her favorite Dick Francis books. "These are classics in the mystery genre. They may be a bit difficult for you in the beginning, but I think you'll enjoy them."

Tate turned the paperback copy of *The Danger* over and read the back cover blurb. "His business is kidnapping?" He sounded unsure as he raised his eyes to hers.

"Trust me. It's good."

"I'll give it a try. But it looks like it'll take me a while."

"Practice makes perfect."

Tate laughed in the low, lazy manner she enjoyed so much. "I've never known anyone who has an automatic comeback the way you do." He took a cold can of soda and tossed it to her. "Let's drink to your wit."

"And have a celebration of words." She settled her back against the trunk of a massive elm and closed her eyes as

Tate haltingly read the first lines of the book she'd given him. It seemed impossible that only a few weeks before he'd been unable to identify the letters of the alphabet. But his difficulty wasn't attributed to any learning disability, such as she'd encountered in the past with others. He was already at a junior level and advancing so quickly she had trouble keeping him in material, which was why she'd started him on a novel. Unfortunately, his writing and spelling skills were advancing at a slower pace. Abby calculated that it wouldn't take more than a month or two before she could set him on his own with the promise to help when he needed it. Already he'd voiced his concerns about an application he'd be filling out for the bank to obtain a business loan. She'd assured him they'd go over it together.

Abby hadn't been home fifteen minutes when Logan showed up at her building. She buzzed him in and opened the door, but for all the emotion he revealed, his face might have been carved in stone.

"Are you going to let me inside today?" he asked, peering into her apartment.

"I suppose I'll have to."

"Not necessarily. You could make a fool of me the way you did last night."

"Me?" she gasped. "You don't need *me* to make you look like a fool. You do a bang-up job of it yourself."

His mouth tightened as he stepped into her apartment and sank down on the sofa.

Abby sat as far away from him as possible. "Well?" She was determined not to make this easy.

"Patty was in a lot of pain when I drove her to the hospital the night of the accident," he began.

"Uh-huh." She sympathized with Patty but didn't know why he was bringing this up.

Logan's voice was indifferent. "I was talking to her, trying to take her mind off how much she was hurting. It seems that in all the garble I rashly said I'd take her to dinner."

"I suppose you also—rashly—suggested the Sofitel?" She felt chilled by his aloofness and she wasn't going to let him off lightly.

An awkward silence followed. "I don't remember that part, but apparently I did."

"Apparently so," she returned with forced calm. "Maybe I could forget the dinner date, but not the perfume. Honestly, Logan, that was a rotten thing to do."

Impatience shadowed his tired features. "It's not what you think. I got her cologne. Not perfume."

"For heaven's sake," she said, exasperated. "Can't you be more original than that?"

"But it's the truth."

"I know that. But you can't go through life giving women perfume and cologne every time the occasion calls for a gift. And, even worse, you chose the same scent!"

"It's the only one I know." He shook his head. "All right, the next time I buy a woman a gift, I'll take you along."

"The next time you buy a woman a gift," she interrupted in a stern voice, "it had better be me."

He ignored her statement. "Abby, how could you believe I'm attracted to Patty?"

She opened her mouth and closed it again. "Maybe I can believe that you really do care about me. But I've seen the way Patty looks at you. It wouldn't take more than a word to have her fall in love with you. I don't want to see her hurt." Or any of them for that matter, Abby mused. "I don't believe you're using Patty to make me jealous," she said honestly. "I mean, I wondered about it but then decided you weren't."

"I'm glad you realize that much." He breathed out in obvious relief.

"But I recognize the looks she's giving you, Logan. She wants you."

"And Tate wants you!"

Abby's shoulders sagged. "Don't go bringing him into this discussion. It's not right. We were talking about you, not me."

"Why not? Isn't turnabout fair play?" The contempt in his expression made her want to cry.

"That's tiddlywinks, not love," she said saucily.

"But if Patty looks at me with adoring eyes, it only mirrors the way Tate looks at you."

"Now you're being ridiculous," she said, annoyed by his false logic.

Slowly Logan rubbed his chin. "It's always amazed me that you can twist a conversation any way you want."

"That's not true," she said, hating the fact that he'd turned the situation around to suit himself.

"All right, let's put it like this—if you mention Patty Martin, then I mention Tate Harding. That sounds fair to me."

"Fine." She flipped a strand of hair over her shoulder. "I won't mention Patty again."

"Are you still seeing him?"

"Who?" Abby widened her eyes innocently.

Logan's jaw tightened grimly. "I want you to promise me that you won't date Harding again."

Abby stared at him.

"A simple yes or no. That's all I want."

The answer wasn't even difficult. She *wasn't* dating him. "And what do I get in return?"

He bent his head to study his hands. "Something that's been yours for over a year. My heart."

At his words, all of Abby's defensive anger melted. "Oh, Logan," she whispered, emotion bringing a misty happiness to her eyes.

"I've loved you so long, Abby, I can't bear to lose you." There could be no doubt of his sincerity.

"I love you, too."

"Then why are you on the other side of the room when all I want to do is hold you and kiss you?"

The well of tenderness inside her overflowed. She rose from her sitting position. "In the interests of fairness, I think we should meet halfway. Okay?"

He chuckled as he stood, coming to her, but his eyes revealed a longing that was deep and intense. A low groan rumbled from his throat as he swept her into his arms and held her as if he never wanted to let her go. He kissed her eyes, her cheeks, the corner of her mouth until she moaned and begged for more.

"Abby." His voice was muffled against her hair. "You're not going to sidestep my question?"

"What question?" She smiled against his throat as she gave him nibbling, biting kisses.

His hands gripped her shoulders as he pulled her slightly away from him so he could look into her face. "You won't be seeing Tate again?"

She decided not to make an issue of semantics. He *meant* date, not see. What she said in response was the truth. "I promise never to date anyone else again. Does that satisfy you?"

He linked his hands at the small of her back and smiled

deeply into her eyes. "I suppose it'll have to," he said, echoing her remark when she'd let him in.

"Now it's your turn."

"What would you like?"

"No more dating Patty, okay?"

"I agree," he replied without hesitation.

"Inventive gift ideas."

He hesitated. "I'll try."

"You're going to have to do better than that."

"All right, all right, I agree."

"And—"

"There's more?" he interrupted with mock impatience.

"And at some point in our lives I want to drive to Des Moines."

"Fine. Shall we seal this agreement with a kiss?"

"I think it would be only proper," Abby said eagerly as she slid her arms around his waist and fit her body to his.

His large hands framed her face, lifting her lips to meet his. It lacked the urgency of their first kiss, but was filled with promise. His breathing was ragged when he released her, but Abby noted that her own wasn't any calmer.

Not surprisingly, their truce held. Maybe it was because they both wanted it so badly. The next Sunday they met at her place for breakfast, which Abby cooked. Later, they drove over to her parents' house and during their visit Frank Carpenter speculated that the two of them would be married by the end of the year. A few not-so-subtle questions about the "date" popped up here and there in the conversation. But neither of them seemed to mind. Logan was included in Abby's every thought. This was the way love was supposed to be, Abby mused as they returned to her apartment.

After changing clothes, they rode their bikes to the park and ate a picnic lunch. After that, with Logan's head resting in her lap, Abby leaned against an elm tree and closed her eyes. This was the same tree that had supported her back during more than one reading session with Tate. A guilty sensation attacked the pit of her stomach, but she successfully fended it off.

"Did you hear that Dick Snyder wants to climb Mount Rainier this summer?" Logan asked unexpectedly, as he chewed lazily on a long blade of grass.

In addition to softball, Dick's passion was mountains. She'd heard rumors about his latest venture, but hadn't been all that interested.

"Yeah, I heard that," she murmured. "So?"

"So, what do you think?"

"What do I think about what?" Abby asked.

"They need an extra man. It sounds like the expedition will be cancelled otherwise." Logan frowned as he looked up at her.

"Climbing the highest mountain in Washington State should be a thrill—for some people. They won't have any trouble finding someone. Personally, I have trouble making it over speed bumps," she teased, leaning forward to kiss his forehead. "What's wrong?"

He smiled up at her and raised his hands to direct her mouth to his. "What could possibly be wrong?" he whispered as he moved his mouth onto her lips for a kiss that left her breathless.

The next week was the happiest of Abby's life. Logan saw her daily. Monday they went to dinner at the same Mexican restaurant Tate had taken her to weeks before. The food was good, but Abby's appetite wasn't up to par. Again, Abby dismissed the twinge of guilt. Tuesday he picked her up for class, but they decided to skip school. Instead they sat in the parking lot and talked until late. From there they drove until they found a café where they could enjoy their drinks outside. The communication between them had never been stronger.

Tate phoned Abby at work on Wednesday and asked her to meet him at the park before the softball game. He wanted to be sure his application for the business loan had been filled out correctly. Uneasy about being in public with him, for fear Logan would see or hear about it, Abby promised to stop off at his garage.

Later, when Logan picked her up for the game she was short-tempered and restless.

"What's the matter with you tonight?" he complained as they reached the park. "You're as jumpy as a bank robber."

"Me?" She feigned innocence. "Nervous about the game, I guess."

"You?" He looked at her with disbelief. "Ms. Confidence? You'd better tell me what's really bothering you. Fess up, kid."

She felt her face heat with a guilty blush. "Nothing's wrong."

"Abby, I thought we'd come a long way recently. Won't you tell me what's bothering you?"

Logan was so sincere that Abby wanted to kick herself. "Nothing. Honest," she lied and tried to swallow the lump in her throat. She hated this deception, no matter how minor it really was.

"Obviously you're not telling the truth," he insisted, and a muscle twitched in his jaw.

"What makes you say that?" She gave him a look of pure innocence.

"Well, for one thing, your face is bright red."

"It's just hot, that's all."

He released a low breath. "Okay, if that's the way you want it."

Patty was in the bleachers when they arrived, and waved eagerly when she saw Logan. Abby doubted she'd noticed that Abby was with him.

"Your girlfriend's here," Abby murmured sarcastically.

"My girlfriend is walking beside me," Logan said. "What's gotten into you lately?"

Abby sighed. "Don't tell me we're going over all of that again?" She didn't wait for him to answer. Instead she ran onto the field, shouting for Dick to pitch her the ball.

The game went smoothly. Patty basked in the attention everyone was giving her and had the team sign her cast. Abby readily agreed to add her own comment, eager to see what Logan had written on the plaster. But she couldn't locate it without being obvious. Maybe he'd done that on purpose. Maybe he'd written Patty a sweet message on the underside of her arm, where no one else could read it. The thought was so ridiculous that Abby almost laughed out loud.

They lost the game by a slim margin, and Abby realized she hadn't been much help. During the get-together at the pizza place afterward she listened to the others joke and laugh. She wanted to join in, but tonight she simply didn't feel like partying.

"Are you feeling all right?" Logan sat beside her, holding her hand. He studied her with worried eyes.

"I'm fine," she answered and managed a halfhearted smile. "But I'm a little tired. Would you mind taking me home?"

"Not at all."

They got up and, with Logan's hand at the small of her back, they made their excuses and left.

The silence in the car was deafening, but Abby did her best to ignore the unspoken questions Logan was sending her way.

"How about if I cook dinner tomorrow?" Abby said brightly. "I've been terrible tonight and I want to make it up to you."

"If you're not feeling well, maybe you should wait."

"I'm fine. Just don't expect anything more complicated than hot dogs on a bun." She was teasing and Logan knew it.

He parked outside her building and kissed her gently. Abby held on to him compulsively as if she couldn't bear to let him go. She felt caught in a game of cat and mouse between Tate and Logan—a game in which she was quickly becoming the loser.

The following evening, Abby was putting the finishing touches on a salad when Logan came over.

"Surprise," he said as he held out a small bouquet of flowers. "Is this more original than perfume?" he asked with laughing eyes.

"Hardly." She gave him a soft brushing kiss across his freshly shaven cheek as she took the carnations from his hand. "Mmm, you smell good."

Logan picked a tomato slice out of the salad and popped it into his mouth. "So do you."

"Well, if you don't like the fragrance, you have only yourself to blame."

"Me? You smell like pork chops." He slipped his arms around her waist from behind and nuzzled her neck. "You know I could get used to having dinner with you every single night." The teasing quality left his eyes.

Abby dropped her gaze as her heart went skyrocketing

into space. She knew what he was saying. The question had entered her mind several times during the past few days. These feelings they were experiencing were the kind to last a lifetime. Abby wanted to share Logan's life. The desire to wake up with him at her side every morning, to marry him and have his children, was stronger than any instinct. She loved this man and wanted to be with him always.

"I think I could get used to that, too," she admitted softly.

Someone knocked at the door, breaking into their conversation. Impatiently Logan glanced at it. "Are you expecting anyone? One of your neighbors?"

"You," she said. "Here, turn these. I'll see who it is and get rid of them." She handed him the spatula.

Abby's hand was shaking as she grasped the knob, praying it wouldn't be Tate. If she was lucky, she could ask him to leave before Logan knew what was happening.

Her worst fears were realized when she pulled the door open halfway.

"Hi. Someone let me into the lobby."

"Hello, how are you?" she asked in a hushed whisper.

"I'm returning the books you lent me. I really enjoyed them." Tate gave her a funny look. "Is this a bad time or something?"

"You might say that," she breathed. "Could you come back tomorrow?"

"Sure, no problem. Is it Logan?"

Abby nodded, and as she did, the door was opened all the way.

"Hello, Tate," Logan greeted him stiffly. "I've been half-expecting you. Why don't you come inside where we can all visit?"

Eight

The two men regarded each other with open hostility.

Glancing from one to the other, Abby paused to swallow a lump of apprehension. Her worst fears had become reality. She wanted to blurt out the truth, explain to Logan exactly why she was seeing Tate. But one look at the two of them standing on either side of the door and Abby recognized the impossibility of making any kind of explanation. Like rival warlords, the two blatantly dared each other to make the first move.

Logan loomed at her side exuding bitterness, surprise, hurt and anger. He held himself still and rigid.

"I'll see you tomorrow, Abby?" Tate spoke at last, making the statement a question.

"Fine." Abby managed to find her voice, which was low and urgent. She wanted to scream at him to leave. If pride wasn't dominating his actions, he'd recognize what a horrible position he was putting her in. Apparently maintaining his pride was more important than the problem he was causing her. Abby's eyes pleaded with Tate, but either he chose to ignore the silent entreaty or he didn't understand what she was asking.

The enigmatic look on Tate's face moved from Logan to Abby. "Will you be all right? Do you want me to stay?"

"Yes. No!" She nearly shouted with frustration. He'd read the look in her eyes as a plea for help. This was crazy. This whole situation was unreal.

"Tomorrow, then," Tate said as he took a step in retreat.

"Tomorrow," Abby confirmed and gestured with her hand, begging him to leave.

He turned and stalked away.

Immobile, Abby stood where she was, waiting for Logan's backlash.

"How long have you been seeing each other?" he asked with infuriating calm.

If he'd shouted and decried her actions, Abby would have felt better; she could have responded the same way. But his composed manner relayed far more adequately the extent of his anger.

"How long, Abby?" he repeated.

Her chin trembled and she shrugged.

His short laugh was derisive. "Your answer says quite a bit."

"It's not what you think," she said hoarsely, desperately wanting to set everything straight.

His jaw tightened forbiddingly. "I suppose you're going to tell me you and Tate are just good friends. If that's the case, you can save your breath."

"Logan." Fighting back tears of frustration, Abby moved away the door and turned to face him. "I need you to trust me in this."

"Trust you!" His laugh was mocking. "I asked you to decide which one of us you wanted. You claimed you'd made your decision. You even went so far as to assure me you wouldn't be seeing Tate again." The intense anger darkened the shadows across his face, making the curve of his jaw look sharp and abrupt.

"I said I wouldn't *date* him again," she corrected.

"Don't play word games with me," he threw back at her. "You knew what I meant."

She merely shook her head, incapable of arguing. Why *couldn't* he trust her? Why hadn't Tate just *told* him? Why, why, why.

"I suspected something yesterday at the game," Logan continued wryly. "That guilty look was in your eyes again. But I didn't want to believe what I was seeing."

Abby lowered her gaze at the onrush of pain. This deception hadn't been easy for her. But she was bound by her promise to Tate. She couldn't explain the circumstances of their meetings to Logan; only Tate's permission would allow her to do that. But Tate couldn't risk his pride to that extent and she wouldn't ask him to.

Logan's short laugh was bitter with irony. "Yet, when the doorbell rang, I knew immediately it was Tate. To be honest, I was almost glad, because it clears away the doubts in my mind."

Determinedly he started for the door, but Abby's hand delayed him. "Don't go," she whispered. "Please." Her fingers tightened around his arm, wanting to bind him to her forever, beginning with this moment. "I love you and...and if you love me, then you'll trust me."

"Love?" he repeated in a contemptuous voice. "You don't know the meaning of the word."

Stunned, Abby dropped her hand and with a supreme effort met his gaze without emotion. "If that's what you think, maybe it would be better if you did leave."

Logan paused, his troubled expression revealing the inner storm raging within him.

"I may be wrong, but I was brought up to believe that love between two people required mutual trust," Abby added.

One corner of his mouth quirked upward. "And I assumed, erroneously it seems, that love required honesty."

"I... I bent the truth a little."

"Why?" he demanded. "No." He stopped her from explaining. "I don't want to know. Because it's over. I told you before that I wouldn't be kept dangling like a schoolboy while you made up your mind."

"But I *can't* explain now! I may never be able to tell you why."

"It doesn't matter, Abby, it's over," Logan said starkly, his expression impassive.

Abby's stomach lurched with shock and disbelief. Logan didn't mean that. He wouldn't do that to them.

Without another word he walked from the room. The door slammed as he left the apartment. He didn't hesitate or look back.

Abby held out her hand in a weak gesture that pleaded with him to turn around, to trust her. But he couldn't see her, and she doubted it would've had any effect on him if he had. Unshed tears were dammed in her throat, but Abby held her head up in a defiant gesture of pride. The pretense was important for the moment, as she calmly moved into the kitchen and turned off the stove.

Only fifteen minutes before, she had stared lovingly into Logan's eyes, letting her own eyes tell him how much she wanted to share his life. Now, swiftly and without apparent concern, Logan had rejected her as carelessly and thoughtlessly as he would an old pair of shoes. Yet Abby knew that wasn't true. He *did* love her. He couldn't hold her and kiss her the way he did without loving her. Abby knew him as well as he knew her. But then, Abby mused, she had reason to doubt that Logan knew her at all.

Even worse was the fact that Abby recognized she was wrong. Logan deserved an explanation. But her hands were bound by her promise to Tate. And Tate had no idea what that pledge was doing to her and to her relationship with Logan. She couldn't believe he'd purposely do this, but Tate was caught in his own trap. He viewed her as his friend and trusted teacher. He felt fiercely protective of her, wanting in his own way to repay her for the second chance she was giving him by teaching him to read.

Logan and Tate had disliked each other on sight. The friction between them wasn't completely her fault, Abby realized. The ironic part was that for all their outward differences they were actually quite a bit alike.

When Abby had first met Tate that day in the park she'd found him compelling. She'd been magnetically drawn to the same strength that had unconsciously bound her to Logan. This insight had taken Abby weeks to discover, but it had come too late.

The weekend arrived in a haze of emotional pain. Tate phoned Friday afternoon to tell her he wouldn't be able to meet her on Saturday because he was going to the bank to sign the final papers for his loan. He invited her to dinner in celebration, but she declined. Not meeting him gave Abby a reprieve. She wasn't up to facing anyone right now. But each minute, each hour, the hurt grew less intense and life became more bearable. At least, that was what she tried to tell herself.

She didn't see Logan on Sunday, and forced herself not to search for him in the crowded park as she took a late-afternoon stroll. This was supposed to be their day. Now it looked as if there wouldn't be any more lazy Sunday afternoons for them.

Involved in her melancholy thoughts, Abby wandered the paths and trails of the park, hardly noticing the people around her.

Early that evening, as the sun was lowering in a purple sky, Abby felt the urge to sit on the damp earth and take in the beauty of the world around her. She needed the tranquillity of the moment and the assurance that another day had come and gone and she'd made it through the sadness and uncertainty. She reflected on her feelings and actions, admitting she'd often been headstrong and at times insensitive. But she was learning, and although the pain of that growth dominated her mind now, it, too, would fade. Abby stared at the darkening sky and, for the first time in several long days, a sense of peace settled over her.

Sitting on the lush grass, enjoying the richness of the park grounds, Abby gazed up at the sky. These rare, peaceful minutes soothed her soul and quieted her troubled heart. If she were never to see Logan again, she'd always be glad for the good year they'd shared. Too late she'd come to realize all that Logan meant to her. She'd carelessly tossed his love aside—with agonizing consequences.

The following afternoon Abby called Dick Snyder about Wednesday's softball game. Although she was dying for the sight of Logan, it would be an uncomfortable situation for both of them.

"Dick, it's Abby," she said when he answered. She suddenly felt awkward and uneasy.

"Abby," Dick greeted her cheerfully. "It's good to hear from you. What's up?"

An involuntary smile touched the corners of her mouth.

No-nonsense Dick. He climbed mountains, coached soft-ball teams, ran a business with the effectiveness of a tycoon and raised a family; it was all in a day's work, as he often said. "Nothing much, but I wanted you to know I won't be able to make the game on Wednesday."

"You, too?"

"Pardon?" Abby didn't know what he meant.

"Logan phoned earlier and said he wouldn't be at the game, either. Are you two up to something we should know about?" he teased. "Like running off and getting married?"

Abby felt the color flow out of her face, and her heart raced. "No," she breathed, hardly able to find her voice. "That's not it at all."

Her hand was trembling when she replaced the receiver a couple of minutes later. So Logan had decided not to play on Wednesday. If he was quitting softball, she could assume he'd also stop attending classes on Tuesday nights. The possibility of their running into each other at work was still present, since their offices were only half a block apart, but he must be going out of his way to avoid any possible meeting. For that matter, she was doing the same thing.

Soon Abby's apartment began to feel like her prison. She did everything she could to take her mind off Logan, but as the weeks progressed, it became more and more difficult. Much as she didn't want to talk to anyone or provide long explanations about Logan's absence, Abby couldn't tolerate another night alone. She had to get out. So after work the following Wednesday, she got in her car and started to drive.

Before she realized where she was headed, Abby pulled into her parents' driveway.

"Hi, Mom," Abby said as she let herself in the front door.

Her father was reading the paper, and Abby paused at

his side. She placed her hand on his shoulder, kissing him lightly on the forehead. "What's that for?" Frank Carpenter grumbled as his arm curved around her waist. "Do you need a loan?"

"Nope," Abby said with forced cheer. "I was just thinking that I don't say *I love you* nearly enough." She glanced up at her mother. "I'm fortunate to have such good parents."

"How sweet," Glenna murmured softly, but her eyes were clouded with obvious worry. "Is everything all right?"

Abby restrained the compulsion to cry out that *nothing* was right anymore. Not without Logan. She left almost as quickly as she'd come, making an excuse about hurrying home to feed Dano. That weak explanation hadn't fooled her perceptive mother. Abby was grateful Glenna didn't pry.

Another week passed and Abby didn't see Logan. Not that she'd expected to. He was avoiding her as determinedly as she did him. Seeing him would only mean pain. She lost weight, and the dark circles under her eyes testified to her inability to sleep.

Sunday morning, Abby headed straight for the park, intent on finding Logan. Even a glimpse would ease the pain she'd suffered without him. She wondered if his face would reveal any of the same torment she had endured. Surely he regretted his lack of trust. He must miss her—perhaps even enough to set aside their differences and talk to her. And if he did, Abby knew she'd readily respond. She imagined the possible scenes that might play out—from complete acceptance on his part to total rejection.

There was a certain irony in her predicament. Tate had been exceptionally busy and she hadn't tutored him at all that week. He was doing so well now that it wouldn't be more than a month before he'd be reading and writing at an adult level. Once he'd completed the lessons, Abby doubted she'd see him very often, despite the friendship that had developed between them. They had little in common and Tate had placed her on such a high pedestal that Abby didn't think he'd ever truly see her as a woman. He saw her as his rescuer, his salvation—not a position Abby felt she deserved.

She sat near the front entrance of the park so she wouldn't miss Logan if he showed up. She made a pretense of reading, but her eyes followed each person entering the park. By noon, she'd been waiting for three hours and Logan had yet to arrive. Abby felt sick with disappointment. Logan came to the park every Sunday morning. Certainly he wouldn't change that, too—would he?

Defeated, Abby closed her book and meandered down the path. She'd been sitting there since nine, so she was sure she hadn't missed him. As she strolled through the park, Abby saw several people she knew and paused to wave but walked on, not wanting to be drawn into conversation.

Dick Snyder's wife was there with her two school-aged children. She called out Abby's name.

"Hi! Come on over and join me. It'll be nice to have an adult to talk to for a while." Betty Snyder chatted easily, patting an empty space on the park bench. "I keep telling Dick that one of these days *I'm* going mountain climbing and leaving him with the kids." Her smile was bright.

Abby sat on the bench beside Betty, deciding she could do with a little conversation herself. "Is he at it again?" she asked, already knowing the answer. Dick thrived on challenge. Abby couldn't understand how anyone could climb anything. Heights bothered her too much. She remembered once—

"Dick and Logan."

"Logan?" His name cut into her thoughts and a tightness twisted her stomach. "He's not climbing, is he?" She didn't even try to hide the alarm in her voice. Logan was no mountaineer! Oh, he enjoyed a hike in the woods, but he'd never shown any interest in conquering anything higher than a sand dune.

Betty looked at her in surprise. She'd obviously assumed Abby would know who Logan was with and what he was up to.

"Well, yes," Betty hedged. "I thought you knew. The Rainier climb is in two weeks."

"No, I didn't." Abby swallowed. "Logan hasn't said anything."

"He was probably waiting until he'd finished learning the basics from Dick."

"Probably," Abby replied weakly, her voice fading as terror overwhelmed her. Logan climbing mountains? With a dignity she didn't realize she possessed, Abby met Betty's gaze head-on. It would sound ridiculous to tell Betty that this latest adventure had slipped Logan's mind. The fact was, Abby knew it hadn't. She recalled Logan's telling her that Dick was looking for an extra climber. But he hadn't said it as though he was considering it *himself.*

Betty continued, apparently trying to fill the stunned silence. "You don't need to worry. Dick's a good climber. I'd go crazy if he weren't. I have complete and utter confidence in him. You shouldn't worry about Logan. He and Dick have been spending a lot of time together preparing for this. Rainier is an excellent climb for a first ascent."

Abby heard almost nothing of Betty's pep talk and her heart sank. This had to be some cruel hoax. Logan was an accountant. He didn't have the physical endurance needed to ascend fourteen thousand feet. He wasn't qualified to do any kind of climbing, let alone a whole mountain. Someone else should go. Not Logan.

Not the man she loved.

Betty's two rambunctious boys returned and closed around the women, chatting excitedly about a squirrel they'd seen. The minute she could do so politely, Abby slipped away from the family and hurried out of the park. She had to get to Logan—talk some sense into him.

Abby returned to her apartment and got in her car. She drove around, dredging up the nerve to confront Logan. If he was out practicing with Dick, he wouldn't be back until dark. Twice she drove by his place, but his parking space was empty.

After a frustrating hour in a shopping mall, Abby sat through a boring movie and immediately drove back to Logan's. For the third time she saw that he hadn't returned. She drove around again—for how long she was unsure.

Abby couldn't comprehend what had made him decide to do this. A hasty decision wasn't like him. She wondered if this crazy mountain-climbing expedition was his way of punishing her; if so, he'd succeeded beyond his expectations. The only thing left to do was confront him.

Abby drove back to Logan's building, telling herself that the sooner they got this settled, the better. Relief washed over her at the familiar sight of his car.

She pressed his apartment buzzer, but Logan didn't respond. She tried again, keeping her finger on it for at least a minute. And still Logan didn't answer.

Abby decided she could sit this out if he could. Logan wasn't fooling her. He was there.

When he finally answered and let her into the building lobby, Abby ran in, rushing up to his third-floor apartment. He'd opened the door and she stumbled ungracefully across the threshold. Regaining her balance—and her breath—she turned to glare angrily at him.

"Abby." Logan was holding a pair of headphones. "Were you waiting long?" He closed the door, placing the headset on a shelf. "I'm sorry I didn't hear you, but I was listening to a CD."

Regaining her composure, Abby straightened. "Now listen here, Logan Fletcher." She punctuated her speech with a finger pointed at him. "I know why you're doing this, and I won't let you."

"Abby, listen." He murmured her name in the soft way she loved.

"No," she cried. "I *won't* listen!"

He held her away from him, one hand on each shoulder. Abby didn't know if this was meant to comfort her or to keep her out of his arms. Desperately she wanted his arms around her, craved the comfort she knew was waiting for her there.

"You don't need to prove anything to me," she continued, her voice gaining in volume and intensity. "I love you just the way you are. Logan, you're more of a hero than any man I know, and I can't—no," she corrected emotionally, "I *won't* let you do this."

"Do what?"

She looked at him in stunned disbelief. "Climb that stupid mountain."

"So you did hear." He sighed. "I was hoping none of this would get back to you."

"Logan," she gasped. "You weren't planning to let me know? You're doing this to prove some egotistical point to me and you weren't even going to let me know until it was too late? I can't believe you'd do that. I simply can't believe it. You've always been so logical and all of a sudden you're falling off the deep end."

Now it was his turn to look flabbergasted. "Abby, sit down. You're becoming irrational."

"I am not," she denied hotly, but she did as he suggested. "Logan, please listen to me. You can't go traipsing off to Washington on this wild scheme. The whole idea is ludicrous. Crazy!"

He knelt beside her and she framed his face with both hands, her eyes pleading with his.

"Don't you understand?" she said. "You've never climbed before. You need experience, endurance and sheer nerve to take on a mountain. You don't have to prove anything to me. I love you just the way you are. Please don't do this."

"Abby," Logan said sternly and pulled her hand free, holding her fingers against his chest. "This decision is mine. You have nothing to do with it. I'm sorry this upsets you, but I'm doing something I've wanted to do for years."

"Haven't you listened to a word I've said?" She yanked her hands away and took in several deep breaths. "You could be killed!"

"You seem to be confusing the issues. My desire to make this climb with Dick and his friends has nothing to do with you."

"Nothing to do with me?" she repeated frantically. Had Logan gone mad? "If you think for one instant that I'm going to let you do this, then you don't know me, Logan Fletcher."

He stood up, and smoothed the side of his hair with one hand as he regarded her quizzically. "You seem to be under the mistaken impression that I'm doing this to prove something to you."

"You may not have admitted it to yourself, but that's exactly the reason you are." She shook her head frantically. "You're climbing this crazy mountain because you want to impress me."

Logan's short laugh was filled with amusement. "I'm doing this, Abby, because I want to. My reasons are as simple as that. You're making it sound like I'm going in front of a firing squad. Dick's an experienced climber. I expect to be perfectly safe," he said matter-of-factly.

"I don't believe you could be so naive," she told him flatly, "about the danger of mountain-climbing *or* about your own motivations."

"Then that's your problem."

"But...you could end up dead!"

"I could walk across the street and be hit by a car tomorrow," Logan replied with infuriating calm.

Abby couldn't stand his quiet confidence another second. She leaped to her feet and stalked across the floor, gesturing wildly with her hands, unable to clarify her thoughts enough to reason with him. Pausing, she took a moment to compose herself. "If this is something you always wanted to do, how come I've never heard about it before?"

"Because I knew what your reaction would be—and I was right. I—"

"You're so caught up in the excitement of this adventure, you can't see how crazy it is," Abby interrupted, not wanting him to argue with her. He *had* to listen.

Logan took her gently by the shoulders and turned her around. "I think you should realize that nothing you say is going to change my mind."

"I drove you to this—" Her voice throbbed painfully.

"No," he cut in abruptly and brushed a hand across his face. "As I keep telling you, this is something I've always wanted to do, whether you like it or not."

"I don't like it and I don't believe it."

"That's too bad." Logan breathed in harshly. "But unlike certain people I know, I don't bend the truth. It's true, Abby."

Abby's mouth twisted in a smile. "And you weren't even going to tell me."

His look was grudging. "I think you can understand why."

Abby shut her eyes and groaned inwardly.

"Now if you'll excuse me, I really do need to get back to the audio book I'm listening to. It's on climbing. Dick recommended it."

"I thought you were smarter than this. I've never heard of anything so stupid in my life," she said waspishly, lashing out at him in her pain.

His smile was mirthless as if he'd expected that kind of statement from her.

"I'm sorry," she mumbled as she studied the scuffed-up toe of her shoe. The entire day had been crazy. "I didn't mean that."

A finger under her chin lifted her eyes to his. "I know you didn't." For that instant all time came to a halt. His eyes burned into hers with an intensity that stole her breath.

Seemingly of their own volition, her hands slid over his chest. She wound her arms around his neck and stood on the tips of her toes as she fitted her mouth over his. The slow-burning fire of his kiss melted her heart. Every part of her seemed to be vibrantly alive. Her nerves tingled and flared to life.

Angrily Logan broke the kiss. "What's this?" he said harshly. "My last kiss before I face the firing squad?"

"Hardly. I expect you to come back alive." She paused, frowning at him. "If you don't, I swear I'll never forgive you."

He rammed his hands into his pants pockets. Then, as if he couldn't bear to look at her, he stalked to the other side of the room. "If I don't come back, why would it matter? We're not on speaking terms as it is."

From somewhere deep inside her, Abby found the strength to swallow her pride and smile. "That's something I'd like to change."

"No," he said without meeting her gaze.

"You're not leaving for two weeks. During that time you won't be able to avoid seeing me," she went on. "I don't mind telling you that I plan to use every one of those days to change your mind."

"It won't work, Abby," he murmured.

"I can try. I—"

"What I mean is that I have two weeks before the climb, but we're flying in early to explore several other mountains in the Cascade Range."

"The Cascades?" From school, Abby remembered that parts of the Cascade mountain range in Washington State had never been explored. This made the whole foolish expedition even more frightening.

"My flight leaves tomorrow night."

"No," she mumbled miserably, the taste of defeat filling her.

"There's a whole troop who'll be seeing us off. If you're free, you might want to come, too."

Abby noted that he didn't ask her to come, but merely informed her of what was happening. Sadly she shook her head. "I don't think so, Logan. I refuse to be a part of it. Besides, I'm not keen on tearful farewells and good wishes."

"I won't ask anything from you anymore, Abby."

"That's fine," she returned more flippantly than she intended. Involuntary tears gathered in her eyes. "But you'd better come back to me, Logan Fletcher. That's all I can say."

"I'll be back," he told her confidently.

Not until Abby was halfway home did she realize that Logan hadn't said he was coming back *to her*.

Later that night Abby lay in bed while a kaleidoscope of memories went through her mind. She recalled the most memorable scenes of her year-long relationship with Logan. One thing was clear: she'd been blind and stupid not to have appreciated him, or recognized how much she loved him.

Staring at the blank ceiling, she felt a tear roll from the corner of her eye and fall onto the pillow. Abby was intensely afraid for Logan.

The following afternoon, when Abby let herself into her apartment, the phone was ringing.

Abby's heart hammered in her throat. Maybe Logan was calling to say goodbye. Maybe he'd changed his mind and would ask her to come to the airport after all.

But it was her mother.

"Abby." Glenna's raised voice came over the line. "I just heard that Logan's joining Dick Snyder on his latest climb."

"Yes," Abby confirmed in a shaky voice, wondering how her mother had found out about it. "His plane's leaving in—" she paused to check her watch "—three hours and fifteen minutes. Not that I care."

"Oh, dear, I was afraid of that. You're taking this hard."

"Me? Why would I?" Abby attempted to sound cool and confident. She didn't want her mother to worry about her. But her voice cracked and she inhaled a quivering breath before she was able to continue. "He's in Dick's capable hands, Mother. All you or I or anyone can do is wait."

The hesitation was only slight. "Sometimes you amaze me, Ab."

"Is that good or bad?" Some of her sense of humor was returning.

"Good," her mother whispered. "It's very good."

* * *

The more Abby told herself she wouldn't break down and go to the airport, the more she realized there was nothing that could stop her.

A cold feeling of apprehension crept up her back and extended all the way to the tips of her fingers as Abby drove. Her hands felt clammy, but that was nothing compared to her stomach. The churning pain was almost more than she could endure. Because she hadn't been able to eat all day, she felt light-headed now.

Abby arrived at the airport and the appropriate concourse in plenty of time to see the small crowd of well-wishers surrounding Dick, Logan and company. They obviously hadn't checked in for their flight. Standing off to one side, Abby chose not to involve herself. She didn't want Logan to know she'd come. Almost everyone from the softball team was there, including Patty. She seemed more quiet and subdued than normal, Abby noted, and was undoubtedly just as worried about Logan's sudden penchant for danger as she herself was.

Once Abby thought Logan was looking into the crowd as if seeking someone. Desperately she wanted to run to him, hold him and kiss him before he left. But she was afraid she'd burst into tears and embarrass them both. Logan wouldn't want that. And her pride wouldn't allow her to show her feelings.

When it came time for Logan and the others to check in and go through security, there was a flurry of embraces, farewells and best wishes. Then almost everyone departed en masse.

Abby waited, studying the departures board until she knew his plane had left.

Nine

Abby rolled out of bed, stumbled into the kitchen and turned on the radio, anxious to hear the weather report. They were in the midst of a July heatwave.

Cradling a cup of coffee in her hands, Abby eyed the calendar. In a few days Logan would be home. Each miserable, apprehensive day brought him closer to her.

Betty Snyder continued to hear regularly from Dick about the group's progress as they trekked over some of the most difficult of the Cascade mountains. Trying not to be obvious, Abby phoned Betty every other day or so, to hear whatever information she could impart. Abby still didn't know the true reasons Logan had joined this venture, but believed they were the wrong ones.

The first week after his departure, Abby received a postcard. She'd laughed and cried and hugged it to her breast. An email would've been nice. Or a phone call. But she'd settle—happily—for a postcard. Crazy, wonderful Logan. Anyone else would have sent her a scene of picturesque Seattle or at least the famous mountain he was about to climb. Not Logan. Instead he sent her a picture of a salmon.

His message was simple:

How are you? Wish you were here. I saw you at the
airport. Thank you for coming. See you soon.
Love, Logan

Abby treasured the card more than the bottles of expensive French perfume he'd given her. Even when several other people on the team received similar messages,
it didn't negate her pleasure. The postcard was tucked in
her purse as a constant reminder of Logan. Not that Abby
needed anything to jog her memory; Logan was continu-
ally in her thoughts. And although the message on the postcard was impersonal, Abby noted that he'd signed it with
his love. It was a minor thing, but she held on to it with all
her might. Logan did love her, and somehow, some way,
they were going to overcome their differences because what
they shared was too precious to relinquish.

"Disturbing news out of Washington State for climbers
on Mount Rainier..." the radio announced.

Abby felt her knees go weak as she pulled out a kitchen
chair and sat down. She immediately turned up the volume.

"An avalanche has buried eleven climbers. The risk of
another avalanche is hampering the chances of rescue. Six
men from the Minneapolis area were making a southern
ascent at the time of the avalanche. Details at the hour."

A slow, sinking sensation attacked Abby as she placed
a trembling hand over her mouth.

During the news, the announcer related the sketchy
details available about the avalanche and fatalities and
concluded the report with the promise of updates as they
became available. Abby ran for the TV and turned it to an
all-news channel. She heard the same report over and over.
Each word struck Abby like a body blow, robbing her lungs
of oxygen. Pain constricted her chest. Fear, anger and a

hundred emotions she couldn't identify were all swelling violently within her. When the telephone rang, she nearly tumbled off the chair in her rush to answer it.

Please, oh, please don't let this be a call telling me Logan's dead, her mind screamed. *He promised he'd come back.*

It was Betty Snyder.

"Abby, do you have your radio or TV on?" she asked urgently. Her usual calm manner had evaporated.

"Yes… I know," Abby managed shakily. "Have you heard from Dick?"

"No." Her soft voice trembled. "Abby, the team was making a southern ascent. If they survived the avalanche, there's a possibility they'll be trapped on the mountain for days before a rescue team can reach them." Betty sounded as shocked as Abby.

"We'll know soon if it's them."

"It's not them," Betty continued on a desperate note, striving for humor. "And if it isn't, I'll personally kill Dick for putting me through this. We should hear something soon."

"I hope so."

"Abby," Betty asked with concern, "are you going to be all right?"

"I'll be fine." But hearing the worry in her friend's voice did little to reassure her. "Do you want me to come over? I can take the day off…"

"Dick's mother is coming and she's a handful. You go on to work and I'll call you if I hear from Dick—or anyone."

"Okay." Her friends at the clinic and on the team would need reassurance themselves and Abby could quickly relay whatever messages came through. She'd check her computer regularly for any breaking news.

"Everything's going to work out fine." Betty's tone was

low and wavering and Abby realized her friend expected
the worst.

The day was a living nightmare; every nerve was
stretched taut. With each ring of the office phone her pulse
thundered before she could bring it under control and react
normally.

Keeping busy was essential for her sanity those first few
hours. But by quarter to five she'd managed to settle her emotions. The worst that could've happened was that Logan was
dead. The worst. But according to the news, no one from the
Minneapolis area was listed among those missing and pre-
sumed dead. Abby decided to believe they were fine; there
was no need to face any other possibility until necessary.

After work Abby drove directly to Betty's. She hadn't realized how emotionally and physically drained she was until
she got there. But she forced herself to relax before entering her friend's home, more for Betty's sake than her own.

"Have you heard anything?" she asked calmly as Betty
let her in the front door. She could hear the TV in the background.

"Not a word." Betty studied Abby closely. "Just what's
on the news. The hardest part is not knowing."

Abby nodded and bit her bottom lip. "And the waiting.
I won't give up my belief that Logan's alive and well. He
must be, because I'm alive and breathing. If anything happened to Logan, I'd know. My heart would know if he was
dead." Abby recognized that her logic was questionable,
but she expected her friend to understand better than anyone else exactly what she was saying.

"I feel the same thing," Betty confirmed.

Dick's mother had gone home and Abby stayed for a
while to keep Betty and the kids company. Then she went
to her apartment to change clothes and watch the latest

update on TV. The television reporter wasn't able to relate much more than what had been available that morning.

Tate was waiting for her at the little Mexican restaurant where they met occasionally and raised his hand when she entered. They'd arranged this on the weekend, and Abby had decided not to change their plans. She needed the distraction.

Her relationship with Tate had changed in the past weeks. He'd changed. Confident and secure now, he often came to her with minor problems related to the business material he was reading. She was his friend as well as his teacher.

"I didn't know if you'd cancel," Tate said as he pulled out a chair for her. "I heard about the accident on Mount Rainier."

"To be honest, I wasn't sure I should come. But I would've gone crazy sitting at home brooding about it," Abby admitted.

"Any news about Logan?"

Abby released a slow, agonizing breath. "Nothing."

"He'll be fine," Tate said. "If anyone could take care of himself, I'd say it was Logan. He wouldn't have gone if he didn't know what to expect and couldn't protect himself."

Abby was surprised by Tate's insights. She wouldn't have thought that Tate would be so generous in his comments.

"I thought you didn't like Logan." She broached the subject boldly. "It seemed that every time you two were around each other, fireworks went off."

Tate lifted one shoulder in a dismissive shrug. "That's because I didn't like his attitude toward you."

"How's that?"

"You know. He acted like he owned you."

The problem was that he held claim to her heart and it had taken Tate to show Abby how much she loved Logan. Her fingers circled the rim of the glass and she smiled into her water. "In a way he does," she whispered. "Because I love him, and I know he loves me."

Tate picked up the menu and studied it. "I'm beginning to realize that...." he murmured. "Look, I'll try to talk to him, if that'll help."

Abby reached across the table and squeezed his hand "Thanks, Tate."

The waitress approached them. "Are you ready to order?"

Abby glanced at the menu and nodded. "I'll have the cheese enchiladas."

"Make that two," Tate said absently. "No." He paused. "I've changed my mind. I'll have the pork burrito."

Abby tried unsuccessfully to disguise her amusement.

"What's so funny?" Tate asked.

"You. Do you remember the first few times we went out to eat? You always ordered the same thing I did. I'm pleased to see you're not still doing it."

"It became a habit." He paused. "I owe you a great deal, Abby, more than I'll ever be able to repay."

"Nonsense." They were friends, and their friendship had evolved from what it had been in those early days, but his gratitude sometimes made her uncomfortable.

"Maybe this will help show a little of my appreciation." Tate pulled a small package from inside his pocket and handed it to her.

Abby was stunned, her fingers numb as she accepted the beautifully wrapped box. She raised her eyes to his. "Tate, please. This isn't necessary."

"Hush and open your gift," he instructed, obviously enjoying her surprise.

When she pulled the paper away, Abby was even more astonished to see the name of a well-known and expensive jeweler embossed across the top of the case. Her heart was in her throat as she shook her head disbelievingly. "Tate," she began. "I—"

"Open it." An impish light glinted in his eyes.

Slowly she raised the lid to discover a lovely intricately woven gold chain on a bed of blue velvet. Even with her untrained eye, Abby recognized that the chain was of the highest quality. A small cry of undisguised pleasure escaped before she could hold it back.

"Tate!" She could hardly take in its beauty. For the first time in months she found herself utterly speechless.

"Abby?"

"I... I can't believe it. It's beautiful."

"I knew you'd like it."

"Like it! It's the most beautiful necklace I've ever seen. Thank you." Abby smiled at him. "But you shouldn't have. You know that, don't you?"

"If you say so."

"*Now* he's agreeable." Abby smiled as she spoke to the empty chair beside her. "Here, help me put it on."

Tate stood and came around to her side of the table. He took the chain from its plush bed and laid it against the hollow of her throat. Abby bowed her head and lifted the hair from the back of her neck to make it easier for Tate to fasten the necklace.

When he returned to his chair, Abby felt a warm glow. "I still think you shouldn't have done this, but to be honest, I'm glad you did."

"I knew the minute I saw it in the jeweler's window that it was exactly what I was looking for. If you want the truth, I'd been searching for weeks for something special to give you. I want to thank you for everything you've done for me."

Abby didn't think Tate realized what a small part she'd played in his tutoring. He'd done all the real work himself.

He was the one who'd sought her out with a need and admitted that need—something he'd never been able to do before, having always hidden his inability. Abby doubted Tate recognized how far he'd come from the day he'd followed her home from the park.

Later, when Abby undressed for bed, she fingered the elegant chain, remembering Tate's promise. Maybe now he'd be willing to explain to Logan why Abby had met with him. The chain represented his willingness to help repair her relationship with Logan. That would be the most significant gift he could possibly give her.

Before leaving for work the next morning, Abby checked the news. Nothing. Then she phoned Betty in case there'd been any calls during the night. There hadn't been, and discouragement sounded in Betty's voice as she promised to phone Abby's office if she heard anything.

At about ten that morning, Abby had just finished updating the chart on a young teen who'd visited the clinic, when she glanced up and saw Betty in the doorway.

Abby straightened and stood immobile, her heart pumping at a furious rate. Suddenly, she went cold with fear. She couldn't move or think. Even breathing became impossible. Betty would've come to the office for only one reason, she thought. Logan was dead.

"Betty," she pleaded in a tortured whisper, "tell me. What is it?"

"He's fine! Everyone is. They were stuck on the slopes an extra night, but made it safely to camp early this morning. I just heard—Dick called me."

Abby closed her eyes and exhaled a breath of pure release. Her heart skipped a beat as she moved across the room. The two women hugged each other fiercely as tears of happiness streaked their faces.

"They're on their way home. The flight will land sometime tomorrow evening. Everyone's planning to meet them at the airport. You'll come, won't you?"

In her anger and pain Abby had refused to see him off with the others…until the last minute. She wouldn't be so stubborn about welcoming him home. Abby doubted she'd be able to resist hurling herself into his arms the instant she saw him. And once she was in his arms, Abby defied anyone to tear her away.

"Abby? You'll come, won't you?" Betty's soft voice broke into her musings.

"I'll be there," Abby replied, as the image of their reunion played in her mind.

"I thought you'd want to be." Her friend gave her a knowing look.

Logan was safe and coming home. Abby's heart leaped with excitement and she waited until it resumed its normal pace before returning to her desk.

"Tonight," Abby explained to Tate at lunch on Thursday. She swallowed a bite of her pastrami sandwich. "Their flight's arriving around nine-thirty. The team's planning a get-together with him and Dick on Friday night. You're invited to attend if you'd like."

"I just might come."

Tate surprised her with his easy acceptance. Abby had issued the invitation thoughtlessly, not expecting Tate to take her up on it. For that matter, it might even have been the wrong thing to do, since Logan would almost certainly be offended.

"I was beginning to wonder if you were ever going to

invite me to any of those social functions your team's always having."

"Tate." Abby glanced up in surprise. "I had no idea you wanted to come. I wish you'd said something earlier." Now she felt guilty for having excluded him in the past.

"Sure," Tate chimed in defensively. "They'll take one look at a mechanic and decide they've got something better to do."

"Tate, that's simply not true." And it wasn't. He'd be accepted as would anyone who wished to join them. Plenty of friends and coworkers attended the team's social events.

"It might turn a few heads." Tate expelled his breath as if he found the thought amusing.

"Oh, hardly."

"You don't think so?" he asked hopefully.

Tate's lack of self-confidence was a by-product of his inability to read. Now that reading was no longer a problem, he would gain that new maturity. She was already seeing it evolve in him.

Moonlight flooded the ground. The evening was glorious. Not a cloud could be seen in the crystal-blue sky as it darkened into night. Slowly, Abby released a long, drawn-out sigh. Logan would land in a couple of hours and the world had never been more beautiful. She paused to hum a love ballad playing on the radio, thrilled by the romantic words.

She must have changed her clothes three times, but everything had to be perfect. When Logan saw her at the airport, she wanted to look as close to an angel as anything he would find this side of heaven.

She spent half an hour on her hair and makeup. Nothing satisfied her. Tight-lipped, Abby realized she couldn't suddenly make herself into an extraordinarily beautiful woman. Sad but true. She could only be herself. She dressed in a soft, plum-colored linen suit and a pink silk blouse. Dissatisfied with her hair, Abby pulled it free of the confining pins and brushed it until it shimmered and fell in deep natural waves down the middle of her back. Logan had always loved her hair loose....

A quick glance at her watch showed her that she was ten minutes behind schedule. Grabbing her purse, Abby hurried out to her car—and she noticed that it was running on empty. Everything seemed to be going wrong....

Abby pulled into a service station, splurging on full service for once instead of pumping her own. *Hurry*, she muttered to herself as the teenager took his time.

"Do you want me to check your oil?"

"No, thanks." Abby handed him the correct change, plus a tip. "And don't bother washing the window."

Inhaling deep breaths helped take the edge off her impatience as she merged onto the freeway. A mile later an accident caused a minor slowdown.

By the time she arrived at the airport, her heart was pounding. Checking the arrivals board revealed that Logan's flight was on schedule.

Abby ran down the concourse. Within minutes the team, as well as Karen, Logan's assistant, came into sight.

Warmth stole over Abby as she saw Logan, a large backpack slung over one shoulder. His face was badly sunburned, the skin around his eyes white from his protective eye gear. He looked tanned and more muscular than she could remember. His eyes searched the crowd and paused on her, his look thoughtful and intense.

Abby beamed, wearing her brightest smile. He was so close. Close enough to reach out and touch if it weren't for the people crowding around. Abby's heart swelled with the depth of her love. His own eyes mirrored the longing she was sure he could see in hers. These past weeks were all either of them would need to recognize that they should never be apart again.

Abby edged her way toward him and Dick. The others who'd come to greet Logan were chatting excitedly, but Abby heard none of their conversation. Logan was back! Here. Now. And she loved him. After today he'd never doubt the strength of her feelings again.

In her desire to get to Logan quickly, Abby nearly stumbled over an elderly man. She stopped and apologized profusely, making sure the white-haired gentleman wasn't hurt. As she straightened, she heard someone call out Logan's name.

In shocked disbelief, Abby watched as Patty Martin ran across the room and threw herself dramatically into Logan's arms. He dropped his pack. Sobbing, she clung to him as if he'd returned from the dead. Soon the others gathered around, and Dick and Logan were completely blocked from Abby's view.

The bitter taste of disappointment filled her mouth. Logan should have pushed the others aside and come to her. *Her* arms should be the ones around him. *Her* lips should be the ones kissing his.

Proudly Abby decided she wouldn't fight her way through the throng of well-wishers. If Logan wanted her, then she was here. And he knew it.

But apparently he didn't care. Five minutes later, the small party moved out of the airport and progressed to the parking lot. As far as Abby could tell, Logan hadn't so much as looked around to see where she was.

After all the lonely days of waiting for Logan, Abby had a difficult time deciding if she should attend the party being held at a local buffet restaurant in his and Dick's honor the following evening. If he hadn't come to her at the airport, then what guarantee did she have that he wouldn't shun her a second time? The pain lingered from his first rejection. Abby didn't know if she could bear another one.

To protect her ego on Friday night Abby dressed casually in jeans and a cotton top. She timed her arrival so she wouldn't cause a stir when she entered the restaurant. As she'd expected, and as was fitting, Logan and Dick were the focus of attention while they relived their tales of danger on the high slopes.

Abby filled her plate and took a seat where she could see Logan. She knew she wouldn't be able to force down any dinner; occasionally she rearranged the food in front of her in a pretence of eating.

Sitting where she was, Abby could observe Logan covertly. Every once in a while he'd glance up and search the room. He seemed to be waiting for someone. Abby would've liked to believe he was looking for her, but she could only speculate. The tension flowed out of her as she witnessed again the strength and vitality he exuded. That experience on the mountain had changed him, just as it had changed her.

Unable to endure being separated any longer, Abby pushed her plate aside and crossed the room to his table. Logan's eyes locked with hers as she approached. Someone was speaking to him, but Abby doubted that Logan heard a word of what was being said.

"Hello, Logan," she said softly. Her arms hung nervously at her sides. "Welcome home."

"It's good to see you, Abby." His gaze roamed her face lovingly. He didn't need to pull her into his arms for Abby to know what he was feeling. It was all there for her to read. Her doubts, confusion and anxiety were all wiped out in that one moment.

"I'm sorry about what happened at the airport." His hand clasped hers. "There wasn't anything I could do."

Their eyes held as she studied his face. Every line, every

groove, was so familiar. "Don't apologize. I understand."
Who would've believed a simple touch could cause such a
wild array of sensations? Abby felt shaky and weak just being
this close to him. A tingling warmth ran up the length of her
arm as he gently enclosed her in his embrace.

"Can I see you later?"

"You must be exhausted." She wanted desperately to
be with him, but she could wait another day. After all this
time, a few more hours wouldn't matter.

"Seeing you again is all the rest I need."

"I'll be here," she promised.

Dick Snyder tapped Logan on the shoulder and led him
to the front row of tables. After a few words from Dick
about their adventure, Logan stood and thanked everyone
for their support. He relayed part of what he'd seen and the
group's close brush with death.

The tables of friends and relatives listened enthralled
as Logan and Dick spoke. Hearing him talk so casually
about their adventures was enough to make Abby's blood
run cold. She'd come so close to losing him.

Abby stood apart from Dick and Logan while they shook
everyone's hand as they filed out the door and thanked them
for coming. When the restaurant began to empty Logan
hurried across the room and brought Abby to his side. She
wasn't proud of feeling this way, but she was glad Patty
hadn't come. Abby was also grateful that Tate had called
to say he couldn't make it. In an effort to assure him he'd
be welcome another time, Abby invited him to the team
picnic scheduled that Sunday in Diamond Lake Park. Tate
promised to be there if possible.

Logan led her into the semidarkened parking lot and
turned Abby into his arms. There was a tormented look in
his eyes as he gazed down on her upturned face.

"Crazy as it sounds, the whole time we were trapped on that mountain, I was thinking that if I didn't come back alive you'd never forgive me." With infinite tenderness he kissed her.

"I wouldn't have forgiven you," she murmured and smiled up at him in the dim light.

"Abby, I love you," he said. "It took a brush with death to prove how much I wanted to come home to you."

His mouth sought hers and with a joyful cry, Abby wrapped her arms around him and clung. Tears of happiness clouded her eyes as Logan slipped his hands into the length of her hair. He couldn't seem to take enough or give enough as he kissed her again and again. Finally he buried his face in the slope of her neck.

He held her face as he inhaled a steadying breath. "When I saw you across the restaurant tonight, it was all I could do to be polite and stay with the others."

Abby lowered her eyes. "I wasn't sure you wanted to see me."

"You weren't sure?" Logan said disbelievingly. He slid his hands down to rest on the curve of her shoulders. His finger caught on the delicate gold chain and he pulled it up from beneath her blouse.

Abby went completely still. Logan seemed to sense that something wasn't right as his eyes searched hers.

"What's wrong?"

"Nothing."

His eyes fell on the chain. "This is lovely and it's far more expensive than you could afford. Who gave it to you, Abby? Tate?"

Ten

Abby pressed her lips so tightly together that they hurt. "Yes, Tate gave me the necklace."

"You're still seeing him, aren't you?" Logan dropped his hands to his sides and didn't wait for her to respond. "After everything I've said, you still haven't been able to break off this relationship with Tate, have you?"

"Tate has nothing to do with you and me," she insisted, inhaling deeply to hide her frustration. After the long, trying days apart, they *couldn't* argue! Abby wanted to cry out that she loved him and nothing else should matter. She should be able to be friends with a hundred men if she loved only him. Her voice shaking, she attempted to salvage their reunion. "I know this is difficult for you to understand. To be honest, I don't know how I'd feel if you were to continue seeing Patty Martin."

His mouth hardened. "Then maybe I should."

Abby realized Logan was tired and impatient, but an angry retort sprang readily to her lips. "You certainly seem to have a lot in common with Patty—far more than you do with me."

"The last thing I want to do is argue."

"I don't, either. My intention in coming tonight wasn't to defend my actions while you were away. And yes—" she paused to compose herself, knowing her face was flushed "—I did see Tate."

The area became charged with an electricity that seemed to spark and crackle. The atmosphere was heavy and still, pressing down on her like the stagnant air before a thunderstorm.

"I think that says everything I need to know," he said with quiet harshness.

Abby nodded sharply, forcing herself to meet his piercing gaze. "Yes, I suppose it does." She took a step backward.

"It was kind of you to come and welcome me back this evening." A muscle twitched in his jaw. "But as you can imagine, the trip was exhausting. I'd like to go home and sleep for a week."

Abby nodded, trying to appear nonchalant. "Perhaps we can discuss this another time."

Logan shook his head. "There won't be another time, Abby."

"That decision is yours," she said calmly, although her voice trembled with reaction. "Good night, Logan."

"Goodbye, Abby."

Goodbye! She knew what he was saying as plainly as if he'd screamed it at her. Whatever had been between them was now completely over.

"I expect you'll be seeing a lot more of Logan now that he's back," Tate commented from her living room the following afternoon.

Abby brought out a sandwich from the kitchen and handed it to him before taking a seat. "We've decided to let things cool between us," she said with as much aplomb as she could manage. "Cool" was an inadequate word. Their relationship was in Antarctica. They'd accidentally run into each other that morning while Abby was doing some grocery shopping and had exchanged a few stilted sentences. After a minute Abby could think of nothing more to say.

"You know what I think, Tate?" Abby paid an inordinate amount of attention to her sandwich. "I've come to the belief that love is a highly overrated emotion."

"Why?"

Abby didn't need to glance up to see the amusement in Tate's face. Instead she took the first bite of her lunch. How could she explain that from the moment she realized how much she loved Logan, all she'd endured was deep emotional pain. "Never mind," she said at last, regretting that she'd brought it up.

"Abby?" Tate's look was thoughtful.

She leaped to her feet. "I forgot the iced tea." She hurried into the kitchen, hoping Tate would let the subject drop.

"Did I tell you the bank approved my loan?"

Returning with their drinks, Abby grinned. "That's great!"

"They phoned yesterday afternoon. Bessler's pleased, but not half as much as I am. I have a lot to thank you for, Abby."

"I'm so happy for you," Abby said with a quick nod. "You've worked hard and deserve this." Abby knew how relieved Tate was that the loan had gone through. He'd called Abby twice out of pure nerves, just to talk through his doubts.

Tomorrow afternoon they were going to attend the picnic together and although Abby was grateful for Tate's friendship, she didn't want to give her friends the wrong impression. Logan had already jumped to conclusions. There was nothing to say the others wouldn't, too. Tate was a friend—a special friend—but their relationship didn't go beyond that. It couldn't, not when she was in love with Logan.

"Abby," Tate said quietly. "I'm going to talk to him."

Sunday afternoon Abby was preoccupied as she dressed in shorts and a Twins T-shirt for the picnic. She was glad Tate was going with her, glad he'd promised to explain, but she hoped Logan didn't do or say anything to make him uncomfortable.

Logan. The unhappiness weighed down on her heart. Her thoughts were filled with him every waking minute. Even her dreams involved him. This misunderstanding, this lack of trust, had to stop once and for all. From the moment Logan had left for Washington, Abby had longed for Tate to explain the situation and heal her relationship with Logan. She'd assumed that as time went on they'd naturally get back together. Now, just the opposite was proving to be true. With every passing hour, Logan was drifting further and further out of her life. Yet her love was just as strong. Perhaps stronger. Whether Tate went through with his confession and whether it changed things remained to be seen.

Since Tate was meeting her at the park, Abby got there early and found a picnic table for them. When Logan came, he claimed the table directly across from hers and Abby felt the first bit of encouragement since they'd last spoken. As quickly as the feeling came, it vanished. Logan set out a tablecloth and unpacked his cooler without so much as glancing her way. Only a few feet separated her from him, but it felt as if their distance had never been greater. He gave no indication that he'd seen her. Even her weak smile had gone unacknowledged.

Soon they were joined by the others, chatting and laughing. A few men played horseshoes while the women sat and visited. The day was glorious, birds trilled their songs from the tree branches and soft music came from someone's CD player. Busy putting the finishing touches on a salad, Abby sang along with the music. The last thing in the world she felt like doing was singing, but if she didn't, she'd start crying.

Tate arrived and Abby could see by the way he walked that he was nervous. He'd met some of the people at the softball game. Still, he looked surprised when one of the guys called out a greeting. The two men talked for a minute and Tate joined her soon afterward.

"Hi."

"There's no need to be nervous," she said, smiling at him.

"What? Me nervous?" he joked. "They're nice people, aren't they?"

"The best."

"Even Logan?"

"Especially Logan."

Tate was silent for a moment. "Like I said, I'll see what I can do to patch things up between you two."

Unhurriedly, she raised her gaze to his. "I'd appreciate that."

His returning smile told her how difficult revealing his past would be. Abby hated to ask him to do it, but there didn't seem to be any other way.

As he wandered off, Abby laced her fingers tightly and sat there, searching for Logan. He was standing alone with his back to her, staring out over the still, quiet lake.

Abby spread out a blanket between the two picnic tables and lay down on it, pretending to sunbathe. She must have drifted off, because the low-pitched voices of Tate and Logan were what stirred her into wakefulness.

"Seems to me you've got the wrong table," Logan was saying. "Your girlfriend's over there."

"I was hoping we could talk."

"I can't see that there's much to talk about. Abby's made her decision."

The noises that followed suggested that Logan was arranging drinks on the table and ignoring Tate as much as possible. Abby resisted the urge to roll over and see exactly what was happening.

"Abby's a friend," Tate said next. "No more and no less."

"You two keep saying that." Logan sounded bored.

"It's the truth."

"Sure."

There was a rustling sound and faintly Abby could hear Tate stumbling over the awkward words in the list of ingredients on the side of a soda can.

"What are you doing?" Logan asked.

"Reading," Tate explained. "And for me that's some kind of miracle. You see, until I met Abby here in the park helping Mai-Ling, I couldn't read."

A shocked silence followed his announcement.

"For a lot of reasons, I never properly learned," Tate continued. "Then I found Abby. Until I met her, I didn't know there were good people like her who'd be willing to teach me."

"Abby taught you to read?" Logan was obviously stunned.

"I asked her not to tell anyone. I suppose that was selfish of me in light of what's happened between you two. I don't have any excuse except pride."

Someone called Logan's name and the conversation was

abruptly cut off. Minutes later someone else announced that it was time to eat. Abby joined the others, helping where she could. She and Tate were sitting with Dick and Betty when she felt Logan's eyes on her. The conversation around her faded away. The space between them seemed to evaporate as she turned and boldly met his look. In his eyes she read anger, regret and a great deal of inner pain.

When it came time to pack up her things and head home, Abby found Tate surrounded by a group of single women. He glanced up and waved. "I'll call you later," he told her cheerfully, clearly enjoying the attention he was receiving.

"Fine," she assured him. She hadn't gotten as far as the parking lot when Logan caught up with her.

He grabbed her shoulder as he turned her around. The anger she'd thought had been directed inward was now focused on her.

"Why didn't you tell me?" he demanded.

"I couldn't," she said simply. "Tate asked me not to."

"That's no excuse," he began, then paused to inhale a shuddering breath. "All the times I questioned you about meeting Tate, you were tutoring him. The least you could've done was tell me!"

"I already told you Tate was uncomfortable with that. Even now, I don't think you appreciate what it took for him to admit it to you," she explained slowly, enunciating each word so there'd be no misunderstanding. "I was the first person he'd ever told about this problem. It was traumatic for him and I couldn't go around telling others. Surely you can understand that."

"What about me? What about *us*?"

"My hands were tied. I asked you to trust me. A hundred times I pleaded with you to look beyond the obvious."

Logan closed his eyes and emitted a low groan. "How could I have been so stupid?"

"We've both been stupid and we've both learned valuable lessons. Isn't it time to put all that behind us?" She wanted to tell him again how much she loved him, but something stopped her.

Hands buried deep in his pockets, Logan turned away from her, but not before Abby saw that his eyes were narrowed. The pride in his expression seemed to block her out.

Abby watched in disbelief. The way he was behaving implied that *she'd* been the unreasonable, untrusting one. The more Abby thought about their short conversation as she drove home, the angrier she got.

Pacing her living room, she folded her arms around her waist to ward off a sudden chill. "Of all the nerve," she snapped at Dano, who paraded in front of her. The cat shot into her bedroom, smart enough to know when to avoid his mistress.

Yanking her car keys out of her purse, Abby hurried outside. She'd be darned if she'd let Logan end things like this.

His car was in its usual space, and he'd just opened the driver's door. She marched over, standing directly in front of him.

Logan frowned. "What's going on?"

She pointed her index finger at his chest until he backed up against the car.

"Now listen here, Logan Fletcher. I've had about all I can take from you." Every word was punctuated with a jab of her finger.

"Abby? What's the problem?"

"You and that stubborn pride of yours."

"Me?" he shouted in return.

"When we're married, you can bet I won't put up with this kind of behavior."

"Married?" he repeated incredulously. "Who said anything about marriage?"

"I did."

"Doesn't the man usually do the asking?" he said in a sarcastic voice.

"Not necessarily." Some of her anger was dissipating and she began to realize what a fool she was making of herself. "And...and while we're on the subject, you owe me an apology."

"You weren't entirely innocent in any of this."

"All right. I apologize. Does that make it easier on your fragile ego?"

"I also prefer to make my own marriage proposals."

Abby paled and crossed her arms. She wouldn't back down now. "Fine. I'm waiting."

Logan squared his shoulders and cleared his throat. "Abby Carpenter." His voice softened measurably. "I want to express my sincere apology for my behavior these past weeks."

"Months," she inserted with a low breath.

"All right, months," Logan amended. "Although you seem to be rushing the moment, I don't suppose it would do any harm to give you this." He pulled a diamond ring from his pocket.

Abby nearly fell over. Her mouth dropped open and she was speechless as he lifted her hand and slipped the solitaire diamond on her ring finger. "I was on my way to your place," he explained as he pulled her into his embrace. "I've loved you for a long time. You know that. I hadn't worked out a plan to steal your heart away from Tate. But you can be assured I wasn't going to let you go without a struggle."

"But I love—"

His lips interrupted her declaration of love. Abby released a small cry of wonder and wound her arms around his neck, giving herself to the kiss as his mouth closed over hers.

Gradually Logan raised his head, and his eyes were filled with the same wonder she was experiencing. "I talked to Tate again after you left the park," Logan said in a husky murmur. "I was a complete fool."

"No more than usual." Her small laugh was breathless.

"I'll need at least thirty years to make it up to you."

"Change that to forty and you've got yourself a deal."

His eyes smiled deeply into hers. "Where would you like to honeymoon?"

Abby's eyes sparkled. "Des Moines—where else?"

* * * * *

LOVE BY DEGREE

One

The melodious sounds of a love ballad drifted through the huge three-storey house in Seattle's Capitol Hill. Ellen Cunningham hummed along as she rubbed her wet curls with a thick towel. These late-afternoon hours before her housemates returned were the only time she had the place to herself, so she'd taken advantage of the peaceful interlude to wash her hair. Privacy was at a premium with three men in the house, and she couldn't always count on the upstairs bathroom being available later in the evening.

Twisting the fire-engine-red towel around her head, turban style, Ellen walked barefoot across the hallway toward her bedroom to retrieve her blouse. Halfway there, she heard the faint ding of the oven timer, signalling that her apple pie was ready to come out.

She altered her course and bounded down the wide stairway. Her classes that day had gone exceptionally well. She couldn't remember ever being happier, even though she still missed Yakima, the small apple-growing community in central Washington, where she'd been raised. But she was adjusting well to life in the big city. She'd waited impatiently for the right time—and enough money—to complete her education, and she'd been gratified by the way everything had fallen into place during the past summer. Her older sister had married, and her "baby" brother had entered the military. For a while, Ellen was worried that her widowed mother might suffer from empty nest syndrome, so she'd decided to delay her education another year. But her worries had been groundless, as it turned out. James Simonson, a widower friend of her mother's, had started dropping by the house often enough for Ellen to recognize a romance brewing between them. The time had finally come for Ellen to make the break, and she did it without guilt or self-reproach.

Clutching a pot holder in one hand, she opened the oven door and lifted out the steaming pie. The fragrance of spicy apples spread through the kitchen, mingling with the savory aroma of the stew that simmered on top of the stove. Carefully, Ellen set the pie on a wire rack. Her housemates appreciated her culinary efforts and she enjoyed doing little things to please them. As the oldest, Ellen fit easily into this household of young men; in fact, she felt that the arrangement was ideal. In exchange for cooking, a little mothering on the side and a share of the cleaning, Ellen paid only a nominal rent.

The unexpected sound of the back door opening made her swivel around.

"What's going on?" Standing in the doorway was a man with the most piercing green eyes Ellen had ever seen. She noticed immediately that the rest of his features were strongly defined and perfectly balanced. His cheekbones were high and wide, yet his face was lean and appealing. He frowned, and his mouth twisted in an unspoken question.

In one clenched hand he held a small leather suitcase, which he slowly lowered to the kitchen floor. "Who are you?" He spoke sharply, but it wasn't anger or disdain that edged his voice; it was genuine bewilderment.

Ellen was too shocked to move. When she'd whirled around, the towel had slipped from her head and covered one eye, blocking her vision. But even a one-eyed view of this stranger was enough to intimidate her. She had to admit that his impeccable business suit didn't look very threatening—but then she glanced at his glowering face again.

With as much poise as possible, she raised a hand to straighten the turban and realized that she was standing in the kitchen wearing washed-out jeans and a white bra. Grabbing the towel from her head, she clasped it to her chest for protection. "Who are *you?*" she snapped back.

She must have made a laughable sight, holding a red bath towel in front of her like a matador before a charging bull. This man reminded her of a bull. He was tall, muscular and solidly built. And she somehow knew that when he moved, it would be with effortless power and sudden speed. Not exactly the type of man she'd want to meet in a dark alley. Or a deserted house, for that matter. Already Ellen could see the headlines: Small-Town Girl Assaulted in Capitol Hill Kitchen.

"What are you doing here?" she asked in her sternest voice.

"This is my home!" The words vibrated against the walls like claps of thunder.

"Your home?" Ellen choked out. "But... I live here."

"Not anymore, you don't."

"Who are you?" she demanded a second time.

"Reed Morgan."

Ellen relaxed. "Derek's brother?"

"Half-brother."

No wonder they didn't look anything alike. Derek was

a lanky, easy-going nineteen-year-old, with dark hair and equally dark eyes. Ellen would certainly never have expected Derek to have a brother—even a half-brother—like this.

"I—I didn't know you were coming," she hedged, feeling utterly foolish.

"Apparently." He cocked one eyebrow ever so slightly as he stared at her bare shoulders. He shoved his bag out of the doorway, then sighed deeply and ran his hands through his hair. Ellen couldn't help making the irrelevant observation that it was a dark auburn, thick and lustrous with health.

He looked tired and irritable, and he obviously wasn't in the best frame of mind for any explanation as to why she was running around his kitchen half-naked. "Would you like a cup of coffee?" she offered congenially, hoping to ease the shock of her presence.

"What I'd like is for you to put some clothes on."

"Yes, of course." Forcing a smile, Ellen turned abruptly and left the kitchen, feeling humiliated that she could stand there discussing coffee with a stranger when she was practically naked. Running up the stairs, she entered her room and removed her shirt from the end of the bed. Her fingers were trembling as she fastened the buttons.

Her thoughts spun in confusion. If this house was indeed Reed Morgan's, then he had every right to ask her to leave. She sincerely hoped he'd made some mistake. Or that she'd misunderstood. It would be difficult to find another place to share this far into the school term. And her meager savings would be quickly wiped out if she had to live somewhere on her own. Ellen's brow wrinkled with worry as she dragged a brush through her short, bouncy curls, still slightly damp. Being forced to move wouldn't be a tragedy, but definitely a problem, and she was understandably apprehensive. The role of housemother came naturally to Ellen. The boys could hardly boil water without her. She'd only recently broken them in to using the vacuum cleaner and the washing machine without her assistance.

When she returned to the kitchen, she found Reed leaning against the counter, holding a mug of coffee.

"How long has this cozy set-up with you and Derek been going on?"

"About two months now," she answered, pouring herself a cup of coffee. Although she rarely drank it she felt she needed something to occupy her hands. "But it's not what you're implying. Derek and I are nothing more than friends."

"I'll just bet."

Ellen could deal with almost anything except sarcasm. Gritting her teeth until her jaws ached, she replied in an even, controlled voice. "I'm not going to stand here and argue with you. Derek advertised for a housemate and I answered the ad. I came to live here with him and the others and—"

"The *others?*" Reed choked on his mouthful of coffee. "You mean there's more of you around?"

Expelling her breath slowly, Ellen met his scowl. "There's Derek, Pat and—"

"Is Pat male or female?" The sheer strength of his personality seemed to fill the kitchen. But Ellen refused to be intimidated.

"Pat is a male friend who attends classes at the university with Derek and me."

"So you're all students?"

"Yes."

"All freshmen?"

"Yes."

He eyed her curiously. "Aren't you a bit old for that?"

"I'm twenty-five." She wasn't about to explain her circumstances to this man.

The sound of the front door opening and closing drew their attention to the opposite end of the house. Carrying an armload of books, Derek Morgan sauntered into the kitchen and stopped cold when he caught sight of his older brother.

"Hi, Reed." Uncertain eyes flew to Ellen as if seeking reassurance. A worried look pinched the boyishly handsome face. Slowly, he placed his books on the counter.

"Derek."

"I see you've met Ellen." Derek's welcoming smile was decidedly forced.

"We more or less stumbled into each other." Derek's stiff shoulders relaxed as Reed straightened and set the mug aside.

"I didn't expect you back so soon."

Momentarily, Reed's gaze slid to Ellen. "That much is obvious. Do you want to tell me what's going on here, little brother?"

"It's not as bad is it looks."

"Right now it doesn't look particularly good."

"I can explain everything."

"I hope so."

Nervously swinging her arms, Ellen stepped forward. "If you two will excuse me, I'll be up in my room." The last thing she wanted was to find herself stuck between the two brothers while they settled their differences.

"No, don't go," Derek said quickly. His dark eyes pleaded with her to stay.

Almost involuntarily Ellen glanced at Reed for guidance.

"By all means, stay." But his expression wasn't encouraging.

A growing sense of resentment made her arch her back and thrust out her chin defiantly. Who was this...this *man* to burst into their tranquil lives and raise havoc? The four of them lived congenially together, all doing their parts in the smooth running of the household.

"Are you charging rent?" Reed asked.

Briefly Derek's eyes met Ellen's. "It makes sense, doesn't it? This big old house has practically as many bedrooms as a dorm. I didn't think it would hurt." He swallowed. "I mean, with you being in the Middle East and all. The house was...so empty."

"How much are you paying?" Reed directed the question at Ellen. That sarcastic look was back and Ellen hesitated.

"How much?" Reed repeated.

Ellen knew from the way Derek's eyes widened that they were entering into dangerous territory.

"It's different with Ellen," Derek hurried to explain. "She does all the shopping and the cooking, so the rest of us—"

"Are you sure that's all she provides?" Reed interrupted harshly.

Ellen's gaze didn't waver. "I pay thirty dollars a week, but believe me, I earn my keep." The second the words slipped out, Ellen wanted to take them back.

"I'm sure you do."

Ellen was too furious and outraged to speak. How dared he barge into this house and immediately assume the worst? All right, she'd been walking around half-naked, but she hadn't exactly been expecting company.

Angrily Derek stepped forward. "It's not like that, Reed."

"I discovered her prancing around the kitchen in her bra. What else am I supposed to think?"

Derek groaned and cast an accusing look at Ellen. "I

just ran down to get the pie out of the oven," she said in her own defence.

"Let me assure you," Derek said, his voice quavering with righteousness. "You've got this all wrong." He glared indignantly at his older brother. "Ellen isn't that kind of woman. I resent the implication. You owe us both an apology."

From the stunned look on Reed's face, Ellen surmised that this could well be the first time Derek had stood up to his domineering brother. Her impulse was to clap her hands and shout: "Attaboy!" With immense effort she restrained herself.

Reed wiped a hand over his face and pinched the bridge of his nose. "Perhaps I do."

The front door opened and closed again. "Anyone here?" Monte's eager voice rang from the living room. The slam of his books hitting the stairs echoed through the hallway that led to the kitchen. "Something smells good." Skidding to an abrupt halt just inside the room, the tall student looked around at the somber faces. "What's up? You three look like you're about to attend a funeral."

"Are you Pat?" Reed asked.

"No, Monte."

Reed closed his eyes and wearily rubbed the back of his neck. "Just how many bedrooms have you rented out?"

Derek lowered his gaze to his hands. "Three."

"My room?" Reed asked.

"Yes, well, Ellen needed a place and it seemed logical to give her that one. You were supposed to be gone for a year. What happened?"

"I came home early."

Stepping forward, her fingers nervously laced together, Ellen broke into the tense interchange. "I'll move up a floor.

I don't mind." No one was using the third floor of the house, which had at one time been reserved for the servants. The rooms were small and airless, but sleeping there was preferable to suffering the wrath of Derek's brother. Or worse, having to find somewhere else to live.

Reed responded with a dismissive gesture of his hand. "Don't worry about it. Until things are straightened out, I'll sleep up there. Once I've taken a long, hot shower and gotten some rest I might be able to make sense out of this mess."

"No, please," Ellen persisted. "If I'm in your room, then I should move."

"No," Reed grumbled on his way out the door, waving aside her offer. "It's only my house. I'll sleep in the servants' quarters."

Before Ellen could argue further, Reed was out of the kitchen and halfway up the stairs.

"Is there a problem?" Monte asked, opening the refrigerator. He didn't seem very concerned, but then he rarely worried about anything unless it directly affected his stomach. Ellen didn't know how any one person could eat so much. He never seemed to gain weight, but if it were up to him he'd feed himself exclusively on pizza and french fries.

"Do you want to tell me what's going on?" Ellen pressed Derek, feeling guilty but not quite knowing why. "I assumed your family owned the house."

"Well...sort of." He sank slowly into one of the kitchen chairs.

"It's the *sort of* that worries me." She pulled out the chair across from Derek and looked at him sternly.

"Reed *is* family."

"But he didn't know you were renting out the bedrooms?"

"He told me this job would last nine months to a year. I couldn't see any harm in it. Everywhere I looked there were ads for students wanting rooms to rent. It didn't seem right to live alone in this house with all these bedrooms."

"Maybe I should try to find someplace else to live," Ellen said reluctantly. The more she thought about it, the harder it was to see any other solution now that Reed had returned.

"Not before dinner," Monte protested, bringing a loaf of bread and assorted sandwich makings to the table.

"There's no need for anyone to leave," Derek said with defiant bravado. "Reed will probably only be around for a couple of weeks before he goes away on another assignment."

"Assignment?" Ellen asked, her curiosity piqued.

"Yeah. He travels all over the place—we hardly ever see him. And from what I hear, I don't think Danielle likes him being gone so much, either."

"Danielle?"

"They've been practically engaged for ages and… I don't know the whole story, but apparently Reed's put off tying the knot because he does so much traveling."

"Danielle must really love him if she's willing to wait." Ellen watched as Monte spread several layers of smoked ham over the inch-thick slice of Swiss cheese. She knew better than to warn her housemate that he'd ruin his dinner. After his triple-decker sandwich, Monte could sit down to a five-course meal—and then ask about dessert.

"I guess," Derek answered nonchalantly. "Reed's perfect for her. You'd have to meet Danielle to understand." Reaching into the teddy-bear-shaped cookie jar and helping himself to a handful, Derek continued. "Reed didn't mean to snap at everyone. Usually, he's a great brother. And Danielle's all right," he added without enthusiasm.

"It takes a special kind of woman to stick by a man that long without a commitment."

Derek shrugged. "I suppose. Danielle's got her own reasons, if you know what I mean."

Ellen didn't, but she let it go. "What does Reed do?"

"He's an aeronautical engineer for Boeing. He travels around the world working on different projects. This last one was somewhere in Saudi Arabia."

"What about the house?"

"Well, that's his, an inheritance from his mother's family, but he's gone so much of the time that he asked me if I'd live here and look after the place."

"What about us?" Monte asked. "Will big brother want us to move out?"

"I don't think so. Tomorrow morning I'll ask him. I can't see me all alone in this huge old place. It's not like I'm trying to make a fortune by collecting a lot of rent."

"If Reed wants us to leave, I'm sure something can be arranged." Already Ellen was considering different options. She didn't want her fate to be determined by a whim of Derek's brother.

"Let's not do anything drastic. I doubt he'll mind once he has a chance to think it through," Derek murmured with a thoughtful frown. "At least, I hope he won't."

Later that night as Ellen slipped between the crisply laundered sheets, she wondered about the man whose bed she occupied. Tucking the thick quilt around her shoulders, she fought back a wave of anxiety. Everything had worked out so perfectly that she should've expected *something* to go wrong. If anyone voiced objections to her being in Reed's house, it would probably be his almost-fiancée. Ellen sighed apprehensively. She had to admit that if the positions were reversed, she wouldn't want the man she loved sharing his house with another woman. Tomorrow she'd check around to see if she could find a new place to live.

Ellen was scrambling eggs the next morning when Reed appeared, coming down the narrow stairs that led from the third floor to the kitchen. He'd shaved, which emphasized the chiseled look of his jaw. His handsome face was weathered and everything about him spoke of health and vitality. Ellen paused, her fork suspended with raw egg dripping from the tines. She wouldn't call Reed Morgan handsome so much as striking. He had an unmistakable masculine appeal. Apparently the duties of an aeronautical engineer were more physically demanding than she'd suspected. Strength showed in the wide muscular shoulders and lean, hard build. He looked even more formidable this morning.

"Good morning," she greeted him cheerfully, as she continued to beat the eggs. "I hope you slept well."

Reed poured coffee into the same mug he'd used the day before. A creature of habit, Ellen mused. "Morning," he responded somewhat gruffly.

"Can I fix you some eggs?"

"Derek and I have already talked. You can all stay."

"Is that a yes or a no to the eggs?"

"I'm trying to tell you that you don't need to worry about impressing me with your cooking."

With a grunt of impatience, Ellen set the bowl aside and leaned forward, slapping her open palms on the countertop. "I'm scrambling eggs here. Whether you want some or not is entirely up to you. Believe me, if I was concerned about impressing you, I wouldn't do it with eggs."

For the first time, Ellen saw a hint of amusement touch those brilliant green eyes. "No, I don't suppose you would."

"Now that we've got that settled, would you like breakfast or not?"

"All right."

His eyes boldly searched hers and for an instant Ellen found herself regretting that there was a Danielle. With an effort, she turned away and brought her concentration back to preparing breakfast.

"Do you do all the cooking?" Just the way he asked made it sound as though he was already criticizing their household arrangements. Ellen bit back a sarcastic reply and busied herself melting butter and putting bread in the toaster. She'd bide her time. If Derek was right, his brother would soon be away on another assignment.

"Most of it," Ellen answered, pouring the eggs into the hot skillet.

"Who pays for the groceries?"

Ellen shrugged, hoping to give the appearance of nonchalance. "We all chip in." She did the shopping and most of the cooking. In return, the boys did their share of the housework—now that she'd taught them how.

The bread popped up from the toaster and Ellen reached for the butter knife, doing her best to ignore the overpowering presence of Reed Morgan.

"What about the shopping?"

"I enjoy it," she said simply, putting two more slices of bread in the toaster.

"I thought women all over America were fighting to get out of the kitchen."

"When a replacement is found, I'll be happy to step aside." She wasn't comfortable with the direction this conversation seemed to be taking. Reed was looking at her as though she was some kind of 1950s throwback.

Ellen liked to cook and as it turned out, the boys needed

someone who knew her way around a kitchen, and she needed an inexpensive place to live. Everything had worked out perfectly....

She spooned the cooked eggs onto one plate and piled the toast on another, then carried it to the table, which gave her enough time to control her indignation. She was temporarily playing the role of surrogate mother to a bunch of college-age boys. All right, maybe that made her a little unusual these days, but she enjoyed living with Derek and the others. It helped her feel at home, and for now she needed that.

"Aren't you going to eat?" Reed stopped her on her way out of the kitchen.

"I'll have something later. The only time I can count on the bathroom being free in the mornings is when the boys are having breakfast. That is, unless you were planning to use it?"

Reed's eyes narrowed fractionally. "No."

"What's the matter? You've got that look on your face again."

"What look?"

"The one where you pinch your lips together as if you aren't pleased about something and you're wondering just how much you should say."

His tight expression relaxed into a slow, sensual grin. "Do you always read people this well?"

Ellen shook her head. "Not always. I just want to know what I've done this time."

"Aren't you concerned about living with three men?"

"No. Should I be?" She crossed her arms and leaned against the doorjamb, almost enjoying their conversation. The earlier antagonism had disappeared. She'd agree that her living arrangements were a bit unconventional, but they suited her. The situation was advantageous for her *and* the boys.

"Any one of them could fall in love with you."

With difficulty, Ellen restrained her laughter. "That's unlikely. They see me as their mother."

The corners of his mouth formed deep grooves as he tried—and failed—to suppress a grin. Raising one brow, he did a thorough inspection of her curves.

Hot color flooded her pale cheeks. "All right—a sister. I'm too old for them."

Monte sauntered into the kitchen, followed closely by Pat who muttered, "I thought I smelled breakfast."

"I was just about to call you," she told them and hurried from the room, wanting to avoid a head-on collision with Reed. And that was where this conversation was going.

Fifteen minutes later, Ellen returned to the kitchen. She was dressed in cords and an Irish cable-knit sweater; soft dark curls framed her small oval face. Ellen had no illusions about her looks. Men on the street weren't going to stop and stare, but she knew she was reasonably attractive. With her short, dark hair and deep brown eyes, she considered herself average. Ordinary. Far too ordinary for a man like Reed Morgan. One look at Ellen, and Danielle would feel completely reassured. Angry at the self-pitying thought, she grabbed a pen and tore out a sheet of notebook paper.

Intent on making the shopping list, Ellen was halfway into the kitchen before she noticed Reed standing at the sink, wiping the frying pan dry. The table had been cleared and the dishes were stacked on the counter, ready for the dishwasher.

"Oh," she said, a little startled. "I would've done that."

"While I'm here, I'll do my share." He said it without looking at her, his eyes avoiding hers.

"But this is your home. I certainly don't mind—"

"I wouldn't be comfortable otherwise. Haven't you got a class this morning?" He sounded anxious to be rid of her.

"Not until eleven."

"What's your major?" He'd turned around, leaning against the sink and crossing his arms. He was the picture of nonchalance, but Ellen wasn't fooled. She knew very well that he wasn't pleased about her living in his home, and she felt he'd given his permission reluctantly. She suspected he was even looking for ways to dislike her. Ellen understood that. Reed was bound to face some awkward questions once Danielle discovered there was a woman living in his house. Especially a woman who slept in his bed and took charge of his kitchen. But that would change this afternoon—at least the sleeping in his bed part.

"I'm majoring in education."

"That's the mother in you coming out again."

Ellen hadn't thought of it that way. Reed simply felt more comfortable seeing her in that light—as a maternal, even matronly figure—she decided. She'd let him, if it meant he'd be willing to accept her arrangement with Derek and the others.

"I suppose you're right," she murmured as she began opening and closing cupboard doors, checking the contents on each shelf, and scribbling down several items she'd need the following week.

"What are you doing now?"

Mentally, Ellen counted to ten before answering. She resented his overbearing tone, and despite her earlier resolve to humor him, she snapped, "I'm making a grocery list. Do you have a problem with that?"

"No," he answered gruffly.

"I'll be out of here in just a minute," she said, trying hard to maintain her patience.

"You aren't in my way."

"And while we're on the subject of being in someone's way, I want you to know I plan to move my things out of your room this afternoon."

"Don't. I won't be here long enough to make it worth your while."

Two

So Reed was leaving. Ellen felt guilty and relieved at the same time. Derek had told her Reed would probably be sent on another job soon, but she hadn't expected it to be quite *this* soon.

"There's a project Boeing is sending me on. California this time—the Monterey area."

Resuming her task, Ellen added several more items to the grocery list. "I've heard that's a lovely part of the state."

"It is beautiful." But his voice held no enthusiasm.

Ellen couldn't help feeling a twinge of disappointment for Reed. One look convinced her that he didn't want to leave again. After all, he'd just returned from several months in the Middle East and already he had another assignment in California. If he was dreading this latest job, Ellen could well imagine how Danielle must feel.

"Nonetheless, I think it's important to give you back your room. I'll move my things this afternoon." She'd ask the boys to help and it wouldn't take long.

With his arms crossed, Reed lounged against the door-jamb, watching her.

"And if you feel that my being here is a problem," she

went on, thinking of Danielle, "I'll look for another place. The only thing I ask is that you give me a couple of weeks to find something."

He hesitated as though he was considering the offer, then shook his head, grinning slightly. "I don't think that'll be necessary."

"I don't mind telling you I'm relieved to hear it, but I'm prepared to move if necessary."

His left brow rose a fraction of an inch as the grin spread across his face. "Having you here does have certain advantages."

"Such as?"

"You're an excellent cook, the house hasn't been this clean in months and Derek's mother says you're a good influence on these boys."

Ellen had briefly met Mary Morgan, Derek's mother, a few weeks before. "Thank you."

He sauntered over to the coffeepot and poured himself a cup. "And for that matter, Derek's right. This house is too big to sit empty. I'm often out of town, but there's no reason others shouldn't use it. Especially with someone as... domestically inclined as you around to keep things running smoothly."

So he viewed her as little more than a live-in housekeeper and cook! Ellen felt a flush of anger. Before she could say something she'd regret, she turned quickly and fled out the back door on her way to the local grocery store. Actually, Reed Morgan had interpreted the situation correctly, but it somehow bothered her that he saw her in such an unflattering light.

Ellen didn't see Reed again until late that night. Friday evenings were lazy ones for her. She'd dated Charlie Hanson, a fellow student, a couple of times but usually preferred the company of a good book. With her heavy class schedule, most of Ellen's free time was devoted to her studies. Particularly algebra. This one class was getting her down. It didn't matter how hard she hit the books, she couldn't seem to grasp the theory.

Dressed in her housecoat and a pair of bright purple knee socks, she sat at the kitchen table, her legs propped on the chair across from her. Holding a paperback novel open with one hand, she dipped chocolate-chip cookies in a tall glass of milk with the other. At the unexpected sound of the back door opening, she looked curiously up from her book.

Reed seemed surprised to see her. He frowned as his eyes darted past her to the clock above the stove. "You're up late."

"On weekends my mommy doesn't make me go to bed until midnight," she said sarcastically, doing her best to ignore him. Reed managed to look fantastic without even trying. He didn't need her gawking at him to tell him that. If his expensive sports jacket was anything to judge by, he'd spent the evening with Danielle.

"You've got that look," he grumbled.

"What look?"

"The same one you said I have—wanting to say something and unsure if you should."

"Oh." She couldn't very well deny it.

"And what did you want to tell me?"

"Only that you look good." She paused, wondering how much she should say. "You even smell expensive."

His gaze slid over her. "From the way you're dressed, you look to me as though you'd smell of cotton candy."

"Thank you, but actually it's chocolate chip." She pushed the package of cookies in his direction. "Here. Save me from myself."

"No, thanks," Reed murmured and headed toward the living room.

"Don't go in there," Ellen cried, swinging her legs off the chair and coming abruptly to her feet.

Reed's hand was on the kitchen door, ready to open it. "Don't go into the living room?"

"Derek's got a girl in there."

Reed continued to stare at her blankly. "So?"

"So. He's with Michelle Tanner. *The* Michelle Tanner. The girl he's been crazy about for the last six weeks. She finally agreed to a date with him. They rented a movie."

"That doesn't explain why I can't go in there."

"Yes, it does," Ellen whispered. "The last time I peeked, Derek was getting ready to make his move. You'll ruin everything if you barge in there now."

"His move?" Reed didn't seem to like the sound of this. "What do you mean, 'his move'? The kid's barely nineteen."

Ellen smiled. "Honestly, Reed, you must've been young once. Don't you remember what it's like to have a crush on a girl? All Derek's doing is plotting that first kiss."

Reed dropped his hand as he stared at Ellen. He seemed to focus on her mouth. Then the glittering green eyes skimmed hers, and Ellen's breath caught somewhere between her throat and her lungs as she struggled to pull her gaze away from his. Reed had no business giving her that kind of look. Not when he'd so recently left Danielle's arms. And not when Ellen reacted so profoundly to a mere glance.

"I haven't forgotten," he said. "And as for that remark about being young *once,* I'm not exactly over the hill."

This was ridiculous! With a sigh of annoyance, Ellen sat down again, swinging her feet onto the opposite chair. She picked up her book and forced her eyes—if not her attention—back to the page in front of her. "I'm glad to hear that." If she could get a grip on herself for the next few days everything would be fine. Reed would leave and her life with the boys would settle back into its routine.

She heard the refrigerator opening and watched Reed pour himself a glass of milk, then reach for a handful of chocolate-chip cookies. When he pulled out the chair across from her, Ellen reluctantly lowered her legs.

"What are you reading?"

Feeling irritable and angry for allowing him to affect her, she deliberately waited until she'd finished the page before answering. "A book," she muttered.

"My, my, you're a regular Mary Sunshine. What's wrong—did your boyfriend stand you up tonight?"

With exaggerated patience she slowly lowered the paperback to the table and marked her place. "Listen. I'm twenty-five years old and well beyond the age of *boyfriends.*"

Reed shrugged. "All right. Your lover."

She hadn't meant to imply that at all! And Reed knew it. He'd wanted to fluster her and he'd succeeded.

"Women these days have this habit of letting their mouths hang open," he said pointedly. "I suppose they think it looks sexy, but actually, they resemble beached trout." With that, he deposited his empty glass in the sink and marched briskly up the back stairs.

Ellen closed her eyes and groaned in embarrassment. He must think she was an idiot, and with good reason. She'd done a remarkable job of imitating one. She groaned again, infuriated by the fact that she found Reed Morgan so attractive.

Ellen didn't climb the stairs to her new bedroom on the third floor for another hour. And then it was only after Derek had paid her a quick visit in the kitchen and given her a thumbs-up. At least his night had gone well.

Twenty minutes after she'd turned off her reading light, Ellen lay staring into the silent, shadow-filled room. She wasn't sleepy, and the mystery novel no longer held her interest. Her thoughts were troubled by that brief incident in the kitchen with Reed. Burying her head in her pillow, Ellen yawned and closed her eyes. But sleep still wouldn't come. A half-hour later, she threw back the covers and grabbed her housecoat from the end of the bed. Perhaps another glass of milk would help.

Not bothering to turn on any lights, she took a clean glass from the dishwasher and pulled the carton of milk from the refrigerator. Drink in hand, she stood at the kitchen window, looking out at the huge oak tree in the backyard. Its bare limbs stretched upward like skeletal hands, silhouetted against the full moon.

"I've heard that a woman's work is never done, but this is ridiculous."

She nearly spilled her milk at the sudden sound of Reed's voice behind her. She whirled around and glared at him. "I see there's a full moon tonight. I wonder if it's safe to be alone with you. And wouldn't you know it, I left my silver bullet upstairs."

"No woman's ever accused me of being a werewolf. A number of other things," he murmured, "but never that."

"Maybe that's because you hadn't frightened them half out of their wits."

"I couldn't resist. Sorry," he said, reaching for the milk carton.

"You know, if we'd stop snapping at each other, it might make life a lot easier around here."

"Perhaps," he agreed. "I will admit it's a whole lot easier to talk to you when you're dressed."

Ellen slammed down her empty glass. "I'm getting a little tired of hearing about that."

But Reed went on, clearly unperturbed. "Unfortunately, ever since that first time when I found you in your bra, you've insisted on overdressing. From one extreme to another—too few clothes to too many." He paused. "Do you always wear socks to bed?"

"Usually."

"I pity the man you sleep with."

"Well, you needn't worry—" She expelled a lungful of oxygen. "We're doing it again."

"So, you're suggesting we stop trading insults for the sake of the children."

"I hadn't thought of it that way," she said with an involuntary smile, "but you're right. No one's going to be comfortable if the two of us are constantly sniping at each other. I'm willing to try if you are. Okay?"

"Okay." A smile softened Reed's features, angular and shadowed in the moonlight.

"And I'm not a threat to your relationship with Danielle, am I? In fact, if you'd rather, she need never even know I'm here," Ellen said casually.

"Maybe that would've been best," he conceded, setting aside his empty glass. "But I doubt it. Besides, she already knows. I told her tonight." He muttered something else she didn't catch.

"And?"

"And," he went on, "she says she doesn't mind, but she'd like to meet you."

This was one encounter Ellen wasn't going to enjoy.

The next morning, Ellen brought down her laundry and was using the washing machine and the dryer before Reed and the others were even awake.

She sighed as she tested the iron with the wet tip of her index finger and found that it still wasn't hot, although she'd turned it on at least five minutes earlier. This house was owned by a wealthy engineer, so why were there only two electrical outlets in the kitchen? It meant that she couldn't use the washer, the dryer and the iron at the same time without causing a blow-out.

"Darn it," she groaned, setting the iron upright on the padded board.

"What's the matter?" Reed asked from the doorway leading into the kitchen. He got himself a cup of coffee.

"This iron."

"Hey, Ellen, if you're doing some ironing, would you press a few things for me?" Monte asked, walking barefoot into the kitchen. He peered into the refrigerator and took out a slice of cold pizza.

"I was afraid this would happen," she grumbled, still upset by the house's electrical problems.

"Ellen's not your personal maid," Reed said sharply. "If you've got something you want pressed, do it yourself."

A hand on her hip, Ellen turned to Reed, defiantly meeting his glare. "If you don't mind, I can answer for myself."

"Fine," he snorted and took a sip of his coffee.

She directed her next words to Monte, who stood looking at her expectantly. "I am not your personal maid. If you want something pressed, do it yourself."

Monte glanced from Reed to Ellen and back to Reed again. "Sorry I asked," he mumbled on his way out of the kitchen. The door was left swinging in his wake.

"You said that well," Reed commented with a soft chuckle.

"Believe me, I was conned into enough schemes by my sister and brother to know how to handle Monte and the others."

Reed's gaze was admiring. "If your brother's anything like mine, I don't doubt it."

"All brothers are alike," she said. Unable to hold back a grin, Ellen tested the iron a second time and noticed that it was only slightly warmer. "Have you ever thought about putting another outlet in this kitchen?"

Reed looked at her in surprise. "No. Do you need one?"

"Need one?" she echoed. "There are only two in here. It's ridiculous."

Reed scanned the kitchen. "I hadn't thought about it." Setting his coffee mug aside, he shook his head. "Your mood's not much better today than it was last night." With that remark, he hurried out of the room, following in Monte's footsteps.

Frustrated, Ellen tightened her grip on the iron. Reed was right. She was being unreasonable and she really didn't understand why. But she was honest enough to admit, at least to herself, that she was attracted to this man whose house she occupied. She realized she'd have to erect a wall of reserve between them to protect them both from embarrassment.

"Morning, Ellen," Derek said as he entered the kitchen and threw himself into a chair. As he emptied a box of cornflakes into a huge bowl, he said, "I've got some shirts that need pressing."

"If you want anything pressed, do it yourself," she almost shouted.

Stunned, Derek blinked. "Okay."

Setting the iron upright again, Ellen released a lengthy sigh. "I didn't mean to scream at you."

"That's all right."

Turning off the iron, she joined Derek at the table and reached for the cornflakes.

"Are you still worried about that math paper you're supposed to do?" he asked.

"I'm working my way to an early grave over it."

"I would've thought you'd do well in math."

Ellen snickered. "Hardly."

"Have you come up with a topic?"

"Not yet. I'm going to the library later, where I pray some form of inspiration will strike me."

"Have you asked the other people in your class what they're writing about?" Derek asked as he refilled his bowl, this time with rice puffs.

Ellen nodded. "That's what worries me most. The brain who sits beside me is doing hers on the probability of solving Goldbach's conjecture in our lifetime."

Derek's eyes widened. "That's a tough act to follow."

"Let me tell you about the guy who sits behind me. He's doing his paper on mathematics during World War II."

"You're in the big leagues now," Derek said with a sympathetic shake of his head.

"I know," Ellen lamented. She was taking this course only because it was compulsory; all she wanted out of it was a passing grade. The quadratic formula certainly wasn't going to have any lasting influence on *her* life.

"Good luck," Derek said.

"Thanks. I'm going to need it."

After straightening up the kitchen, Ellen changed into old jeans and a faded sweatshirt. The jeans had been washed so many times they were nearly white. They fit her hips so snugly she could hardly slide her fingers into the pockets, but she hated the idea of throwing them out.

She tied an old red scarf around her hair and headed for the garage. While rooting around for a ladder a few days earlier, she'd discovered some pruning shears. She'd noticed several overgrown bushes in the backyard and decided to tackle those first, before cleaning the drainpipes.

After an hour, she had a pile of underbrush large enough to be worth a haul to the dump. She'd have one of the boys do that later. For now, the drainpipes demanded her attention.

"Derek!" she called as she pushed open the back door. She knew her face was flushed and damp from exertion.

"Yeah?" His voice drifted toward her from the living room.

Ellen wandered in to discover him on the phone. "I'm ready for you now."

"Now?" His eyes pleaded with her as his palm covered the mouthpiece. "It's Michelle."

"All right, I'll ask Monte."

"Thanks." He gave her a smile of appreciation.

But Monte was nowhere to be found, and Pat was at the Y shooting baskets with some friends. When she stuck her head into the living room again, she saw Derek still draped over the sofa, deep in conversation. Unwilling to interfere with the course of young love, she decided she could probably manage to climb onto the roof unaided.

Dragging the aluminum ladder from the garage, she thought she might not need Derek's help anyway. She'd mentioned her plan earlier in the week, and he hadn't looked particularly enthusiastic.

With the extension ladder braced against the side of the house, she climbed onto the roof of the back porch. Very carefully, she reached for the ladder and extended it to the very top of the house.

She maneuvered herself back onto the ladder and climbed slowly and cautiously up.

Once she'd managed to position herself on the slanting roof, she was fine. She even took a moment to enjoy the spectacular view. She could see Lake Washington, with its deep-green water, and the spacious grounds of the university campus.

Using the brush she'd tucked—with some struggle— into her back pocket, Ellen began clearing away the leaves and other debris that clogged the gutters and drainpipes.

She was about half finished when she heard raised voices below. Pausing, she sat down, drawing her knees against her chest, and watched the scene unfolding on the front lawn. Reed and his brother were embroiled in a heated discussion—with Reed doing most of the talking. Derek was raking leaves and didn't seem at all pleased about devoting his Saturday morning to chores. Ellen guessed that Reed had summarily interrupted the telephone conversation between Derek and Michelle.

With a lackadaisical swish of the rake, Derek flung the multicolored leaves skyward. Ellen restrained a laugh. Reed had obviously pulled rank and felt no hesitation about giving him orders.

To her further amusement, Reed then motioned toward his black Porsche, apparently suggesting that his brother wash the car when he'd finished with the leaves. Still chuckling, Ellen grabbed for the brush, but she missed and accidentally sent it tumbling down the side of the roof. It hit the green shingles over the front porch with a loud thump before flying onto the grass only a few feet from where Derek and Reed were standing.

Two pairs of astonished eyes turned swiftly in her direction. "Hi," she called down and waved. "I don't suppose I could talk one of you into bringing that up to me?" She braced her feet and pulled herself into a standing position as she waited for a reply.

Reed pointed his finger at her and yelled, "What do you think you're doing up there?"

"Playing tiddlywinks," she shouted back. "What do *you* think I'm doing?"

"I don't know, but I want you down."

"In a minute."

"Now."

"Yes, *sir.*" She gave him a mocking salute and would have bowed if she hadn't been afraid she might lose her footing.

Derek burst out laughing but was quickly silenced by a scathing glance from his older brother.

"Tell Derek to bring me the broom," Ellen called, moving closer to the edge.

Ellen couldn't decipher Reed's response, but from the way he stormed around the back of the house, she figured it was best to come down before he had a heart attack. She had the ladder lowered to the back-porch roof before she saw him.

"You idiot!" he shouted. He was standing in the driveway, hands on his hips, glaring at her in fury. "I can't believe anyone would do anything so stupid."

"What do you mean?" The calmness of her words belied the way the blood pulsed through her veins. Alarm rang in his voice and that surprised her. She certainly hadn't expected Reed, of all people, to be concerned about her safety. He held the ladder steady until she'd climbed down and was standing squarely in front of him. Then he started pacing. For a minute Ellen didn't know what to think.

"What's wrong?" she asked. "You look as pale as a sheet."

"What's wrong?" he sputtered. "You were on the *roof* and—"

"I wasn't in any danger."

He shook his head, clearly upset. "There are people who specialize in that sort of thing. I don't want you up there again. Understand?"

"Yes, but—"

"No buts. You do anything that stupid again and you're out of here. Have you got that?"

"Yes," she said with forced calm. "I understand."

"Good."

Before she could think of anything else to say, Reed was gone.

"You all right?" Derek asked a minute later. Shocked by Reed's outburst, Ellen hadn't moved. Rarely had anyone been that angry with her. Heavens, she'd cleaned out drainpipes lots of times. Her father had died when Ellen was fourteen, and over the years she'd assumed most of the maintenance duties around the house. She'd learned that, with the help of a good book and a well-stocked hardware store, there wasn't anything she couldn't fix. She'd repaired the plumbing, built bookshelves and done a multitude of household projects. It was just part of her life. Reed had acted as though she'd done something hazardous, as though she'd taken some extraordinary risk, and that seemed totally ridiculous to her. She knew what she was doing. Besides, heights didn't frighten her; they never had.

"Ellen?" Derek prompted.

"I'm fine."

"I've never seen Reed act like that. He didn't mean anything."

"I know," she whispered, brushing the dirt from her knees. Derek drifted off, leaving her to return the ladder to the garage single-handed.

Reed found her an hour later folding laundry in her bedroom. He knocked on the open door.

"Yes?" She looked up expectantly.

"I owe you an apology."

She continued folding towels at the foot of her bed. "Oh?"

"I didn't mean to come at you like Attila the Hun."

Hugging a University of Washington T-shirt to her stomach, she lowered her gaze to the bedspread and nodded. "Apology accepted and I'll offer one of my own. I didn't mean to come back at you like a spoiled brat."

"Accepted." They smiled at each other and she caught her breath as those incredible green eyes gazed into hers. It was a repeat of the scene in the kitchen the night before. For a long, silent moment they did nothing but stare, and she realized that a welter of conflicting emotions must have registered on her face. A similar turmoil raged on his.

"If it'll make you feel any better, I won't go up on the roof again," she said at last.

"I'd appreciate it." His lips barely moved. The words were more of a sigh than a sentence.

She managed a slight nod in response.

At the sound of footsteps, they guiltily looked away.

"Say, Ellen." Pat stopped in the doorway, a basketball under his left arm. "Got time to shoot a few baskets with me?"

"Sure," she whispered, stepping around Reed. At that

moment, she would've agreed to just about anything to escape his company. There was something happening between them and she felt frightened and confused and excited, all at the same time.

The basketball hoop was positioned above the garage door at the end of the long driveway. Pat was attending the University of Washington with the express hope of making the Husky basketball team. His whole life revolved around the game. He was rarely seen without a ball tucked under his arm and sometimes Ellen wondered if he showered with it. She was well aware that the invitation to practice a few free throws with him was not meant to be taken literally. The only slam dunk Ellen had ever accomplished was with a doughnut in her hot chocolate. Her main job was to stand on the sidelines and be awed by Pat's talent.

They hadn't been in the driveway fifteen minutes when the back door opened and Derek strolled out. "Say, Ellen, have you got a minute?" he asked, frowning.

"What's the problem?"

"It's Michelle."

Sitting on the concrete porch step, Derek looked at Ellen with those wide pleading eyes of his.

Ellen sat beside him and wrapped her arms around her bent knees. "What's wrong with Michelle?"

"Nothing. She's beautiful and I think she might even fall in love with me, given the chance." He paused to sigh expressively. "I asked her out to dinner tonight."

"She agreed. Right?" If Michelle was anywhere near as taken with Derek as he was with her, she wasn't likely to refuse.

The boyishly thin shoulders heaved in a gesture of despair. "She can't."

"Why not?" Ellen watched as Pat bounced the basketball across the driveway, pivoted, jumped high in the air and sent the ball through the net.

"Michelle promised her older sister that she'd baby-sit tonight."

"That's too bad." Ellen gave him a sympathetic look.

"The thing is, she'd probably go out with me if there was someone who could watch her niece and nephew for her."

"Uh-huh." Pat made another skillful play and Ellen applauded vigorously. He rewarded her with a triumphant smile.

"Then you will?"

Ellen switched her attention from Pat's antics at the basketball hoop back to Derek. "Will I what?"

"Babysit Michelle's niece and nephew?"

"What?" she exploded. "Not me. I've got to do research for a term paper."

"Ellen, please, please, please."

"No. No. No." She sliced the air forcefully with her hand and got to her feet.

Derek rose with her. "I sense some resistance to this idea."

"The boy's a genius," she mumbled under her breath as she hurried into the kitchen. "I've got to write my term paper. You know that."

Derek followed her inside. "Ellen, please? I promise I'll never ask anything of you again."

"I've heard that before." She tried to ignore him as he trailed her to the refrigerator and watched her take out sandwich makings for lunch.

"It's a matter of the utmost importance," Derek pleaded anew.

"What is?" Reed spoke from behind the paper he was reading at the kitchen table.

"My date with Michelle. Listen, Ellen, I bet Reed would help you. You're not doing anything tonight, are you?"

Reed lowered the newspaper. "Help Ellen with what?"

"Babysitting."

Reed glanced from the intent expression on his younger brother's face to the stubborn look on Ellen's. "You two leave me out of this."

"Ellen. Dear, *sweet* Ellen, you've got to understand that it could be weeks—weeks," he repeated dramatically, "before Michelle will be able to go out with me again."

Ellen put down an armload of cheese, ham and assorted jars of mustard and pickles. "*No!* Can I make it any plainer than that? I'm sorry, Derek, honest. But I can't."

"Reed," Derek pleaded with his brother. "Say something that'll convince her."

"Like I said, I'm out of this one."

He raised the paper again, but Ellen could sense a smile hidden behind it. Still, she doubted that Reed would be foolish enough to involve himself in this situation.

"Ellen, puleease."

"No." Ellen realized that if she wanted any peace, she'd have to forget about lunch and make an immediate escape. She whirled around and headed out of the kitchen, the door swinging in her wake.

"I think she's weakening," she heard Derek say as he followed her.

She was on her way up the stairs when she caught sight of Derek in the dining room, coming toward her on his knees, hands folded in supplication. "Won't you please reconsider?"

Ellen groaned. "What do I need to say to convince you? I've got to get to the library. That paper is due Monday morning."

"I'll write it for you."

"No, thanks."

At just that moment Reed came through the door. "It shouldn't be too difficult to find a reliable sitter. There are a few families with teenagers in the neighbourhood, as I recall."

"I...don't know," Derek hedged.

"If we can't find anyone, then Danielle and I'll manage. It'll be good practice for us. Besides, just how much trouble can two kids be?"

When she heard that, Ellen had to swallow a burst of laughter. Reed obviously hadn't spent much time around children, she thought with a mischievous grin.

"How old did you say these kids are?" she couldn't resist asking.

"Nine and four." Derek's dark eyes brightened as he leaped to his feet and gave his brother a grateful smile. "So I can tell Michelle everything's taken care of?"

"I suppose." Reed turned to Ellen. "I was young once myself," he said pointedly, reminding her of the comment she'd made the night before.

"I really appreciate this, Reed," Derek was saying. "I'll be your slave for life. I'd even lend you money if I had some. By the way, can I borrow your car tonight?"

"Don't press your luck."

"Right." Derek chuckled, bounding up the stairs. He paused for a moment. "Oh, I forgot to tell you. Michelle's bringing the kids over here, okay?"

He didn't wait for a response.

The doorbell chimed close to six o'clock, just as Ellen was gathering up her books and preparing to leave for the library.

"That'll be Michelle," Derek called excitedly. "Can you get it, Ellen?"

"No problem."

Coloring books and crayons were arranged on the coffee table, along with some building blocks Reed must have purchased that afternoon. From bits and pieces of information she'd picked up, she concluded that Reed had discovered it wasn't quite as easy to find a baby-sitter as he'd assumed. And with no other recourse, he and Danielle were apparently taking over the task. Ellen wished him luck, but she really did need to concentrate on this stupid term paper. Reed hadn't suggested that Ellen wait around to meet Danielle. But she had to admit she'd been wondering about the woman from the time Derek had first mentioned her.

"Hello, Ellen." Blonde Michelle greeted Ellen with a warm, eager smile. They'd met briefly the other night, when she'd come over to watch the movie. "This sure is great of Derek's brother and his girlfriend, isn't it?"

"It sure is."

The four-year-old boy was clinging to Michelle's trouser leg so that her gait was stiff-kneed as she limped into the house with the child attached.

"Jimmy, this is Ellen. You'll be staying in her house tonight while Auntie Michelle goes out to dinner with Derek."

"I want my mommy."

"He won't be a problem," Michelle told Ellen confidently.

"I thought there were two children."

"Yeah, the baby's in the car. I'll be right back."

"Baby?" Ellen swallowed down a laugh. "What baby?"

"Jenny's nine months."

"Nine *months?*" A small uncontrollable giggle slid from her throat. This would be marvelous. Reed with a nine-month-old was almost too good to miss.

"Jimmy, you stay here." Somehow Michelle was able to

pry the four-year-old's fingers from her leg and pass the struggling child to Ellen.

Kicking and thrashing, Jimmy broke into loud sobs as Ellen carried him into the living room. "Here's a coloring book. Do you like to color, Jimmy?"

But he refused to talk to Ellen or even look at her as he buried his face in the sofa cushions. "I want my mommy," he wailed again.

By the time Michelle had returned with a baby carrier and a fussing nine-month-old, Derek sauntered out from the kitchen. "Hey, Michelle, you're lookin' good."

Reed, who was following closely behind, came to a shocked standstill when he saw the baby. "I thought you said they were nine and four."

"I did," Derek explained patiently, his eyes devouring the blonde at his side.

"They won't be any trouble," Michelle cooed as Derek placed an arm around her shoulders and led her toward the open door.

"Derek, we need to talk," Reed insisted.

"Haven't got time now. Our reservations are for seven." His hand slid from Michelle's shoulders to her waist. "I'm taking my lady out for a night on the town."

"Derek," Reed demanded.

"Oh." Michelle tore her gaze from Derek's. "The diaper bag is in the entry. Jenny should be dry, but you might want to check her later. She'll probably cry for a few minutes once she sees I'm gone, but that'll stop almost immediately."

Reed's face was grim as he cast a speculative glance at Jimmy, who was still howling for his mother. The happily gurgling Jenny stared up at the unfamiliar dark-haired man and noticed for the first time that she was at the mercy of a stranger. She immediately burst into heart-wrenching tears.

"I want my mommy," Jimmy wailed yet again.

"I can see you've got everything under control," Ellen said, reaching for her coat. "I'm sure Danielle will be here any minute."

"Ellen…"

"Don't expect me back soon. I've got hours of research ahead of me."

"You aren't really going to leave, are you?" Reed gave her a horrified look.

"I wish I could stay," she lied breezily. "Another time." With that, she was out the door, smiling as she bounded down the steps.

Three

An uneasy feeling struck Ellen as she stood waiting at the bus stop. But she resolutely hardened herself against the impulse to rush back to Reed and his disconsolate charges. Danielle would show up any minute and Ellen really was obliged to do the research for her yet-to-be-determined math paper. Besides, she reminded herself, Reed had volunteered to babysit and she wasn't responsible for rescuing him. But his eyes had pleaded with her so earnestly. Ellen felt herself beginning to weaken. *No!* she mumbled under her breath. Reed had Danielle, and as far as Ellen was concerned, they were on their own.

However, by the time she arrived at the undergraduate library, Ellen discovered that she couldn't get Reed's pleading look out of her mind. From everything she'd heard about Danielle, Ellen figured the woman probably didn't know the first thing about babies. As for the term paper, she supposed she could put it off until Sunday. After all, she'd found excuses all day to avoid working on it. She'd done the laundry, trimmed the shrubs, cleaned the drainpipes and washed the upstairs walls in an effort to escape that paper. One more night wasn't going to make much difference.

Hurriedly, she signed out some books and journals that looked as though they might be helpful and headed for the bus stop. Ellen had to admit that she was curious enough to want to meet Danielle. Reed's girlfriend had to be someone very special to put up with his frequent absences—or else a schemer, as Derek had implied. But Ellen couldn't see Reed being duped by a woman, no matter how clever or sophisticated she might be.

Her speculations came to an end as the bus arrived, and she quickly jumped on for the short ride home.

Reed was kneeling on the carpet changing the still-tearful Jenny's diaper when Ellen walked in the front door. He seemed to have aged ten years in the past hour. The long sleeves of his wool shirt were rolled up to the elbows as he struggled with the tape on Jenny's disposable diaper.

Reed shook his head and sagged with relief. "Good thing you're here. She hasn't stopped crying from the minute you left."

"You look like you're doing a good job without me. Where's Danielle?" She glanced around, smiling at Jimmy; the little boy hadn't moved from the sofa, his face still hidden in the cushions.

Reed muttered a few words under his breath. "She couldn't stay." He finally finished with the diaper. "That wasn't so difficult after all," he said, glancing proudly at Ellen as he stood Jenny up on the floor, holding the baby upright by her small arms.

Ellen swallowed a laugh. The diaper hung crookedly, bunched up in front. She was trying to think of a tactful way of pointing it out to Reed when the whole thing began to slide down Jenny's pudgy legs, settling at her ankles.

"Maybe you should try," Reed conceded, handing her the baby. Within minutes, Ellen had successfully secured the diaper. Unfortunately, she didn't manage to soothe the baby any more than Reed had.

Cradling Jenny in her arms, Ellen paced the area in front of the fireplace, at a loss to comfort the sobbing child. "I doubt I'll do any better. It's been a long while since my brother was this size."

"Women are always better at this kind of stuff," Reed argued, rubbing a hand over his face. "Most women," he amended, with such a look of frustration that Ellen smiled.

"I'll bet Jimmy knows what to do," she suggested next, pleased with her inspiration. The little boy might actually come up with something helpful, and involving him in their attempts to comfort Jenny might distract him from his own unhappiness. Or so Ellen hoped. "Jimmy's a good big brother. Isn't that right, honey?"

The child lifted his face from the cushion. "I want my mommy."

"Let's pretend Ellen is your mommy," Reed coaxed.

"No! She's like that other lady who said bad words."

Meanwhile, Jenny wailed all the louder. Digging around in the bag, Reed found a stuffed teddy bear and pressed it into her arms. But Jenny angrily tossed the toy aside, the tears flowing unabated down her face.

"Come on, Jimmy," Reed said desperately. "We need a little help here. Your sister's crying."

Holding his hands over his eyes, Jimmy straightened and peeked through two fingers. The distraught Jenny continued to cry at full volume in spite of Ellen's best efforts.

"Mommy bounces her."

Ellen had been gently doing that from the beginning.

"What else?" she asked.

"She likes her boo-loo."

"What's that?"

"Her teddy bear."

"I've already tried that," Reed said. "What else does your mommy do when she cries like this?"

Jimmy was thoughtful for a moment. "Oh." The four-year-old's eyes sparkled. "Mommy nurses her."

Reed and Ellen glanced at each other and dissolved into giggles. The laughter faded from his eyes and was replaced with a roguish grin. "That could be interesting."

Hiding a smile, Ellen decided to ignore Reed's comment. "Sorry, Jenny," she said softly to the baby girl.

"But maybe he's got an idea," Reed suggested. "Could she be hungry?"

"It's worth a try. At this point, anything is."

Jenny's bellowing had finally dwindled into a few hiccuping sobs. And for some reason, Jimmy suddenly straightened and stared at Reed's craggy face, at his deep auburn hair and brilliant green eyes. Then he pointed to the plaid wool shirt, its long sleeves rolled up to the elbow. "Are you a lumberjack?"

"A lumberjack?" Reed repeated, looking puzzled. He broke into a full laugh. "No, but I imagine I must look like one to you."

Rummaging through the diaper bag, Ellen found a plastic bottle filled with what was presumably formula. Jenny eyed it skeptically, but no sooner had Ellen removed the cap than Jenny grabbed it from her hands and began sucking eagerly at the nipple.

Sighing, Ellen sank into the rocking chair and swayed back and forth with the baby tucked in her arms. "I guess that settles that."

The silence was so blissful that she wanted to wrap it around herself. She felt the tension drain from her muscles as she relaxed in the rocking chair. From what Jimmy had dropped, she surmised that Danielle hadn't been much help. Everything she'd learned about the other woman told Ellen that Danielle would probably find young children frustrating—and apparently she had.

Jimmy had crawled into Reed's lap with a book and demanded the lumberjack read to him. Together the two leafed through the storybook. Several times during the peaceful interlude, Ellen's eyes met Reed's across the room and they exchanged a contented smile.

Jenny sucked tranquilly at the bottle, and her eyes slowly drooped shut. At peace with her world, the baby was satisfied to be held and rocked to sleep. Ellen gazed down at the angelic face and brushed fine wisps of hair from the untroubled forehead. Releasing her breath in a slow, drawnout sigh, she glanced up to discover Reed watching her, the little boy still sitting quietly on his lap.

"Ellen?" Reed spoke in a low voice. "Did you finish your math paper?"

"Finish it?" She groaned. "Are you kidding? I haven't even started it."

"What's a math paper?" Jimmy asked.

Rocking the baby, Ellen looked solemnly over at the boy. "Well, it's something I have to write for a math class. And if I don't write a paper, I haven't got a hope of passing the course." She didn't think he'd understand any algebraic terms. For that matter, neither did she.

"What's math?"

"Numbers," Reed told the boy.

"And, in this case, sometimes letters—like x and y."

"I like numbers," Jimmy declared. "I like three and nine and seven."

"Well, Jimmy, my boy, how would you like to write my paper for me?"

"Can I?"

Ellen grinned at him. "You bet."

Reed got out pencil and paper and set the four-year-old to work.

Glancing up, she gave Reed a smile. "See how easy this is? You're good with kids." Reed smiled in answer as he carefully drew numbers for Jimmy to copy.

After several minutes of this activity, Jimmy decided it was time to put on his pajamas. Seeing him yawn, Reed brought down a pillow and blanket and tucked him into a hastily made bed on the sofa. Then he read a bedtime story until the four-year-old again yawned loudly and fell almost instantly asleep.

Ellen still hadn't moved, fearing that the slightest jolt would rouse the baby.

"Why don't we set her down in the baby seat?" Reed said.

"I'm afraid she'll wake up."

"If she does, you can rock her again."

His suggestion made sense and besides, her arms were beginning to ache. "Okay." He moved to her side and took the sleeping child. Ellen held her breath momentarily when Jenny stirred. But the little girl simply rolled her head against the cushion and returned to sleep.

Ellen rose to her feet and turned the lamp down to its dimmest setting, surrounding them with a warm circle of light.

"I couldn't have done it without you," Reed whispered, coming to stand beside her. He rested his hand at the back of her neck.

An unfamiliar warmth seeped through Ellen, and she began to talk quickly, hoping to conceal her sudden nervousness. "Sure you could have. It looked to me as if you had everything under control."

Reed snorted. "I was ten minutes away from calling the crisis clinic. Thanks for coming to the rescue." He casually withdrew his hand, and Ellen felt both relieved and disappointed.

"You're welcome." She was dying to know what had happened with Danielle, but she didn't want to ask. Apparently, the other woman hadn't stayed around for long.

"Have you eaten?"

Ellen had been so busy that she'd forgotten about dinner, but once Reed mentioned it, she realized how hungry she was. "No, and I'm starved."

"Do you like Chinese food?"

"Love it."

"Good. There's enough for an army out in the kitchen. I ordered it earlier."

Ellen didn't need to be told that he'd made dinner plans with Danielle in mind. He'd expected to share an intimate evening with her. "Listen," she began awkwardly, clasping her hands. "I really have to get going on this term paper. Why don't you call Danielle and invite her back? Now that the kids are asleep, I'm sure everything will be better. I—"

"Children make Danielle nervous. She warned me about it, but I refused to listen. She's home now and has probably taken some aspirin and gone to sleep. I can't see letting good food go to waste. Besides, this gives me an opportunity to thank you."

"Oh." It was the longest speech that Reed had made. "All right," she agreed with a slight nod.

While Reed warmed the food in the microwave, Ellen set out plates and forks and prepared a large pot of green tea, placing it in the middle of the table. The swinging door that connected the kitchen with the living room was left open in case either child woke.

"What do we need plates for?" Reed asked with a questioning arch of his brow.

"Plates are the customary eating device."

"Not tonight."

"Not tonight?" Something amusing glinted in Reed's eyes as he set out several white boxes and brandished two pairs of chopsticks. "Since it's only the two of us, we can eat right out of the boxes."

"I'm not very adept with chopsticks." The smell drifting from the open boxes was tangy and enticing.

"You'll learn if you're hungry."

"I'm famished."

"Good." Deftly he took the first pair of chopsticks and showed her how to work them with her thumb and index finger.

Imitating his movements Ellen discovered that her fingers weren't nearly as agile as his. Two or three tries at picking up small pieces of spicy diced chicken succeeded only in frustrating her.

"Here." Reed fed her a bite from the end of his chopsticks. "Be a little more patient with yourself."

"That's easy for you to say while you're eating your fill and I'm starving to death."

"It'll come."

Ellen grumbled under her breath, but a few tries later she managed to deliver a portion of the hot food to her eager mouth.

"See, I told you you'd pick this up fast enough."

"Do you always tell someone 'I told you so'?" she asked with pretended annoyance. The mood was too congenial for any real discontent. Ellen felt that they'd shared a special time together looking after the two small children. More than special—astonishing. They hadn't clashed once or found a single thing to squabble over.

"I enjoy teasing you. Your eyes have an irresistible way of lighting up when you're angry."

"If you continue to insist that I eat with these absurd pieces of wood, you'll see my eyes brighten the entire room."

"I'm looking forward to that," he murmured with a laugh. "No forks. You can't properly enjoy Chinese food unless you use chopsticks."

"I can't properly *taste* it without a fork."

"Here, I'll feed you." Again he brought a spicy morsel to her mouth.

A drop of the sauce fell onto her chin and Ellen wiped it off. "You aren't any better at this than me." She dipped the chopsticks into the chicken mixture and attempted to transport a tidbit to Reed's mouth. It balanced precariously on the end of her chopsticks, and Reed lowered his mouth to catch it before it could land in his lap.

"You're improving," he told her, his voice low and slightly husky.

Their eyes met. Unable to face the caressing look in his warm gaze, Ellen bent her head and pretended to be engrossed in her dinner. But her appetite was instantly gone—vanished.

A tense silence filled the room. The air between them was so charged that she felt breathless and weak, as though she'd lost the energy to move or speak. Ellen didn't dare raise her eyes for fear of what she'd see in his.

"Ellen."

She took a deep breath and scrambled to her feet. "I think I hear Jimmy," she whispered.

"Maybe it was Jenny," Reed added hurriedly.

Ellen paused in the doorway between the two rooms. They were both overwhelmingly aware that neither child had made a sound. "I guess they're still asleep."

"That's good." The scraping sound of his chair against the floor told her that Reed, too, had risen from the table. When she turned, she found him depositing the leftovers in the refrigerator. His preoccupation with the task gave her a moment to reflect on what had just happened. There were too many problems involved in pursuing this attraction; the best thing was to ignore it and hope the craziness passed. They were mature adults, not adolescents, and besides, this would complicate her life, which was something she didn't need right now. Neither, she was sure, did he. Especially with Danielle in the picture…

"If you don't mind, I'm going to head upstairs," she began awkwardly, taking a step in retreat.

"Okay, then. And thanks. I appreciated the help."

"I appreciated the dinner," she returned.

"See you in the morning."

"Right." Neither seemed eager to bring the evening to an end.

"Good night, Ellen."

"Night, Reed. Call if you need me."

"I will."

Turning decisively, she took the stairs and was panting by the time she'd climbed up the second narrow flight. Since the third floor had originally been built to accommodate servants, the five bedrooms were small and opened onto a large central room, which was where Ellen had placed her bed. She'd chosen the largest of the bedrooms as her study.

She sat resolutely down at her desk and leafed through

several books, hoping to come across an idea she could use for her term paper. But her thoughts were dominated by the man two floors below. Clutching a study on the origins of algebra to her chest, she sighed deeply and wondered whether Danielle truly valued Reed. She must, Ellen decided, or she wouldn't be so willing to sit at home waiting, while her fiancé traipsed around the world directing a variety of projects.

Reed had been so patient and good-natured with Jimmy and Jenny. When the little boy had climbed into his lap, Reed had read to him and held him with a tenderness that stirred her heart. And Reed was generous to a fault. Another man might have told Pat, Monte and Ellen to pack their bags. This was his home, after all, and Derek had been wrong to rent out the rooms without Reed's knowledge. But Reed had let them stay.

Disgruntled with the trend her thoughts were taking, Ellen forced her mind back to the books in front of her. But it wasn't long before her concentration started to drift again. Reed had Danielle, and she had... Charlie Hanson. First thing in the morning, she'd call dependable old Charlie and suggest they get together; he'd probably be as surprised as he was pleased to hear from her. Feeling relieved and a little light-headed, Ellen turned off the light and went to bed.

"What are you doing?" Reed arrived in the kitchen early the next afternoon, looking as though he'd just finished eighteen holes of golf or a vigorous game of tennis. He'd already left by the time she'd wandered down to the kitchen that morning.

"Ellen?" he repeated impatiently.

She'd taken the wall plates off the electrical outlets and pulled the receptacle out of its box, from which two thin colored wires now protruded. "I'm trying to figure out why this outlet won't heat the iron," she answered without looking in his direction.

"You're what!" he bellowed.

She wiped her face to remove a layer of dust before she straightened. "Don't yell at me."

"Good grief, woman. You run around on the roof like a trapeze artist, cook like a dream and do electrical work on the side. Is there anything you *can't* do?"

"Algebra," she muttered.

Reed closed the instruction manual Ellen had propped against the sugar bowl in the middle of the table. He took her by the shoulders and pushed her gently aside, then re-attached the electrical wires and fastened the whole thing back in place.

As he finished securing the wall plate, Ellen burst out, "What did you do that for? I've almost got the problem traced."

"No doubt, but if you don't mind, I'd rather have a real electrician look at this."

"What can I say? It's your house."

"Right. Now sit down." He nudged her into a chair. "How much longer are you going to delay writing that term paper?"

"It's written," she snapped. She wasn't particularly pleased with it, but at least the assignment was done. Her subject matter might impress four-year-old Jimmy, but she wasn't too confident that her professor would feel the same way.

"Do you want me to look it over?"

The offer surprised her. "No, thanks." She stuck the screwdriver in the pocket of her gray-striped coveralls.

"Well, that wasn't so hard, was it?"

"I just don't think I've got a snowball's chance of getting a decent grade on it. Anyway, I have to go and iron a dress. I've got a date."

A dark brow lifted over inscrutable green eyes and he seemed about to say something.

"Reed." Unexpectedly, the kitchen door swung open and a soft, feminine voice purred his name. "What's taking you so long?"

"Danielle, I'd like you to meet Ellen."

"Hello." Ellen resisted the urge to kick Reed. If he was going to introduce her to his friend, the least he could have done was waited until she looked a little more presentable. Just as she'd figured, Danielle was beautiful. No, the word was *gorgeous*. She wore a cute pale blue tennis outfit with a short, pleated skirt. A dark blue silk scarf held back the curly cascade of long blond hair—Ellen should have known the other woman would be blonde. Naturally, Danielle possessed a trim waist, perfect legs and blue eyes to match the heavens. She'd apparently just finished playing golf or tennis with Reed, but she still looked cool and elegant.

"I feel as though I already know you," Danielle was saying with a pleasant smile. "Reed told me how much help you were with the children."

"It was nothing, really." Embarrassed by her ridiculous outfit, Ellen tried to conceal as much of it as possible by grabbing the electrical repair book and clasping it to her stomach.

"Not according to Reed." Danielle slipped her arm around his and smiled adoringly up at him. "Unfortunately, I came down with a terrible headache."

"Danielle doesn't have your knack with young children," Reed said.

"If we decide to have our own, things will be different," Danielle continued sweetly. "But I'm not convinced I'm the maternal type."

Ellen sent the couple a wan smile. "If you'll excuse me, I've got to go change my clothes."

"Of course. It was nice meeting you, Elaine."

"Ellen," Reed and Ellen corrected simultaneously.

"You, too." Gallantly, Ellen stifled the childish impulse to call the other woman Diane. As she turned and hurried up the stairs leading from the kitchen, she heard Danielle whisper that she didn't mind at all if Ellen lived in Reed's home. Of course not, Ellen muttered to herself. How could Danielle possibly be jealous?

Winded by the time she'd marched up both flights, Ellen walked into the tiny bedroom where she stored her clothes. She threw down the electrical manual and slammed the door shut. Then she sighed with despair as she saw her reflection in the full-length mirror on the back of the door; it revealed baggy coveralls, a faded white T-shirt and smudges of dirt across her cheekbone. She struck a seductive pose with her hand on her hip and vampishly puffed up her hair. "Of course I don't mind if sweet little Elaine lives here, darling," she mimicked in a high-pitched falsely sweet voice.

Dropping her coveralls to the ground, Ellen gruffly kicked them aside. Hands on her hips, she glared at her reflection. Her figure was no less attractive than Danielle's, and her face was pretty enough—even if she did say so herself. But Danielle had barely looked at Ellen and certainly hadn't seen her as a potential rival.

As she brushed her hair away from her face, Ellen's shoulders suddenly dropped. She was losing her mind! She liked living with the boys. Their arrangement was ideal, yet here she was, complaining bitterly because her presence hadn't been challenged.

Carefully choosing a light pink blouse and denim skirt, Ellen told herself that Charlie, at least, would appreciate her. And for now, Ellen needed that. Her self-confidence had been shaken by Danielle's casual acceptance of her role in Reed's house. She didn't like Danielle. But then, she hadn't expected to.

"Ellen." Her name was followed by a loud pounding on the bedroom door. "Wake up! There's a phone call for you."

"Okay," she mumbled into her pillow, still caught in the dregs of sleep. It felt so warm and cozy under the blankets that she didn't want to stir. Charlie had taken her to dinner and a movie and they'd returned a little after ten. The boys had stayed in that evening, but Reed was out and Ellen didn't need to ask with whom. She hadn't heard him come home.

"Ellen!"

"I'm awake, I'm awake," she grumbled, slipping one leg free of the covers and dangling it over the edge of the bed. The sudden cold that assailed her bare foot made her eyes flutter open in momentary shock.

"It's long distance."

Her eyes did open then. She knew only one person who could be calling. Her mother!

Hurriedly tossing the covers aside, she grabbed her housecoat and scurried out of the room. "Why didn't you tell me it was long distance?"

"I tried," Pat said. "But you were more interested in sleeping."

A glance at her clock radio told her it was barely seven. Taking a deep, calming breath, Ellen walked quickly down one flight of stairs and picked up the phone at the end of the hallway.

"Good morning, Mom."

"How'd you know it was me?"

Although they emailed each other regularly, this was the first time her mother had actually phoned since she'd left home. "Lucky guess."

"Who was that young man who answered the phone?"

"Patrick."

"The basketball kid."

Her mother had read every word of her emails. "That's him."

"Has Monte eaten you out of house and home yet?"

"Just about."

"And has this Derek kid finally summoned up enough nerve to ask out…what was her name again?"

"Michelle."

"Right. That's the one."

"They saw each other twice this weekend," Ellen told her, feeling a sharp pang of homesickness.

"And what about you, Ellen? Are you dating?" It wasn't an idle question. Through the years, Ellen's mother had often fretted that her oldest child was giving up her youth in order to care for the family. Ellen didn't deny that she'd made sacrifices, but they'd been willing ones.

Her emails had been chatty, but she hadn't mentioned Charlie, and Ellen wasn't sure she wanted her mother to know about him. Her relationship with him was based on friendship and nothing more, although Ellen suspected that Charlie would've liked it to develop into something romantic.

"Mom, you didn't phone me long distance on a Monday morning to discuss my social life."

"You're right. I called to discuss mine."

"And?" Ellen's heart hammered against her ribs. She already knew what was coming. She'd known it months ago, even before she'd moved to Seattle. Her mother was going to remarry. After ten years of widowhood, Barbara Cunningham had found another man to love.

"And—" her mother faltered "—James has asked me to be his wife."

"And?" It seemed to Ellen that her vocabulary had suddenly been reduced to one word.

"And I've said yes."

Ellen closed her eyes, expecting to feel a rush of bittersweet nostalgia for the father she remembered so well and had loved so much. Instead, she felt only gladness that her mother had discovered this new happiness.

"Congratulations, Mom."

"Do you mean that?"

"With all my heart. When's the wedding?"

"Well, actually..." Her mother hedged again. "Honey, don't be angry."

"Angry?"

"We're already married. I'm calling from Reno."

"Oh."

"Are you mad?"

"Of course not."

"James has a winter home in Arizona and we're going to stay there until April."

"April," Ellen repeated, feeling a little dazed.

"If you object, honey, I'll come back to Yakima for Christmas."

"No... I don't object. It's just kind of sudden."

"Dad's been gone ten years."

"I know, Mom. Don't worry, okay?"

"I'll email you soon."

"Do that. And much happiness, Mom. You and James deserve it."

"Thank you, love."

They spoke for a few more minutes before saying goodbye. Ellen walked down the stairs in a state of stunned disbelief, absentmindedly tightening the belt of her housecoat. In a matter of months, her entire family had disintegrated. Her sister and mother had married and Bud had joined the military.

"Good morning," she cautiously greeted Reed, who was sitting at the kitchen table dressed and reading the paper.

"Morning," he responded dryly, as he lowered his paper.

Her hands trembling, Ellen reached for a mug, but it slipped out of her fingers and hit the counter, luckily without breaking.

Reed carefully folded the newspaper and studied her face. "What's wrong? You look like you've just seen a ghost."

"My mom's married," she murmured in a subdued voice. Tears burned in her eyes. She was no longer sure just what she was feeling. Happiness for her mother, yes, but also sadness as she remembered her father and his untimely death.

"Remarried?" he asked.

"Yes." She sat down across from him, holding the mug in both hands and staring into its depths. "It's not like this is sudden. Dad's been gone a lot of years. What surprises me is all the emotion I'm feeling."

"That's only natural. I remember how I felt when my dad remarried. I'd known about Mary and Dad for months. But the day of the wedding I couldn't help feeling, somehow, that my father had betrayed my mother's memory. Those were heavy thoughts for a ten-year-old boy." His hand reached for hers. "As I recall, that was the last time I cried."

Ellen nodded. It was the only way she could thank him, because speaking was impossible just then. She knew instinctively that Reed didn't often share the hurts of his youth.

Just when her throat had relaxed and she felt she could speak, Derek threw open the back door and dashed in, tossing his older brother a set of keys.

"I had them add a quart of oil," Derek said. "Are you sure you can't stay longer?"

The sip of coffee sank to the pit of Ellen's stomach and sat there. "You're leaving?" It seemed as though someone had jerked her chair out from under her.

He released her hand and gave it a gentle pat. "You'll be fine."

Ellen forced her concentration back to her coffee. For days she'd been telling herself that she'd be relieved and delighted when Reed left. Now she dreaded it. More than anything, she wanted him to stay.

Four

"Ellen," Derek shouted as he burst in the front door, his hands full of mail. "Can I invite Michelle to dinner on Friday night?"

Casually, Ellen looked up from the textbook she was studying. By mutual agreement, they all went their separate ways on Friday evenings and Ellen didn't cook. If one of the boys happened to be in the house, he heated up soup or put together a sandwich or made do with leftovers. In Monte's case, he did all three.

"What are you planning to fix?" Ellen responded cagily.

"Cook? Me?" Derek slapped his hand against his chest and looked utterly shocked. "I can't cook. You know that."

"But you're inviting company."

His gaze dropped and he restlessly shuffled his feet. "I was hoping that maybe this one Friday you could…" He paused and his head jerked up. "You don't have a date, do you?" He sounded as if that was the worst possible thing that could happen.

"Not this Friday."

"Oh, good. For a minute there, I thought we might have a problem."

"We?" She rolled her eyes. "I don't have a problem, but it sounds like you do." She wasn't going to let him con her into his schemes quite so easily.

"But you'll be here."

"I was planning on soaking in the tub, giving my hair a hot-oil treatment and hibernating with a good book."

"But you could still make dinner, couldn't you? Something simple like seafood jambalaya with shrimp, stuffed eggplant and pecan pie for dessert."

"Are you planning to rob a bank, as well?" At his blank stare, she elaborated. "Honestly, Derek, have you checked out the price of seafood lately?"

"No, but you cooked that Cajun meal not long ago and—"

"Shrimp was on sale," she broke in.

He continued undaunted. "And it was probably the most delicious meal I've ever tasted in my whole life. I was kicking myself because Reed wasn't here and he would have loved it as much as everyone else."

At the mention of Reed's name, Ellen's lashes fell, hiding the confusion and longing in her eyes. The house had been full of college boys, yet it had seemed astonishingly empty without Reed. He'd been with them barely a week and Ellen couldn't believe how much his presence had affected her. The morning he'd left, she'd walked him out to his truck, trying to think of a way to say goodbye and to thank him for understanding the emotions that raged through her at the news of her mother's remarriage. But nothing had turned out quite as she'd expected. Reed had seemed just as reluctant to say goodbye as she was, and before climbing into the truck, he'd leaned forward and lightly brushed his lips over hers. The kiss had been so spontaneous that Ellen wasn't sure if he'd really meant to do it. But intentional or not, he *had,* and the memory of that kiss stayed with her. Now hardly a day passed that he didn't enter her thoughts.

A couple of times when she was on the second floor she'd wandered into her old bedroom, forgetting that it now belonged to Reed. Both times, she'd lingered there, enjoying the sensation of remembering Reed and their verbal battles.

Repeatedly Ellen told herself that it was because Derek's brother was over twenty-one and she could therefore carry on an adult conversation with him. Although she was genuinely fond of the boys, she'd discovered that a constant diet of their antics and their adolescent preoccupations—Pat's basketball, Monte's appetite and Derek's Michelle—didn't exactly make for stimulating conversation.

"You really are a fantastic cook," Derek went on. "Even better than my mother. You know, only the other day Monte was saying—"

"Don't you think you're putting it on a little thick, Derek?"

He blinked. "I just wanted to tell you how much I'd appreciate it if you decided to do me this tiny favor."

"You'll buy the ingredients yourself?"

"The grocery budget couldn't manage it?"

"Not unless everyone else is willing to eat oatmeal three times a week for the remainder of the month."

"I don't suppose they would be," he muttered. "All right, make me a list and I'll buy what you need."

Ellen was half hoping that once he saw the price of fresh shrimp, he'd realize it might be cheaper to take Michelle to a seafood restaurant.

"Oh, by the way," Derek said, examining one of the envelopes in his hand. "You got a letter. Looks like it's from Reed."

"Reed?" Her lungs slowly contracted as she said his name, and it was all she could do not to snatch the envelope out of Derek's hand. The instant he gave it to her, she tore it open.

"What does he say?" Derek asked, sorting through the rest of the mail. "He didn't write me."

Ellen quickly scanned the contents. "He's asking if the electrician has showed up yet. That's all."

"Oh? Then why didn't he just call? Or send an email?"

She didn't respond, but made a show of putting the letter back inside the envelope. "I'll go into the kitchen and make that grocery list before I forget."

"I'm really grateful, Ellen, honest."

"Sure," she grumbled.

As soon as the kitchen door swung shut, Ellen took out Reed's letter again, intent on savoring every word.

Dear Ellen,

I realized I don't have your email address, so I thought I'd do this the old-fashioned way—by mail. There's something so leisurely and personal about writing a letter, isn't there?

You're right, the Monterey area is beautiful. I wish I could say that everything else is as peaceful as the scenery here. Unfortunately it's not. Things have been hectic. But if all goes well, I should be back at the house by Saturday, which is earlier than I expected.

Have you become accustomed to the idea that your mother's remarried? I know it was a shock. Like I said, I remember how I felt, and that was many years ago. I've been thinking about it all—and wondering about you. If I'd known what was happening, I might have been able to postpone this trip. You looked like you needed someone. And knowing you, it isn't often that you're willing to lean on anyone. Not the independent, self-sufficient woman I discovered walking around my kitchen half-naked. I can almost see your face getting red when you read that. I shouldn't tease you, but I can't help it.

By the way, I contacted a friend of mine who owns an electrical business and told him about the problem with the kitchen outlet. He said he'd try to stop by soon. He'll call first.

I wanted you to know that I was thinking about you—and the boys, but mostly you. Actually, I'm pleased you're there to keep those kids in line.

Take care and I'll see you late Saturday.

Say hi to the boys for me. I'm trusting that they aren't giving you any problems.

Reed

Ellen folded the letter and slipped it into her pocket. She crossed her arms, smiling to herself, feeling incredibly good. So Reed had been thinking about her. And she sensed that it was more than the troublesome kitchen outlet that had prompted his letter. Although she knew it would be dangerous for her to read too much into Reed's message, Ellen couldn't help feeling encouraged.

She propped open her cookbook, compiling the list of items Derek would need for his fancy dinner with Michelle. A few minutes later, her spirits soared still higher when the electrical contractor phoned and arranged a date and a time to check the faulty outlet. Somehow, that seemed like a good omen to her—a kind of proof that she really was in Reed's thoughts.

"Was the phone for me?" Derek called from halfway down the stairs.

Ellen finished writing the information on the pad by the phone before answering. "It was the electrician."

"Oh. I'm expecting a call from Michelle."

"Speaking of your true love, here's your grocery list."

Derek took it and slowly ran his finger down the items she'd need for his dinner with Michelle. "Is this going to cost more than twenty-five dollars?" He glanced up, his face doubtful.

"The pecans alone will be that much," she exaggerated.

With only a hint of disappointment, Derek shook his head. "I think maybe Michelle and I should find a nice, cozy, *inexpensive* restaurant."

Satisfied that her plan had worked so well, Ellen hid a smile. "Good idea. By the way," she added, "Reed says he'll be home Saturday."

"So soon? He's just been gone two weeks."

"Apparently it's a short job."

"Apparently," Derek grumbled. "I don't have to be here, do I? Michelle wanted me to help her and her sister paint."

"Derek," Ellen said. "I didn't even know you could wield a brush. The upstairs hallway—"

"Forget it," he told her sharply. "I'm only doing this to help Michelle."

"Right, but I'm sure Michelle would be willing to help you in exchange."

"Hey, we're students, not slaves."

The following afternoon, the electrician arrived and was in and out of the house within thirty minutes. Ellen felt proud that she'd correctly traced the problem. She could probably have fixed it if Reed hadn't become so frantic at the thought of her fumbling around with the wiring. Still, recalling his reaction made her smile.

That evening, Ellen had finished loading the dishwasher and had just settled down at the kitchen table to study when the phone rang. Pat, who happened to be walking past it, answered.

"It's Reed," he told Ellen. "He wants to talk to you."

With reflexes that surprised even her, Ellen bounded out of her chair.

"Reed," she said into the receiver, holding it tightly against her ear. "Hello, how are you?"

"Fine. Did the electrician come?"

"He was here this afternoon."

"Any problems?"

"No," she breathed. He sounded wonderfully close, his voice warm and vibrant. "In fact, I was on the right track. I probably could've handled it myself."

"I don't want you to even think about fixing anything like that. You could end up killing yourself or someone else. I absolutely forbid it."

"Aye, aye, sir." His words had the immediate effect of igniting her temper, sending the hot blood roaring through her veins. She hadn't been able to stop thinking about Reed since he'd left, but two minutes after picking up the phone, she was ready to argue with him again.

There was a long, awkward silence. Reed was the first to speak, expelling his breath sharply. "I didn't mean to snap your head off," he said. "I'm sorry."

"Thank you," she responded, instantly soothed.

"How's everything else going?"

"Fine."

"Have the boys talked you into any more of their schemes?"

"They keep trying."

"They wouldn't be college kids if they didn't."

"I know." It piqued her a little that Reed assumed she could be manipulated by three teenagers. "Don't worry about me. I can hold my own with these guys."

His low sensuous chuckle did funny things to her pulse. "It's not you I'm concerned about."

"Just what are you implying?" she asked with mock seriousness.

"I'm going to play this one smart and leave that last comment open-ended."

"Clever of you, my friend, very clever."

"I thought as much."

After a short pause, Ellen quickly asked, "How's everything with you?" She knew there really wasn't anything more to say, but she didn't want the conversation to end. Talking to Reed was almost as good as having him there.

"Much better, thanks. I shouldn't have any problem getting home by Saturday."

"Good."

Another short silence followed.

"Well, I guess that's all I've got to say. If I'm going to be any later than Saturday, I'll give you a call."

"Drive carefully."

"I will. Bye, Ellen."

"Goodbye, Reed." Smiling, she replaced the receiver. When she glanced up, all three boys were staring at her, their arms crossed dramatically over their chests.

"I think something's going on here." Pat spoke first. "I answered the phone and Reed asked for Ellen. He didn't even ask for Derek—his own brother."

"Right." Derek nodded vigorously.

"I'm wondering," Monte said, rubbing his chin. "Could we have the makings of a romance on our hands?"

"I think we do," Pat concurred.

"Stop it." Ellen did her best to join in the banter, although she felt the color flooding her cheeks. "It makes sense that Reed would want to talk to me. I'm the oldest."

"But I'm his brother," Derek countered.

"I refuse to listen to any of this," she said with a small laugh and turned back to the kitchen. "You three are being ridiculous. Reed's dating Danielle."

All three followed her. "He could have married Danielle months ago if he was really interested," Derek informed the small gathering.

"Be still, my beating heart," Monte joked, melodramatically folding both hands over his chest and pretending to swoon.

Not to be outdone, Pat rested the back of his hand against his forehead and rolled his eyes. "Ah, love."

"I'm out of here." Before anyone could argue, Ellen ran up the back stairs to her room, laughing as she went. She had to admit she'd found the boys' little performances quite funny. But if they pulled any of their pranks around Reed, it would be extremely embarrassing. Ellen resolved to say something to them when the time seemed appropriate.

Friday afternoon, Ellen walked into the kitchen, her book bag clutched tightly to her chest.

"What's the matter? You're as pale as a ghost," Monte remarked, cramming a chocolate-chip cookie in his mouth.

Derek and Pat turned toward her, their faces revealing concern.

"I got my algebra paper back today."

"And?" Derek prompted.

"I don't know. I haven't looked."

"Why not?"

"Because I know how tough Engstrom was on the others. The girl who wrote about solving that oddball conjecture got a C-minus and the guy who was so enthusiastic about Mathematics in World War II got a D. With impressive subjects like that getting low grades, I'm doomed."

"But you worked hard on that paper." Loyally, Derek defended her and placed a consoling arm around her shoulders. "You found out a whole bunch of interesting facts about the number nine."

"You did your paper on that?" Pat asked, his smooth brow wrinkling with amusement.

"Don't laugh." She already felt enough of a fool.

"It isn't going to do any good to worry," Monte insisted, pulling the folded assignment from between her fingers.

Ellen watched his expression intently as he looked at the paper, then handed it to Derek who raised his brows and gave it to Pat.

"Well?"

"You got a B-minus," Pat said in obvious surprise. "I don't believe it."

"Me neither." Ellen reveled in the delicious feeling of relief. She sank luxuriously into a chair. "I'm calling Charlie." Almost immediately she jumped up again and dashed to the phone. "This is too exciting! I'm celebrating."

The other three had drifted into the living room and two minutes later, she joined them there. "Charlie's out, but his roommate said he'd give him the message." Too happy to contain her excitement, she added, "But I'm not sitting home alone. How about if we go out for pizza tonight? My treat."

"Sorry, Ellen." Derek looked up with a frown. "I've already made plans with Michelle."

"I'm getting together with a bunch of guys at the gym," Pat informed her. "Throw a few baskets."

"And I told my mom I'd be home for dinner."

Some of the excitement drained from her, but she put on a brave front. "No problem. We'll do it another night."

"I'll go."

The small group whirled around, shocked to discover Reed standing there, framed in the living-room doorway.

Five

"Reed," Ellen burst out, astonished. "When did you get here?" The instant she'd finished speaking, she realized how stupid the question was. He'd just walked in the back door.

With a grin, he checked his wristwatch. "About fifteen seconds ago."

"How was the trip?" Derek asked.

"Did you drive straight through?" Pat asked, then said, "I don't suppose you had a chance to see the Lakers play, did you?"

"You must be exhausted," Ellen murmured, noting how tired his eyes looked.

As his smiling gaze met hers, the fine laugh lines that fanned out from his eyes became more pronounced. "I'm hungry *and* tired. Didn't I just hear you offer to buy me pizza?"

"Ellen got a B-minus on her crazy algebra paper," Monte said with pride.

Rolling her eyes playfully toward the ceiling, Ellen laughed. "Who would have guessed it—I'm a mathematical genius!"

"So that's the reason for this dinner. I thought you might have won the lottery."

He was more deeply tanned than Ellen remembered. Handsome. Vital. And incredibly male. He seemed glad to be home, she thought. Not a hint of hostility showed in the eyes that smiled back at her.

"No such luck."

Derek made a show of glancing at his watch. "I gotta go or I'll be late picking up Michelle. It's good to see you, Reed."

"Yeah, welcome home," Pat said, reaching for his basketball. "I'll see you later."

Reed raised his right hand in salute and picked up his suitcase, then headed up the wide stairs. "Give me fifteen minutes to shower and I'll meet you down here."

The minute Reed's back was turned, Monte placed his hand over his heart and batted his lashes wildly as he mouthed something about love, true love. Ellen practically threw him out of the house, slamming the door after him.

At the top of the stairs, Reed turned and glanced down at her. "What was that all about?"

Ellen leaned against the closed door, one hand covering her mouth to smother her giggles. But the laughter drained from her as she looked at his puzzled face, and she slowly straightened. She cleared her throat. "Nothing. Did you want me to order pizza? Or do you want to go out?"

"Whatever you prefer."

"If you leave it up to me, my choice would be to get away from these four walls."

"I'll be ready in a few minutes."

Ellen suppressed a shudder at the thought of what would've happened had Reed caught a glimpse of Monte's antics. She herself handled the boys' teasing with good-natured indulgence, but she was fairly sure that Reed would take offense at their nonsense. And heaven forbid that Danielle should ever catch a hint of what was going on—not that anything *was* going on.

With her thoughts becoming more muddled every minute, Ellen made her way to the third floor to change into a pair of gray tailored pants and a frilly pale blue silk blouse. One glance in the mirror and she sadly shook her head. They were only going out for pizza—there was no need to wear anything so elaborate. Hurriedly, she changed into dark brown cords and a turtleneck sweater the color of summer wheat. Then she ran a brush through her short curls and freshened her lipstick.

When Ellen returned to the living room, Reed was already waiting for her. "You're sure you don't mind going out?" she asked again.

"Are you dodging your pizza offer?"

He was so serious that Ellen couldn't help laughing. "Not at all."

"Good. I hope you like spicy sausage with lots of olives."

"Love it."

His hand rested on her shoulder. "And a cold beer."

"This is sounding better all the time." Ellen would have guessed that Reed was the type of man who drank martinis or expensive cocktails. In some ways, he was completely down-to-earth and in others, surprisingly complex. Perceptive, unpretentious and unpredictable—she knew that much about him, but she didn't expect to understand him anytime soon.

Reed helped her into his pickup, which was parked in the driveway. The evening sky was already dark and Ellen regretted not having brought her coat.

"Cold?" Reed asked her when they stopped at a red light.

"Only a little."

He adjusted the switches for the heater and soon a rush of warm air filled the cab. Reed chatted easily, telling her about his project in California and explaining why his work demanded so much travel. "That's changing now."

"Oh?" She couldn't restrain a little shiver of gladness at his announcement. "Will you be coming home more often?"

"Not for another three or four months. I'm up for promotion and then I'll be able to pick and choose my assignments more carefully. Over the past four years, I've traveled enough to last me a lifetime."

"Then it's true that there's no place like home."

"Be it ever so humble," he added with a chuckle.

"I don't exactly consider a three-storey, twenty-room turn-of-the-century mansion all that humble."

"Throw in four college students and you'll quickly discover how unassuming it can become."

"Oh?"

"You like that word, don't you?"

"Yes," she agreed, her mouth curving into a lazy smile. "It's amazing how much you can say with that one little sound."

Reed exited the freeway close to the Seattle Center and continued north. At her questioning glance, he explained, "The best pizza in Seattle is made at a small place near the Center. You don't mind coming this far, do you?"

"Of course not. I'll travel a whole lot farther than this for a good pizza." Suddenly slouching forward, she dropped her forehead into her hand. "Oh, no. It's happening."

"What is?"

"I'm beginning to sound like Monte."

They both laughed. It felt so good to be sitting there with

Reed, sharing an easy, relaxed companionship, that Ellen could almost forget about Danielle. Almost, but not quite.

Although Ellen had said she'd pay for the pizza, Reed insisted on picking up the tab. They sat across from each other at a narrow booth in the corner of the semidarkened room. A lighted red candle in a glass bowl flickered on the table between them and Ellen decided this was the perfect atmosphere. The old-fashioned jukebox blared out the latest country hits, drowning out the possibility of any audible conversation, but that seemed just as well since she was feeling strangely tongue-tied.

When their number was called, Reed slid from the booth and returned a minute later with two frothy beers in ice-cold mugs and a huge steaming pizza.

"I hope you don't expect us to eat all this?" Ellen said, shouting above the music. The pizza certainly smelled enticing, but Ellen doubted she'd manage to eat more than two or three pieces.

"We'll put a dent in it, anyway," Reed said, resuming his seat. "I bought the largest, figuring the boys would enjoy the leftovers."

"You're a terrific older brother."

The song on the jukebox was fading into silence at last.

"There are times I'd like to shake some sense into Derek, though," Reed said.

Ellen looked down at the spicy pizza and put a small slice on her plate. Strings of melted cheese still linked the piece to the rest of the pie. She pulled them loose and licked her fingers. "I can imagine how you felt when you discovered that Derek had accidentally-on-purpose forgotten to tell you about renting out rooms."

Reed shrugged noncommittally. "I was thinking more

about the time he let you climb on top of the roof," he muttered.

"He didn't *let* me, I went all by myself."

"But you won't do it again. Right?"

"Right." Ellen nodded reluctantly. Behind Reed's slow smiles and easy banter, she recognized his unrelenting male pride. "You still haven't forgiven me for that, have you?"

"Not you. Derek."

"I think this is one of those subjects on which we should agree to disagree."

"Have you heard from your mother?" Reed asked, apparently just as willing to change the subject.

"Yes. She's emailed me several times. She seems very happy and after a day or two, I discovered I couldn't be more pleased for her. She deserves a lot of contentment."

"I knew you'd realize that." Warmth briefly showed in his green eyes.

"I felt a lot better after talking to you. I was surprised when Mom announced her marriage, but I shouldn't have been. The signs were there all along. I suppose once the three of us kids were gone, she felt free to remarry. And I suppose she thought that presenting it to the family as a fait accompli would make it easier for all of us."

There was a comfortable silence as they finished eating. The pizza was thick with sausage and cheese, and Ellen placed her hands on her stomach after leisurely eating two narrow pieces. "I'm stuffed," she declared, leaning back. "But you're right, this has got to be the best pizza in town."

"I thought you'd like it."

Reed brought over a carry-out box and Ellen carefully put the leftovers inside.

"How about a movie?" he asked once they were in the car park.

Astounded, Ellen darted him a sideways glance, but his features were unreadable. "You're kidding, aren't you?"

"I wouldn't have asked you if I was."

"But you must be exhausted." Ellen guessed he'd probably spent most of the day driving.

"A little," he admitted.

Her frown deepened. Suddenly, it no longer seemed right for them to be together—because of Danielle. The problem was that Ellen had been so pleased to see him that she hadn't stopped to think about the consequences of their going out together. "Thanks anyway, but it's been a long week. I think I'll call it a night."

When they reached the house, Reed parked on the street rather than the driveway. The light from the stars and the silvery moon penetrated the branches that hung overhead and created shadows on his face. Neither of them seemed eager to leave the warm cab of the pickup truck. The mood was intimate and Ellen didn't want to disturb this moment of tranquillity. Lowering her gaze, she admitted to herself how attracted she was to Reed and how much she liked him. She admitted, too, that it was wrong for her to feel this way about him.

"You're quiet all of a sudden."

Ellen's smile was decidedly forced. She turned toward him to apologise for putting a damper on their evening, but the words never left her lips. Instead, her eyes met his. Paralyzed, she stared at Reed, fighting to disguise the intense attraction she felt for him. It seemed the most natural thing in the world to lean toward him and brush her lips against his. She could smell the woodsy scent of his aftershave and could almost taste his mouth on hers. With determination, she pulled her gaze away and reached for the door, like a drowning person grasping a life preserver.

She was on the front porch by the time Reed joined her. Her fingers shook as she inserted the key in the lock.

"Ellen." He spoke her name softly and placed his hand on her shoulder.

"I don't know why we went out tonight." Her voice was high and strained as she drew free of his touch. "We shouldn't have been together."

In response, Reed mockingly lifted one eyebrow. "I believe it was you who asked me."

"Be serious, will you," she snapped irritably and shoved open the door.

Reed slammed it shut behind him and followed her into the kitchen. He set the pizza on the counter, then turned to face her. "What the hell do you mean? I *was* being serious."

"You shouldn't have been with me tonight."

"Why not?"

"Where's Danielle? I'm not the one who's been patiently waiting around for you. *She* is. You had no business taking me out to dinner and then suggesting a movie. You're my landlord, not my boyfriend."

"Let's get two things straight here. First, what's between Danielle and me is none of *your* business. And second, you invited *me* out. Remember?"

"But…it wasn't like that and you know it."

"Besides, I thought you said you were far too old for *boyfriends*." She detected an undertone of amusement in his voice.

Confused, Ellen marched into the living room and immediately busied herself straightening magazines. Reed charged in after her, leaving the kitchen door swinging in his wake. Clutching a sofa pillow, she searched for some witty retort. Naturally, whenever she needed a clever comeback, her mind was a total blank.

"You're making a joke out of everything," she told him, angry that her voice was shaking. "And I don't like that. If you want to play games, do it with someone other than me."

"Ellen, listen—"

The phone rang and she jerked her attention to the hall-way.

"I didn't mean—" Reed paused and raked his fingers through his hair. The phone pealed a second time. "Go ahead and answer that."

She hurried away, relieved to interrupt this disturbing conversation. "Hello." Her voice sounded breathless, as though she'd raced down the stairs.

"Ellen? This is Charlie. I got a message that you phoned."

For one crazy instant, Ellen forgot why she'd wanted to talk to Charlie. "I phoned? Oh, right. Remember that algebra paper I was struggling with? Well, I got it back today."

"How'd you do?"

A little of the surprised pleasure returned. "I still can't believe it. I got a B-minus. My simple paper about the wonders of the number nine received one of the highest marks in the class. I'm still in shock."

Charlie's delighted chuckle came over the wire. "This calls for a celebration. How about if we go out tomorrow night? Dinner, drinks, the works."

Ellen almost regretted the impulse to contact Charlie. She sincerely liked him, and she hated the thought of stringing him along or taking advantage of his attraction to her. "Nothing so elaborate. Chinese food and a movie would be great."

"You let me worry about that. Just be ready by seven."

"Charlie."

"No arguing. I'll see you at seven."

By the time Ellen got off the phone, Reed was nowhere

to be seen. Nor was he around the following afternoon. The boys didn't comment and she couldn't very well ask about him without arousing their suspicions. As it was, the less she mentioned Reed around them, the better. The boys had obviously read more into the letter, phone call and dinner than Reed had intended. But she couldn't blame them; she'd read enough into it herself to be frightened by what was happening between them. He'd almost kissed her when he'd parked in front of the house. And she'd wanted him to—that was what disturbed her most. But if she allowed her emotions to get involved, she knew that someone would probably end up being hurt. And the most likely *someone* was Ellen herself.

Besides, if Reed was attracted to Danielle's sleek elegance, then he would hardly be interested in her own more homespun qualities.

A few minutes before seven, Ellen was ready for her evening with Charlie. She stood before the downstairs hallway mirror to put the finishing touches on her appearance, fastening her gold earrings and straightening the single chain necklace.

"Where's Reed been today?" Pat inquired of no one in particular.

"His sports car is gone," Monte said, munching on a chocolate bar. "I noticed it wasn't in the garage when I took out the garbage."

Slowly Ellen sauntered into the living room. She didn't want to appear too curious, but at the same time, she was definitely interested in the conversation.

She had flopped into a chair and picked up a two-month-old magazine before she noticed all three boys staring at her.

"What are you looking at me for?"

"We thought you might know something."

"About what?" she asked, playing dumb.

"Reed," all three said simultaneously.

"Why should I know anything?" Her gaze flittered from them to the magazine and back again.

"You went out with him last night."

"We didn't *go out* the way you're implying."

Pat pointed an accusing finger at her. "The two of you were alone together, and both of you have been acting weird ever since."

"And I say the three of you have overactive imaginations."

"All I know is that Reed was like a wounded bear this morning," Derek volunteered.

"Everyone's entitled to an off day." Hoping to give a casual impression, she leafed through the magazine, idly fanning the pages with her thumb.

"That might explain Reed. But what about you?"

"Me?"

"For the first time since you moved in, you weren't downstairs until after ten."

"I slept in. Is that a crime?"

"It just might be. You and Reed are both acting really strange. It's like the two of you are avoiding each other and we want to know why."

"It's your imagination. Believe me, if there was anything to tell you, I would."

"Sure, you would," Derek mocked.

From the corner of her eye, Ellen saw Charlie's car pull up in front of the house. Releasing a sigh of relief, she quickly stood and gave the boys a falsely bright smile. "If you'll excuse me, my date has arrived."

"Should we tell Reed you're out with Charlie if he wants

to know where you are?" Monte looked uncomfortable asking the question.

"Of course. Besides, he probably already knows. He's free to see anyone he wants and so am I. For that matter, so are you." She whirled around and made her way to the front door, pulling it open before Charlie even got a chance to ring the doorbell.

The evening didn't go well. Charlie took her out for a steak dinner and spent more money than Ellen knew he could afford. She regretted having phoned him. Charlie had obviously interpreted her call as a sign that she was interested in becoming romantically involved. She wasn't, and didn't know how to make it clear without offending him.

"Did you have a good time?" he asked as they drove back toward Capitol Hill.

"Lovely, thank you, Charlie."

His hand reached for hers and squeezed it reassuringly. "We don't go out enough."

"Neither of us can afford it too often."

"We don't need to go to a fancy restaurant to be together," he said lightly. "Just being with you is a joy."

"Thank you." If only Charlie weren't so nice. She hated the idea of hurting him. But she couldn't allow him to go on hoping that she would ever return his feelings. As much as she dreaded it, she knew she had to disillusion him. Anything else would be cruel and dishonest.

"I don't think I've made a secret of how I feel about you, Ellen. You're wonderful."

"Come on, Charlie, I'm not that different from a thousand other girls on campus." She tried to swallow the tightness in her throat. "In fact, I saw the way that girl in our sociology class—what's her name—Lisa, has been looking at you lately."

"I hadn't noticed."

"I believe you've got yourself an admirer."

"But I'm only interested in you."

"Charlie, listen. I think you're a very special person. I—"

"Shh," he demanded softly as he parked in front of Ellen's house and turned off the engine. He slid his arm along the back of the seat and caressed her shoulder. "I don't want you to say anything."

"But I feel I may have—"

"Ellen," he whispered seductively. "Be quiet and just let me kiss you."

Before she could utter another word, Charlie claimed her mouth in a short but surprisingly ardent kiss. Charlie had kissed her on several occasions, but that was as far as things had ever gone.

When his arms tightened around her, Ellen resisted.

"Invite me in for coffee," he whispered urgently in her ear.

She pressed her forehead against his shirt collar. "Not tonight."

He tensed. "Can I see you again soon?"

"I don't know. We see each other every day. Why don't we just meet after class for coffee one day next week?"

"But I want more than that," he protested.

"I know," she answered, dropping her eyes. She felt confused and miserable.

Ellen could tell he was disappointed from the way he climbed out of the car and trudged around to her side. There was tense silence between them as he walked her up to the front door and kissed her a second time. Again, Ellen had to break away from him by pushing her hands against his chest.

"Thank you for everything," she whispered.

"Right. Thanks, but no thanks."

"Oh, Charlie, don't start that. Not now."

Eyes downcast, he wearily rubbed a hand along the side of his face. "I guess I'll see you Monday," he said with a sigh.

"Thanks for the lovely evening." She didn't let herself inside until Charlie had climbed into his car and driven away.

Releasing a jagged breath, Ellen had just started to unbutton her coat when she glanced up to find Reed standing in the living room, glowering at her.

"Is something wrong?" The undisguised anger that twisted his mouth and hardened his gaze was a shock.

"Do you always linger outside with your boyfriends?"

"We didn't linger."

"Right." He dragged one hand roughly through his hair and marched a few paces toward her, only to do an abrupt about-face. "I saw the two of you necking."

"Necking?" Ellen was so startled by his unreasonable anger that she didn't know whether to laugh or argue. "Be serious, will you? Two chaste kisses hardly constitute necking."

"What kind of influence are you on Derek and the others?" He couldn't seem to stand still and paced back and forth in agitation.

He was obviously furious, but Ellen didn't understand why. He couldn't possibly believe these absurd insinuations. Perhaps he was upset about something else and merely taking it out on her. "Reed, what's wrong?" she finally asked.

"I saw you out there."

"You were spying on me?"

"I wasn't spying," he snapped.

"Charlie and I were in his car. You must've been staring out the window to have seen us."

He didn't answer her, but instead hurled another accusation in her direction. "You're corrupting the boys."

"I'm *what?*" She couldn't believe what she was hearing. "What year do you think this is?" She shook her head, bewildered. "They're nineteen. Trust me, they've kissed girls before."

"You can kiss anyone you like. Just don't do it in front of the boys."

From the way this conversation was going, Ellen could see that Reed was in no mood to listen to reason. "I think we should discuss this some other time," she said quietly.

"We'll talk about it right now."

Ignoring his domineering tone as much as possible, Ellen forced a smile. "Good night, Reed. I'll see you in the morning."

She was halfway to the stairs when he called her, his voice calm. "Ellen."

She turned around, holding herself tense, watching him stride quickly across the short distance that separated them. With his thumb and forefinger, he caught her chin, tilting it slightly so he could study her face. He rubbed his thumb across her lips. "Funny, you don't look kissed."

In one breath he was accusing her of necking and in the next, claiming she was unkissed. Not knowing how to respond, Ellen didn't. She merely gazed at him, her eyes wide and questioning.

"If you're going to engage in that sort of activity, the least you can do—" He paused. With each word his mouth drew closer and closer to hers until his lips hovered over her own and their breath mingled. "The least you can do is look kissed." His hand located the vein pounding wildly in her throat as his mouth settled over hers.

Slowly, patiently, his mouth moved over hers with an exquisite tenderness that left her quivering with anticipation and delight. Timidly, her hands crept across his chest to link behind his neck. Again his lips descended on hers, more hungrily now, as he groaned and pulled her even closer.

Ellen felt her face grow hot as she surrendered to the sensations that stole through her. Yet all the while, her mind was telling her she had no right to feel this contentment, this warmth. Reed belonged to another woman. Not to her...to someone else.

Color seeped into her face. When she'd understood that he intended to kiss her, her first thought had been to resist. But once she'd felt his mouth on hers, all her resolve had drained away. Embarrassed now, she realized she'd pliantly wrapped her arms around his neck. And worse, she'd responded with enough enthusiasm for him to know exactly what she was feeling.

He pressed his mouth to her forehead as though he couldn't bear to release her.

Ellen struggled to breathe normally. She let her arms slip from his neck to his chest and through the palm of her hand she could feel the rapid beating of his heart. She closed her eyes, knowing that her own pulse was pounding no less wildly.

She could feel his mouth move against her temple. "I've been wanting to do that for days." The grudging admission came in a voice that was low and taut.

The words to tell him that she'd wanted it just as much were quickly silenced by the sound of someone walking into the room.

Guiltily Reed and Ellen jerked apart. Her face turned a deep shade of red as Derek stopped in his tracks, staring at them.

"Hi."

"Hi," Reed and Ellen said together.

"Hey, I'm not interrupting anything, am I? If you like, I could turn around and pretend I didn't see a thing."

"Do it," Reed ordered.

"No," Ellen said in the same moment.

Derek's eyes sparkled with boyish delight. "You know," he said, "I had a feeling about the two of you." While he spoke, he was taking small steps backward until he stood pressed against the polished kitchen door. He gave his brother a thumbs-up as he nudged open the door with one foot and hurriedly backed out of the room.

"Now look what you've done," Ellen wailed.

"Me? As I recall you were just as eager for this as I was."

"It was a mistake," she blurted out. A ridiculous, illogical mistake. He'd accused her of being a bad influence on the boys and then proceeded to kiss her senseless.

"You're telling me." A distinct coolness entered his eyes. "It's probably a good thing I'm leaving."

There was no hiding her stricken look. "Again? So soon?"

"After what's just happened, I'd say it wasn't soon enough."

"But…where to this time?"

"Denver. I'll be back before Thanksgiving."

Mentally, Ellen calculated that he'd be away another two weeks.

When he spoke again, his voice was gentle. "It's just as well, don't you think?"

Six

"Looks like rain." Pat stood in front of the window above the kitchen sink and frowned at the thick black clouds that darkened the late-afternoon sky. "Why does it have to rain?"

Ellen glanced up at him. "Are you seeking a scientific response or will a simple 'I don't know' suffice?"

The kitchen door swung open and Derek sauntered in. "Has anyone seen Reed?"

Instantly, Ellen's gaze dropped to her textbook. Reed had returned to Seattle two days earlier and so far, they'd done an admirable job of avoiding each other. Both mornings, he'd left for his office before she was up. Each evening, he'd come home, showered, changed and then gone off again. It didn't require much detective work to figure out that he was with Danielle. Ellen had attempted—unsuccessfully—not to think of Reed at all. And especially not of him and Danielle together.

She secretly wished she'd had the nerve to arrange an opportunity to talk to Reed. So much remained unclear in her mind. Reed had kissed her and it had been wonderful, yet that was something neither seemed willing to admit. It was as if they'd tacitly agreed that the kiss had been a terrible mistake and should be forgotten. The problem was, Ellen *couldn't* forget it.

"Reed hasn't been around the house much," Pat answered.

"I know." Derek sounded slightly disgruntled and cast an accusing look in Ellen's direction. "It's almost like he doesn't live here anymore."

"He doesn't. Not really." Pat stepped away from the window and gently set his basketball on a chair. "It's sort of like he's a guest who stops in now and then."

Ellen preferred not to be drawn into this conversation. She hastily closed her book and stood up to leave.

"Hey, Ellen." Pat stopped her.

She sighed and met his questioning gaze with a nervous smile. "Yes?"

"I'll be leaving in a few minutes. Have a nice Thanksgiving."

Relieved that the subject of Reed had been dropped, she threw him a brilliant smile. "You, too."

"Where are you having dinner tomorrow?" Derek asked, as if the thought had unexpectedly occurred to him.

Her mother was still in Arizona, her sister had gone to visit her in-laws and Bud couldn't get leave, so Ellen had decided to stay in Seattle. "Here."

"In this house?" Derek's eyes widened with concern. "But why? Shouldn't you be with your family?"

"My family is going in different directions this year. It's no problem. In fact, I'm looking forward to having the whole house to myself."

"There's no reason to spend the day alone," Derek argued. "My parents wouldn't mind putting out an extra plate. There's always plenty of food."

Her heart was touched by the sincerity of his invitation. "Thank you, but honestly, I prefer it this way."

"It's because of Reed, isn't it?" Both boys studied her with inquisitive eyes.

"Nonsense."

"But, Ellen, he isn't going to be there."

"Reed isn't the reason," she assured him. Undoubtedly, Reed would be spending the holiday with Danielle. She made an effort to ignore the flash of pain that accompanied the thought; she knew she had no right to feel hurt if Reed chose to spend Thanksgiving with his "almost" fiancée.

"You're sure?" Derek didn't look convinced.

"You could come and spend the day with my family," Pat offered next.

"Will you two quit acting like it's such a terrible tragedy? I'm going to *enjoy* an entire day alone. Look at these nails." She fanned her fingers and held them up for their inspection. "For once, I'll have an uninterrupted block of time to do all the things I've delayed for weeks."

"All right, but if you change your mind, give me a call."

"I asked her first," Derek argued. "You'll call me. Right?"

"Right to you both."

Thanksgiving morning, Ellen woke to a torrential downpour. Rain pelted against the window and the day seemed destined to be a melancholy one. She lounged in her room and read, enjoying the luxury of not having to rush around, preparing breakfast for the whole household.

She wandered down to the kitchen, where she was greeted by a heavy silence. The house was definitely empty. Apparently, Reed, too, had started his day early. Ellen couldn't decide whether she was pleased or annoyed that she had seen so little of him since his return from Denver. He'd been the one to avoid her, and she'd concluded that two could play his silly game. So she'd purposely stayed out of his way. She smiled sadly as she reflected on the past few days. She and Reed had been acting like a couple of adolescents.

She ate a bowl of cornflakes and spent the next hour wiping down the cupboards, with the radio tuned to the soft-rock music station. Whenever a particularly romantic ballad aired, she danced around the kitchen with an imaginary partner. Not so imaginary, really. In her mind, she was in Reed's arms.

The silence became more oppressive during the afternoon, while Ellen busied herself fussing over her nails. When the final layer of polish had dried, she decided to turn on the television to drown out the quiet. An hour into the football game, Ellen noticed that it was nearly dinnertime, and she suddenly felt hungry.

She made popcorn in the microwave and splurged by dripping melted butter over the top. She carried the bowl into the living room and got back on the sofa, tucking her legs beneath her. She'd just found a comfortable position when she heard a noise in the kitchen.

Frowning, she twisted around, wondering who it could be.

The door into the living room swung open and Ellen's heart rate soared into double time.

"Reed?" She blinked to make sure he wasn't an apparition.

"Hello."

He didn't vanish. Instead he took several steps in her direction. "That popcorn smells great."

Without considering the wisdom of her offer, she held out the bowl to him. "Help yourself."

"Thanks." He took off his jacket and tossed it over the back of a chair before joining her on the sofa. He leaned forward, studying the TV. "Who's winning?"

Ellen was momentarily confused, until she realized he was asking about the football game. "I don't know. I haven't paid that much attention."

Reed reached for another handful of popcorn and Ellen set the bowl on the coffee table. Her emotions were muddled. She couldn't imagine what Reed was doing here when he was supposed to be at Danielle's. Although the question burned in her mind, she couldn't bring herself to ask. She glanced at him covertly, but Reed was staring at the TV as though he was alone in the room.

"I'll get us something to drink," she volunteered.

"Great."

Even while she was speaking, Reed hadn't looked in her direction. Slightly piqued by his attitude, she stalked into the kitchen and took two Pepsis out of the refrigerator.

When she returned with the soft drinks and two glasses filled with ice, Reed took one set from her. "Thanks," he murmured, popping open the can. He carefully poured his soda over the ice and set the can aside before taking a sip.

"You're welcome." She flopped down again, pretending to watch television. But her mind was spinning in a hundred different directions. When she couldn't tolerate it any longer, she blurted out the question that dominated her thoughts.

"Reed, what are you doing here?"

He took a long swallow before answering her. "I happen to live here."

"You know what I mean. You should be with Danielle."

"I was earlier, but I decided I preferred your company."

"I don't need your sympathy," she snapped, then swallowed painfully and averted her gaze. Her fingers tightened around the cold glass until the chill extended up her arm. "I'm perfectly content to spend the day alone. I just wish everyone would quit saving me from myself."

His low chuckle was unexpected. "That wasn't my intention."

"Then why are you here?"

"I already told you."

"I can't accept that," she said shakily. He was toying with her emotions, and the thought made her all the more furious.

"All right." Determinedly, he set down his drink and turned toward her. "I felt this was the perfect opportunity for us to talk."

"You haven't said more than ten words to me in three days. What makes this one day so special?"

"We're alone, aren't we, and that's more than we can usually say." His voice was strained. He hesitated a moment, his lips pressed together in a thin, hard line. "I don't know what's happening with us."

"Nothing's happening," she said wildly. "You kissed me, and we both admitted it was a mistake. Can't we leave it at that?"

"No," he answered dryly. "I don't believe it was such a major tragedy, and neither do you."

If it had really been a mistake, Ellen wouldn't have remembered it with such vivid clarity. Nor would she yearn for the taste of him again and again, or hurt so much when she knew he was with Danielle.

Swiftly she turned her eyes away from the disturbing intensity of his, unwilling to reveal the depth of her feelings.

"It wasn't a mistake, was it, Ellen?" he prompted in a husky voice.

She squeezed her eyes shut and shook her head. "No," she whispered, but the word was barely audible.

He gathered her close and she felt his deep shudder of satisfaction as he buried his face in her hair. Long moments passed before he spoke. "Nothing that felt so right could have been a mistake."

Tenderly he kissed her, his lips touching hers with a gentleness she hadn't expected. As if he feared she was somehow fragile; as if he found her highly precious. Without conscious decision, she slipped her arms around him.

"The whole time Danielle and I were together this afternoon, I was wishing it was you. Today, of all days, it seemed important to be with you."

Ellen gazed up into his eyes and saw not only his gentleness, but his confusion. Her fingers slid into the thick hair around his lean, rugged face. "Danielle couldn't have been pleased when you left."

"She wasn't. I didn't even know how to explain it to her. I don't know how to explain it to myself."

Ellen swallowed the dryness that constricted her throat. "Do you want me to move out of the house?"

"No," he said forcefully, then added more quietly, "I think I'd go crazy if you did. Are you a witch who's cast some spell over me?"

She tried unsuccessfully to answer him, but no words of denial came. The knowledge that he was experiencing these strange whirling emotions was enough to overwhelm her.

"If so, the spell is working," he murmured, although he didn't sound particularly happy about the idea.

"I'm confused, too," she admitted and leaned her forehead against his chest. She could feel his heart pounding beneath her open hand.

His long fingers stroked her hair. "I know." He leaned

down and kissed the top of her head. "The night you went out with Charlie, I was completely unreasonable. I need to apologize for the things I said. To put it simply, I was jealous. I've acknowledged that, these last weeks in Denver." Some of the tightness left his voice, as though the events of that night had weighed heavily on his mind. "I didn't like the idea of another man holding you, and when I saw the two of you kissing, I think I went a little berserk."

"I…we don't date often."

"I won't ask you not to see him again," he said reluctantly. "I can't ask anything of you."

"Nor can I ask anything of you."

His grip around her tightened. "Let's give this time."

"It's the only thing we can do."

Reed straightened and draped his arm around Ellen's shoulders, drawing her close to his side. Her head nestled against his chest. "I'd like us to start going out together," he said, his chin resting on the crown of her head. "Will that cause a problem for you?"

"Cause a problem?" she repeated uncertainly.

"I'm thinking about the boys."

Remembering their earlier buffoonery and the way they'd taken such delight in teasing her, Ellen shrugged. If those three had any evidence of a romance between her and Reed, they could make everyone's lives miserable. "I don't know."

"Then let's play it cool for a while. We'll move into this gradually until they become accustomed to seeing us together. That way it won't be any big deal."

"I think you might be right." She didn't like pretence or deceit, but she'd be the one subjected to their heckling. They wouldn't dare try it with Reed.

"Can I take you to dinner tomorrow night?"

"I'd like that."

"Not as much as I will. But how are we going to do this? It'll be obvious that we're going out," he mused aloud.

"Not if we leave the house at different times," she said.

She could feel his frown. "Is that really necessary?"

"I'm afraid so...."

Ellen and Reed spent the rest of the evening doing nothing more exciting than watching television. His arm remained securely around her shoulders and she felt a sense of deep contentment that was new to her. It was a peaceful interlude during a time that had become increasingly wrought with stress.

Derek got back to the house close to nine-thirty. They both heard him lope in through the kitchen and Reed gave Ellen a quick kiss before withdrawing his arm.

"Hi." Derek entered the room and stood beside the sofa, shuffling his feet. "Dad wondered where you were." His gaze flitted from Ellen to his brother.

"I told them I wouldn't be there for dinner."

"I know. But Danielle called looking for you."

"She knew where I was."

"Apparently not." Reed's younger brother gestured with one hand. "Are you two friends again?"

Reed's eyes found Ellen's and he smiled. "You could say that."

"Good. You haven't been the easiest people to be around lately." Without giving them a chance to respond, he whirled around and marched upstairs.

Ellen placed a hand over her mouth to smother her giggles. "Well, he certainly told us."

Amusement flared in Reed's eyes, and he chuckled softly. "I guess he did, at that." His arm slid around Ellen's shoulders once again. "Have you been difficult lately?"

"I'm never difficult," she said.

"Me neither."

They exchanged smiles and went back to watching their movie.

As much as Ellen tried to concentrate on the television, her mind unwillingly returned to Derek's announcement. "Do you think you should call Danielle?" She cast her eyes down, disguising her discomfort. Spending these past few hours with Reed had been like an unexpected Christmas gift, granted early. But she felt guilty that it had been at the other woman's expense.

Impatience tightened Reed's mouth. "Maybe I'd better. I didn't mean to offend her or her family by leaving early." He paused a moment, then added, "Danielle's kind of high-strung."

Ellen had noticed that, but she had no intention of mentioning it. And she had no intention of listening in on their conversation, either. "While you're doing that, I'll wash up the popcorn dishes, then go to bed."

Reed's eyes widened slightly in a mock reprimand. "It's a little early, isn't it?"

"Perhaps," she said, faking a yawn, "but I've got this hot date tomorrow night and I want to be well rested for it."

The front door opened and Pat sauntered in, carrying his duffel bag. "Hi." He stopped and studied them curiously. "Hi," he repeated.

"I thought you were staying at your parents' for the weekend." Ellen remembered that he'd said something about being gone for the entire four-day holiday.

"Mom gave my bedroom to one of my aunts. I can't see any reason to sleep on the floor when I've got a bed here."

"Makes sense," Reed said with a grin.

"Are you two getting along again?"

"We never fought."

"Yeah, sure," Pat mumbled sarcastically. "And a basket isn't worth two points."

Ellen had been unaware how much her disagreement with Reed had affected the boys. Apparently, Reed's reaction was the same as hers; their eyes met briefly in silent communication.

"I'll go up with you," she told Pat. "See you in the morning, Reed."

"Sure thing."

She left Pat on the second floor to trudge up to the third.

It shouldn't have been a surprise that she slept so well. Her mind was at ease and she awoke feeling contented and hopeful. Neither she nor Reed had made any commitments yet. They didn't know if what they felt would last a day or a lifetime. They were explorers, discovering the uncharted territory of a new relationship.

She hurried down the stairs early the next morning. Reed was already up, sitting at the kitchen table drinking coffee and reading the paper.

"Morning," she said, pouring water into the tea kettle and setting it on the burner.

"Morning." His eyes didn't leave the paper.

Ellen got a mug from the cupboard and walked past Reed on her way to get the canister of tea. His hand reached out and clasped her around the waist, pulling her down into his lap.

Before she could protest, his mouth firmly covered hers. When the kiss was over, Ellen straightened, resting her hands on his shoulders. "What was that for?" she asked to disguise how flustered he made her feel.

"Just to say good morning," he said in a warm, husky voice. "I don't imagine I'll have too many opportunities to do it in such a pleasant manner."

"No," she said and cleared her throat. "Probably not."

Ellen was sitting at the table, with a section of the paper propped up in front of her, when the boys came into the kitchen.

"Morning," Monte murmured vaguely as he opened the refrigerator. He was barefoot, his hair was uncombed and his shirt was still unbuttoned. "What's for breakfast?"

"Whatever your little heart desires," she told him, neatly folding over a page of the paper.

"Does this mean you're not cooking?"

"That's right."

"But—"

Reed lowered the sports page and glared openly at Monte.

"Cold cereal will be fine," Monte grumbled and took down a large serving bowl, emptying half the contents of a box of rice crisps inside.

"Hey, save some for me," Pat hollered from the doorway. "That's my favorite."

"I was here first."

Derek strolled into the kitchen. "Does everyone have to argue?"

"Everyone?" Reed cocked a brow in his brother's direction.

"First it was you and Ellen, and now it's Pat and Monte."

"Hey, that's right," Monte cried. "You two aren't fighting. That's great." He set his serving bowl of rice crisps on the table. "Does this mean…you're…you know?"

Lowering the paper, Ellen eyed him sardonically. "No, I don't know."

"Are you…seeing each other?" A deep flush darkened Monte's face.

"We see each other every day."

"That's not what I'm asking."

"But that's all I'm answering." From the corner of her eye, she caught sight of Pat pantomiming a fiddler, and she groaned inwardly. The boys were going to make it difficult to maintain any kind of romantic relationship with Reed. She cast him a speculative glance. But if Reed had noticed the activity around him, he wasn't letting on, and Ellen was grateful.

"I've got a practice game tonight," Pat told Ellen as he buttered a piece of toast. "Do you want to come?"

Flustered, she automatically sought out Reed. "Sorry... I'd like to come, but I've got a date."

"Bring him along."

"I...don't know if he likes basketball."

"Yeah, he does," Derek supplied. "Charlie and I were talking about it recently and he said it's one of his favorite games."

She didn't want to tell an outright lie. But she would save herself a lot of aggravation if she simply let Derek and the others assume it was Charlie she'd be seeing.

"What about you, Reed?" Derek asked.

His gaze didn't flicker from the paper and Ellen marveled at his ability to appear so dispassionate. "Not tonight. Thanks anyway."

"Have you got a date, too?" Derek pressed.

It seemed as though everyone in the kitchen was watching Reed, waiting for his response. "I generally go out on Friday nights."

"Well," Ellen said, coming to her feet. "I think I'll get moving. I want to take advantage of the holiday to do some errands. Does anybody need anything picked up at the cleaners?"

"I do," Monte said, raising his hand. "If you'll wait a minute, I'll get the slip."

"Sure."

By some miracle, Ellen was able to avoid any more questions for the remainder of the day. She went about her errands and didn't see Reed until late in the afternoon, when their paths happened to cross in the kitchen. He quickly whispered a time and meeting place and explained that he'd leave first. Ellen didn't have a chance to do more than agree before the boys were upon them.

At precisely seven, Ellen met Reed at the grocery store parking lot two blocks from the house. He'd left ten minutes earlier to wait for her there. As soon as he spotted her, he leaned across the cab of the pickup and opened the door on her side. Ellen found it slightly amusing that when he was with her he drove the pickup, and when he was with Danielle he took the sports car. She wondered whether or not this was a conscious decision. In any event, it told her quite a bit about the way Reed viewed the two women in his life.

"Did you get away unscathed?" he asked, chuckling softly.

She slid into the seat beside him in the cab and shook her head. "Not entirely. All three of them were curious about why Charlie wasn't coming to the house to pick me up. I didn't want to lie, so I told them they'd have to ask him."

"Will they?"

"I certainly hope not."

Reed's hand reached for hers and his eyes grew serious. "I'm not convinced that keeping this a secret is the right thing to do."

"I don't like it, either, but it's better than their constant teasing."

"I'll put a stop to that." His voice dropped ominously and Ellen didn't doubt that he'd quickly handle the situation.

"But, Reed, they don't mean any harm. I was hoping we

could lead them gradually into accepting us as a couple. Let them get used to seeing us together before we spring it on them that we're...dating."

"Ellen, I don't know."

"Trust me on this," she pleaded, her eyes imploring him. This arrangement, with its furtiveness and deception, was far from ideal, but for now it seemed necessary. She hoped the secrecy could end soon.

His kiss was brief and ardent. "I don't think I could deny you anything." But he didn't sound happy about it.

The restaurant he took her to was located in the south end of Seattle, thirty minutes from Capitol Hill. At first, Ellen was surprised that he'd chosen one so far from home but the food was fantastic and the view from the Des Moines Marina alone would have been worth the drive.

Reed ordered a bottle of an award-winning wine, a sauvignon blanc from a local winery. It was satisfyingly clear and crisp.

"I spoke to Danielle," Reed began.

"Reed." She stopped him, placing her hand over his. "What goes on between you and Danielle has nothing to do with me. We've made no promises and no commitments." In fact, of course, she was dying to know about the other woman Reed had dated for so long. She hoped that if she pretended no interest in his relationship with Danielle, she'd seem more mature and sophisticated than she really was. She didn't want Reid to think she was threatened by Danielle or that she expected anything from him. Hoped, yes. Expected, no.

He looked a little stunned. "But—"

Swiftly she lowered her gaze. "I don't want to know." Naturally, she was longing to hear every detail. As it was, she felt guilty about the other woman. Danielle might have had her faults, but she loved Reed. She must love him to be so patient with his traveling all these months. And when Derek had first mentioned her, he'd spoken as though Reed and Danielle's relationship was a permanent one.

Danielle and Ellen couldn't have been more different. Ellen was practical and down-to-earth. She'd had to be. After her father's death, she'd become the cornerstone that held the family together.

Danielle, on the other hand, had obviously been pampered and indulged all her life. Ellen guessed that she'd been destined from birth to be a wealthy socialite, someone who might, in time, turn to charitable works to occupy herself. They were obviously women with completely dissimilar backgrounds, she and Danielle.

"I'll be in Atlanta the latter part of next week," Reed was saying.

"You're full of good news, aren't you?"

"It's my work, Ellen."

"I wasn't complaining. It just seems that five minutes after you get home, you're off again."

"I won't be long this time. A couple of days. I'll fly in for the meeting and be back soon afterward."

"You'll be here for Christmas?" Her thoughts flew to her family and how much she wished they could meet Reed. Bud, especially. He'd be in Yakima over the holidays and Ellen was planning to take the bus home to spend some time with him. But first she had to get through her exams.

"I'll be here."

"Good." But it was too soon to ask Reed to join her for the trip. He might misinterpret her invitation, see something that wasn't there. She had no desire to pressure him into the sort of commitment that meeting her family might imply.

After their meal, they walked along the pier, holding

hands. The evening air was chilly and when Ellen shivered, Reed wrapped his arm around her shoulders.

"I enjoyed tonight," he murmured.

"I did, too." She bent her arm so that her fingers linked with his.

"Tomorrow night—"

"No." She stopped him, turning so that her arm slid around his middle. Tilting her head back, she stared into the troubled green eyes. "Let's not talk about tomorrow. For right now, let's take one day at a time."

His mouth met hers before she could finish speaking. A gentle brushing of lips. Then he deepened the kiss, and his arms tightened around her, and her whole body hummed with joy.

Ellen was lost, irretrievably lost, in the taste and scent of this man. She felt frightened by her response to him— it would be so easy to fall in love with Reed. *Completely* in love. But she couldn't allow that to happen. Not yet. It was too soon.

Her words about taking each day as it came were forcefully brought to Ellen's mind the following evening. She'd gone to the store and noticed Reed's Porsche parked in the driveway. When she returned, both Reed and the sports car had disappeared.

He was with Danielle.

Seven

"Why couldn't I see that?" Ellen moaned, looking over the algebraic equation Reed had worked out. "If I can fix a stopped-up sink, tune a car engine and manage a budget, why can't I understand something this simple?" She was quickly losing a grip on the more advanced theories they were now studying.

"Here, let me show it to you again."

Her hand lifted the curls off her forehead. "Do you think it'll do any good?"

"Yes, I do." Reed obviously had more faith in her powers of comprehension than she did. Step by step, he led her through another problem. When he explained the textbook examples, the whole process seemed so logical. Yet when she set out to solve a similar equation on her own, nothing went right.

"I give up." Throwing her hands over her head, she leaned back in the kitchen chair and groaned. "I should've realized that algebra would be too much for me. I had difficulty memorizing the multiplication tables, for heaven's sake."

"What you need is a break."

"I couldn't agree more. Twenty years?" She stood up and brought the cookie jar to the table. "Here, this will help ease the suffering." She offered him a chocolate-chip cookie and took one herself.

"Be more patient with yourself," Reed urged.

"There's only two weeks left in this term—and then exams. I need to understand this stuff and I need to understand it now."

He laid his hands on her shoulders, massaging gently. "No, you don't. Come on, I'm taking you to a movie."

"I've got to study," she protested, but not too strenuously. Escaping for an hour or two sounded infinitely more appealing than struggling with these impossible equations.

"There's a wonderful foreign film showing at the Moore Egyptian Theatre and we're going. We can worry about that assignment once we get back."

"But, Reed—"

"No buts. We're going." He took her firmly by the hand and led her into the front hall. Derek and Monte were watching TV and the staccato sounds of machine guns firing could be heard in the background. Neither boy noticed them until Reed opened the hall closet.

"Where are you two headed?" Derek asked, peering around the living-room door as Reed handed Ellen her jacket.

"A movie."

Instantly Derek muted the television. "The two of you alone? Together?"

"I imagine there'll be one or two others at the cinema," Reed responded dryly.

"Can I come?" Monte had joined Derek in the doorway. Instantly Derek's elbow shoved the other boy in the ribs.

"On second thought, just bring me back some popcorn, okay?"

"Sure."

Ellen pulled a knit cap over her ears. "Do either of you want anything else? I'd buy out the concession stand if one of you felt inclined to do my algebra assignment."

"No way."

"Bribing them won't help," Reed commented.

"I know, but I was hoping...."

It was a cold, blustery night. An icy north wind whipped against them as they hurried to Reed's truck. He opened the door for her before running around to the driver's side.

"Brr." Ellen shoved her hands inside her pockets. "If I doubted it was winter before, now I know."

"Come here and I'll warm you." He patted the seat beside him, indicating that she should slide closer.

Willingly she complied, until she sat so near him that her thigh pressed against his. Neither of them moved. It had been several days since they'd been completely alone together and longer still since he'd held or kissed her without interruption. The past week had been filled with frustration. Often she'd noticed Reed's gaze on her, studying her face and her movements, but it seemed that every time he touched her one of the boys would unexpectedly appear.

Reed turned to her. Their thoughts seemed to echo each other's; their eyes locked hungrily. Ellen required no invitation. She'd been longing for his touch. With a tiny cry she reached for him just as his arms came out to encircle her, drawing her even closer.

"This is crazy," he whispered fervently into her hair.

"I know."

As though he couldn't deny himself any longer, he cradled her face with both hands and he slowly lowered his mouth to hers.

Their lips clung and Reed's hand went around her ribs as he held her tight. The kiss was long and thoroughly satisfying.

Panting, he tore his mouth from hers and buried his face in her neck. "We'd better get to that movie."

It was all Ellen could do to nod her head in agreement.

They moved apart and fastened their seat belts, both of them silent.

When Reed started the truck, she saw that his hand was trembling. She was shaking too, but no longer from the cold. Reed had promised to warm her and he had, but not quite in the way she'd expected.

They were silent as Reed pulled onto the street. After days of carefully avoiding any kind of touch, any lingering glances, they'd sat in the driveway kissing in direct view of curious eyes. She realized the boys could easily have been watching them.

Ellen felt caught up in a tide that tossed her closer and closer to a long stretch of rocky beach. Powerless to alter the course of her emotions, she feared for her heart, afraid of being caught in the undertow.

"The engineering department is having a Christmas party this weekend at the Space Needle," Reed murmured.

Ellen nodded. Twice in the past week he'd left the house wearing formal evening clothes. He hadn't told her where he was going, but she knew. He'd driven the Porsche and he'd come back smelling of expensive perfume. For a Christmas party with his peers, Reed would escort Danielle. She understood that and tried to accept it.

"I want you to come with me."

"Reed," she breathed, uncertain. "Are you sure?"

"Yes." His hand reached for hers. "I want you with me."

"The boys—"

"Forget the boys. I'm tired of playing games with them."

Her smile came from her heart. "I am, too," she whispered.

"I'm going to have a talk with them."

"Don't," she pleaded. "It's not necessary to say anything."

"They'll start in with their teasing," he warned. "I thought you hated that."

"I don't care as much anymore. And if they do, we can say something then."

He frowned briefly. "All right."

The Moore Egyptian was located in the heart of downtown Seattle, so parking was limited. They finally found a spot on the street three blocks away. They left the truck and hurried through the cold, arm in arm, not talking. The French film was a popular one; by the time they got to the cinema, a long line had already formed outside.

A blast of wind sliced through Ellen's jacket and she buried her hands in her pockets. Reed leaned close to ask her something, then paused, slowly straightening.

"Morgan." A tall, brusque-looking man approached Reed.

"Dailey," Reed said, quickly stepping away from Ellen.

"I wouldn't have expected to see you out on a night like this," the man Reed had called Dailey was saying.

"I'm surprised to see you, too."

"This film is supposed to be good," Dailey said.

"Yeah. It's got great reviews."

Dailey's eyes returned to the line and rested on Ellen, seeking an introduction. Reed didn't give him one. Reed was obviously pretending he wasn't with Ellen.

She offered the man a feeble smile, wondering why Reed

would move away from her, why he wouldn't introduce her to his acquaintance. The line moved slowly toward the ticket booth and Ellen went with it, leaving Reed talking to Dailey on the pavement. She felt a flare of resentment when he rejoined her a few minutes later.

"That was a friend of a friend."

Ellen didn't respond. Somehow she didn't believe him. And she resented the fact that he'd ignored the most basic of courtesies and left her standing on the sidewalk alone, while he spoke with a friend. The way he'd acted, anyone would assume Reed didn't want the man to know Ellen was with him. That hurt. Fifteen minutes earlier she'd been soaring with happiness at his unexpected invitation to the Christmas party, and now she was consumed with doubt and bitterness. Perhaps this Dailey was a friend of Danielle's and Reed didn't want the other woman to know he was out with Ellen. But that didn't really sound like Reed.

Once inside the cinema, Reed bought a huge bucket of buttered popcorn. They located good seats, despite the crowd, and sat down, neither of them speaking. As the lights went down, Reed placed his hand on the back of her neck.

Ellen stiffened. "Are you sure you want to do that?"

"What?"

"Touch me. Someone you know might recognize you."

"Ellen, listen…"

The credits started to roll on the huge screen and she shook her head, not wanting to hear any of his excuses.

But maintaining her bad mood was impossible with the comedy that played out before them. Unable to stop herself, Ellen laughed until tears formed in her eyes; she was clutching her stomach because it hurt from laughing. Reed seemed just as amused as she was, and a couple of times during the film, their smiling gazes met. Before she knew it, Reed was holding her hand and she didn't resist when he draped his arm over her shoulders.

Afterward, as they strolled outside, he tucked her hand in the crook of his elbow. "I told you a movie would make you feel better."

It had and it hadn't. Yes, she'd needed the break, but Reed's behavior outside the cinema earlier had revived the insecurities she was trying so hard to suppress. She knew she wasn't nearly as beautiful or sophisticated as Danielle.

"You *do* feel better?" His finger lifted her chin to study her eyes.

There was no denying that the film had been wonderful. "I haven't laughed so hard in ages," she told him, smiling.

"Good."

Friday night, Ellen wore her most elaborate outfit— slim black velvet pants and a silver lamé top. She'd spent hours debating whether an evening gown would have been more appropriate, but had finally decided on the pants. Examining herself from every direction in the full-length mirror that hung from her closet door, Ellen released a pent-up breath and closed her eyes. This one night, she wanted everything to be perfect. Her heels felt a little uncomfortable, but she'd get used to them. She rarely had any reason to wear heels. She'd chosen them now because Reed had said there'd be dancing and she wanted to adjust her height to his.

By the time she reached the foot of the stairs, Reed was waiting for her. His eyes softened as he looked at her. "You're lovely."

"Oh, Reed, are you sure? I don't mind changing if you'd rather I wear something else."

His eyes held hers for a long moment. "I don't want you to change a thing."

"Hey, Ellen." Derek burst out of the kitchen, and stopped abruptly. "Wow." For an instant he looked as though he'd lost his breath. "Hey, guys," he called eagerly. "Come and see Ellen."

The other two joined Derek. "You look like a movie star," Pat breathed.

Monte closed his mouth and opened it again. "You're *pretty.*"

"Don't sound so shocked."

"It's just that we've never seen you dressed…like this," Pat mumbled.

"Are you going out with Charlie?"

Ellen glanced at Reed, suddenly unsure. She hadn't dated Charlie in weeks. She hadn't wanted to.

"She's going out with me," Reed explained in an even voice that didn't invite comment.

"With you? Where?" Derek's eyes got that mischievous twinkle Ellen recognized immediately.

"A party."

"What about—" He stopped suddenly, swallowing several times.

"You had a comment?" Reed lifted his eyebrows.

"I thought I was going to say something," Derek muttered, clearly embarrassed, "but then I realized I wasn't."

Hiding a smile, Reed held Ellen's coat for her.

She slipped her arms into the satin-lined sleeves and reached for her beaded bag. "Good night, guys, and don't wait up."

"Right." Monte raised his index finger. "We won't wait up."

Derek took a step forward. "Should I say anything to someone…anyone…in case either of you gets a phone call?"

"Try *hello,*" Reed answered, shaking his head.

"Right." Derek stuck his hand in his jeans pocket. "Have a good time."

"We intend to."

Ellen managed to hold back her laughter until they were on the front porch. But when the door clicked shut the giggles escaped and she pressed a hand to her mouth. "Derek *thought* he was going to say something."

"Then he realized he wasn't," Reed finished for her, chuckling. His hand at her elbow guided her down the steps. "They're right about one thing. You do look gorgeous."

"Thank you, but I hadn't expected it to be such a shock."

"The problem is, the boys are used to seeing you as a substitute mother. It's suddenly dawned on them what an attractive woman you are."

"And how was it *you* noticed?"

"The day I arrived and found you in my kitchen wearing only a bra, I knew."

"I was wearing more than that," she argued.

"Maybe, but at the time that was all I saw." He stroked her cheek with the tip of his finger, then tucked her arm in his.

Ellen felt a warm contentment as Reed led her to the sports car. This was the first time she'd been inside, and the significance of that seemed unmistakable. She sensed that somewhere in the past two weeks Reed had made an unconscious decision about their relationship. Maybe she was being silly in judging the strength of their bond by what car he chose to drive. And maybe not. Reed was escorting her to this party in his Porsche because he viewed her in a new light. He saw her now as a beautiful, alluring woman—no longer as the college student who seemed capable of mastering everything but algebra.

The Space Needle came into view as Reed pulled onto

Denny Street. The world-famous Needle, which had been built for the 1962 World's Fair, rose 605 feet above the Seattle skyline. Ellen had taken the trip up to the observation deck only once and she'd been thrilled at the unobstructed view of the Olympic and Cascade mountain ranges. Looking out at the unspoiled beauty of Puget Sound, she'd understood immediately why Seattle was described as one of the world's most livable cities.

For this evening, Reed explained, his office had booked the convention rooms on the hundred-foot level of the Needle. The banquet facilities had been an addition, and Ellen wondered what sort of view would be available.

As Reed stopped in front of the Needle, a valet appeared, opening Ellen's door and offering her his gloved hand. She climbed as gracefully as she could from the low-built vehicle. Her smile felt a little strained, and she took a deep breath to dispel the gathering tension. She wanted everything about the evening to be perfect; she longed for Reed to be proud of her, to feel that she belonged in his life— and in his world.

Her curiosity about the view was answered as soon as they stepped from the elevator into the large room. She glanced at the darkened sky that resembled folds of black velvet, sprinkled with glittering gems. When she had a chance she'd walk over toward the windows. For now, she was more concerned with fitting into Reed's circle and being accepted by his friends and colleagues.

Bracing herself for the inevitable round of introductions, she scanned the crowd for the man she'd seen outside the cinema. He didn't seem to be at the party and Ellen breathed easier. If Dailey was there, he would surely make a comment about seeing her with Reed that night, and she wouldn't know how to respond.

As they made their way through the large room, several people called out to Reed. When he introduced Ellen, two or three of them appeared to have trouble concealing their surprise that he wasn't with Danielle. But no one mentioned Danielle and they all seemed to accept Ellen freely, although a couple of people gave her curious looks. Eventually, Ellen relaxed and smiled up at Reed.

"That wasn't so bad, was it?" he asked, his voice tender.

"Not at all."

"Would you like something to drink?"

"Please."

"Wine okay?"

"Of course."

"I'll be right back."

Ellen watched Reed cross the room toward the bar. She was absurdly proud of him and made no attempt to disguise her feelings when he returned to her, carrying two glasses of white wine.

"You shouldn't look at me like that," he murmured, handing her a glass.

"Why?" she teased, her eyes sparkling. "Does it embarrass you?"

"No. It makes me wish I could ignore everyone in this room and kiss you right this minute." A slow, almost boyish grin spread across his features.

"That would certainly cause quite a commotion."

"But not half the commotion it would cause if they knew what else I was thinking."

"Oh?" She hid a smile by taking another sip of wine.

"Are we back to that word again?"

"Just what do you have in mind?"

He dipped his head so that he appeared to be whispering something in her ear, although actually his lips brushed her face. "I'll show you later."

"I'll be waiting."

They stood together, listening to the music and the laughter. Ellen found it curious that he'd introduced her to so few people and then only to those who'd approached him. But she dismissed her qualms as petty and, worse, paranoid. After all, she told herself, she was here to be with Reed, not to make small talk with his friends.

He finished his drink and suggested another. While he returned to the bar for refills, Ellen wandered through the crowd, walking over to the windows for a glimpse of the magnificent view. But as she moved, she kept her gaze trained on Reed.

A group of men stopped him before he could reach the bar. His head was inclined toward them, and he seemed to be giving them his rapt attention. Yet periodically his eyes would flicker through the crowd, searching for her. When he located her by the huge floor-to-ceiling windows, he smiled as though he felt relieved. With an abruptness that bordered on rudeness, he excused himself from the group and strolled in her direction.

"I didn't see where you'd gone."

"I wasn't about to leave you," she told him. Turning, she faced the window, watching the lights of the ferry boats gliding across the dark green waters of Puget Sound.

His hands rested on her shoulders and Ellen leaned back against him, warmed by his nearness. "It's lovely from up here."

"Exquisite," he agreed, his mouth close to her ear. "But I'm not talking about the view." His hands slid lazily down her arms. "Dance with me," he said, taking her hand and leading her to the dance floor.

Ellen walked obediently into his arms, loving the feel of being close to Reed. She pressed her cheek against the smooth fabric of his jacket as they swayed gently to the slow, dreamy music.

"I don't normally do a lot of dancing," he whispered.

Ellen wouldn't have guessed that. He moved with confident grace, and she assumed he'd escorted Danielle around a dance floor more than once. At the thought of the other woman, Ellen grew uneasy, but she forced her tense body to relax. Reed had chosen to bring *her,* and not Danielle, to this party. That had to mean something—something exciting.

"Dancing was just an excuse to hold you."

"You don't need an excuse," she whispered.

"In a room full of people, I do."

"Shall we wish them away?" She closed her eyes, savoring the feel of his hard, lithe body against her own.

He maneuvered them into the darkest corner of the dance floor and immediately claimed her mouth in a kiss that sent her world spinning into orbit.

Mindless of where they were, Ellen arched upward, Reed responded by sliding his hands down her back, down to her hips, drawing her even closer.

He dragged his mouth across her cheek. "I'm sorry we came."

"Why?"

"I don't want to waste time with all these people around. We're hardly ever alone. I want you, Ellen."

His honest, straightforward statement sent the fire roaring through her veins. "I know. I want you, too." Her voice was unsteady. "But it's a good thing we aren't alone very often." At the rate things were progressing between them, Ellen felt relieved that the boys were at the house. Otherwise—

"Hey, Reed." A friendly voice boomed out a few feet away. "Aren't you going to introduce me to your friend?"

Reed stiffened and for a moment Ellen wondered if he was going to pretend he hadn't heard. He looked at her through half-closed eyes, and she grinned up at him, mutely telling him she didn't mind. Their private world couldn't last forever. She knew that. They were at a party, an office party, and Reed was expected to mingle with his colleagues.

"Hello, Ralph." Reed's arm slid around Ellen's waist, keeping her close.

"Hello there." But Ralph wasn't watching Reed. "Well, aren't you going to introduce me?"

"Ellen Cunningham, Ralph Forester."

Ralph extended his hand and held Ellen's in both of his for a long moment. His eyes were frankly admiring.

"I don't suppose you'd let me steal this beauty away for a dance, would you?" Although the question was directed at Reed, Ralph didn't take his eyes from Ellen. "Leave it to you to be with the most beautiful woman here," the other man teased. "You sure do attract them."

Reed's hand tightened around Ellen. "Ellen?" He left the choice to her.

"I don't mind." She glanced at Reed and noted that his expression was carefully blank. But she knew him too well to be fooled. She could see that his jaw was rigid with tension and that his eyes showed annoyance at the other man's intrusion. Gradually he lowered his arm, releasing her.

Ralph stepped forward and claimed Ellen's hand, leading her onto the dance floor.

She swallowed as she placed her left hand on his shoulder and her right hand in his. Wordlessly they moved to the soft music. But when Ralph tried to bring her closer, Ellen resisted.

"Have you known Reed long?" Ralph asked, his hand trailing sensuously up and down her back.

She tensed. "Several months now." Despite her efforts to keep her voice even and controlled, she sounded slightly breathless.

"How'd you meet?"

"Through his brother." The less said about their living arrangements, the better. Ellen could just guess what Ralph would say if he knew they were living in the same house. "Do you two work together?"

"For the last six years."

They whirled around, and Ellen caught a glimpse of Reed standing against the opposite wall, studying them like a hawk zeroing in on its prey. Ralph apparently noticed him, as well.

"I don't think Reed was all that anxious to have you dance with me."

Ellen merely shrugged.

Ralph chortled gleefully, obviously enjoying Reed's reaction. "Not if the looks he's giving me are any indication. I can't believe it. Reed Morgan is jealous," he said with another chuckle, leading her out of Reed's sight and into the dimly lit center of the floor.

"I'm sure you're mistaken."

"Well, look at him."

All Ellen could see was Reed peering suspiciously at them across the crowded dance floor.

"This is too good to be true," Ralph murmured.

"What do you mean?"

"There isn't a woman in our department who wouldn't give her eyeteeth to go out with Reed."

Ellen was shocked, yet somehow unsurprised. "Oh?"

"Half the women are in love with him and he ignores

them. He's friendly, don't get me wrong. But it's all business. Every time a single woman gets transferred into our area it takes her a week, maybe two, to fall for Reed. The rest of us guys just stand back and shake our heads. But with Reed otherwise occupied, we might have a chance."

"He *is* wonderful," Ellen admitted, managing to keep a courteous smile on her face. What Ralph was describing sounded so much like her own feelings that she couldn't doubt the truth of what he said.

Ralph arched his brows and studied her. "You too?"

"I'm afraid so."

"What's this guy got?" He sighed expressively, shaking his head. "Can we bottle it?"

"Unfortunately, I don't think so," Ellen responded lightly, liking Ralph more. His approach might have been a bit overpowering at first, but he was honest and compelling in his own right. "I don't imagine you have much trouble attracting women."

"As long as I don't bring them around Reed, I'm fine." A smile swept his face. "The best thing that could happen would be if he got married. I don't suppose that's in the offing between you two?"

He was so blithely serious that Ellen laughed. "Sorry."

"You're sure?"

Ralph was probably thinking of some rumor he'd heard about Danielle. "There's another woman he's seeing. They've known each other for a long time and apparently, they're quite serious," she explained, keeping her voice calmly detached.

"I don't believe it," Ralph countered, frowning. "Reed wouldn't be tossing daggers at my back if he was involved with someone else. One thing I suspect about this guy, he's a one-woman man."

Ellen closed her eyes, trying to shut out the pain. She didn't know what to believe about Reed anymore. All she could do was hold on to the moment. Wasn't that what she'd told him earlier—that they'd have to take things day by day? She was the one who hadn't wanted to talk about Danielle. In any case, she didn't want to read too much into his actions. She couldn't. She was on the brink of falling in love with him...if she hadn't already. To allow herself to think he might feel the same way was asking for trouble. For heartbreak.

The music ended and Ralph gently let her go. "I'd better return you to Reed or he's likely to come after me."

"Thank you for...everything."

"You're welcome, Ellen." With one hand at her waist, he steered her toward Reed.

They were within a few feet of him when Danielle suddenly appeared. She seemed to have come out of nowhere. "Reed!" She was laughing delightedly, flinging herself into his arms and kissing him intimately. "Oh, darling, you're so right. Being together is more important than any ski trip. I'm so sorry. Will you forgive me?"

Eight

"Ellen," Ralph asked. "Are you all right?"

"I'm fine," she lied.

"Sure you are," he mocked, sliding his arm around her waist and guiding her back to the dance floor. "I take it the blonde is Woman Number One?"

"You got it." The anger was beginning to build inside her. "Beautiful, too, you'll notice."

"Well, you aren't exactly chopped liver."

She gave a small, mirthless laugh. "Nice of you to say so, but by comparison, I come in a poor second."

"I wouldn't say that."

"Then why can't you take your eyes off Danielle?"

"Danielle. Hmm." He looked away from the other woman and stared blankly into Ellen's face. "Sorry." For her part, Ellen instinctively turned her back on Reed, unable to bear the sight of him holding and kissing another woman.

"Someone must have got their wires crossed."

"Like me," Ellen muttered. She'd been an idiot to assume that Reed had meant anything by his invitation. He'd just needed someone to take to this party, and his first choice hadn't been available. She was a substitute, and a second-rate one at that.

"What do you want to do?"

Ellen frowned, her thoughts fragmented. "I don't know yet. Give me a minute to think."

"You two could always fight for him."

"The stronger woman takes the spoils? No, thanks." Despite herself she laughed. It certainly would've created a diversion at this formal, rather staid party.

Craning his neck, Ralph peered over at the other couple. "Reed doesn't seem too pleased to see her."

"I can imagine. The situation's put him in a bit of a bind."

"I admit it's unpleasant for you, but, otherwise, I'm enjoying this immensely."

Who wouldn't? The scene was just short of comical. "I thought you said Reed was a one-woman man."

"I guess I stand corrected."

Ellen was making a few corrections herself, revising some cherished ideas about Reed Morgan.

"I don't suppose you'd consider staying with me for the rest of the evening?" Ralph suggested hopefully.

"Consider it? I'd say it's the best offer I've had in weeks." She might feel like a fool, but she didn't plan to hang around looking like one.

Ralph nudged her and bent his head to whisper in her ear. "Reed's staring at us. And like I said, he doesn't seem pleased."

With a determination born of anger and pride, she forced a smile to her lips and gazed adoringly up at Ralph. "How am I doing?" she asked, batting her lashes at him.

"Wonderful, wonderful." He swung her energetically around to the beat of the music. "Uh-oh, here he comes."

Reed weaved his way through the dancing couples and tapped Ralph on the shoulder. "I'm cutting in."

Ellen tightened her grip on Reed's colleague, silently pleading with him to stay. "Sorry, buddy, but Ellen's with me now that your lady friend has arrived."

"Ellen?" Reed's eyes narrowed as he stared at her intently. The other couples were dancing around them and curiously watching the party of three that had formed in the center of the room.

She couldn't remember ever seeing anyone look more furious than Reed did at this moment. "Maybe I'd better leave," she said in a low, faltering voice.

"I'll take you home," Ralph offered, dropping his hand to her waist.

"You came with me. You'll leave with me." Reed grasped her hand, pulling her toward him.

"Obviously you were making provisions," Ellen said, "on the off-chance Danielle showed up. How else did she get in here?"

"How am I supposed to know? She probably told the manager she was with me."

"And apparently she is," Ellen hissed.

"Maybe Reed and I should wrestle to decide the winner," Ralph suggested, glancing at Ellen and sharing a comical grin.

"Maybe."

Obviously, Reed saw no humor in the situation. Anger darkened his handsome face, and a muscle twitched in his jaw as the tight rein on his patience slipped.

Ralph withdrew his hand. "Go ahead and dance. It's obvious you two have a lot to talk about."

Reed took Ellen in his arms. "I suppose you're furious," he muttered.

"Have I got anything to be angry about?" she asked calmly. Now that the initial shock had worn off, she felt somewhat distanced from the whole predicament.

"Of course you do. But I want a chance to explain."

"Don't bother. I've got the picture."

"I'm sure you don't."

Ellen stubbornly refused to look up at him, resisting for as long as she could, but eventually she gave in. "It doesn't matter. Ralph said he'd take me home and—"

"I've already made my feelings on that subject quite clear."

"Listen, Reed. Your Porsche seats two. Is Danielle supposed to sit on my lap?"

"She came uninvited. Let her find her own way home."

"You don't mean that."

"I certainly do."

"You can't humiliate Danielle like that." Ellen didn't mention how *she* felt. What was the point? "Don't—"

"She deserves it," he broke in.

"Reed, no." Her hold on his forearm tightened. "This is unpleasant enough for all of us. Don't compound it."

The song ended and the music faded from the room. Reed fastened his hand on Ellen's elbow, guiding her across the floor to where Danielle was standing with Ralph. The two of them were sipping champagne.

"Hello again," Ellen began amicably, doing her utmost to appear friendly, trying to smooth over an already awkward situation.

"Hello." Danielle stared at Ellen curiously, apparently not recognizing her.

"You remember Ellen Cunningham, don't you?" Reed said.

"Not that college girl your brother's renting a room to—"

Danielle stopped abruptly, shock etched on her perfect features. "*You're* Ellen Cunningham?"

"In the flesh." Still trying to keep things light, she cocked her head toward Ralph and spoke stagily out of the side of her mouth, turning the remark into a farcical aside. "I wasn't at my best when we met the first time."

"You were fiddling around with that electrical outlet and Reed was horrified," Danielle inserted, her voice completely humorless, her eyes narrowed assessingly. "You didn't even look like a girl."

"She does now." Ralph beamed her a brilliant smile.

"Yes." Danielle swallowed, her face puckered with concern. "She looks very…nice."

"Thank you." Ellen bowed her head.

"I've made a terrible mess of things," Danielle continued, casually handing her half-empty glass to a passing waiter. "Reed mentioned the party weeks ago, and Mom and I had this ski party planned. I told him I couldn't attend and then I felt guilty because Reed's been so sweet, escorting me to all the charity balls."

Ellen didn't hear a word of explanation beyond the fact that Reed had originally asked Danielle to the party. The other woman had just confirmed Ellen's suspicions, and the hurt went through her like a thousand needles. He'd invited her only because Danielle couldn't attend.

"There's no problem," Ellen said in a bland voice. "I understand how these things happen. He asked you first, so you stay and I'll leave."

"I couldn't do that," Danielle murmured.

Reed's eyes were saying the same thing. Ellen ignored him, and she ignored Danielle. Slipping her hand around Ralph's arm, she looked up at him and smiled, silently thanking him for being her friend. "As I said, it's not a problem. Ralph's already offered to take me home."

Reed's expression was impassive, almost aloof, as she turned toward him. "I'm sure you won't mind."

"How understanding of you," Danielle simpered, locking her arm around Reed's.

"It's better than hand-to-hand combat. I don't really care for fighting."

Danielle looked puzzled, while Ralph choked on a swallow of his drink, his face turning several shades of red as he struggled to hide his amusement. The only one who revealed no sense of humor was Reed, whose face grew more and more shadowed.

The band struck up a lively song and the dance floor quickly filled. "Come on, Reed," Danielle said, her blue eyes eager. "Let's dance." She tugged at Reed's hand and gave a little wriggle of her hips. "You know how much I love to dance."

So Reed *had* done his share of dancing with Danielle—probably at all those charity balls she'd mentioned. Ellen had guessed as much and yet he'd tried to give her the impression that he rarely danced.

But noticing the stiff way Reed held himself now, Ellen could almost believe him.

Ralph placed a gentle hand on her shoulder. "I don't know about you, but I'm ready to get out of here."

Watching Reed with Danielle in his arms was absurdly painful; her throat muscles constricted in an effort to hold back tears and she simply nodded.

"Since we'll be skipping the banquet, shall we go have dinner somewhere?"

Ellen blinked. Dinner. "I'm not really hungry," she said.

"Sure you're hungry," Ralph insisted. "We'll stop at a

nice restaurant before I drive you home. I know where Reed's place is, so I know where you live. Don't look so shocked. I figured it out from what you and Danielle were saying. But don't worry, I understand—impoverished students sharing a house and all that. So, what do you say? We'll have a leisurely dinner and get home two hours after Reed. That should set him thinking."

Ellen didn't feel in any mood to play games at Reed's expense. "I'd rather not."

Ralph's jovial expression sobered. "You've got it bad."

"I'll be fine."

He smiled. "I know you will. Come on, let's go."

The night that had begun with such promise had evaporated so quickly, leaving a residue of uncertainty and suspicion. As they neared the house, her composure gradually crumbled until she was nervously twisting the delicate strap of her evening bag over and over between her fingers. To his credit, Ralph attempted to carry the conversation, but her responses became less and less animated. She just wanted to get home and bury her head in her pillow.

By the time Ralph pulled up in front of the Capitol Hill house, they were both silent.

"Would you like to come in for coffee?" she asked. The illusion she'd created earlier of flippant humor was gone now. She hurt, and every time she blinked, a picture of Danielle dancing with Reed came to mind. How easy it was to visualize the other woman's arms around his neck, her voluptuous body pressed against his. The image tormented Ellen with every breath she took.

"No, I think I'll make it an early night."

"Thank you," she said affectionately. "I couldn't have handled this without you."

"I was happy to help. And, Ellen, if you want a shoulder to cry on, I'm available."

She dropped her gaze to the tightly coiled strap of her bag. "I'm fine. Really."

He patted her hand. "Somehow I don't quite believe that." Opening the car door, he came around to her side and handed her out.

On the top step of the porch, Ellen kissed his cheek. "Thanks again."

"Good night, Ellen."

"Night." She took out her keys and unlocked the front door. Pushing it open, she discovered that the house was oddly dark and oddly deserted. It was still relatively early and she would've expected the boys to be around. But not having to make excuses to them was a blessing she wasn't about to question.

As she removed her coat and headed for the stairs, she noticed the shadows bouncing around the darkened living room. She walked over to investigate and, two steps into the room, heard soft violin music.

Ellen stood there paralyzed, taking in the romantic scene before her. A bottle of wine and two glasses were set out on the coffee table. A fire blazed in the brick fireplace. And the music seemed to assault her from all sides.

"Derek," she called out.

Silence.

"All right, Pat and Monte. I know you're here somewhere."

Silence.

"I'd suggest the three of you get rid of this...stuff before Reed comes home. He's with Danielle." With that, she marched up the stairs, uncaring if they heard her.

"With Danielle?" she heard a male voice shout after her.

"What happened?"

Ellen pretended not to hear.

The morning sun sneaked into her window, splashing the pillow where Ellen lay awake staring sightlessly at the ceiling. Sooner or later she'd have to get out of bed, but she couldn't see any reason to rush the process. Besides, the longer she stayed up here, the greater her chances of missing Reed. The unpleasantness of facing him wasn't going to vanish, but she might be able to postpone it for a morning. Although she had to wonder whether Reed was any more keen on seeing her than she was on seeing him. She could always kill time by dragging out her algebra books and studying for the exam—but that was almost as distasteful as facing Reed.

No, she decided suddenly, she'd stay in her room until she was weak with hunger. Checking her wristwatch, she figured that would be about another five minutes.

Someone knocked on her bedroom door. Sitting up, Ellen pulled the sheet to her neck. "Who is it?" she shouted, not particularly eager to talk to anyone.

Reed threw open the door and stalked inside. He stood in the middle of the room with his hands on his hips. "Are you planning to stay up here for the rest of your life?"

"The idea has distinct possibilities." She glared back at him, her eyes flashing with outrage and ill humor. "By the way, you'll note that I asked who was at the door. I didn't say, 'come in.'" Her voice rose to a mockingly high pitch. "You might have walked in on me when I was dressing."

A smile crossed his mouth. "Is that an invitation?"

"Absolutely not." She rose to a kneeling position, taking the sheets and blankets with her, and pointed a finger in the direction of the door. "Would you kindly leave? I'd like to get dressed."

"Don't let me stop you."

"Reed, please," she said irritably. "I'm not in any mood to talk to you."

"I'm not leaving until we do."

"Unfair. I haven't had my cup of tea and my mouth feels like the bottom of Puget Sound."

"All right," he agreed reluctantly. "I'll give you ten minutes."

"How generous of you."

"Considering my frame of mind since you walked out on me last night, I consider it pretty generous."

"Walked out on you!" She flew off the bed. "That's a bit much!"

"Ten minutes," he repeated, his voice low.

The whole time Ellen was dressing, she fumed. Reed had some nerve accusing her of walking out on him. He obviously didn't have any idea what it had cost her to leave him at that party with Danielle. He was thinking only of his own feelings, showing no regard for hers. He hadn't even acknowledged that she'd swallowed her pride to save them all from an extremely embarrassing situation.

Four male faces met hers when she appeared in the kitchen. "Good morning," she said with false enthusiasm.

The three boys looked sheepishly away. "Morning," they droned. Each found something at the table to occupy his hands. Pat, who was holding his basketball, carefully examined its grooves. Monte read the back of the cereal box and Derek folded the front page of the paper, pretending to read it.

"Ellen and I would like a few minutes of privacy," Reed announced, frowning at the three boys.

Derek, Monte and Pat stood up simultaneously.

"I don't think there's anything we have to say that the boys can't hear," she said.

The three boys reclaimed their chairs, looking with interest first at Reed and then at Ellen.

Reed's scowl deepened. "Can't you see that Ellen and I need to talk?"

"There's nothing to discuss," Ellen insisted, pouring boiling water into her mug and dipping a tea bag in the water.

"Yes, there is," Reed countered.

"Maybe it would be best if we did leave," Derek hedged, noticeably uneasy with his brother's anger and Ellen's feigned composure.

"You walk out of this room and there will be no packed lunches next week," Ellen said, leaning against the counter. She threw out the bag and began sipping her tea.

"I'm staying." Monte crossed his arms over his chest as though preparing for a long standoff.

Ellen knew she could count on Monte; his stomach would always take precedence. Childishly, she flashed Reed a saucy grin. He wasn't going to bulldoze her into any confrontation.

"Either you're out of here *now*, or you won't have a place to *live* next week," Reed flared back. At Derek's smug expression, Reed added, "And that includes you, little brother."

The boys exchanged shocked glances. "Sorry, Ellen," Derek mumbled on his way out of the kitchen. "I told Michelle I'd be over in a few minutes anyway." Without another moment's hesitation, Reed's brother was out the door.

"Well?" Reed stared at Monte and Pat.

"Yeah, well... I guess I should probably..." Pat looked to Ellen for guidance, his resolve wavering.

"Go ahead." She dismissed them both with a wave of her hand.

"Are you sure you want us to go?" Monte asked anxiously.

Ellen smiled her appreciation at this small display of mettle. "Thanks, but I'll be okay."

The sound of the door swinging back and forth echoed through the kitchen. Ellen drew a deep, calming breath and turned to Reed, who didn't look all that pleased to have her alone, although he'd gone to some lengths to arrange it. His face was pinched, and fine lines fanned out from his eyes and mouth. Either he'd had a late night or he hadn't slept at all. Ellen decided it must have been the former.

"Well, I'm here within ten minutes, just as you decreed. If you've got something to say, then say it."

"Don't rush me," he snapped.

Ellen released an exaggerated sigh. "First you want to talk to me—and then you're not sure. This sounds like someone who asked me to a party once. First he wanted me with him—and then he didn't."

"I wanted you there last night."

"Oh, was I talking about you?" she asked in fake innocence.

"You're not making this easy." He ploughed his fingers through his hair, the abrupt movement at odds with the self-control he usually exhibited.

"Listen," she breathed, casting her eyes down. "You don't need to explain anything. I have a fairly accurate picture of what happened."

"I doubt that." But he didn't elaborate.

"I can understand why you'd prefer Danielle's company."

"I didn't. That had to be one of the most awkward moments of my life. I wanted you—not Danielle."

Sure, she mused sarcastically. That was why he'd introduced her to so few people. She'd had plenty of time in the past twelve hours to think. If she hadn't been so blinded by the stars in her eyes, she would have figured it out sooner. Reed had taken her to his company party and kept her shielded from the other guests; he hadn't wanted her talking to his friends and colleagues. At the time, she'd assumed he wanted her all to himself. Now she understood the reason. The others knew he'd invited Danielle; they knew that Danielle usually accompanied him to these functions. The other woman had an official status in Reed's life. Ellen didn't.

"It wasn't your fault," she told him. "Unfortunately, under the circumstances, this was unavoidable."

"I'd rather Danielle had left instead of you." He walked to her side, deliberately taking the mug of tea from her hand and setting it on the counter. Slowly his arms came around her.

Ellen lacked the will to resist. She closed her eyes as her arms reached around him, almost of their own accord. He felt so warm and vital.

"I want us to spend the day together."

Her earlier intention of studying for her algebra exam went out the window. Despite all her hesitations, all her doubts and fears, she couldn't refuse this chance to be with him. Alone, the two of them. "All right," she answered softly.

"Ellen." His breath stirred her hair. "There's something you should know."

"Hmm?"

"I'm flying out tomorrow morning for two days."

Her eyes flew open. "How long?"

"Two days, but after that, I won't be leaving again until the Christmas holidays are over."

She nodded. Traveling was part of his job, and any woman

in his life would have to accept that. She was touched that he felt so concerned for her. "That's fine," she whispered. "I understand."

Ellen couldn't fault Reed's behavior for the remainder of the weekend. Saturday afternoon, they went Christmas shopping at the Tacoma Mall. His choice of shopping area surprised her, since there were several in the immediate area, much closer than Tacoma, which was a forty-five-minute drive away. But they had a good time, wandering from store to store. Before she knew it, Christmas would be upon them and this was the first opportunity she'd had to do any real shopping. With Reed's help, she picked out gifts for the boys and her brother.

"You'll like Bud," she told him, licking a chocolate ice-cream cone. They found a place to sit, with their packages gathered around them, and took a fifteen-minute break.

"I imagine I will." A flash of amusement lit his eyes, then he abruptly looked away.

Ellen lowered her ice-cream cone. "What's so funny? Have I got chocolate on my nose?"

"No."

"What, then?"

"You must have forgiven me for what happened at the party."

"What do you mean?"

"The way you looked into the future and said I'd like your brother, as though you and I are going to have a long relationship."

The ice cream suddenly became very important and Ellen licked away at it with an all-consuming energy. "I told you before that I feel things have to be one day at a time with us. There are too many variables in our...relationship." She waved the ice cream in his direction. "And I use that term loosely."

"There *is* a future for us."

"You seem sure of yourself."

"I'm more sure of you." He said it so smoothly that Ellen wondered if she heard him right. She would have challenged his arrogant assumption, but just then, he glanced at his wristwatch and suggested a movie.

By the time they returned to the house it was close to midnight. He kissed her with a tenderness that somehow reminded her of an early-summer dawn, but his touch was as potent as a sultry August afternoon.

"Ellen?" he murmured into her hair.

"Hmm?"

"I think you'd better go upstairs now."

The warmth of his touch had melted away the last traces of icy reserve. She didn't want to leave him. "Why?"

His hands gripped her shoulders, pushing her away from him, putting an arm's length between them. "Because if you don't leave now, I may climb those stairs with you."

At his straightforward, honest statement, Ellen swallowed hard. "I enjoyed today. Thank you, Reed." He dropped his arms and she placed a trembling hand on the railing. "Have a safe trip."

"I will." He took a step toward her. "I wish I didn't have to go." His hand cupped her chin and he drew her face toward his, kissing her with a hunger that shook Ellen to the core. She needed all her strength not to throw her arms around him again.

Monday afternoon, when Ellen walked into the house after her classes, the three boys were waiting for her. They looked up at her with peculiar expressions on their faces, as though they'd never seen her before and they couldn't understand how she'd wandered into their kitchen.

"All right, what's up?"

"Up?" Derek asked.

"You've got that guilty look."

"*We're* not the guilty party," Pat said.

She sighed. "You'd better let me know what's going on so I can deal with it before Reed gets back."

Monte swung open the kitchen door so that the dining-room table came into view. In the center of the table stood the largest bouquet of red roses Ellen had ever seen.

A shocked gasp slid from the back of her throat. "Who... who sent those?"

"We thought you'd ask so we took the liberty of reading the card."

Their prying barely registered in her numbed brain as she walked slowly into the room and removed the small card pinned to the bright red ribbon. It could have been Bud— but he didn't have the kind of money to buy roses. And if he did, Ellen suspected he wouldn't get them for his sister.

"Reed did it," Pat inserted eagerly.

"Reed?"

"We were as surprised as you."

Her gaze fell to the tiny envelope. She removed the card, biting her lip when she read the message. *I miss you. Reed.*

"He said he misses you," Derek added.

"I see that."

"Good grief, he'll be back tomorrow. How can he possibly miss you in such a short time?"

"I don't know." Her finger lovingly caressed the petals of a dewy rosebud. They were so beautiful, but their message was even more so.

"I'll bet this is his way of telling you he's sorry about the party," Derek murmured.

"Not that any of us actually knows what happened. We'd like to, but it'd be considered bad manners to ask," Pat explained. "That is, unless you'd like to tell us why he'd take you to the party and then come back alone."

"He didn't get in until three that morning," Monte said accusingly. "You aren't going to let him off so easy are you, Ellen?"

Bowing her head to smell the sweet fragrance, she closed her eyes. "Roses cover a multitude of sins."

"Reed's feeling guilty, I think," Derek said with authority. "But he cares, or else he wouldn't have gone to this much trouble."

"Maybe he just wants to keep the peace," Monte suggested. "My dad bought my mom flowers once for no reason."

"We all live together. Reed's probably figured out that he had to do something if he wanted to maintain the status quo."

"Right," Ellen agreed tartly, scooping up the flowers to take to her room. Maybe it was selfish to deprive the boys of their beauty, but she didn't care. They'd been meant for her, as a private message from Reed, and she wanted them close.

The following day, Ellen cut her last morning class, knowing that Reed's flight was getting in around noon. She could ill afford to skip algebra, but it wouldn't have done her any good to stay. She would've spent the entire time thinking about Reed—so it made more sense to hurry home.

She stepped off the bus a block from the house and even from that distance she could see his truck parked in the driveway. It was the first—and only—thing she noticed. She sprinted toward the house and dashed up the front steps.

Flinging open the door, she called breathlessly, "Anyone here?"

Both Reed and Derek came out of the kitchen.

Her eyes met Reed's from across the room. "Hi," she said in a low, husky voice. "Welcome home."

He advanced toward her, his gaze holding hers.

Neither spoke as Ellen threw her bag of books on the sofa and moved just as quickly toward him.

He caught her around the waist as though he'd been away for months instead of days, hugging her fiercely.

Ellen savored the warmth of his embrace, closing her eyes to the overwhelming emotion she suddenly felt. Reed was becoming far too important in her life. But she no longer had the power to resist him. If she ever had…

"His plane was right on time," Derek was saying. "And the airport was hardly busy. And—"

Irritably, Reed tossed a look over his shoulder. "Little brother, get lost."

Nine

"I've got a game today," Pat said, his fork cutting into the syrup-laden pancakes. "Can you come?"

Ellen's eyes met Reed's in mute communication. No longer did they bother to hide their attraction to each other from the boys. They couldn't. "What time?"

"Six."

"I can be there."

"What about you, Reed?"

Reed wiped the corners of his mouth with the paper napkin. "Sorry, I've got a meeting. But I should be home in time for the victory celebration."

Ellen thrilled at the way the boys automatically linked her name and Reed's. It had been like that from the time he'd returned from his most recent trip. But then, they'd given the boys plenty of reason to think of her and Reed as a couple. He and Ellen were with each other every free moment; the time they spent together was exclusively theirs. And Ellen loved it. She loved Reed, she loved being with him…and she loved every single thing about him. Almost. His reticence on the subject of Danielle had her a little worried, but she pushed it to the back of her mind. She couldn't bring herself to question him, especially after her own insistence that they not discuss Danielle. She no longer felt that way—she wanted reassurance—but she'd decided she'd just assume that the relationship was over. As far as she knew, Reed hadn't spoken to Danielle since the night of the Christmas party. Even stronger evidence was the fact that he drove his truck every day. The Porsche sat in the garage, gathering dust.

Reed stood up and delivered his breakfast plate to the sink. "Ellen, walk me to the door?"

"Sure."

"For Pete's sake, the door's only two feet away," Derek scoffed. "You travel all over the world and all of a sudden you need someone to show you where the back door is?"

Ellen didn't see the look the two brothers exchanged, but Derek's mouth curved upward in a knowing grin. "Oh, I get it. Hey, guys, they want to be alone."

"Just a minute." Monte wolfed down the last of his breakfast, still chewing as he carried his plate to the counter.

Ellen was mildly surprised that Reed didn't comment on Derek's needling, but she supposed they were both accustomed to it.

One by one, the boys left the kitchen. Silently, Reed stood by the back door, waiting. When the last one had departed, he slipped his arms around Ellen.

"You're getting mighty brave," she whispered, smiling into his intense green eyes. Lately, Reed almost seemed to invite the boys' comments. And when they responded, the teasing rolled off his back like rain off a well-waxed car.

"It's torture being around you every day and not touching you," he said just before his mouth descended on hers in an excruciatingly slow kiss that seemed to melt Ellen's very bones.

Reality seemed light-years away as she clung to him, and she struggled to recover her equilibrium. "Reed," she whispered, "you have to get to work."

"Right." But he didn't stop kissing her.

"And I've got classes." If he didn't end this soon, they'd both reach the point of no return. Each time he held and kissed her, it became more difficult to break away.

"I know. I know." His voice echoed through the fog that held her captive. "Now isn't the time or place."

Her arms tightened around his middle as she burrowed her face into his chest. One second, she was telling Reed they had to stop and in the next, she refused to let him go.

"I'll be late tonight," he murmured into her hair.

She remembered that he'd told Pat something about a meeting. "Me, too," she said. "I'm going to the basketball game."

"Right. Want to go out to dinner afterward?" His breath fanned her temple. "Just the two of us. I love being alone with you."

Ellen wanted to cry with frustration. "I can't. I promised the boys dinner. Plus exams start next week and I've got to study."

"Need any help?"

"Only with one subject." She looked up at him and sadly shook her head. "I don't suppose you can guess which one."

"Aren't you glad you've got me?"

"Eternally grateful." Ellen would never have believed that algebra could be both her downfall and her greatest ally. If it weren't for that one subject, she wouldn't have had the excuse to sit down with Reed every night to work through her assignments. But then, she didn't really need an excuse anymore....

"We'll see how grateful you are when grades come out."

"I hate to disappoint you, but it's going to take a lot more than your excellent tutoring to rescue me from my fate this time." The exam was crucial. If she didn't do well, she'd probably end up repeating the class. The thought filled her with dread. It would be a waste of her time and, even worse, a waste of precious funds.

Reed kissed her lightly before releasing her. "Have a good day."

"You, too." She stood at the door until he'd climbed inside the pickup and waved when he backed out of the driveway.

Ellen loaded the dirty dishes into the dishwasher and cleaned off the counter, humming a Christmas carol as she worked.

One of the boys knocked on the door. "Is it safe to come in yet?"

"Sure. Come on in."

All three innocently strolled into the kitchen. "You and Reed are getting kind of friendly, aren't you?"

Running hot tap water into the sink, Ellen nodded. "I suppose."

"Reed hasn't seen Danielle in a while."

Ellen didn't comment, but she did feel encouraged that Derek's conclusion was the same as hers.

"You know what I think?" he asked, hopping onto the counter so she was forced to look at him.

"I can only guess."

"I think Reed's getting serious about you."

"That's nice."

"*Nice*—is that all you can say?" He gave her a look of disgust. "That's my brother you're talking about. He could have any woman he wanted."

"I know." She poured soap into the dishwasher, then

closed the door and turned the dial. The sound of rushing water drowned out Derek's next comment.

"Sorry, I have to get to class. I'll talk to you later." She sauntered past Pat and Monte, offering them a cheerful smile.

"She's got it bad," Ellen heard Monte comment. That was the same thing Ralph had said the night of the party. "She hardly even bakes anymore. Remember how she used to make cookies every week?"

"I didn't know love did that to a person," Pat grumbled.

"I'm not sure I like Ellen in love," Monte flung after her as she stepped out the door.

"I just hope she doesn't get hurt."

The boy's remarks echoed in her mind as the day wore on. Ellen didn't need to hear their doubts; she had more than enough of her own. Qualms assailed her when she least expected it—like during the morning's algebra class, or during the long afternoon that followed.

But one look at Reed that evening and all her anxieties evaporated. As soon as she entered the house, she walked straight into the living room, hoping to find him there, and she did.

He put some papers back in a file when she walked in. "How was the game?"

"Pat scored seventeen points and is a hero. Unfortunately, the Huskies lost." Sometimes, that was just the way life went—winning small victories yet losing the war.

She hurried into the kitchen to begin dinner preparations.

"Something smells good." Monte bounded in half an hour later, sniffing appreciatively.

"There's a roast in the oven and an apple pie on the counter," she answered him. She'd bought the pie in hopes of celebrating the Huskies' victory. Now it would soothe their loss. "I imagine everyone's starved."

"I am," Monte announced.

"That goes without saying," Reed called from the living room.

Gradually, the other boys trailed in, and it was time to eat.

After dinner, the evening was spent at the kitchen table, poring over her textbooks. Reed came in twice to make her a fresh cup of tea. Standing behind her chair, he glanced over her shoulder at the psychology book.

"Do you want me to get you anything?" she asked. She was studying in the kitchen, rather than in her room, just to be close to Reed. Admittedly, her room offered more seclusion, but she preferred being around people—one person, actually.

"I don't need a thing." He kissed the top of her head. "And if I did, I'd get it myself. You study."

"Thanks."

"When's the first exam?"

"Monday."

He nodded. "You'll do fine."

"I don't want fine," she countered nervously. "I want fantastic."

"Then you'll do fantastic."

"Where are the boys?" The house was uncommonly silent for a weekday evening.

"Studying. I'm pleased to see they're taking exams as seriously as you are."

"We have to," she mumbled, her gaze dropping to her notebook.

"All right. I get the message. I'll quit pestering you."

"You're not pestering me."

"Right." He bent to kiss the side of her neck as his fingers stroked her arms.

Shivers raced down her spine and Ellen closed her eyes, unconsciously swaying toward him. "Now…now you're pestering me."

He chuckled, leaving her alone at the kitchen table when she would much rather have had him with her every minute of every day.

The next morning, Ellen stood by the door, watching Reed pull out of the driveway.

"Why do you do that?" Pat asked, giving her a glance that said she looked foolish standing there.

· "Do what?" She decided the best reaction was to pretend she didn't have any idea what he was talking about.

"Watch Reed leave every morning. He's not likely to have an accident pulling out of the driveway."

Ellen didn't have the courage to confess that she watched so she could see whether Reed drove the pickup or the Porsche. It would sound ridiculous to admit that she gauged their relationship by which vehicle he chose to drive that day.

"She watches because she can't bear to see him go," Derek answered when she didn't. "From what I hear, Michelle does the same thing. What can I say? The woman's crazy about me."

"Oh, yeah?" Monte snickered. "And that's the reason she was with Rick Bloomfield the other day?"

"She was?" Derek sounded completely shocked. "There's an explanation for that. Michelle and I have an understanding."

"Sure you do," Monte teased. "She can date whoever

she wants and you can date whoever you want. Some *understanding.*"

To prove to the boys that she wasn't as infatuated as they assumed—and maybe to prove the same thing to herself—Ellen didn't watch Reed leave for work the next two mornings. It was pointless, anyway. So what if he drove his Porsche? He had the car, and she could see no reason for him to not drive it. Except for her unspoken insecurities. And there seemed to be plenty of those. As Derek had said earlier in the week, Reed could have any woman he wanted.

She was the first one home that afternoon. Derek was probably sorting things out with Michelle, Pat had basketball practice and no doubt Monte was in someone's kitchen.

Gathering the ingredients for spaghetti sauce, she arranged them neatly on the counter. She was busy reading over her recipe when the phone rang.

"Hello," she said absently.

"This is Capitol Hill Cleaners. Mr. Morgan's evening suit is ready."

"Pardon?" Reed hadn't told her he was having anything cleaned. Ellen usually picked up his dry cleaning because it was no inconvenience to stop there on her way home from school. And she hadn't minded at all. As silly as it seemed, she'd felt very wifely doing that for him.

"Is it for Reed or Derek?" It was just like Derek to forget something like that.

"The slip says it's for Mr. Reed Morgan."

"Oh?"

"Is there a problem with picking it up? He brought it in yesterday and told us he had to have it this evening."

This evening? Reed was going out tonight?

"From what he said, this is for some special event."

Well, he wouldn't wear a suit to a barbecue. "I'll let him know."

"Thank you. Oh, and be sure to mention that we close at six tonight."

"Yes, I will."

A strange numbness overpowered Ellen as she hung up. Something was wrong. Something was very, very wrong. Without even realizing it, she moved rapidly through the kitchen and then outside.

Reed had often told her the importance of reading a problem in algebra. Read it carefully, he always said, and don't make any quick assumptions. It seemed crazy to remember that now. But he was right. She couldn't jump to conclusions just because he was going out for the evening. He had every right to do so. She was suddenly furious with herself. All those times he'd offered information about Danielle and she'd refused to listen, trying to play it so cool, trying to appear so unconcerned when on the inside she was dying to know.

By the time she reached the garage she was trembling, but it wasn't from the cold December air. She knew without looking that Reed had driven his sports car to work. The door creaked as she pushed it open to discover the pickup, sitting there in all its glory.

"Okay, he drove his Porsche. That doesn't have to mean anything. He isn't necessarily seeing Danielle. There's a logical explanation for this." Even if he *was* seeing Danielle, she had no right to say anything. They'd made no promises to each other.

Rubbing the chill from her arms, Ellen returned to the house. But the kitchen's warmth did little to chase away the bitter cold that cut her to the heart. Ellen moved numbly toward the phone and ran her finger down the long list of numbers that hung on the wall beside it. When she located the one for Reed's office, she punched out the seven numbers, then waited, her mind in turmoil.

"Mr. Morgan's office," came the efficient voice.

"Hello…this is Ellen Cunningham. I live, that is, I'm a friend of Mr. Morgan's."

"Yes, I remember seeing you the night of the Christmas party," the voice responded warmly. "We didn't have a chance to meet. Would you like me to put you through to Mr. Morgan?"

"No," she said hastily. "Could you give him a message?" Not waiting for a reply, she continued, "Tell him his suit is ready at the cleaners for that…party tonight."

"Oh, good, he wanted me to call. Thanks for saving me the trouble. Was there anything else?"

Tears welled in Ellen's eyes. "No, that's it."

Being reminded by Reed's assistant that they hadn't met the night of the Christmas party forcefully brought to Ellen's attention how few of his friends she did know. None, really. He'd gone out of his way *not* to introduce her to people.

"Just a minute," Ellen cried, her hand clenching the receiver. "There *is* something else you can tell Mr. Morgan. Tell him goodbye." With that, she severed the connection.

A tear rolled down her cheek, searing a path as it made its way to her chin. She'd been a fool not to have seen the situation more clearly. Reed had a good thing going, with her living at the house. She was close to falling in love with him. In fact, she was already there and anyone looking at her could tell. It certainly wasn't any secret from the boys. She cooked his meals, ran his errands, vacuumed his rugs. How convenient she'd become. How useful she'd been to the smooth running of his household.

But Reed had never said a word about his feelings. Sure, they'd gone out, but always to places where no one was likely to recognize him. And the one time Reed did see someone he knew, he'd pretended he wasn't with her. When he *had* included her in a social event, he'd only introduced her to a handful of people, as though...as though he didn't really want others to know her. As it turned out, that evening had been a disaster, and this time he'd apparently decided to take Danielle. The other woman was far more familiar with the social graces.

Fine. She'd let Reed escort Danielle tonight. But she was going to quit making life so pleasant for him. How appropriate that she now used the old servants' quarters, she thought bitterly. Because that was all she was to him—a servant. Well, no more. She would never be content to live a backstairs life. If Reed didn't want to be seen with her, or include her in his life, that was his decision. But she couldn't...she *wouldn't* continue to live this way.

Without analyzing her actions, Ellen punched out a second set of numbers.

"Charlie, it's Ellen," she said quickly, trying to swallow back tears.

"Ellen? It doesn't sound like you."

"I know." The tightness in her chest extended all the way to her throat, choking off her breath until it escaped in a sob.

"Ellen, are you all right?"

"Yes...no." The fact that she'd called Charlie was a sign of her desperation. He was so sweet and she didn't want to do anything to hurt him. "Charlie, I hate to ask, but I need a friend."

"I'm here."

He said it without the least hesitation, and his unquestioning loyalty made her weep all the louder. "Oh, Charlie, I've got to find a new place to live and I need to do it today."

"My sister's got a friend looking for a roommate. Do you want me to call her?"

"Please." Straightening, she wiped the tears from her face. Charlie might have had his faults, but he'd recognized the panic in her voice and immediately assumed control. Just now, that was what she needed—a friend to temporarily take charge of things. "How soon can you talk to her?"

"Now. I'll call her and get right back to you. On second thought, I'll come directly to your place. If you can't move in with Patty's friend, my parents will put you up."

"Oh, Charlie, how can I ever thank you?"

The sound of his chuckle was like a clean, fresh breeze. "I'll come up with a way later." His voice softened. "You know how I feel about you, Ellen. If you only want me for a friend, I understand. But I'm determined to be a good friend."

The back door closed with a bang. "Anyone home?"

Guiltily, Ellen turned around, coming face to face with Monte. She replaced the receiver, took a deep breath and squared her shoulders. She'd hoped to get away without having to talk to anyone.

"Ellen?" Concern clouded his face. "What's wrong? You look like you've been crying." He narrowed his eyes. "You *have* been crying. What happened?"

"Nothing." She took a minute to wipe her eyes with a tissue. "Listen, I'll be up in my room, but I'd appreciate some time alone, so don't get me unless it's important."

"Sure. Anything you say. Are you sick? Should I call Reed?"

"No!" she almost shouted at him, then instantly regretted reacting so harshly. "Please don't contact him…. He's busy tonight anyway." She rubbed a hand over her face. "And listen, about dinner—"

"Hey, don't worry. I can cook."

"You?" This wasn't the time to get into an argument. How messy he made the kitchen was no longer her problem. "There's a recipe on the counter if you want to tackle spaghetti sauce."

"Sure. I can do that. How long am I supposed to boil the noodles?"

One of her lesser concerns at the moment was boiling noodles. "Just read the back of the package."

Already he was rolling up his sleeves. "I'll take care of everything. You go lie down and do whatever women do when they're crying and pretending they're not."

"Thanks," she returned evenly. "I'll do that." Only in this case, she wasn't going to lie on her bed, hiding her face in her pillow. She was going to pack up everything she owned and cart it away before Reed even had a hint that she was leaving.

Sniffling as she worked, Ellen dumped the contents of her drawers into open suitcases. A couple of times she stopped to blow her nose. She detested tears. At the age of fifteen, she'd broken her leg and gritted her teeth against the agony. But she hadn't shed a tear. Now she wept as though it were the end of the world. Why, oh why, did her emotions have to be so unpredictable?

Carrying her suitcases down the first flight of stairs, she paused on the boys' floor to shift the weight. Because she was concentrating on her task and not watching where she was going, she walked headlong into Derek. "Sorry," she muttered.

"Ellen." He glanced at her suitcases and said her name

as though he'd unexpectedly stumbled into the Queen of Sheba. "What...what are you doing?"

"Moving."

"Moving? But...why?"

"It's a long story."

"You're crying." He sounded even more shocked by her tears than by the fact that she was moving out of the house. "It's Reed, isn't it? What did he do?"

"He didn't do a thing. Stay out of it, Derek. I mean that."

He looked stunned. "Sure." He stepped aside and stuck his hand in his pocket. "Anything you say."

She made a second trip downstairs, this time bringing a couple of tote bags and the clothes from her closet, which she draped over the top of the two suitcases. There wasn't room in her luggage for everything. She realized she'd have to put the rest of her belongings in boxes.

Assuming she'd find a few empty boxes in the garage, she stormed through the kitchen and out the back door. Muttering between themselves, Monte and Derek followed her. Soon her movements resembled a small parade.

"Will you two stop it," she shouted, whirling around and confronting them. The tears had dried now and her face burned with the heat of anger and regret.

"We just want to know what happened," Monte interjected.

"Or is this going to be another one of your 'stay tuned' responses?" Derek asked.

"I'm moving out. I don't think I can make it any plainer than that."

"Why?"

"That's none of your business." She left them standing with mouths open as she trooped up the back stairs to her rooms.

Heedlessly she tossed her things into the two boxes, more intent on escaping than on taking care to ensure that nothing was broken. When she got to the vase that had held the roses Reed had sent her, Ellen picked it up and hugged it. She managed to forestall further tears by taking deep breaths and blinking rapidly. Setting the vase down, she decided not to bring it with her. As much as possible, she wanted to leave Reed in this house and not carry the memories of him around with her like a constant, throbbing ache. That would be hard enough without taking the vase along as a constant reminder of what she'd once felt.

The scene that met her at the foot of the stairs made her stop in her tracks. The three boys were involved in a shouting match, each blaming the others for Ellen's unexpected decision to move out.

"It's your fault," Derek accused Monte. "If you weren't so concerned about your stomach, she'd stay."

"My stomach? *You're* the one who's always asking her for favors. Like babysitting and cooking for you and your girlfriend and—"

"If you want my opinion…" Pat began.

"We don't," Monte and Derek shouted.

"Stop it! All of you," Ellen cried. "Now, if you're the least bit interested in helping me, you can take my things outside. Charlie will be here anytime."

"Charlie?" the three echoed in shock.

"Are you moving in with him?"

She didn't bother to respond. Once the suitcases, the bags, two boxes and her clothes had been lugged onto the porch, Ellen sat on the top step and waited.

She could hear the boys pacing back and forth behind her, still bickering quietly. When the black sports car squealed around the corner, Ellen covered her face with both hands and groaned. The last person she wanted to see now was Reed. Her throat was already swollen with the effort of not giving way to tears.

He parked in front of the house and threw open the car door.

She straightened, determined to appear cool and calm.

Seconds later, Reed stood on the bottom step. "What's going on here?"

"Hello, Reed," she said with a breathlessness she couldn't control. "How was your day?"

He jerked his fingers through his hair as he stared back at her in utter confusion. "How am I supposed to know? I get a frantic phone call from Derek telling me to come home right away. As I'm running out the door, my assistant hands me a message. Some absurd thing about you saying goodbye. What is going on? I thought you'd hurt yourself!"

"Sorry to disappoint you."

"Ellen, I don't know what's happening in that overworked mind of yours, but I want some answers and I want them now."

"I'm leaving." Her hands were clenched so tight that her fingers ached.

"I'm not blind," he shouted, quickly losing control of his obviously limited patience. "I can see that. I'm asking you *why.*"

Pride demanded that she raise her chin and meet his probing gaze. "I've decided I'm an unstable person," she told him, her voice low and quavering. "I broke my leg once and didn't shed a tear, but when I learn that you're going to a party tonight, I start to cry."

"Ellen." He said her name gently, then shook his head as if clearing his thoughts. "You're not making any sense."

"I know. That's the worst part."

"In the simplest terms possible, tell me why you're leaving."

"I'm trying to." Furious with herself, she wiped a tear from her cheek. How could she explain it to him when everything was still so muddled in her own mind? "I'm leaving because you're driving the Porsche."

"What!" he exploded.

"You tell me," she burst out. "Why did you drive the Porsche today?"

"Would you believe that my truck was low on fuel?"

"I may be confused," she said, "but I'm not stupid. You're going out with Danielle. Not that I care."

"I can tell." His mocking gaze lingered on her suitcases. "I hate to disillusion you, but Danielle won't be with me."

She didn't know whether to believe him or not. "It doesn't matter."

"None of this is making sense."

"I don't imagine it would. I apologize for acting so unreasonable, but that's exactly how I feel. So, I'm getting out of here with my pride intact."

"Is your pride worth so much?"

"It's the only thing I have left," she said. She'd already given him her heart.

"She's moving in with Charlie," Derek said in a worried voice. "You aren't going to let her, are you, Reed?"

"You can't," Monte added.

"He won't," Pat stated confidently.

For a moment, the three of them stared intently at Reed. Ellen noticed the way his green eyes hardened. "Yes, I can," he said at last. "If this is what you want, then so be it. Goodbye, Ellen." With that, he marched into the house.

Ten

"I'm swearing off men for good," Ellen vowed, taking another long swallow of wine.

"Me, too," Darlene, her new roommate, echoed. To toast the promise, Darlene bent forward to touch the rim of her wineglass against Ellen's and missed. A shocked moment passed before they broke into hysterical laughter.

"Here." Ellen replenished their half-full glasses as tears of mirth rolled down her face. The world seemed to spin off its axis for a moment as she straightened. "You know what? I think we're drunk."

"Maybe you are," Darlene declared, slurring her words, "but not me. I can hold my wine as well as any man."

"I thought we weren't going to talk about men anymore."

"Right, I forgot."

"Do you think they're talking about us?" Ellen asked, putting a hand to her head in an effort to keep the walls from going around and around.

"Nah, we're just a fading memory."

"Right." Ellen pointed her index finger toward the ceiling in emphatic agreement.

The doorbell chimed and both women stared accusingly at the door. "If it's a man, don't answer it," Darlene said.

"Right again." Ellen staggered across the beige carpet. The floor seemed to pitch under her feet and she placed a hand on the back of the sofa to steady herself. Facing the door, she turned around. "How do I know if it's a man or not?"

The doorbell sounded again.

Darlene motioned languidly with her hand to show that she no longer cared who was at the door. "Just open it."

Holding the knob in a death grip, Ellen pulled open the door and found herself glaring at solid male chest. "It's a man," she announced to Darlene.

"Who?"

Squinting, Ellen studied the blurred male figure until she recognized Monte. "Monte," she cried, instantly sobering. "What are you doing here?"

"I… I was in the neighborhood and thought I'd stop by and see how you're doing."

"Come in." She stepped aside to let him enter. "What brings you to this neck of the woods?" She hiccuped despite her frenzied effort to look and act sober. "It's a school night. You shouldn't be out this late."

"It's only ten-thirty. You've been drinking."

"Me?" She slammed her hand against her chest. "Have we been drinking, Darlene?"

Her roommate grabbed the wine bottle—their second—from the table and hid it behind her back. "Not us."

Monte cast them a look of disbelief. "How'd your exams go?" he asked Ellen politely.

"Fine," she answered and hiccuped again. Embarrassed, she covered her mouth with her hand. "I think."

"What about algebra?"

"I'm making it by the skin of my nose."

"Teeth," both Darlene and Monte corrected.

"Right."

Looking uncomfortable, Monte said, "Maybe I should come back another time."

"Okay." Ellen wasn't about to argue. If she was going to run into her former housemates, she'd prefer to do it when she looked and felt her best. Definitely not when she was feeling...tipsy and the walls kept spinning. But on second thought, she couldn't resist asking about the others. "How's...everyone?"

"Fine." But he lowered his gaze to the carpet. "Not really, if you want the truth."

A shaft of fear went through her, tempering the effects of several glasses of wine. "It's not Reed, is it? Is he ill?"

"No, Reed's fine. I guess. He hasn't been around much lately."

No doubt he was spending a lot of his time at parties and social events with Danielle. Or with any number of other women, all of them far more sophisticated than Ellen.

"Things haven't been the same since you left," Monte added sheepishly.

"Who's doing the cooking?"

He shrugged his shoulders. "We've been taking turns."

"That sounds fair." She hoped that in the months she'd lived with them the three boys had at least learned their way around the kitchen.

"Derek started a fire yesterday."

Ellen couldn't conceal her dismay. "Was there any damage?" As much as she tried to persuade herself that she didn't need to feel guilty over leaving the boys, this news was her undoing. "Was anyone hurt?" she gasped out.

"Not really, and Reed said the insurance would take care of everything."

"What happened?" Ellen was almost afraid to ask.

"Nothing much. Derek forgot to turn off the burner and the fat caught fire. Then he tried to beat it out with a dish towel, but that burst into flames, too. The real mistake was throwing the burning towel into the sink because when he did, it set the curtains on fire."

"Oh, good grief." Ellen dropped her head into her hands.

"It's not too bad, though. Reed said he wanted new kitchen walls, anyway."

"The walls too?"

"Well, the curtains started burning the wallpaper."

Ellen wished she hadn't asked. "Was anyone hurt?"

Monte moved a bandaged hand from behind his back. "Just me, but only a little."

"Oh, Monte," she cried, fighting back her guilt. "What did you do—try and pound out the fire with your fist?" Leave it to Monte. He'd probably tried to rescue whatever it was Derek had been cooking.

"No, I grabbed a hot biscuit from the oven and blistered one finger."

"Then why did you wrap up your whole hand?" From the size of the bandage, it looked as though he'd been lucky not to lose his arm.

"I thought you might feel sorry for me and come back."

"Oh, Monte." She reached up to brush the hair from his temple.

"I didn't realize what a good cook you were until you left. I kept thinking maybe it was something I'd done that caused you to leave."

"Of course not."

"Then you'll come back and make dinners again?"

Good ol' Monte never forgot about his stomach. "The four of you will do fine without me."

"You mean you won't come back?"

"I can't." She felt like crying, but she struggled to hold back the tears stinging her eyes. "I'm really sorry, but I can't."

Hanging his head, Monte nodded. "Well, have a merry Christmas anyway."

"Right. You, too."

"Bye, Ellen." He turned back to the door, his large hand gripping the knob. "You know about Pat making varsity, don't you?"

She'd read it in the *Daily*. "I'm really proud of him. You tell him for me. Okay?"

"Sure."

She closed the door after him and leaned against it while the regrets washed over her like a torrent of rain. Holding back her tears was difficult, but somehow she managed. She'd shed enough tears. It was time to put her grief behind her and to start facing life again.

"I take it Monte is one of the guys," Darlene remarked. She set the wine back on the table, but neither seemed interested in another glass.

Ellen nodded. "The one with the stomach."

"He's so skinny!"

"I know. There's no justice in this world." But she wasn't talking about Monte's appetite in relation to his weight. She was talking about Reed. If she'd had any hope that he really did care for her, that had vanished in the past week. He hadn't even tried to get in touch with her. She knew he wouldn't have had any problem locating her. The obvious conclusion was that he didn't *want* to see her. At first she thought he might have believed the boys' ridiculous claim that she was moving in with Charlie. But if he'd loved her half as much as she loved him, even that shouldn't have stopped him from coming after her.

Apparently, presuming that Reed cared for her was a mistake on her part. She hadn't heard a word from him all week. Exam week, at that. Well, fine. She'd wipe him out of her memory—just as effectively as she'd forgotten every algebraic formula she'd ever learned. A giggle escaped and Darlene sent her a curious look. Ellen carried their wineglasses to the sink, ignoring her new roommate, as she considered her dilemma. The trouble was, she wanted to remember the algebra, which seemed to slip out of her mind as soon as it entered, and she wanted to forget Reed, who never left her thoughts for an instant.

"I think I'll go to bed," Darlene said, holding her hand to her stomach. "I'm not feeling so great."

"Me neither." But Ellen's churning stomach had little to do with the wine. "Night."

"See you in the morning."

Ellen nodded. She was fortunate to have found Darlene. The other woman, who had recently broken up with her fiancé after a two-year engagement, understood how Ellen felt. It seemed natural to drown their sorrows together. But...she missed the boys and—Reed.

One thing she'd learned from this experience was that men and school didn't mix. Darlene might not have been serious about swearing off men, but Ellen was. She was through with them for good—or at least until she obtained her degree. For now, she was determined to bury herself in her books, get her teaching credentials and then become the best first-grade teacher around.

Only she couldn't close her eyes without remembering Reed's touch or how he'd slip up behind her and hold her in his arms. Something as simple as a passing glance from him had been enough to thrill her. Well, that relationship was over. And just in the nick of time. She could have been hurt. Really hurt. She could be feeling terrible. Really terrible.

Just like she did right now.

Signs of Christmas were everywhere. Huge decorations adorned the streetlights down University Way. Store windows displayed a variety of Christmas themes, and the streets were jammed with holiday traffic. Ellen tried to absorb some of the good cheer that surrounded her, with little success.

She'd gone to the university library to return some books and was headed back to Darlene's place. Her place, too, even though it didn't feel that way.

She planned to leave for Yakima the next morning. But instead of feeling the pull toward home and family, Ellen's thoughts drifted to Reed and the boys. They'd been her surrogate family since September and she couldn't erase them from her mind as easily as she'd hoped.

As she walked across campus, sharp gusts of wind tousled her hair. Her face felt numb with cold. All day she'd been debating what to do with the Christmas gifts she'd bought for the boys. Her first inclination had been to bring them over herself—when Reed wasn't home, of course. But just the idea of returning to the lovely old house had proved so painful that Ellen abandoned it. Instead, Darlene had promised to deliver them the next day, after Ellen had left for Yakima.

Hugging her purse, Ellen trudged toward the bus stop. According to her watch, she had about ten minutes to wait. Now her feet felt as numb as her face. She frowned at her pumps, cursing the decrees of fashion and her insane willingness to wear elegant shoes at this time of year. It wasn't as though a handsome prince was likely to come galloping by only to be overwhelmed by her attractive shoes. Even if one did swoop Ellen and her frozen toes onto his silver steed, she'd be highly suspicious of his character.

Smiling, she took a shortcut across the lawn in the Quad.

"Is something funny?"

A pair of men's leather loafers had joined her fashionable gray pumps, matching her stride. Stunned, Ellen glanced up. Reed.

"Well?" he asked again in an achingly gentle voice. "Something seems to amuse you."

"My…shoes. I was thinking about attracting a prince… a man." Oh heavens, why had she said that? "I mean," she mumbled on, trying to cover her embarrassment, "my feet are numb."

"You need to get out of the cold." His hands were thrust into his pockets and he was so compellingly handsome that Ellen forced her eyes away. She was afraid that if she stared at him long enough, she'd give him whatever he asked. She remembered the way his face had looked the last time she'd seen him, how cold and steely his eyes had been the day she'd announced she was moving out. One word from him and she would've stayed. But the "might-have-beens" didn't matter anymore. He hadn't asked her to stay, so she'd gone. Pure and simple. Or so it had seemed at the time.

Determination strengthened her trembling voice as she finally spoke. "The bus will be at the corner in seven minutes."

Her statement was met with silence. Together they reached the pavement and strolled toward the sheltered bus area.

Much as she wished to appear cool and composed, Ellen's gaze was riveted on the man at her side. She noticed how straight and dark Reed's brows were and how his chin jutted out with stubborn pride. Every line of his beloved face emanated strength and unflinching resolve.

Abruptly, she looked away. Pride was no stranger to her, either. Her methods might have been wrong, she told herself, but she'd been right to let Reed know he'd hurt her. She wasn't willing to be a victim of her love for him.

"Ellen," he said softly, "I was hoping we could talk."

She made a show of glancing at her watch. "Go ahead. You've got six and a half minutes."

"Here?"

"As you so recently said, I need to get out of the cold."

"I'll take you to lunch."

"I'm not hungry." To further her embarrassment, her stomach growled and she pressed a firm hand over it, commanding it to be quiet.

"When was the last time you ate a decent meal?"

"Yesterday. No," she corrected, "today."

"Come on, we're getting out of here."

"No way."

"I'm not arguing with you, Ellen. I've given you a week to come to your senses. I still haven't figured out what went wrong. And I'm not waiting any longer for the answers. Got that?"

She ignored him, looking instead in the direction of the traffic. She could see the bus approaching, though it was still several blocks away. "I believe everything that needed to be said—" she motioned dramatically with her hand "—was already said."

"And what's this I hear about you succumbing to the demon rum?"

"I was only a little drunk," she spat out, furious at Monte's loose tongue. "Darlene and I were celebrating. We've sworn off men for life." Or at least until Reed freely admitted he loved her and needed her. At the moment that didn't appear likely.

"I see." His eyes seemed to be looking all the way into her soul. "If that's how you want it, fine. Just answer a couple of questions and I'll leave you alone. Agreed?"

"All right."

"First, what were you talking about when you flew off the handle about me driving the Porsche?"

"Oh, that." Now it just seemed silly.

"Yes, that."

"Well, you only drove the Porsche when you were seeing Danielle."

"But I wasn't! It's been completely over between us since the night of the Christmas party."

"It has?" The words came out in a squeak.

Reed dragged his fingers through his hair. "I haven't seen Danielle in weeks."

Ellen stared at the sidewalk. "But the cleaners phoned about your suit. You were attending some fancy party."

"So? I wasn't taking another woman."

"It doesn't matter," she insisted. "You weren't taking me, either."

"Of course not!" he shouted, his raised voice attracting the attention of several passersby. "You were studying for your exams. I couldn't very well ask you to attend an extremely boring business dinner with me. Not when you were spending every available minute hitting the books." He lowered his voice to a calm, even pitch.

The least he could do was be more unreasonable, Ellen thought irritably. She simply wasn't in the mood for logic.

"Did you hear what I said?"

She nodded.

"There is only one woman in my life. You. To be honest, Ellen, I can't understand any of this. You may be many things, but I know you're not the jealous type. I wanted to talk about Danielle with you. Any other woman would've loved hearing all the details. But not you." His voice was slightly raised. "Then you make these ridiculous accusations about the truck and the Porsche, and I'm at a loss to understand."

Now she felt even more foolish. "Then why were you driving the Porsche?" Her arms tightened around her purse. "Forget I asked that."

"You really have a thing for that sports car, don't you?"

"It's not the car."

"I'm glad to hear that."

Squaring her shoulders, Ellen decided it was time to be forthright, time to face things squarely rather than skirt around them. "My feelings are that you would rather not be seen with me," she said bluntly.

"What?" he exploded.

"You kept taking me to these out-of-the-way restaurants."

"I did it for privacy."

"You didn't want to be seen with me," she countered.

"I can't believe this." He took three steps away from her, then turned around sharply.

"Don't you think the Des Moines Marina is a bit far to go for a meal?"

"I was afraid we'd run into one of the boys."

More logic, and she was in no mood for it. "You didn't introduce me to your friend the night we went to that French film."

His eyes narrowed. "You can bet I wasn't going to introduce you to Tom Dailey. He's a lecher. I was protecting you."

"What about the night of the Christmas party? You only introduced me to a handful of people."

"Of course. Every man in the place was looking for an excuse to take you away from me. If you'd wanted to flirt with them, you should've said something."

"I only wanted to be with you."

"Then why bring up that evening now?"

"I was offended."

"I apologize," he shouted.

"Fine. But I didn't even meet your assistant…."

"You left so fast, I didn't exactly have a chance to introduce you, did I?"

He was being logical again, and she couldn't really argue.

The bus arrived then, its doors parting with a swish. But Ellen didn't move. Reed's gaze commanded her to stay with him, and she was torn. Her strongest impulse, though, was not to board the bus. It didn't matter that she was cold and the wind was cutting through her thin coat or that she could barely feel her toes. Her heart was telling her one thing and her head another.

"You coming or not?" the driver called out to her.

"She won't be taking the bus," Reed answered, slipping his hand under her elbow. "She's coming with me."

"Whatever." The doors swished shut and the bus roared away, leaving a trail of black diesel smoke in its wake.

"You *are* coming with me, aren't you?" he coaxed.

"I suppose."

His hand was at the small of her back, directing her across the busy street to a coffee shop, festooned with tinsel and tired-looking decorations. "I wasn't kidding about lunch."

"When was the last time *you* had a decent meal?" she couldn't resist asking.

"About a week ago," he grumbled. "Derek's cooking is a poor substitute for real food."

They found a table at the back of the café. The waitress handed them each a menu and filled their water glasses.

"I heard about the fire."

Reed groaned. "That was a comedy of errors."

"Is there much damage?"

"Enough." The look he gave her was mildly accusing.

The guilt returned. Trying to disguise it, Ellen made a show of glancing through the menu. The last thing on her mind at the moment was food. When the waitress returned, Ellen ordered the daily special without knowing what it was. The day was destined to be full of surprises.

"Ellen," Reed began, then cleared his throat. "Come back."

Her heart melted at the hint of anguish in his low voice. Her gaze was magnetically drawn to his. She wanted to tell him how much she longed to be…home. She wanted to say that the house on Capitol Hill was the only real home she had now, that she longed to walk through its front door again. With him.

"Nothing's been the same since you left."

The knot in her stomach pushed its way up to her throat, choking her.

"The boys are miserable."

Resolutely she shook her head. If she went back, it had to be for Reed.

"Why not?"

Tears blurred her vision. "Because."

"That makes about as much sense as you being angry because I drove the Porsche."

Taking several deep, measured breaths, Ellen said, "If all you need is a cook, I can suggest several who—"

"I couldn't care less about the cooking."

The café went silent as every head turned curiously in their direction. "I wasn't talking about the cooking *here,*" Reed explained to the roomful of shocked faces.

The normal noise of the café resumed.

"Good grief, Ellen, you've got me so tied up in knots I'm about to get kicked out of here."

"Me, tie *you* in knots?" She was astonished that Reed felt she had so much power over him.

"If you won't come back for the boys, will you consider doing it for me?" The intense green eyes demanded a response.

"I want to know why you want me back. So I can cook your meals and—"

"I told you I don't care about that. I don't care if you never do another thing around the house. I want you there because I love you, damn it."

Her eyes widened. "You love me, damn it?"

"You're not making this any easier." He ripped the napkin from around the silverware and slammed it down on his lap. "You must have known. I didn't bother keeping it secret."

"You didn't bother keeping it secret…from anyone but me," she repeated hotly.

"Come on. Don't tell me you didn't know."

"I didn't know."

"Well, you do now," he yelled back.

The waitress cautiously approached their table, standing

back until Reed glanced in her direction. Hurriedly the girl set their plates in front of them and promptly moved away.

"You frightened her," Ellen accused him.

"I'm the one in a panic here. Do you or do you not love me?"

Again, it seemed as though every customer there had fallen silent, awaiting her reply.

"You'd better answer him, miss," the elderly gentleman sitting at the table next to theirs suggested. "Fact is, we're all curious."

"Yes, I love him."

Reed cast her a look of utter disbelief. "You'll tell a stranger but not me?"

"I love you, Reed Morgan. There, are you happy?"

"Overjoyed."

"I can tell." Ellen had thought that when she admitted her feelings, Reed would jump up from the table and throw his arms around her. Instead, he looked as angry as she'd ever seen him.

"I think you'd better ask her to marry you while she's in a friendly mood," the older man suggested next.

"Well?" Reed looked at her. "What do you think?"

"You want to get married?"

"It's the time of year to be generous," the waitress said shyly. "He's handsome enough."

"He is, isn't he?" Ellen agreed, her sense of humor restored by this unexpected turn of events. "But he can be a little hard to understand."

"All men are, believe me," a woman across the room shouted. "But he looks like a decent guy. Go ahead and give him another chance."

The anger washed from Reed's dark eyes as he reached

for Ellen's hand. "I love you. I want to marry you. Won't you put me out of my misery?"

Tears dampened her eyes as she nodded wildly.

"Let's go home." Standing, Reed took out his wallet and threw a couple of twenties on the table.

Ellen quickly buttoned her jacket and picked up her purse. "Goodbye, everyone," she called with a cheerful wave. "Thank you—and Merry Christmas!"

The amused customers broke into a round of applause as Reed took Ellen's hand and pulled her outside.

She was no sooner out the door when Reed hauled her into his arms. "Oh, Ellen, I've missed you."

Reveling in the warmth of his arms, she nuzzled closer. "I've missed you, too. I've even missed the boys."

"As far as I'm concerned, they're on their own. I want you back for myself. That house was full of people, yet it's never felt so empty." Suddenly he looked around, as though he'd only now realized that their private moment was taking place in the middle of a busy street. "Let's get out of here." He slipped an arm about her waist, steering her toward the campus car park. "But I think I'd better tell you something important."

"What?"

"I didn't bring the truck."

"Oh?" She swallowed her disappointment. She could try, but she doubted she'd ever be the Porsche type.

"I traded in the truck last week."

"For what?"

"Maybe it was presumptuous of me, but I was hoping you'd accept my marriage proposal."

"What's the truck got to do with whether I marry you or not?"

"*You're* asking me that? The woman who left me—"

"All right, all right, I get the picture."

"Okay, I don't have the truck *or* the Porsche. I gave it to Derek."

"I'm sure he's thrilled."

"He is. And…"

"And?"

"I traded the truck for an SUV. More of a family-friendly vehicle, wouldn't you say?"

"Oh, Reed." With a small cry of joy, she flung her arms around this man she knew she'd love for a lifetime. No matter what kind of car he drove.

* * * * *

Get 4 FREE REWARDS!

We'll send you 2 FREE Books plus 2 FREE Mystery Gifts.

Both the **Romance** and **Suspense** collections feature compelling novels written by many of today's bestselling authors.

YES! Please send me 2 FREE novels from the Essential Romance or Essential Suspense Collection and my 2 FREE gifts (gifts are worth about $10 retail). After receiving them, if I don't wish to receive any more books, I can return the shipping statement marked "cancel." If I don't cancel, I will receive 4 brand-new novels every month and be billed just $7.24 each in the U.S. or $7.49 each in Canada. That's a savings of up to 28% off the cover price. It's quite a bargain! Shipping and handling is just 50¢ per book in the U.S. and $1.25 per book in Canada.* I understand that accepting the 2 free books and gifts places me under no obligation to buy anything. I can always return a shipment and cancel at any time. The free books and gifts are mine to keep no matter what I decide.

Choose one: ☐ **Essential Romance**
(194/394 MDN GQ6M)

☐ **Essential Suspense**
(191/391 MDN GQ6M)

Name (please print)

Address _____ Apt. #

City _____ State/Province _____ Zip/Postal Code

Email: Please check this box ☐ if you would like to receive newsletters and promotional emails from Harlequin Enterprises ULC and its affiliates. You can unsubscribe anytime.

> #### Mail to the **Reader Service:**
> **IN U.S.A.:** P.O. Box 1341, Buffalo, NY 14240-8531
> **IN CANADA:** P.O. Box 603, Fort Erie, Ontario L2A 5X3

Want to try 2 free books from another series? Call **1-800-873-8635** or visit www.ReaderService.com.

*Terms and prices subject to change without notice. Prices do not include sales taxes, which will be charged (if applicable) based on your state or country of residence. Canadian residents will be charged applicable taxes. Offer not valid in Quebec. This offer is limited to one order per household. Books received may not be as shown. Not valid for current subscribers to the Essential Romance or Essential Suspense Collection. All orders subject to approval. Credit or debit balances in a customer's account(s) may be offset by any other outstanding balance owed by or to the customer. Please allow 4 to 6 weeks for delivery. Offer available while quantities last.

Your Privacy—Your information is being collected by Harlequin Enterprises ULC, operating as Reader Service. For a complete summary of the information we collect, how we use this information and to whom it is disclosed, please visit our privacy notice located at corporate.harlequin.com/privacy-notice. From time to time we may also exchange your personal information with reputable third parties. If you wish to opt out of this sharing of your personal information, please visit readerservice.com/consumerschoice or call 1-800-873-8635. **Notice to California Residents**—Under California law, you have specific rights to control and access your data. For more information on these rights and how to exercise them, visit corporate.harlequin.com/california-privacy.

STRS20MAX